ARNOLD GRUNDVIG

AN HISTORICAL NOVEL

I *Am*
PETER

BONNEVILLE BOOKS
SPRINGVILLE, UTAH

The views expressed within this work are the sole responsibility of the author and do not necessarily reflect the position of Cedar Fort, Inc., or any other entity.

ISBN 13: 978-1-59955-791-5

Published by Bonneville Books, an imprint of Cedar Fort, Inc.,
2373 W. 700 S., Springville, UT 84663
Distributed by Cedar Fort, Inc., www.cedarfort.com

LIBRARY OF CONGRESS CATALOGING-IN-PUBLICATION DATA

Grundvig, Arnold S., Jr., 1948- , author.
  I am Peter : disciple, apostle, and witness of the Son of God / Arnold S. Grundvig Jr.
    p. cm.
  Includes bibliographical references.
  Summary: A first-person narrative on the Apostle Peter's life, based on scriptural and historical documentation.
  ISBN 978-1-59955-791-5
  1. Peter, the Apostle, Saint. 2. Jesus Christ. 3. Bible.
N.T.--Biography. I. Title.
  BS2515.G74 2011
  225.9'2--dc22

                                        2011001580

Cover design by Angela Olsen
Cover design © 2011 by Lyle Mortimer
Edited and typeset by Megan E. Welton
Interior artwork by Rembrandt Harmenszoon van Rijn

Printed in the United States of America
10 9 8 7 6 5 4 3 2 1

Printed on acid-free paper

For my dad, Arnold S. Grundvig, Sr.

JERUSALEM AND
SURROUNDING ENVIRONS

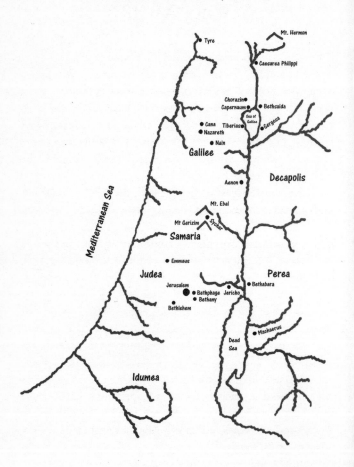

WHO AM I?

I am Peter.

I was born Simon, the son of Jonah. My father was a fisherman, and, by tradition, I was a fisherman, just as my sons would become fishermen too. I was raised in the small fishing village of Bethsaida in Galilee, on the northernmost shore of the life-giving Sea of Galilee. Galileans were more impressed by the calluses on a man's hands than by the clothes on his back.

I was in the fishing business with my brother, Andrew, and our partners and good friends, James and John, the sons of Zebedee. Fishing was an important and gainful industry in our time, and our fleet made a comfortable living on the Sea of Galilee. Because we employed a number of hard-working fishermen, we had the ability to be away from our work and still provide for our families. Successful or not, we were not men of leisure. We worked as hard as any fisherman on our boats.

We fished from the port of Bethsaida, but I made my home in the village of Capernaum, located about two miles west of Bethsaida, also on the rocky shores of Galilee. I was able to afford a spacious home in Capernaum, where there was more than ample room for my family—including my wife's mother—Andrew's family, and a number of guests, when the need arose.

I might add one more important fact: I am of the Tribe of Judah, a Jew. Jews, and all of the house of Israel, looked forward to the coming of the Messiah with great anticipation. We believed that the Messiah, the Anointed One, would be a military leader who would lead Israel to independence. We were not looking for a political change, but for liberation. The Romans had occupied Israel for nearly a century, and they had dominated us with burdensome taxes, merciless cruelty, and torturous executions. It could be said that we coexisted, but there was no peace by anyone's definition. The coming of the Messiah was on our minds constantly.

As I tell my story, there will be times when words are inadequate to express the feelings in my heart, but I shall do my best. There will also be times when some shall say that I am too brief, while others will complain that I am too wordy. These are my shortcomings. Please overlook them and focus on what I am sharing, not how I do so. With experience, I have found it useful to periodically interrupt my story to explain traditions and history or make other observations that make the events easier to understand. It is my desire that everyone see what I saw, as if they were there beside me, seeing these events through their own eyes so they can know what I know, that Jesus is the Son of God.

I've disclosed more than enough about me. The remarkable things I have to share are not about me but about what I experienced. Please allow me to tell of my life as a disciple, Apostle, and witness of the Messiah, the Lord Jesus Christ, the Son of the Living God.

Rumors of The Messiah

I shall begin during the fifteenth year of the reign of the Roman Emperor Tiberius Caesar. It was the early spring of the year A.D. 29, according to the way years are counted in modern times. Many rumors came from Judea reporting that the Messiah had finally come. Some people claimed they had actually seen and spoken to Him. Others repeated stories about Him from someone they knew or trusted. The reports kept coming, so I paid more attention than I had to the countless tales of the many Messiahs I had heard in Galilee so many times before.

I looked forward to the coming of the Messiah as much as any man, but I confess that I was not easily convinced by a man's words. I also knew that just because a man gathered followers, it did not prove he spoke the truth. For generations, impostors had claimed to be the Messiah. These false messiahs gathered large followings of dedicated believers. Desperate people are easily deceived, so deceivers prey on desperate people.

It was my experience that a pretender would eventually ask for silver or gold or some other kind of tribute. Or worse, he would abuse the power granted him by his followers. One thing was certain, these self-anointed messiahs depended on their followers for food, clothing, and shelter. As a result, they usually stayed in the same general location once they built a following, assuring themselves that they would no longer need to work for their daily bread, at least until they were

3

exposed as frauds. In addition, this dependence on their followers meant that these wicked men had a financial incentive to preach what their followers wanted to hear, to pander to them, independent of whether what they taught was true. This way of making a living—attracting followers and being paid to preach what they wanted to hear—has always been profitable.

If the things we heard about this man were true, he asked for nothing, lived in the desert, wore crude clothing, and ate only what the land provided. He went about the eastern wilderness of Judea preaching repentance, claiming that the kingdom of heaven was at hand. His message seemed pure, but what appealed to me was that he was not one of those educated as a "master of the law." He was not granted any elite social status or religious office for his great knowledge of the law of Moses. He may or may not have been the Messiah we were looking for, but I grew more curious about Him.

Being a man of responsibility, I stayed in Capernaum to work in our fishing business and sent Andrew and young John, the son of Zebedee, to learn what they could about this man. Andrew was my younger brother, and John was the younger brother of James. I knew that Andrew would be an excellent companion for John, so I sent them on their way, knowing they would be all right.

John was an enthusiastic young man with strong convictions, which he freely expressed—characteristics common to many youth. John followed the example of his older brother, who never hesitated to boldly express his opinion.

I am not embarrassed to say that I was at least as bold as James and my young friend John, but my brother Andrew was gentle man of soft-spoken wisdom. He was a perfect balance for me and John. That should give a fair picture of us four Galilean fishermen. We were ordinary men who found ourselves in extraordinary times.

It didn't seem like it took many days for Andrew and John to return from their journey to the wilderness area of northern Judea. In the short time they were gone, they became disciples of a man named John, the son of Zacharias. Because of his much baptizing, he was known to many as John the Baptist.

Perhaps out of respect for Andrew and John, I never said anything critical of their belief in John the Baptist, but it was my nature to be a skeptical man. I was confident that if he were another deceiver, I should easily recognize it, so I decided to journey to Judea with my brother and friend. If this John the Baptist were the Messiah, as they believed, I would know it for myself. Andrew and John wanted to be there when I met the man they hoped was the Christ. We left James and his father, Zebedee, to manage the fishing business, and we journeyed south.

As we approached Jericho, we split up. Andrew and John continued east to find John the Baptist, while I went on into Jericho. I did not hide my skepticism about John the Baptist from my brother Andrew. He suggested that contrary to the way I usually did things, I should go into Jericho to hear what local citizens had to say about John the Baptist before I met— or confronted—the man. In fact, Andrew insisted—something rare for him—so I sought out the followers of John the Baptist to inquire what he had asked of them. All I had to do was talk to the people in the markets, where John the Baptist was a popular subject. Everyone knew of him, and many there had heard him preach.

We learned that he asked nothing material or financial of the people, but he told them to repent and be baptized. John the Baptist had apparently come from the mountainous wilderness in the southeastern part of the land of Judah, or Judea, as the Romans called it, but no one knew exactly where he lived before. The gossip was that John preferred living in the wilderness to being in the city. Other than that, no one knew very much about him. The one thing I heard over and over was that people firmly believed John the Baptist was the Messiah.

In the meantime, it did not take Andrew and John long to locate John the Baptist. He frequented the other side of the River Jordan near a village called Bethabara. People came great distances to hear him preach and to be baptized by him. He was easy to find because of his large following.

On that day, Andrew and John heard the priests and Levites who had been charged by the Pharisees and Sadducees of Jerusalem to interrogate John the Baptist. They demanded to know if he was the Christ, the Messiah. This was a question that John and Andrew had not dared ask.

Standing in the river, John assured everyone, including the Pharisees and Sadducees, that he was not the Messiah. Once he had their attention, he boldly told everyone to repent and be baptized. In response to their questioning of his authority, he tantalized them with the declaration that the Messiah was among them. John intentionally insulted the Jewish leadership further by pointing out that neither the Pharisees nor the Sadducees knew who the Messiah was. John finished with his humble observation that "He who is coming after me is preferred above me. I am not worthy even to untie His shoelaces."

Neither Andrew nor John doubted or questioned John the Baptist's teachings. Instead, they absorbed his every word. They listened quietly as the Pharisees and the Sadducees badgered him with even more questions about his authority to baptize and about the identity of the Messiah. The tone of their questioning was sharp and antagonistic. It was obvious that they were unhappy with John's growing popularity. Even as John the Baptist spoke with the Pharisees and Sadducees, people went down into the river to have John baptize them.

It was at this gathering where my friend John met Caiaphas, the chief priest. Caiaphas was the powerful Sadducee who presided over the great Sanhedrin, the Israelite civil and religious court, since A.D. 18. In time, that acquaintance would prove useful.

Hearing that John the Baptist knew who Christ was, Andrew and John hoped the Baptist might reveal where to find Him or possibly even introduce them. However, it became obvious that John was very cautious in his remarks about the Messiah, at least in the presence of the Pharisees and the Sadducees. John was preparing the way for the Messiah, but he would not speak for Him.

Being serious-minded disciples, Andrew and John treated John the Baptist with quiet respect, unlike the insufferable Pharisees and Sadducees. Andrew and John were there to gather all the information they could so they could share it with me.

When John the Baptist said that he was not the Messiah, Andrew and John concluded that there was no reason for me to meet him. Hoping to learn something more about the Messiah, they stayed at Bethabara, listening to John preach. The crowd surrounding him grew as more and more people came to hear him and to be baptized by him.

Late in the afternoon, as John the Baptist preached repentance, he spied someone walking along the river bank. John abruptly halted what he was saying, gestured toward the man, and boldly announced, "Behold, the Lamb of God, which takes away the sin of the world." If John the Baptist spoke the truth, this was the Messiah, and Andrew and John were in His presence!

John the Baptist loudly repeated his testimony that this man was the Christ, explaining that Jesus was the One he had been talking about, the One who would come after him, the One preferred before him. John recognized Jesus as the

Christ, saying, "I know Him, not as a man, but as the Son of God." He added that Christ would make Himself known throughout all of Israel. John explained that his own mission was to baptize with water to prepare the way for Christ.

John the Baptist also bore witness that earlier, as he baptized Jesus in the river, he saw the Holy Ghost descend from heaven like a dove upon Jesus. John explained, "God spoke, and I heard His voice saying, 'This is my beloved Son, in whom I am well pleased.' I knew both by the voice of God and by this sign of the dove that Jesus was the Son of God. The angel who sent me to baptize with water told me that I would recognize the Messiah by that sign."

What a powerful testimony! I like to imagine what great joy and wonder lifted the hearts of Andrew and John as they saw Jesus for the first time. They told me later that they stood frozen as the long-awaited Messiah, Jesus the Christ, approached them. Then He passed by and was lost into the crowd. Knowing Andrew and John as I do, I suspect they were speechless. I might have been the same way, but I doubt it.

Andrew and John had found the Christ, but they were in such awe that they had let Him slip away, and they didn't know where to find Him. They then faced the problem of what to tell me. They had convinced me to leave Galilee to see the Messiah with my own eyes, and they let Him get away. They didn't dare go to Jericho and tell me of their folly, so they stayed in the wilderness that night.

Fortunately, they got another chance the following day. Later in the afternoon, as he stood in the river, inviting people to be baptized, John the Baptist stopped and repeated his earlier proclamation, "Behold, the Lamb of God!"

Calling Jesus "the Lamb of God" had specific meaning to Jews. The house of Israel had been sacrificing lambs at Passover for many generations in anticipation of the coming of the Lamb of God. Those listening with honest hearts and open minds understood exactly what John the Baptist meant and to whom he was referring. Certainly, Andrew and John understood him.

This time, as soon as John the Baptist announced the Messiah, both Andrew and John immediately followed Him. They were directly behind Him as He walked away. Of course, the Lord knew who they were and why they were there, but He turned and asked them what they wanted. I think it was His way of introducing Himself. Andrew and John called Him "Master" and asked where He lived. They explained that they needed to know where to find Him, so they could take me to Him.

Jesus motioned and invited them to follow Him as He has invited all men, saying, "Come and see." They gratefully accepted His invitation and followed Him away from the multitude. It was later in the afternoon, about four o'clock, when they arrived at the small village of Bethabara, so they stayed the rest of the day and listened as He taught them into the night.

The next morning, Andrew and John came to Jericho to find me. As they approached, Andrew boldly exclaimed, "We have found the Messiah!"

Without waiting to hear the rest of their explanation, we immediately set out to find Him. Bethabara was approximately five miles west of Jericho, and on the way, Andrew and John related everything that John the Baptist had said leading up to his proclamation that the man we were on our way to see was the Messiah. I confess that I completely forgot my skepticism in the exhilaration of the moment. In fact, I admit that I almost ran to where they said I would meet the Messiah. I was as excited as a child running home for a surprise promised by his parents.

WHEN I MET JESUS

The first time I saw Jesus, it was from a distance. That moment remains fresh in my memory—as if it were only a few moments ago. I may say this often, but I do not have the vocabulary to express the feelings that filled my soul. My heart beat rapidly, my mouth was dry, and my ears were ringing. Skeptic or not, I admit that my heart wanted this man to be the Christ, even if it seemed too good to be true.

As John and Andrew led me into Bethabara, we saw a handful of people surrounding someone sitting on a stone outcropping. Whoever He was, it looked as though He had far fewer followers than John the Baptist. As we approached, I tried to catch a glimpse of Him, but the small crowd blocked my view. When we arrived, those around Him made way for us, and that was the first time I saw Jesus. He sat on a large rock, talking to those around Him, explaining something in the law of Moses. He continued His discourse until He had made His point.

John drew nearer to Jesus, said nothing, and then gestured toward me as if to say, "Here is the one I told you about."

Jesus turned toward me and said, "You are Simon, son of Jonah." Then, with a smile on His face, He patted the rock He was sitting on and added, "You shall be called 'Peter.'"

I immediately knew Him to be the Messiah. I felt it. I can't explain how I knew, but I knew that this man sitting in front of me was the Messiah! There was a feeling of loving warmth that descended on me, similar to how John the Baptist described the Holy Ghost descending on Jesus at His baptism. Under the influence of that tender, sweet Spirit, I immediately knew that Jesus was the Christ. I apologize that I cannot explain it better, but it was unlike any feeling I had ever experienced. Tears fill my eyes whenever I remember the emotions of that singular moment in my life. I would never be the same. I would never want to be the same.

I realized that Jesus knew my given name from His earlier conversations with Andrew and John, but He also knew my heart. When the Son of God gives you a name, it is not merely a name, it is a title. When he called me a "rock," I confess it was an apt description.

In those days, it was a tradition to give a child a name with spiritual significance. My given name of Simon meant "God hears" or "God listens," referring to God hearing the prayers of my mother. However, being called a "rock" would have been an insult if it had been uttered by anyone other than Jesus, because it meant that I "listened like a rock." To be precise, Jesus was suggesting that God listened, but I did not.

I did not take His comment as an insult because it was true. I didn't listen to very many people, perhaps with the exception of my brother . . . now and then. So when Jesus called me a rock, I knew exactly what He meant. He knew that I truly was stubbornly immovable once I fixed my mind on something, and nothing anyone could say would change that. Jesus knew my heart. So, I ask, would the Son of God know anything less?

I am Peter.

WHAT DID JESUS LOOK LIKE?

One of the things people often ask is what Jesus looked like. Well, He was a Jew in His early thirties, the traditional age for Jewish men to begin religious service.

Other than what Isaiah mentioned nearly seven centuries before Jesus was born, there is absolutely nothing in the written record that describes Him physically. Isaiah counseled that it is not for His looks that we should desire Him.

I will note one thing though. He had the muscular body expected of one who was raised as the son of a carpenter. His powerful build was nothing like the emaciated weaklings portrayed in Renaissance paintings and sculptures. He was a "manly man."

Here is something those who await his return should know: as Isaiah suggested, it isn't His physical description by which men will recognize Him, but by His divine Spirit, just as it was when I met Him. To me, the power of His Spirit made His physical appearance inconsequential. He looked very much like a common man because we were created in His image.

As is often the case, the written record does not include what else was said when I met Jesus. What took place shall remain between us.

After our conversation, Jesus asked the three of us to follow Him on a journey to Galilee. He was the Son of God, so we followed Him.

GATHERING FOLLOWERS IN GALILEE

The next day, we all left Bethabara, walking north on the dusty, rocky pathway back to my beloved Galilee. As we traveled, Jesus explained that He had reasons to be in Galilee, and He wanted us to be there with Him.

Shortly after we entered the land of Galilee, we passed near, but did not enter into, the village of Nazareth. Jesus had told us that He had been raised in Nazareth, so I wondered why we passed it by, but I did not ask. Not wanting to act like a lawyer who asks endless questions, I often left it to Jesus to tell me what He wanted me to know when He wanted me to know it. About four miles beyond Nazareth, we entered Cana. We had traveled about twenty miles north from Bethabara, and we were about twenty miles southwest of my hometown of Capernaum. I knew Cana to be a beautiful little village, watered by many springs and surrounded by rolling hills, which were dotted with olive orchards.

As soon as we arrived in Cana, Jesus sought out and spoke to Philip, a man I knew because he was from Bethsaida. We heard Jesus invite Philip to join us, using His wonderful words, "Follow me."

I told Philip who it was that had invited him to be a follower, and he agreed to join our company without hesitation. He immediately excused himself and went in search of his good friend, Nathanael. When he located him, Philip told Nathanael that he had found the Christ, the One written about by Moses in the book of the law, the One written about by the prophets.

When Philip told him that the Messiah was Jesus of Nazareth, the son of Joseph, Nathanael was unimpressed and jokingly asked, "Can anything good come out of Nazareth?"

In those days, Galilee was ridiculed as culturally impure because many of its citizens were from Greece, Rome, Phoenicia, Syria, and other areas. Galileans spoke with an accent and dialect that Judeans mocked as being crude, corrupted by the idioms of the Syrians and the Samaritans. In turn, the people of Galilee looked down on those from Nazareth. It was considered either an insult or a joke to say someone was from Nazareth.

Nathanael's teasing did not discourage his dear friend. Instead, Philip confidently responded with a challenge appropriate for anyone wanting to learn of Jesus, which is, "Come and see."

As Philip and Nathanael approached us, Jesus proclaimed, "Behold an Israelite indeed, in whom there is no guile!" His observation took us by surprise. He knew Nathanael's heart just as He had known ours.

Expressing his wonder, Nathanael asked, "Where do you know me from?"

Jesus looked at Nathanael and said, "Before Philip asked you to come here, you were under a fig tree, and I saw you." Jesus had been nowhere near Nathanael, so He didn't see Nathanael the way we would think. Jesus saw him because He was a prophet—a seer—able to see things no ordinary man can see. This would not be the last time we would see Jesus do such a marvelous thing.

Only Nathanael and Jesus knew what happened under that fig tree and why it was so important to Nathanael, but it was meaningful enough that it immediately convinced Nathanael that Jesus was the Christ. With the greatest of reverence, Nathanael exclaimed, "You are the Son of God! You are the King of Israel!"

Jesus smiled at Nathanael and responded, "You believe in me just because I said I saw you under that fig tree?" Then Jesus turned to the rest of us. "You shall see greater things than this," he promised. "Here is the truth. I tell you now you shall see the heavens open and the angels of God ascending and descending upon the Son of Man."

That was the first time I heard Jesus call Himself "the Son of Man." I recognized the expression from what I had been taught from the law and the prophets. When I asked Jesus about it later, He confirmed that those verses referred specifically to Him. From then on, I understood that when Jesus said "Son of Man" it was the same as saying "the Son of God." He didn't explain further, but there were a lot of things He didn't explain in detail. It was up to me to learn a little at a time. It was up to me to pay attention.

As to His comment about the angels, I did not know then what He meant. I testify that in time I would see Him in the presence of angels. There was a lot that I would yet learn and experience, but I already knew the most important thing I would ever know: that the Messiah had come and He had invited us to walk with Him! Why He chose us instead of one of the many great and learned men in Israel was a mystery to me. I was a crude fisherman, a man without formal training, but I was walking beside the Son of God.

A WEDDING AT CANA

We were invited to attend a wedding feast the next day in Cana, where I met Jesus's family, including His half brothers, James, Joseph, Simon, and Judah, and His half sisters. I call them half brothers and sisters because they had the same mother, but not the same father. Jesus was the Son of God, not Joseph the carpenter.

I met Mary, the remarkable mother of Jesus. What an incredibly beautiful lady she was. An unmistakable glow in her countenance and the brightness of the light in her eyes touched me. There have never been any as blessed as she. Following Jesus's example, we accorded her even greater respect. I was privileged to witness the tender love and genuine thoughtfulness Jesus showed His mother. Truly, it can be said that He honored her.

A traditional wedding feast was a social event that could last more than a week. Friends and family would bring food and wine for the guests. Each contribution was received as a gift to the groom, whose family was responsible for hosting the wedding. I overheard that they were running short on wine because guests had brought more food than wine. Without wine, the wedding feast would end early, and Mary's family would be humiliated.

Another of our traditions was that wine was not acceptable for drinking unless it had been greatly diluted with water. In our time, unless water came from a fresh well, it was not safe to drink because it was often filled with bacteria, and it usually tasted bad. We used wine to make water safe to drink because the alcohol killed most of the bacteria, and it effectively masked the water's bad flavor. Depending on the tradition of the locality, Israelite wine had to be diluted with at least three and as much as ten parts of water before it was acceptable to drink. The Greek culture, whose influence was found throughout Galilee, mixed twenty parts of water with wine. Undiluted wine was called "strong drink," and anyone who drank it was looked down upon.

I heard one of the servants tell Mary that the wine was running low and that he saw no arriving guests with any more to present to the groom. Mary approached Jesus out of the hearing of the other guests. Pointing to the friends and family who were yet to give their gifts to the groom, she said, "They have no wine." It was clear to me that she expected Him to do something. I didn't know what miracles Jesus had performed as a youth, but it was clear to me that Mary was confident He could and would solve the problem.

Jesus addressed her with a term you might misunderstand; He called her "Woman." In those days, "Woman" was the ultimate title of respect. He went on to ask, "What would you have me do for you?" I didn't hear her answer, but after they spoke, Jesus assured her that He would help when it was His turn to present an offering to the groom, saying, "It is not yet my turn."

She responded by telling the servants, "Whatever He tells you to do, you do it!"

Jesus instructed the servants to gather stone pots from the house. They brought six stone water pots of different sizes, each holding from eighteen to twenty-seven gallons. He then told them to fill the pots with water. We watched as the servants filled each pot to the brim. When they finished, Jesus directed them to draw from the pots and take the drink to the "governor" of the feast for him to taste. The servants were shocked that Jesus would tell them to have the governor taste the water. As the "master of ceremonies," it was the governor's duty to dilute the wine with the appropriate amount of water and taste it to make sure it was acceptable. But following Mary's orders, the servants did as Jesus instructed.

The governor had the servants pour the water, thinking it was wine, into the crater, or mixing bowl. The nervous servants said nothing and did as they were told. The governor then ordered the servants to dilute the wine with water. The servants were amazed at what they saw. When the governor tasted it, he was astonished at its excellent quality. He found the bridegroom and complimented him in front of all the guests, announcing, "Most hosts serve the best wine first and save the lesser wine until everyone has had a lot to drink, but you saved the best for last." The governor had no idea the wine was the product of a miracle, but the servants did, and so did we. The servants told everyone, and the story of water being turned into wine spread throughout Cana.

After the feast, we accompanied Jesus, Mary, and the rest of their family as they traveled the twenty miles east to their homes in Capernaum. Mary and her family had recently moved there from Nazareth.

I never met Joseph, the husband of Mary, and the written record makes only one reference to him after Jesus was born, when He was twelve years old. I know that Jesus was taught by Joseph to be a carpenter, but I do not know when Joseph died.

At this time, the Passover was at hand, so after only a few days in Capernaum, Jesus left His family to journey to Jerusalem to observe the Passover. We went with Him, leaving James in charge of our fishing business. Our business continued to support our families, so we didn't leave them without income. We were responsible men.

I should also explain that every holy day, or holiday,

including Passover, was treated as a Sabbath day and observed from sundown on Friday until three stars were visible in the Saturday night sky. Moses was commanded that whenever the house of Israel observed a feast day, each such holy day was to be a Sabbath day in which no work was performed. So whenever a holy day occurred, we observed two Sabbaths the same week. Only occasionally did the "holy day Sabbath" fall on the day of the "weekly Sabbath."

CLEARING THE TEMPLE

As soon as we arrived in Jerusalem, Jesus went directly to the temple, the center of all religious observances. In those days, Jews were expected to make an annual pilgrimage to the temple to offer an animal sacrifice and to pay a temple tax of half a shekel—no more, no less.

Worshippers were only permitted to give certain silver coins, known as "temple shekels," which had the exact amount of silver. Taking advantage of the demand for this specific coin, money changers set up stalls in the outer courtyard of the temple grounds, known as the Court of the Gentiles. This is where they exchanged the money used in public commerce for the approved temple coins—at a liberal profit, of course. Others set up shops to sell a variety of sacrificial animals at appallingly high prices. Truly, they had turned the outer courtyard of the temple into a bazaar of discordance, filled with thieves who competed to take advantage of vulnerable customers. This had been the tradition for so long, we were numb to how inappropriate it was.

Unlike the rest of us, Jesus did not ignore or tolerate it. He did something that should have been done long before but something we did not expect. He told us not to interfere and pointed to where He wanted us to stand and watch. Then He thoughtfully surveyed the situation and prepared to expel the animal merchandisers and the numerous money changers from the Temple Mount.

What Jesus was about to do was not the first "purification"

of the temple. In fact, it was reminiscent of the purification of the temple that we celebrated every year, also known as Hanukkah. That holy day acknowledged the rededication of the temple that occurred after the Maccabees recaptured it from the Syrians. The house of Israel had celebrated the rededication of the temple for nearly two hundred years. The purity of the temple was something we took seriously. At least, we thought we did until we saw what Jesus did to clear it.

Some people may have the impression that Jesus acted in a fit of anger. Not so. After He surveyed the outer courtyard, He gathered a few small discarded cords from the floor of the courtyard and took the time to weave them into a short scourge, a kind of whip. He rapidly drove the sheep and the oxen from the Temple Mount. The men selling the animals grudgingly followed them, but none of them dared challenge Jesus. It was orderly, if herding cattle could ever be described as orderly. After the sheep and oxen were gone, Jesus commanded those who were selling caged doves to pick them up and carry them from the temple grounds immediately. They obeyed without resistance. His act was not a fit of violent rage as some may suggest, but instead it was an expression of His deep passion about the sacredness and the purity of the temple.

After Jesus methodically expelled all of the animals and their merchants, He had yet to "convince" the money changers to depart. Noticing their indifference to His request to leave the courtyard, Jesus did something to get their attention. Rather than condescend to a physical confrontation, He simply tipped over their tables, spilling their precious coins everywhere. They quickly scrambled to retrieve their scattered money, making sure no one took what was theirs. Then they hastily retreated from the temple grounds, clutching their money to their bodies. As a commentary on the character of money changers, they were held with the same regard as liars, cheats, and thieves. They were not trusted, their testimony was not allowed in court, and yet the Pharisees allowed them to do business at the temple. As the money changers exited the courtyard, grumbling and whining, Jesus boldly commanded them to stay away, saying, "Do not make my Father's house a house of merchandise!"

To some, the scene may seem chaotic, but Jesus simply purged the temple courtyard of what did not belong there, systematically and completely.

When He cleared the courtyard that day, everyone yielded or quickly got out of His way. There was a reason no one tried to argue with or overpower Him; He had an obvious physical strength, gained from a life as a carpenter, that no one wanted to quarrel with. In spite of His physical presence, His demeanor as He cleared the temple grounds was purposeful and controlled.

After He finished his task, those of us who stood and watched in stunned silence were reminded of the psalm that says, "The zeal of Thine house hath eaten me up." Zeal is a good word. His emotion was that of unrelenting energy and enthusiasm, not of rage or anger.

Almost as soon as the courtyard was cleared, the peaceful silence was broken. A group of Pharisees and chief priests, wicked men that they were, came bustling out of the temple to confront Jesus. Dressed in their long, colorful robes, they demanded that Jesus show them a sign to prove that His claim of authority over the temple was superior to theirs.

I observed to my friends that they didn't question why He did it; they only wanted a sign of His authority. The truth was that the chief priests were actually profiting from the merchandising done on the temple grounds. They knew it was wrong—everyone knew it was wrong—but they did it because it was profitable. In my opinion, the Pharisees were no better than the despised money changers.

In response to their pathetic request for a sign, Jesus assured the chief priests they would see a sign. Standing in front of the temple, He gestured toward Himself and said, "Destroy this temple, and in three days I will raise it up." He didn't say, "Destroy the temple." They clearly understood His one-word parable.

Jesus would use a word with its literal meaning in one instance, and then he would use it again with a symbolic meaning in the same breath. Part of it was the poetic language we used in those days, but more important, it was one of the methods Jesus used to teach. He often used metaphors and figurative language.

Quite often, He would refer to something nearby, such as bread, the light, water, or a shepherd, and then repeat the word symbolically in what I like to call "one-line parables" or even "one-word parables." Because of the way we spoke, we expected and understood this kind of symbolic imagery. I came to know Jesus as a master of language because He used words as tools to effectively communicate different things to different people. At other times, He used parables to hide the meanings of His teachings from certain people.

The leaders of the Jews later pretended that they did not understand the symbolism Jesus was using, but they clearly knew He was not referring to the edifice of the temple but to His own body. That day in the temple, the chief priests were only concerned about the money they would lose, and they resented Jesus as a threat to their corrupt enterprise.

Following the tactics used by arrogant "masters of the law" throughout history, they took the opportunity to distort His words to mean something other than what He said. They sarcastically observed that the temple had been under construction for forty-six years. This allowed them to mock a nonexistent claim that He could rebuild "the temple" in three days. In His wisdom, Jesus did not waste His breath in a debate with these wicked men. His insight into the hearts of men both comforted and alarmed me.

At that moment, I did not fully understand what He meant about raising up "this temple." It was not until the day He was resurrected that I came to comprehend what He meant that day. I make no excuses, but I was a fisherman, not a scholar of the law and the prophets. At that time, none of us understood what it meant to be resurrected. We all believed in the doctrine, but no one had ever been resurrected.

There was a time when I was hard on myself because I did not fully understand what was happening until after it unfolded. None of us knew that his body of flesh and bones would be raised from the grave. But He came out of the grave and walked with us. We touched His wounds, and we ate food with Him. The meaning of those events is essential to our understanding of God.

In the days following the clearing of the temple, we were with Jesus as He walked about Jerusalem. He taught the people in the open spaces. He taught in the shade of trees. He taught on stairways and porches. He taught at springs and pools of water. He taught from rock outcroppings around the city. He taught merchants in their stalls. He taught people wherever they would gather. What He said and the many miracles He performed are not found in the written record, but they happened. I was there, and I saw and heard them.

This was the first time Jesus went about teaching and healing. Rumors about Him and what He was doing spread quickly. People sought Him out to hear Him teach and to be healed. It was a time of wonders. It is a sad thing that the written record does not include all of the many things He said and did.

Because of His rapidly growing popularity, it did not take long for the corrupt rulers of the Jews to hear of Jesus. Their initial resentment turned to fear because His followers were rapidly growing in number, which was another threat to them.

Believers witnessed the miracles and recognized them for what they were, accepting Jesus for who He was. This was the beginning of His ministry, a ministry that would take us many places. I was there to see it, so I might testify of it to all who will listen. Jesus is the Son of God. Do not doubt it.

The days were filled with work, but the nights did not mean He rested from His labors. Jesus never seemed to weary as He filled every day with miracles. I was amazed at the power of the Son of God. My heart overflows as I remember it.

As His popularity grew, I observed a growing opposition from the wicked chief priests of Israel, the Pharisees and the Sadducees. They followed Him everywhere, standing at the back of the crowds, talking among themselves. Their faces betrayed their anger and hatred. I could also see fear in their eyes.

I began to be concerned for the safety of Jesus. I suspected they might try to harm Him or even kill Him. I carried a sword on my left hip, as many men did in our time. I resolved that I would not hesitate to defend Jesus if He were threatened. If I were to sacrifice my life for Him, it would be a privilege. No one would harm the Son of God as long as I was at His side.

Nicodemus of the Sanhedrin,
a Pharisee

As I watched the Pharisees and Sadducees in Judea, I became deeply suspicious of these so-called "rulers" of the Jews, the members of the Great Sanhedrin of Jerusalem. This powerful council had the authority to interpret and enforce both civil and religious law, even to execute someone, if they chose. I believed that this concentration of power had corrupted them. The council had a membership of seventy Pharisees and Sadducees plus a "chief priest," a man selected by the Roman Procurator. I observed that at least one member of this council was usually nearby, watching and listening, wherever Jesus taught in Judea.

The Great Sanhedrin was patterned after the Council of Seventy, which Moses was commanded to form to assist him in governing the Israelites. However, it seemed to me that the Sanhedrin were more interested in protecting their entrenched power than in serving God. From what I gathered, membership in the Sanhedrin and wealth was more than mere coincidence. I suspected that the love of money and what it could purchase were part of the Sanhedrin's "charter." There were also powerful local councils, with only twenty-three members, located in larger cities throughout Israel, including my own city of Capernaum, but the council in Jerusalem actively dominated the people.

That year, the Great Sanhedrin still had the authority to order executions—authority they would lose the following year—so it was still best to avoid them. Whenever I thought we had escaped them, one of their ranks would suddenly show up to watch Jesus, no matter where we were. I concluded that they perceived Jesus as a threat to their power because He was quickly gaining a large following of people who loved Him. He taught compliance with the law, which somehow infringed on the Sanhedrin's "religious" franchise.

One evening, we were gathered after dark, listening to Jesus as He taught us about His mission and explained the role of the Messiah. Jesus dismissed the long-held Jewish tradition that the Messiah would be a military leader who would lead Israel in revolution and overthrow the Romans. It was a common belief, and I confess that was why I left Capernaum to seek Him out. Jesus assured us that His mission was to change His countrymen's hearts, not their political leadership.

He had just started discussing the necessity of a man being "born again" when a member of the Great Sanhedrin boldly stepped out of the darkness to join our little gathering. I clenched my jaw as soon as I saw him come forward in the flickering glow from our fire. In the dim light, I could not see the colors of his long woolen robe, but its elaborate fringes testified that he was a Pharisee. Pharisees proclaimed their piousness by the expensive clothing they wore.

I was confident that I recognized this man. I had noticed him earlier, watching from the back of the crowd as Jesus taught and performed miracles in Jerusalem. After seeing him a few times, I had asked around and learned that His name was Nicodemus. It seemed to me that Nicodemus had followed Jesus more than anyone else. Now, he had followed us here. I was not pleased to see him, not pleased at all.

Nicodemus stood behind us, just as he had done before in the streets of Jerusalem. Then I noticed that his head was bowed slightly, a traditional display of respect. He listened courteously, without interrupting, possibly waiting for Jesus to acknowledge him. As soon as Jesus finished making His point, He gestured for Nicodemus to come forward and join us, which the Pharisee did without apology or comment.

I was curious to know why such an influential man would wait until dark to visit this insignificant congregation of disciples. With his power and position, if he wanted to make trouble for Jesus, he could have done it anywhere at any time. In my experience, the presence of a Pharisee at a congregation of believers inevitably led to antagonistic, mocking, or insulting comments. I expected this man to bring hostility to our peaceful gathering, so I wondered why Jesus had invited him to join us.

Nicodemus obediently sat down with the rest of us, choosing a spot between me and Jesus. I thought I detected the odor of incense on his clothing. As he prepared to speak, I observed a subtle smile. I expected him to offer an insult, but in an unexpectedly respectful tone, this imposing man humbly said, "Master, we all know that you are a teacher sent from God, because no man could do the miracles you do except God be with Him."

I was stunned. Nicodemus referred to himself as a believer—at least for the moment. Then Nicodemus sat in silence, waiting with the rest of us to hear what Jesus would say in response. I quickly recovered from my shock to wonder if Nicodemus was sincere or if he was acting as spy for the Sanhedrin.

Jesus paused only briefly before He resumed teaching. He knew that Nicodemus had missed the first few minutes of His discourse on the meaning of being born again, so He repeated what He had told us, turning His head and speaking directly to Nicodemus.

Jesus started by saying that He was there to correct the foolish traditions of our fathers. He spoke of being baptized by John the Baptist and said He had been immersed in water as an example for all men. He explained that all men needed to be baptized, and all men, including those of the house of Israel, needed to be "born again." This was a new concept. We had been taught that only Gentiles needed to be "born again" because they were not born into the house of Israel.

I should add that many Jews were truly arrogant in their belief in Jewish superiority to the point that Israelites openly detested Gentiles. This attitude was returned in kind by the Gentiles. Traditionally, Israelites hated everyone, and everyone hated Israelites.

Jesus refuted the Jewish tradition that being descended of Abraham was all that was required of a man to qualify for citizenship in the kingdom of God. I was certain this Pharisee would feel insulted, so I was surprised when he offered no objection. Jesus took a few more minutes to summarize the essentials of what Nicodemus had missed. Then, turning fully toward Nicodemus, the Lord continued to address him, adding, "Here is the truth that I would have you know, except a man be born again, he cannot see the kingdom of God."

Nicodemus seemed perplexed and asked his first questions: "How can a man be born when he is old? Can he enter into his mother's womb a second time and be born?"

Frankly, Nicodemus knew better than his questions might suggest. He could not break the lawyer's habit of twisting a man's words and repeating them back as a question, but I understood that it was simply his method of asking Jesus to expand on His teaching.

Jesus knew exactly what Nicodemus meant. "This is the truth I want you to know: every man must be born of the water, which is being immersed in the water, then be lifted out again as if symbolically coming out of the grave," He explained. "This is baptism. Every man must also be born of the Spirit. He must do both or he cannot enter into the kingdom of God.

"That which is born of the flesh is flesh, and that which is born of the Spirit is spiritual. Do not marvel that I have said you must 'be born again' because you know what it means." Jesus paused for the Pharisee to absorb what He had just said.

To Nicodemus, Jesus's point of view was a new—and unsettling—application of an old precept. Jews thought of baptism as a ceremonial cleansing, a token of our covenant to obey the law of Moses. That it was required of Jews as a symbolic death and rebirth was new. After all, Nicodemus had been taught that being born of the house of Israel was enough. We all remained quiet, wondering what Jesus would say next to enlighten us.

During the silence, a night breeze blew through the trees, causing a noticeable whooshing sound as it passed through the leaves. Sparks rose from our little fire as the breeze twisted the flames into a small whirlwind, making the fire crackle. Jesus gestured toward the trees and said, "The wind blows wherever it will. You hear the sound the wind makes, but you do not know where it came from, nor do you know where it is going. It is the same with being born of the Spirit. Your earthly knowledge cannot help you understand spiritual things."

Nicodemus seemed to struggle with this new information, which required him to rethink and reorder his long-held beliefs. He asked, "How can these things be?"

Jesus challenged this learned man to be open-minded and to listen to what He was saying. Jesus said, "You are a rabbi in Israel and you don't know these things? In truth, I speak only of that which I know, and I testify only of that which I have seen, but you do not accept what I tell you. If you will not believe the truths I tell you about earthly things, how will you ever believe if I tell you truths about heavenly things? No man can bear witness as I have, because no man has ever ascended up to heaven except the One which came down from heaven, that is, the Son of Man."

Jesus had just testified to Nicodemus that He was the Son of God. Jesus paused and Nicodemus sat quietly, stroking his graying beard as he contemplated His testimony. We watched him but said nothing. Finally, Nicodemus looked up and changed the subject, saying, "I have heard talk among the Pharisees that you said you expect to be killed."

Jesus nodded His head as if agreeing, but He persisted in His testimony that He was the Son of God. Jesus spoke softly, "As Moses lifted up the serpent in the wilderness and those who looked upon it were saved from the bites of the fiery serpents, so shall the Son of Man be lifted up. And those who believe on Him shall not perish but shall have eternal life."

That comment was a "beginning" for me. I saw how much of our Israelite tradition and history symbolically pointed toward Jesus. I marveled that a crude fisherman such as I could understand such a marvelous thing.

I was surprised that Nicodemus was still confused. His head was tipped slightly to the side, and he leaned forward as if to ask, "Why must these things be?" He started to ask his question but stopped, expressing his confusion with a furrowed brow.

Jesus responded to his unasked question by rephrasing His earlier comment: "Because God so loved His children, He gave His only fathered Son, that whosoever shall believe in Him shall not perish, but shall have everlasting life. God did not send His Son into the world to condemn it, but that through His Son, His children might be saved."

Nicodemus sat motionless with the puzzled look of "Why?" still on his face.

Jesus continued, "Those who believe in the Son of God are not condemned, but those who do not believe are condemned because they do not believe in the name of the only Son fathered by God."

Jesus used the darkness of the night to explain. Pointing to Himself, He said, "This is their condemnation: the Light has come into the world." Then gesturing to the darkness surrounding us, He added, "But they love the darkness instead of the Light—because their deeds are evil. Those who love evil hate the Light. Tonight, Nicodemus, you came out of the darkness into the Light, but evil men do not come to the Light because they fear that their deeds will be known and reproved. Those who love the truth come to the Light because their deeds will be known as being done in obedience to God."

I was listening too, and I now understood that four things were required of a follower of Christ. First, belief in Him as the Messiah, the actual Son of God; second, repentance by turning away from evil and coming into the Light of Christ; third, being born of the water, which is being baptized by immersion; and fourth, being born of the Spirit, the final part of what Jesus called "being born again."

We all pondered what Jesus had just shared with us as we watched the fire slowly burn itself out until we had only the moon to light the night. I sat quietly as I judged myself, and, as usual, I judged harshly.

After a while, we arose to retire for the night. Nicodemus spoke privately to Jesus before he left, but we could not hear what words passed between them. Nicodemus seemed to be a believer, but I still wasn't confident he was to be trusted. Later, I learned that Nicodemus had joined us that night at the request of some of his fellow members of the Great Sanhedrin, not as a spy. I was greatly surprised to learn that there were other believers within the Sanhedrin, but they were afraid to say anything. They feared that the wicked Pharisees would expel them from the synagogue and that they would lose their status and the source of their income. That was why Nicodemus came to Jesus in the night. He did not want to be seen by the Pharisees or the Sadducees.

Nicodemus was like many who called themselves believers. They loved the praise of men more than the praise of God. Sadly, nothing has changed from that time to this. One cannot follow Jesus without offending those who oppose Him. Some people, like Nicodemus once did, may believe in Jesus, but they do not follow Him. As Jesus said, it is not enough just to believe.

I know that some are offended when they learn they are expected to believe in and follow Christ to receive eternal life. They insist that if they are "good people," that is all that should be necessary to be granted eternal life. I only have one question of them: if you reject Christ, why would you want to be with Him in the eternities? That, after all, is what eternal life is.

I testify to you that it is because of Him that you will be resurrected, and it is because of Him that your sins will be taken from you, but only if you repent of those sins.

Jesus is the Son of God. What He says is the Word of God. Believe Him.

TEACHING IN JUDEA

The next day we traveled together into Judea, the land surrounding and just to the south of Jerusalem, where Jesus continued teaching and we continued baptizing for the next several weeks. I was glad to be out of Jerusalem, away from the Great Sanhedrin and the city's great numbers of Pharisees and Sadducees. Jesus baptized some but not as many as His disciples. Those with good hearts found us and came to the Light, just as Jesus had told Nicodemus they would. They came to be baptized, so we baptized them, being authorized to do so by Jesus. These people were following the four steps Jesus had outlined to Nicodemus.

All this time, John the Baptist continued baptizing people too. He had not yet been cast into prison. When we left Jerusalem, John was at the springs and the many pools of water near Salim, not far west of the River Jordan, where Andrew and John had found him. Believers continued to seek him out, and he baptized them in the water. He did not merely wash them, nor did he sprinkle water on them, and he did not carry a pitcher with him and pour water over their heads. He baptized them, immersing them under the water and then lifting them out, just as he had baptized Jesus and just as Jesus had taught us to do, symbolically representing their death and resurrection.

John the Baptist's disciples told us that some of the Pharisees tried to confront them over purification rites. The Pharisees were concerned that traditional Jewish purification rituals were being discarded in favor of John's baptism.

They also told us that the Pharisees followed John, asking him about Jesus, trying to irritate him, saying, "Rabbi, do you remember the One which was with you beyond Jordan? Behold, He baptizes also, and all men go to Him."

The Pharisees were trying to stir up trouble, so John's answer was not what they expected. Addressing all who could hear, John said, "A man can receive nothing from heaven, except it is given to him from heaven. You heard for yourself that I said, 'I am not the Christ.' I also told you, 'I am sent before Him.' The bride is for the Bridegroom. I am the friend of the Bridegroom, and I stand and hear Him, rejoicing greatly at the sound of the Bridegroom's voice. In that, my joy is full."

The Pharisees continued, implying that Jesus was somehow usurping John's authority by baptizing. John quickly enlightened them. "His following must increase, but mine must decrease," he said. "He that came from above is above all." Then, gesturing to himself, John continued humbly, "He that is of the earth is earthly and speaks of the earth."

When the Pharisees continued pushing John to condemn Jesus, he recognized their strategy and again acknowledged Jesus as the Christ, repeating his testimony. "He who comes from heaven is above all," he proclaimed. "He testifies of that which He has seen and heard. No man receives a testimony of Him by himself. He can only receive a testimony of Him by the Holy Spirit, sealed by God, to know that His testimony is true. He whom God sent speaks the words of God. God did not give Him only a measure of the Spirit, but because the Father loves His Son, He gave all things into His hands. Any man who believes on the Son has eternal life, but he who does not believe on the Son shall not see eternal life. Instead, the wrath of God will be upon him."

After hearing John's explanation to the Pharisees, several

more of John's disciples left his side and joined us to follow Jesus. They told us that everyone knew Jesus was baptizing in Judea and that He was gathering believers. Over several weeks, it became known throughout Judea that Jesus now had more followers than John, just as John prophesied.

John the Baptist's disciples also told us that John put their minds at ease by continually reminding them that his only mission was to prepare the way, continually bearing witness that Jesus was the promised Messiah, the Son of God. A few days earlier, John had warned them, saying prophetically, "Now that Jesus is teaching, my work of preparing the way for Him is coming to its conclusion."

It was while we were in Judea that word came to us that the Tetrarch, Herod Antipas, had arrested John the Baptist and cast him into prison. Herod Antipas was a wicked man, the son of an even more wicked man. His father was the king who was known by some as "Herod the Great." To others, Herod's father was secretly called "Herod the Great Murderer" because he killed his own sons and other family members, not to mention the many children he ordered murdered in his futile attempt to kill the newborn Messiah.

John the Baptist had publicly denounced Herod Antipas because the Tetrarch had divorced his wife to marry his brother's daughter, his niece Herodias. She, in turn, had divorced one of Herod's half-brothers, Herod II Boethus. Herod Antipas arrested John the Baptist to stop John's public condemnation of their divorces and their incestuous relationship.

I grew increasingly concerned that the Pharisees and Sadducees of the Great Sanhedrin might arrest Jesus to stop Him from preaching, just as Herod had arrested John the Baptist. I was certain that the members of the Sanhedrin wanted to have Jesus killed, and they had the authority to do it. I feared for Jesus, knowing that wicked men with hatred in their hearts had the power to execute Him. In order to distance Himself from these wicked men and allow Himself to teach freely, Jesus told us that we were going to journey to Galilee.

I was greatly relieved.

THE WOMAN AT THE WELL

Jesus told us it was time to leave Judea, but instead of going around Samaria, the traditional route, He headed north, traveling directly through Samaria. I quickly appreciated the wisdom of His decision; this was certainly not the route favored by most Jews. I knew that His choice would discourage spies from the Sanhedrin because Jews did everything possible to avoid contact with Samaritans.

Jews hated Samaritans because of their connection to the Assyrians. This time-honored hostility had two sources. First, Samaritan blood was of the house of Israel, but it was mingled with the blood of Assyrians and other traditional enemies of Israel. Being of mixed blood, Samaritans were detested by Jews. Second, because the prophets wrote harshly of the Assyrians and of intermarriage, the Samaritans flatly rejected anything the prophets had written. Socially, Samaritans were dealt with as if they were "beneath" the Jews, inferior even to Gentiles. The Samaritans reciprocated this hatred, piously claiming religious superiority.

At the same time, it was a curious fact that Samaritans observed the law of Moses more faithfully than Jews, adding to the mutual distrust that existed between the two groups. In addition, the Samaritans had a better understanding of the nature of the Messiah than the Jews because the Samaritans expected Him to be a spiritual leader, not a military one.

I looked forward to leaving Judea because of its proximity to Jerusalem, but I was equally concerned about how we would be received in Samaria. Because we were Jews, I doubted we would be welcome. I was troubled about how the Samaritans might treat Jesus. Looking back, this was probably the beginning of my resolve to protect Him from anyone who might do Him harm, whether they be Jew, Samaritan, or Roman.

It was about noon when Jesus, tired and thirsty from the journey along the rocky road from Jerusalem, stopped at Jacob's well near Sychar of Samaria. It was located in the fertile valley between Mount Ebal and Mount Gerizim, both of which stood less than a thousand feet above the valley floor.

John the son of Zebedee and I remained with Jesus while the rest of the disciples went onto Sychar to buy something to eat. I stayed because I felt that I should be near Jesus in case He needed protection from the Samaritans. He was certainly not a physical weakling, but I carried a sword, and He did not. As Jesus paused to rest, once more He did the unexpected and asked a Samaritan woman for a drink of water.

We were not the only ones surprised at His request. The woman at the well was astonished too. She responded, "How is it that you, being a Jew, ask me, a Samaritan woman, for a drink? After all, Jews have no dealings with Samaritans." This woman knew that the accepted "etiquette" between Jews and Samaritans was to treat one other as if they were invisible. She was wary of a Jew bold enough to ask her for a drink of water, so she began to verbally spar with Jesus.

Jesus understood the origin of her feelings and answered as if there were no differences between them. "If you knew about the gift of God and whom it is that is asking you to 'Give me something to drink,' you would have asked of me, and I would have given you living water."

The woman was so preoccupied with what she might say to insult Jesus that she completely ignored His symbolism. "Sir, you have nothing to draw water out of the well, and this well is deep," she retorted. "From what well will you draw living water?" Then, without waiting for His answer, she continued her scornful interrogation. "Are you greater than our father Jacob, who gave us this well and drank from it himself, along with his children and his cattle?"

Instead of accepting her challenge to argue, Jesus patiently gestured toward the well and continued, "Whosoever drinks of the water from this well shall thirst again, but whosoever drinks of the water that I shall give him shall never thirst because the water I shall give him shall be within him a well of water springing up into everlasting life."

His patience and courtesy disarmed her, and she softened her disposition. She said, "Sir, please give me the water of which you speak, so I will not thirst and will not have to come here to draw water." She had stopped her attack, but she still did not understand His symbolic reference to water, His one-word parable.

Now that she was listening, Jesus quickly drew her out,

saying, "Go, call your husband, and then return."

The woman turned her head in shame and replied quietly, "I have no husband."

Of course, Jesus knew her situation. Bringing her another step closer to understanding who He was, Jesus continued, "You spoke well when you said, 'I have no husband,' because you have had five husbands, and the man you are with now is not your husband. In that, you spoke honestly."

The woman's eyes widened in wonder, her anxiety disappeared, and a smile appeared on her face. She exclaimed, "Sir, I know from what you have said that you are a prophet!"

Filled with unquestioning faith in this discerning Jew, the Samaritan woman immediately asked Jesus to resolve one of the fundamental issues that separated Samaritans from Jews. To the south of where she stood, Mount Gerizim was within her view. As a Samaritan, she had been taught that Mount Gerizim was the true center of religious observance because there was once a temple there. Because the temple stood in Jerusalem, the Jews taught that Jerusalem was the correct place to worship God. She gestured toward Gerizim and said, "Our fathers worshipped at this mountain, but as a Jew, you say that Jerusalem is the place where men ought to worship."

Before she finished framing her question, Jesus answered her with the same respectful title He used with His own mother, saying, "Woman, believe me, the time is coming when you shall worship the Father neither at this mountain nor at Jerusalem. Because of your fathers' traditions, you do not know what you worship. Jews do know what we worship. Further, salvation will come from a Jew. The time, which has been so long in coming, has now arrived. True worshippers shall worship the Father—not by outward ritual, but spiritually and in truth. These are the ones the Father seeks to worship Him, and this is how He wants them to worship Him.

God is spiritual, so those who would worship Him must worship Him spiritually, knowing who He truly is."

The woman seemed to understand, expressing her simple faith and an unexpectedly sound understanding of the Messiah. "I know that the Messiah is coming, He that is called Christ," she said. "When He comes, He will teach us all things."

Then Jesus rewarded her unconditional faith, uttering the most wonderful words anyone in search of God would ever hear. Speaking plainly, without symbolism, He said, "I that speak to you am He."

Take a minute and delight in the supreme joy of that moment, just as this Samaritan woman certainly did. At first she was silent, but after a while, she tried to speak but could not form the words. Her chin trembled slightly, and her voice only made a squeaking sound. Tears filled her eyes. Her hands and legs were weak. There, in front of her, was the Christ, and He was speaking to her, a Samaritan woman.

By now, Andrew, Philip, and Nathanael had returned from Sychar to see Jesus courteously conversing with this woman as if she were a Jew and not a lowly Samaritan. They spoke among themselves, marveling that he would lower himself to speak with such a woman. They observed from a distance, without saying anything to Jesus or the woman at the well.

Because they kept their distance, they did not hear what Jesus told her. They watched as she turned and left Jesus. She bounced as she walked, almost as if she were able to walk without touching the ground. She set down her water pot and quickened her pace, speeding up as she ran toward the village. The disciples wondered if she were just trying to get away from this large group of Jews, but I knew better because I had seen it before in Judea. Her inexpressible joy was demonstrated by her childlike desire to run and share what she knew with everyone.

After she left, the disciples offered meat to Jesus, sharing what they had purchased in Sychar. He declined, saying, "I have been nourished in a way that you do not know."

I have since come to know for myself that He was referring to the spiritual fulfillment that comes from serving God, from feeling the presence of His Spirit while edifying those who seek the truth. Physical hunger is the last thing on your mind at those times. I suspect that such a feeling cannot be understood without experiencing it.

The disciples were surprised at His answer but still concerned about His welfare. Everyone knew that Jews were forbidden to eat food prepared by an "unclean" Samaritan, so they doubted that He had eaten anything she might have offered. They also knew that even though Jews were allowed to eat freshly harvested fruit and vegetables from Samaritan fields, it was late in the spring and not yet the harvest season. They said, "Certainly, it is four months too early for anything to be harvested." As they discussed the situation among themselves, I asked, "Has anyone yet given Jesus anything to eat?"

Jesus knew what was troubling me and comforted me, saying, "My nourishment is to do the will of Him that sent me and to finish His work." Then Jesus looked toward the city, and, with a sparkle in His eyes and a smile on His face, He said, "Do not speak of the harvest of the fields being four months away. Lift up your eyes, and you will see fields which are white already to harvest." Then Jesus nodded toward Sychar, His smile becoming even more apparent.

As we turned and looked toward the city, we beheld several large groups of people coming our direction. There were not twenty or thirty, but maybe a hundred or more people, all walking quickly toward us. It was not a mob but a host of believers. I had seen believers before, and I recognized them by the smiles on their faces and the light in their eyes.

They were coming to greet the Messiah. I was surprised and delighted.

Jesus gestured toward the approaching throng and said, "Know that whosoever reaps these fields shall receive wages and shall gather fruit for his eternal life. Know also that both he that sowed and he that reaped shall rejoice together over this harvest. You have heard the saying that 'One man sows and another reaps.' It is true today. You are sent to harvest in fields where you have not labored, where the prophets have labored, but you shall enjoy the results of their labors."

Again, Jesus used more of His powerful one-word parables, this time He referred to "nourishment" with two meanings, to "fields" with two meanings, to "sowing" with two meanings, and to "harvesting" or "reaping" with two meanings. His symbolism was elegant.

As the multitude gathered around Jesus, they told us that the woman at the well had scurried around the village of Sychar. She talked to anyone who would listen, saying, "Come to Jacob's Well and see a man, a man who told me everything I did. Is this not the Christ?" They saw the joy in her face and the tears in her eyes, and their hearts were touched. They were quick to believe her because of the preparatory labors of the prophets in the past. As a result of her testimony, swarms of people left the village of Sychar to meet Jesus at the well.

Many Samaritans listened and believed in Jesus after coming to him in response to the words of the woman at the well. They trusted her account and believed in the coming of Christ, and when He arrived in Samaria, they pleaded with Him to stay. He remained and He taught them.

This "field" was indeed white, just as Jesus said, and He was there to harvest. The next day, there were even more Samaritan believers. They came because of the woman at the well, but they stayed because they believed Jesus. They gained their own testimony of Jesus. "We know that this is indeed the Christ, the Savior of the world."

After two days, Jesus ended His teaching of the Samaritans, and we continued our trip into Galilee. At the beginning of this journey, I was apprehensive about traveling directly through Samaria, but it turned out to be an unforeseen joy, a wonderful experience that I still treasure.

Directly north of Sychar was Nazareth, the village where Jesus grew up. Instead of entering the village, we again went around it without stopping. As we did so, Jesus said something he would repeat later, "A prophet has no honor in his own country." He knew He would not be acknowledged as the Christ in Nazareth. It must have been a disappointment, especially after the way He was received in Samaria.

HEALING THE SICK IN CAPERNAUM

As we traveled in Galilee, Jesus was welcomed by the people in every city and village. He took the time to teach the multitudes whenever they gathered around Him. In fact, He spent His time teaching everywhere we went, always attracting crowds who sought the Messiah or who wanted Him to heal their sick. Some of the people of Galilee had been in Jerusalem months earlier for Passover, so they had seen or heard of the miracles He performed in Jerusalem and in Judea.

We eventually arrived at Cana, where He had turned the water into wine at the wedding feast. Indeed, His reputation for miracles was well known, so word quickly spread from Cana that Jesus was back from Jerusalem. On the Sabbath, He went to the synagogue and taught.

One of those hearing of His return to Galilee was a Roman official who lived in my hometown of Capernaum, nearly twenty miles to the northeast of Cana. The Roman's son was near death, sick with a fever. The morning he heard that Jesus was in Cana, the Roman left Capernaum, finding Jesus at about one o'clock in the afternoon. He pleaded with Jesus to immediately come with him to Capernaum to heal his dying son.

Jesus turned to the multitude and said, "Except you see signs and wonders, you will not believe." To some, Jesus might have appeared to be speaking to the Roman nobleman, but His comments were clearly directed to the crowd, which had gathered out of curiosity to see Jesus perform a miracle.

Knowing that the journey to Capernaum would take precious time that his dying son did not have, the Roman official urgently pleaded with Jesus again, "Please sir, come to Capernaum before my son dies."

Because it was the Sabbath, travel to Capernaum would violate the commandments. Even if it were not the Sabbath, Jesus knew the boy's condition was too serious for Him to travel to Capernaum before the boy would die. Prior to this, I had seen Him heal many people, but they were always in His presence. This time, He chose to heal the boy without leaving Cana. He comforted the Roman, simply saying, "You may return to your home. Your son shall live."

Without argument or hesitation, the Roman believed Jesus and immediately started his journey back to Capernaum. His faith was simple and complete, very much like that of the woman at the well.

My friends in Capernaum told me that the next morning the Roman's servants met him on the road and said, "Your son is still alive, and he is doing better."

They also told me that the Roman affirmed his confidence in Jesus by asking, "When did my son begin to get better?"

And they answered, "The fever left him yesterday at one o'clock in the afternoon."

The Roman father testified to everyone in his house—his family, his friends, and his servants—that Jesus declared his healing words, and they all believed in Christ. This was the second miracle Jesus did in Galilee.

I had seen many miracles and many faithful believers. This time, He performed a miracle that the multitudes could not see. I was saddened that two of the most faithful believers—the Samaritan woman and this Roman—were not of the house of Israel. Why were the Jews so reluctant to accept Jesus as the Messiah? They accepted false Messiahs but not the true Son of God. I marveled.

ONE SABBATH IN NAZARETH
AND CAPERNAUM

W e were only in Cana a few days before Jesus told us that the time had come for Him to return to Nazareth, the small town where He had been raised. He took me aside and told me that He would go alone. That night, He walked to Nazareth and stayed with someone He knew from the days of His youth.

The following day was the Sabbath, and Jesus went into the Synagogue to read. Following the custom of the time, He stood to read and asked for the scroll of the Book of Isaiah. He read the following verse in Hebrew, "The Spirit of the Lord God is upon me because the Lord has anointed me to preach good tidings unto the meek. He has sent me to bind up the brokenhearted, to proclaim liberty to the captives, and for the opening of the prison to them that are bound; to proclaim the acceptable year of the Lord."

When He finished reading this short passage, He closed the scroll, handed it back, and sat down. Sitting was the signal He was going to comment on what He had read. One of the traditions of our time was that individuals were not allowed to stand in the front of the room but were required to sit if they chose to translate or expound on the scriptures. Every eye was fastened on Jesus as all listened to His commentary.

Jesus spoke in Aramaic—the language of His hometown—slowly, carefully, and in a voice just loud enough for everyone to hear. Instead of translating the scripture or commenting on it, He said only, "This day, this scripture is fulfilled in your ears."

Jesus told us that everyone clearly heard and understood what He said. At first, the tenderness and sincerity of His spirit offset the shock of His statement. He had just borne personal witness that He was the Messiah. The gracious tone of His voice and the presence of His divine spirit filled those present with a feeling of peace, but Jesus said that their doubting hearts forced them to immediately question the words He had spoken. A skeptic broke the silence and asked, "Is not this Joseph's son?"

Jesus, knowing their thoughts, replied, "You will surely quote the proverb, 'Physician, heal thyself.' And you will also say, 'We have heard from Capernaum about the miracles you did. Do those things here, in your own country, so we can see them.' I know that you wish to see a sign, but I tell you this truth, no prophet is accepted in his own country."

Jesus continued, "I remind you of the fact that in the days of Elijah, there were many widows in Israel when the heavens were shut up three years and six months, and there was a great famine throughout all the land. This is the fact I would have you remember: Elijah was not sent to an Israelite but to a Gentile, a widow in the city Sarepta, a city near Sidon."

His comments sounded like an insult to the ears of the arrogant Jews in the crowd. Jesus continued with another observation that added to their insult. He said, "And there were many lepers in Israel during the time of Elisha the prophet. Elisha did not cleanse any of them, but he did cleanse Naaman the Syrian.

His point was clear: Gentiles have faith also, sometimes even greater than that of Israelites. Later, when He related this event to us, I savored the experience of the Samaritan woman and the Roman nobleman in Capernaum. They were marvelous examples of the faith He told them about.

To the Jews in Nazareth, Jesus was nothing more than the son of a carpenter, not the Messiah, and His claims were offensive. Enraged, they jumped to their feet, grabbed Jesus by His arms, pulled Him out of the synagogue, and forcefully took Him to the edge of the city. Jesus said they intended to throw Him headfirst from the rocky cliffs of the Nazareth Ridge to murder Him.

When Jesus related the events to me, I nearly exploded with my own rage. Jesus calmed me, assuring me that they could have no power over Him, but what He allowed them to have. When they had done everything they would, up to actually killing Him, they had fully proven the wicked intent of their hearts. At that moment, He loosed Himself and walked away from them because they had no more power over Him. He left them bewildered, looking for Him, and He went to stay in the home of His old friend. The following day, He returned to us, His friends in Capernaum. When Jesus left Nazareth for Capernaum, He fulfilled the prophesy of Isaiah that He would be afflicted in the land of Zebulon and Naphtali, and afterwards be at the sea beyond Jordan, in Galilee. This also fulfilled the prophecy that the people of Galilee that walked in the darkness would see a great Light, and the Light would shine on those who walked in the shadow of death. The prophecies of old were being fulfilled.

Had I been in the synagogue with Jesus when they took hold of Him on that Sabbath day, my sword would surely have drawn blood. I am certain that is why Jesus left me and went alone, only to tell me about the event afterward. He knew that I was resolved in my heart that any who would harm Him would lay dead at my feet. I was resolved that I would be struck down before I would allow anyone to harm Jesus.

I admit that I am a man of action with a tendency to be a

bit hasty. My friend and fellow disciple, James, had cautioned me about this particular weakness because he knew that even though I made my living as a fisherman, I was a warrior at heart. It would not be easy for me to change or ignore what was in me if Jesus were threatened.

Yet Jesus never appeared to feel threatened. He taught the people of Capernaum in the synagogue that Sabbath day as He would do on any Sabbath. He acted as if nothing of importance had happened the week before in His childhood village. Still, I knew by the way He talked that it saddened Him greatly, which is why I suspected He avoided Nazareth when we traveled. Unlike the people of Nazareth, the people of Capernaum were amazed at the divine power by which He delivered his words. His message and His spirit touched their hearts. Many people came to Jesus to be near him, to see and hear Him, and to be healed. I know it was a pleasant contrast to His experience in Nazareth.

Casting out a Devil

That Sabbath day, as Jesus taught in the synagogue, there was a man possessed by an evil spirit. His friends held his arms and carefully led him toward Jesus. As he approached the Lord, the man cried out with a loud voice, shouting, "Let us alone! What business do you have with us, Jesus of Nazareth? Did you come here to destroy us? O, I know who you are; the Holy One of God!"

I was stunned. I had just heard an evil spirit, a servant of the devil, bear testimony that Jesus was the Son of God. This devil recognized Jesus and physically trembled in His presence. I learned two things that day. First, Satan and his minions knew and feared Jesus from a time before the world was. Second, the fact that a man knows and testifies that Jesus is the Son of God does not necessarily differentiate him from the devil. I knew that the devil knew Jesus and testified of Him too. Sadly, this latter truth may offend those who believe that testifying of Him saves them from their sins. It certainly didn't save that evil spirit that day in Capernaum.

James, the unbelieving brother of Jesus, was in the synagogue that day also. He was similarly impressed with this testimony, and the time would yet come when he would accept his brother as the Messiah and would testify of Him. He said later that the difference between the devil and a faithful man is not his testimony of Jesus but what he does with that knowledge.

Without hesitation, Jesus firmly rebuked the demonic

spirit, commanding, "Hold your peace, and come out of him!"

Immediately, the evil spirit forced the man to tear at his filthy, ragged clothing and throw himself to the floor. Then the man was silent. He was alone, unhurt, and no longer possessed. He lay on the floor exhausted, looking around in wonder.

That day, I saw for the first time that Jesus had power and authority over the devil! My heart leapt with joy and a passion that I find difficult to express. Later, Jesus explained why He had silenced this devil. Because Satan's goal is to deceive man, he will first tell a truth to gain a man's trust. Once that confidence is established, Satan will begin to deceive him with cunning lies. Know that anyone who trusts him will be deceived.

The people who saw this spectacle were all in total wonderment and amazement because they had never heard nor seen such a thing. They wondered about the source of the power and the authority that Jesus had over those demonic spirits. They were in awe of Him. Jesus had done miracles in Judea and in Cana, but now He had done a miracle in Capernaum. Word of this miracle spread quickly. Within days, many more people throughout Galilee had heard of Him.

As the multitude gathered closer to hear Jesus, their hearts and ears were open to hear. Jesus taught them, "The kingdom of God is at hand. Repent, change your ways, and believe the gospel." It was a good day.

Being in Capernaum felt safe compared to how Jesus had been received in Jerusalem and Nazareth. We were in my land, surrounded by the kind of people I knew and trusted. I was growing comfortable with letting Jesus go His way without my protection. Perhaps I flattered myself that I could protect Him, but that was what my heart told me I had to do. We all knew that the wicked Jews wanted to kill Him. I would do what I could to prevent that.

Being in our own land also meant that my brethren and I were expected to take care of our fishing business. We were not men of leisure, so we returned to our daily labors as fishermen. I joined my partners, and we sailed out each night on the Sea of Galilee to fish. I did not know what the future might hold for me as a disciple of Christ, but I would always be a fisherman.

FISHERS OF MEN

Very early one morning, my brother Andrew and I were focused on our work, fishing at a spot near the rocky shore that usually yielded fish. We were balancing ourselves in the boat, casting our nets into the sea, when we heard a man call out to us, saying, "Fishermen!" I recognized His voice. It was Jesus. As usual, just hearing Him lifted my heart. We stopped immediately to hear what He had to say.

Jesus called again, saying, "Come, follow me. I will make you fishers of men!" He used another of His wonderful one-word parables. When the Lord said, "Follow me," parable or not, that is exactly what I did. We pulled our empty nets into the boat, stowed them properly, and rowed to shore. We followed Him straightaway.

As we walked with Him along rocky edge of the shore, we saw James and John and their father, Zebedee, along with the men who worked on the boats for us. They were in their boats, not far from where we had been fishing. They were mending their nets, a constant chore for good fishermen. Jesus called to them, repeating the words, "Fishermen, come, follow me. I will make you fishers of men." And like us, they immediately followed, leaving their nets and their boats in the experienced hands of Zebedee and our hired men.

Zebedee had the privilege of hearing both of his sons being called by Jesus, and he rejoiced with them at their opportunity to be in His service. I was especially pleased that Jesus asked my friend James to join us. He had missed out on all that had happened up to now. He was busy taking responsibility for our business. James was a good man.

The following morning, we planned to follow Jesus as He taught in Capernaum. I got up very early to do some last-minute chores before leaving my family and my business. As I walked by the room where Jesus slept, I saw that He was not there. It was very early, not even dawn. I looked around the rest of our home, but He was not to be found. I woke Andrew and asked if he knew where Jesus was, but he had no idea either.

We opened the door to look around the outside of our home. A crowd was already gathering, awaiting the appearance of Jesus, wanting to hear Him or to be healed. Wrapped in blankets, it appeared that many of them had been there several hours, if not all night. Many of them were asleep, but others were awake, watching my home. We tried not to attract any attention as we left, but we failed. Some of the crowd followed us as we walked to the home of James and John. They did not know where Jesus was either.

I knew that no one had come into my home and forcefully taken Jesus away, so I concluded that He had gotten up even earlier than I did and had gone to some secluded place to be alone. He did this often to pray to His Father in Heaven. Earlier, when we walked had toward Capernaum, I told Him about my favorite place to be alone. He seemed to know about it already. It was out of the city in an area best described as a desert. I wondered if He would be there.

I decided to search for Him, just to assure myself that He was all right. As we left with James and John, the crowd that had gathered was even larger than when we arrived. Apparently, they sent the word to others that we were seeking Jesus too. There was no way for Him to go anywhere without a crowd gathering. Today, they followed us in search of Him.

We determined that each of us should go a different direction to give the impression that we were looking for Jesus in several places. If I couldn't lose them, at least I would bring fewer people if I found Him. I was reluctant to lead the crowd to Him. I did not want to interrupt His privacy, but I could not be at peace until I knew He was safe.

I found Him just as I suspected. He was praying, alone at the place we had talked about, and I interrupted Him. Not only that, but I had a small crowd following me. I asked the crowd to stay behind while I spoke to Jesus. Then I approached the Lord. I apologized profoundly for interrupting Him and explained that many people were seeking Him and that some of them had followed me there.

People knew that Jesus had traveled to Jerusalem, Judea, and Samaria, so they feared He would soon leave Capernaum. They wanted Him to stay so they could hear Him preach and bring their sick for Him to heal. They were concerned that He might leave before they could bring all of their friends and family to Him. Even as we spoke, the crowds began to press in on Jesus, pleading with Him to stay in Capernaum. It seemed that only a few minutes passed before the crowds that had followed Andrew, James, and John heard where Jesus was and started collecting around us. It quickly became crowded.

Jesus called me, along with Andrew, James, and John, to His side. He said, "Let us go into the next towns, that I may preach there also because that is what I am here to do." Then Jesus stood on a rock and said to the gathered crowd, "I must preach the kingdom of God to other cities also. That is the reason I have come."

Many were disappointed, but I was surprised that they also seemed to agree with Him. That He was in Capernaum at all was a great blessing. One man spoke to assure the crowd, saying that Jesus had stayed at my home and that I would be traveling with Him, so Jesus would certainly return to Capernaum. That hope seemed to satisfy everyone. Before the morning passed, we left Capernaum.

JESUS TRAVELS
THROUGHOUT GALILEE

We followed Jesus all about Galilee as He preached. During those months, He taught in synagogues in many cities. He preached repentance and the gospel of the kingdom of God. He healed all manner of illnesses and disease, and He cast devils out of those who were possessed.

One day, a group of men came to Jesus, bringing a man that was possessed by the devil and was unable to speak. Jesus promptly cast the devil out, and the man started speaking. The multitude all marveled, saying, "Such things have never before been seen in all of Israel." Well, such things had happened before, all across Israel, all at the hands of Jesus.

By this time, Pharisees had started following Jesus too. Of course, after all of the things Jesus did that day, they conferred among themselves for an explanation of His marvelous power. They finally announced their conclusion, "He has power through Beelzebub, chief of the devils." If any group had a connection with the devil, I was sure it was the Pharisees.

I knew of the greatness of the Lord, and many times I felt unworthy to be at His side. I was an ordinary man, crude in my ways, lowly in my education, and subject to the temperament of men. In a way, His greatness was intimidating to me, but when He asked me to follow Him, I obeyed. I was greatly pleased that He blessed the people of my homeland.

Wherever we traveled in Galilee, people had already heard of Jesus. People with all manner of afflictions awaited

Him, greeted Him warmly, and treated Him with honor and love. His fame went out of Galilee, even to the north throughout all of Syria. People came from many places, and they brought with them all manner of people who suffered from diverse diseases and torments, knowing that Jesus had the power to heal. They brought those who were possessed with devils, those who were insane, and those with tremors and paralysis. Jesus healed them all.

There were more and more followers every day. Great multitudes of people came from Galilee, Decapolis, Jerusalem, Judea, and beyond Jordan. Everywhere He went, there were crowds awaiting Him, and there were always crowds following along behind Him. It was a tiring time for all of the disciples, but Jesus never wearied of doing good works. His strength and energy never seemed to be exhausted. Jesus saw that we were weary and needed to rest, so after a few months, we all returned to Capernaum. It was good to be home.

LET DOWN YOUR NETS

Whenever I was at Capernaum, I took the opportunity to go fishing. Yes, fishing was work, but sometimes work has a restful, refreshing effect. I often retreated to my boat when I had things to ponder or if I needed to focus my thoughts. As I busied myself with the mundane physical activities of being a fisherman, my mind was cleared and invigorated. I loved being a fisherman because I was good at it. At the same time, I loved the Lord with all my heart, but I often feared I was not worthy to be with Him.

Late one evening, I joined Andrew, James, and John, and we went fishing. We fished at night because that was when we had the best results. But that night we caught nothing! In the morning, we retreated to shore with our empty boats. As we washed and mended our nets on the shore of Galilee, Jesus approached Andrew and me. As usual, a huge throng of believers surrounded Him, seeking to hear His words and to be healed. They were closing in on Him, making it difficult for Him to do anything but keep walking.

Our boats were near us, so Jesus asked me to take Him aboard one of them and go out a short distance from the rocky shore. I was pleased to do so, and Andrew joined us in the boat. James and John got in their boat and followed us. When we were only out a short way, Jesus had me cast the anchor. Then He sat down and began preaching to the people on shore, using our boat as His pulpit.

His sermon was wonderful, filled with challenges and

insight. I listened intently, drinking in every word as if it were pure cool water to my dry, weary soul. I was comforted in His love, but I felt unworthy to be one of those allowed to be with Him. Before I was ready for Him to stop preaching, He had finished.

He paused only briefly before He asked me to pull in the anchor and launch the boat into deeper water. He said, "Let down your nets and draw them in one more time." We were physically exhausted from throwing our nets all night without catching a single fish. I said, "Master, we have worked all night and have caught nothing." Humbly and obediently, I added, "Nevertheless, at your word, we will let down our nets."

I expected to pull in our nets and find them empty—again. Instead, our nets did not yield to our pull. It felt as if we had snagged something heavy and could not draw our nets to the surface. Slowly, very slowly, our nets rose. When they approached the surface, they were so full of fish that they were breaking. We beckoned to James and John to come next to us to help us draw in the nets. As we emptied the nets, there were so many fish that both boats were in danger of sinking.

Everyone stood, astonished. Andrew, James, and John said nothing, but I could not remain quiet. I felt unworthy to be in the Lord's presence. Tears filled my eyes, and I fell to my knees. Bowing in front of Jesus, I said, "Depart from me because I am a sinful man, O Lord."

No, I didn't want Him to leave, but there were many better men who could be at His side and serve Him. Jesus knew what was in my heart. In great compassion, He lifted my bearded chin, looked into my tearful eyes, and said, "Fear not, fisherman; from now on you shall catch men." His words warmed my soul, but what gave me peace was knowing that the Lord knew me and He still wanted me with Him. I felt His love.

In silence, we rowed our overloaded boats back to shore, being careful not to overturn them. After we unloaded our catch, we stowed our nets and turned everything over to Zebedee, the father of James and John. That was when we left our lives as fishermen and followed Him. We would be fishers of men from that day on.

Cleansing a Leper

Once again, we left Capernaum and traveled into Galilee. Excited crowds followed behind us and gathered around Jesus whenever we stopped or entered a city. As we entered one city, a man whose body was obviously plagued with leprosy fell at the feet of Jesus and pleaded with Him, saying, "If you will, you can make me clean."

Of all the diseases that afflicted man in our time, leprosy was the worst. There was no hope, no medicine, no cure—nothing but waiting for your body to decay and die. This man's plea was one of simple faith. He knew that Jesus could heal him, and he only asked if He would.

Without hesitation, Jesus bent over him, touched him on his head, and said, "I will. Be clean."

He spoke but four words, but when the man looked up at Jesus, the leprosy was gone from his face and skin. I was startled at what I saw or, rather, at what I didn't see. His body was whole, and when he stood, it was obvious to everyone that the man had been totally cleansed of his leprosy. The man tried to speak, but no sound escaped his mouth. He was overcome with gratitude. Tears spilled from his eyes and ran down his cheeks as he looked down at his healthy hands and arms, then his legs and feet. The man shook his head in disbelief and breathed in deeply, trying to maintain control of his emotions. His body shook as he sobbed uncontrollably. We were all tearful, sharing his joy.

The man stood there as if he didn't know what to do

next. Jesus instructed him, "Tell no man what has happened. Instead, go to the priest and observe the law of Moses to receive the testimony to those who will pronounce that you are cleansed and may again enter society."

The cleansed leper was so ecstatic at being healed that he could not keep his silence. Of course, the best way to be sure a man will share his story is to tell him that it is a secret. He told everyone that he had been cleansed, who had done it, and how He did it. As a consequence, the crowds that followed Jesus about Galilee grew even larger. They came to Jesus to be healed of all their infirmities. The crowds were so large that He found it difficult to enter the smaller villages. Sometimes He stayed outside of those villages and spoke from a hillside, where there was more room.

It was a gratifying time to see Jesus so beloved and so honored in Galilee. At the same time, I was worried that local Pharisees would send word of His amazing popularity back to the Pharisees and the Sadducees in Jerusalem. They would feel even more threatened if they saw how many people were following Jesus and how much they loved Him in Galilee. Sometimes I even feared they would send assassins to kill Jesus. I believed that they were not only corrupt but that they were cowards too. If they could, they would find a way to have someone else kill Jesus for them. For that reason, I was on continual watch for anyone who looked threatening as they approached Jesus. I never told anyone what I was doing. I just did it.

Ordained an Apostle

Jesus always had a crowd following Him. After they were healed, most returned to their homes, but it seemed that greater numbers always replaced them. It comforted me that we were part of His following, but it thrilled me that He had asked us to follow Him. I felt at ease in the presence of the Son of God because He knew my heart and still wanted me at His side. Those feelings prepared me for the historic event that was about to take place.

Later in the afternoon, when He departed from the Galilean city where He had taught, we walked together to a nearby mountainside. Jesus specifically asked the twelve of us to go with Him, but, as usual, many others followed. Along the way, Jesus spoke to us with a tenderness that warmed my heart.

We left the crowd at the bottom of the mountain and followed the trail up the side until we came to a level spot near the top. Jesus went off alone to kneel and pray, far enough that we could see Him, but not so close that we could hear his words. He communicated with His Father in Heaven. I kept watch, making sure no one interrupted Him.

Jesus prayed to His Father in Heaven the whole of the night. He was not on the side of the mountain praying to Himself. As Jesus would say, "Let him with ears hear." I would say, "Let him with a brain think." Jesus and His Father are not the same person. Jesus, the Son of God, knelt and prayed to His Father, not to Himself or some unknown "substance."

I wish to dispel any belief that says Jesus and His Father are the same individual, making Jesus His own Father.

In the early hours of the morning, Jesus called the twelve of us to His side and spoke to us privately. He told us that He was going to ordain us to be Apostles, those He would send to preach the gospel of the kingdom of God and testify of Him.

Starting with me, He laid His hands on each of our heads and gave us very specific priesthood keys, the power and authority to act in His name. He gave each of us power over unclean spirits so that we could cast them out. He also gave us power to heal all manner of sickness and disease.

As the first one ordained, I became the senior Apostle. I mention this not as a boast but as a statement of fact. When He ordained me, He called me Peter, the name He gave me when we first met. Then He ordained my brother Andrew. The next two were James and John, the sons of Zebedee. Just as He had given me the name of Peter, He gave James and John the surname of Boanerges, meaning "sons of thunder," for that is what they were—bold men with little patience for disbelievers.

In order, Jesus then ordained Philip, Nathanael, Thomas, Matthew, James, Thaddeus, Simon, and Judas Iscariot. These were the Twelve Apostles, personally chosen and ordained to the priesthood under the divine hands of the Lord Jesus Christ after His night of prayer. With the single exception of Judas Iscariot of Judea, we were all men of Galilee like Jesus.

Being the senior Apostle came with certain leadership responsibilities. In the absence of the Lord, it was my duty to preside. The commitment this role required was not something I ever took lightly. I also note that it was not until later that I was actually given the rest of the keys of leadership.

I've already given much of my background and confessed a few of my many faults. I would like to add that I believe there is a right and wrong in most things. I believe that shades of gray are where people look for excuses to do what is wrong. I cannot abide people who create a good reason for doing the wrong thing. They are clever, but I do not believe the Lord is ever deceived.

Sometimes I react to evil men without giving the consequences of my actions a lot of consideration. Some have called me "impulsive." I might agree, but I won't. Most of the time, right and wrong do not take a lot of thought to discern. I find no need to waste time debating the obvious. I've always tried to do what needed to be done. I expect the same from anyone claiming to serve the Lord. I make no apologies for my intolerance of sin or those clever devils who hypothecate excuses to commit sin. That should be more than enough about me.

I would like to introduce the rest of my brother Apostles, in the order they were ordained. Andrew, my brother, made himself responsible to keep me in check when he felt it was necessary. Men with no brother may not understand the relationship between us. We were brothers by blood and in the Apostleship.

James and John were my good friends and partners in our fishing business. Like me, and possibly in part because of my example, they were not pleased with any who rejected the Lord. Jesus called them "sons of thunder" for good reason. They were men of strong faith and belief. Given the Lord's approval, they would have destroyed evil from the face of the earth, but that was not part of the Lord's plan. They loved Jesus in a way that can only be appreciated by someone who has served Him. They wanted to be with Him, one on each side of Him, in heaven. They were bold men, and I respect them for it.

James, John, and I were often alone with Jesus. There was a reason for that. Rather than have me preside alone in His absence, Jesus asked them to serve with me, to counsel me, and He often taught us privately.

My young friend John loved the Lord, and the Lord loved him. I love these men as brothers too. John grew to be such a dedicated follower of Jesus that he asked if he might remain on earth until Jesus returned in His glory.

The next Apostle was Philip. He is only mentioned briefly in the written record because his contribution and presence were low profile most of the time. He was a follower. Still, he was an important part of our group, important enough that Jesus traveled from Jericho to Galilee to find him and invite him to join us as a disciple.

Philip's friend was Nathanael, or Bartholomew, as many people called him, because he was the son of a farmer. Like Philip, he is only mentioned briefly in the written record.

Thomas, also known as Didymus, meaning he was a twin, was next. Thomas, like the rest of us, lacked an understanding of the Lord's mission as it unfolded before us. Unlike the rest of us, who listened patiently and learned, Thomas spoke out and betrayed his lack of understanding. Thomas did not lack faith in or love for the Lord. In a way, Thomas and I were much alike in our temperaments. Thomas spoke; I acted.

Matthew, also known as Levi, was the son of Alphaeus. He was a publican, a living for which the Jews held him in great contempt and barred him from the synagogue. Publicans purchased the position of tax collector from the Romans and thereby had the authority to levy and collect taxes. In effect, publicans left the ranks of the oppressed to become one of the oppressors. Matthew also authored the book given the first position in the written record of Jesus. With the exception of the feast where Jesus was Matthew's honored guest, he humbly wrote very little about himself. Matthew felt that giving that feast was the privilege of a lifetime. Who among us would not find it an extraordinary honor to feed the Son of God?

James the son of Alphaeus is traditionally referred to as

"James the Less," to distinguish the two men. As I noted earlier, they were not actually named James, but Jacob, and their name was pronounced "Ya'akov" in Aramaic.

Thaddeus, also known as Lebbeus Thaddeus, was sometimes referred to as Judas the son of James.

Simon Zelotes was one of the zealots, a deeply patriotic, nationalistic group who held all Romans in contempt. Candidly, we all held Romans in contempt, but the zealots did so with a public passion, something that was not always wise to do. Simon's heart, as with the rest of the Apostles', was softened by the love of the Lord.

The last Apostle was Judas Iscariot. Judas acted as "treasurer" for the Apostles, handling what little money we received. Jesus knew the heart of Judas, just as He knew the hearts of all men.

After Jesus ordained us, we all went down from the mountainside and into the village, where we were invited to have supper in the home of a believer. We were tired, and we had not eaten for some time. Along the way, the multitudes surrounded Jesus and followed Him. They overflowed the house so that our host could not serve us any food, nor could we even sit to rest. I worked my way through the crowd, hoping to lead Jesus out of the multitude, but when I got to Him, He was busily healing the sick and afflicted. I wondered if He were beside Himself, filled with a compulsion to help everyone within His reach while ignoring His own well-being. I had benefited from His great love too, but I was greatly concerned for Him.

TRAINING NEW APOSTLES

We remained at the house in Galilee until later in the day when the crowd began to disperse. Our host provided us with food to take to the mountainside where we could be alone with the Master. Jesus sometimes taught us at my home, other times as we walked, and, many times, overnight on a mountainside, where we spent the whole night being taught privately by Jesus.

That night, we learned that the nature of our calling as Apostles was to stand as witnesses of the Lord Jesus Christ, to go out among the house of Israel and teach the Jews about the kingdom of God. He forbade us to teach either the Gentiles or the Samaritans. Instead, we were instructed to seek only the lost sheep of the house of Israel and preach to them that "the kingdom of heaven is at hand."

The priesthood we had received was given freely, and we were to use its power freely. Jesus told us to go out two by two. He instructed us that we were to use the priesthood to heal the sick, to cleanse the lepers, to cast out devils, and, he added, to raise the dead. That's right, He instructed us to raise the dead!

Was I concerned? As a crude fisherman, I admit I was not comfortable with this responsibility. However, as an Apostle of the Lord Jesus Christ, I did not stop to consider if there were any limitations to what we could do. My calling as an Apostle made me a different man. Later, I would have the opportunity to raise a good woman named Tabitha, also called Dorcas, from the dead in Joppa.

Jesus challenged us to take nothing with us as we journeyed. He told us to go without purse or scrip. We were not to take pouches for money or for food. Even more, He told us to take only one pair of shoes and one coat. If we were used to carrying a staff, we were to leave it home. After all, He said, as workmen, we would earn what we needed to eat. I trusted the Lord completely, but I didn't trust people that much.

In His instructions, Jesus gave us very specific things to say and do. As we entered into a village, we were to inquire who in the village were believers, seeking those who were faithful to the Lord. If there were believers, we were to go to them, announce ourselves, and ask to stay with them while we were in their village. If we were well received at those homes and if they were faithful, we were to bless them with peace. If we were well received, but the people were not faithful, we were to accept their hospitality, but we were not to bless them.

Finally, if we were turned away from a home or a village, we were to perform a specific task. We were to shake the dust off our feet as we left as a testimony against them. Jesus said, "Here is a truth to know: it shall be easier for the land of Sodom and Gomorrah in the day of judgment than for that village or that house where you have dusted off your feet."

Jesus then warned us to be cautious in our dealings. He said, "Behold, I am sending you out as sheep among the wolves. Be as wise as serpents but as harmless as doves." This time, instead of using His usual one-line parables, He used similes.

As Jesus continued, He watched the Pharisees below us, and then He took the opportunity to caution us about what would happen to us in the future. He told us it was not to happen in the immediate future but soon enough. He said, "Be cautious of evil men because they shall take you captive, deliver you up to their councils, and scourge you in their synagogues. There will be wicked men who take you before governors and kings because you preach in my name, but their acts will be a testimony against themselves and against the Gentiles. When they deliver you up to their councils, take no thought about how you might defend yourself or what to say, for it shall be given you in the very hour what to say. Know this truth, the words you shall say will not be your own but the words of your Father in Heaven, speaking through you by His Holy Spirit."

Jesus continued prophesying about what we would one day see in Israel. The opposition we were to see would be from Satan and those who follow him. Jesus said, "One brother will deliver up his own brother to death for believing in me, and the father will deliver up his child for believing in me, and children will rise up against their parents and cause them to be put to death for believing in me."

Then Jesus warned us about what we should expect to experience as Apostles, saying, "You shall be hated by all men because you will be healing and teaching in my name, but those of you who endure to the end shall be saved. When they persecute you in one village, abandon it and go to another. Here is a truth I want you to know: you shall meet again with the Son of Man before you can finish visiting the cities of Israel."

I was relieved to know that we were not being sent out permanently. We would gather again with Jesus before we had gone to all of Israel. I resolved to teach as many people as possible in whatever time we would have. I had no idea how much time would pass before we were with Jesus again, but I would make it productive. I would not be embarrassed to report my actions to Him when we met.

Then, just to remind us that we were in His service and that we should expect to receive the same treatment as He had received, Jesus said, "The disciple is not above the Master nor the servant above his Lord. It is enough for the disciple to be treated as well as—but not better than—his Master and for the servant to be treated as well as—but not better than—his Lord. If they call me the prince of demons, Beelzebub, they are likely to call you the same."

He was preparing us to be defamed, spat upon, accused, tried, and beaten. One cannot serve God without offending Satan. If that were all He had to say, we might have been fearful of our futures, but He had more.

As the stars faded from the morning sky, we saw that a multitude had gathered at the foot of the mountain during the night. As the light filled the valley, the size of the crowd became more apparent, so large I could not number them. In the early morning light, they were stirring, waking, and arising from the blankets where they had spent the night. From our spot on the side of the mountain, I noticed a group of Pharisees working its way through the multitude, causing people to scatter and to trample those who had not yet arisen from their sleep. I suspected the Pharisees were offering insults to those in the multitude who had come to see Jesus and be healed by Him.

As I was thus observing, another of the Apostles was preparing bread for our breakfast. He was cooking the leavened bread on the coals of the fire that had kept the chill of the night from us. The sweet smell of cooking bread filled our nostrils.

Referring to the bread and the darkness of the night, Jesus spoke two more of His one-word parables, "Beware of the leaven of the Pharisees, which is hypocrisy. Do not fear them for what they might do. They can do nothing in secret because anything they cover shall be uncovered; anything they hide will be revealed. Whatever is spoken in darkness shall be heard in the light, and that which is whispered in the ear in private places shall be proclaimed from the housetops."

Then Jesus both warned and comforted us about being killed by the wicked Jews. He said, "My friends, do not be afraid of them who might kill your bodies because they can do nothing to you after that. However, I forewarn you about whom you should fear; it is God, who has power to cast you into hell after He has taken your life. I tell you to fear God."

He continued, "Are not five sparrows sold for the price of two mites, yet not one sparrow is forgotten by God? Even the very hairs of your head are numbered by Him, so do not fear. You are of infinitely greater value to Him than many sparrows."

Gesturing toward the Pharisees below us in the multitude, Jesus said, "When they take you into the synagogues before their magistrates and authorities, do not worry what you are going to say or how you are going to say it because the Holy Ghost will give you the words to say at that time."

Then, as the sun began to shine on our gathering, Jesus challenged us to share what He had taught: "What I have spoken in our nightly discourses, teach in the light of day. What I have spoken quietly, preach from the rooftops."

He made us a promise, saying, "If you testify before men that I am the Son of God, I will testify before my Father which is in heaven that you are mine. Likewise, if you deny that I am the Son of God before men, I will deny that you are mine before my Father which is in heaven.

"Whosoever shall utter a word against the Son of Man shall be forgiven, but he who blasphemes against the Holy Ghost shall not be forgiven."

I would never think to speak against Jesus, nor would I ever deny the Holy Ghost. In my heart was the hope that our testimonies of Jesus would help bring peace to my people. I knew of the corruption and treachery of the Pharisees and the Sadducees, but I wanted to believe that the ordinary people of the house of Israel were better than that. I confess that I have been overly optimistic at times—and this was one of those times. Jesus brought me back to reality.

Jesus pointed to our fire and said, "Do not think I came

to spread peace on earth. I have come to spread fire on the earth. What will I do if the fire is already kindled? I have a baptism that I am yet to be baptized with, and I am greatly distressed until it shall be accomplished." Then, pointing to my sword, Jesus said, "My presence on earth will be as a sword dividing families. A father shall be divided against his son, a son will oppose his father, a mother will be divided against her daughter, a daughter will oppose her mother, and a daughter-in-law will oppose her mother-in-law, because of me. A man who believes in me shall find that his worst foes are in his own household. And when that happens, if a man forsakes me for the love of his father or for the love of his mother, that man is not worthy to be called mine. And if that man loves his son or his daughter more than he loves me, he is not worthy to be called mine."

I understood what He was talking about. I had seen families split over one member professing belief in Jesus. It was heartbreaking to see. He added, "Following me has a price: rejection by the world and rejection of the world. It is a 'cross' that the faithful must bear. He who takes this cross and follows me is worthy of the eternal rewards that I have for him. He who does not take this cross and does not follow me is not worthy of the eternal rewards that I have for him."

I was aware of the significance of His reference to the cross. It was the method the Romans used for execution. It was a long, painful, humiliating death. Before they executed a man, they would tie him to a post and beat him with a leather whip with metal balls and pieces of broken bone that were designed to shred the skin and the underlying muscle. This "scourging" was intended to weaken a man before his crucifixion to quicken his death, but the whipping was so severe that it would often kill him before he was crucified. If a man did survive the scourging, the Romans would force him to carry the crossbar, or the "cross," to the place where he was to be crucified. Sometimes men died along the way. When Jesus referred to "bearing a cross," we clearly understood that following Him would not be an easy task.

Some people are under the mistaken impression that if they follow Jesus, He will make their life easy. Some even demand it. It is not so, and it never was. Cain murdered Abel because Abel did well in the sight of God, and Cain did not. I understood completely that we could not follow Jesus without offending those who did not, and that would be the "cross" we would bear. It was our choice to follow Him, but He was preparing us to make an informed choice.

Jesus said, "Which of you, intending to build a tower, will not sit down first and count the cost of building that tower to know whether you have what it takes to finish the project?" He wanted us to know the cost of choosing to follow Him and to make our decisions in the light of that knowledge.

Then Jesus expounded on the eternal reward of making that choice, of what we should expect if we take up our cross and follow Him. He said, "He who 'finds' his life, shall 'lose' it, and he who 'loses' his life for my sake, shall 'find' it." This time, Jesus was using a two-word parable. My first thought was that as Apostles, we had already "lost" our lives; we had given up the lives we had before we became Apostles. We did it because the Son of God asked us to, not because of the reward we hoped to earn. He let us know that some of our number would be murdered. It was sobering; we were quiet.

Jesus said, "He who will receive you will receive me, and he who will receive me will receive Him who sent me." We were going out and representing the Son of God and His Father. Our tasks were weightier than I initially thought.

Still, my heart was full in the presence of Jesus. Knowledge that He was the Messiah, the Son of God, was the most uplifting, most important, most joyful knowledge in my mortal and eternal life. I felt compelled to testify of Jesus to my family, my friends, and even those I did not know. I truly was His Apostle.

As Apostles, we were all sent to do what we all wanted to do anyway—to testify of Him. We would be hated for it, but we would share the eternal joy we had with those who were seeking Him. Not everyone would receive our message gratefully. Some would be indifferent; some would hate us. Being defamed, mocked, and beaten would be the price we would pay, but it would be worth it. Opposition served as a confirmation that we were doing His work.

I knew that if we kept our knowledge secret, we would be withholding the joy of knowing that the Son of God was on earth and that His name was Jesus. The very nature of who I was and what I knew compelled me to testify of Jesus to every soul who would listen. Now it was our duty, given us by the Messiah. Those who would not hear would not share the joy we had. We were not to impose our beliefs on anyone, but those seeking the truth would listen and recognize it. We were not to threaten anyone into submission; the fear of man or fear of death is not obedience to God. We were to share our joy. Those who would choose to follow Jesus could receive that same joy. To me, it was simple.

As Jesus explained, "He who shall recognize a prophet and receive him as a prophet shall receive a prophet's reward. He who shall recognize a righteous man and receive him as a righteous man shall receive a righteous man's reward. Further, even the one who but gives a cup of cold water to these 'little ones' will receive a reward."

Jesus often referred to us as His children, or His "little ones." It was a loving term, not a demeaning one. He loved us. To those who have given a cup of cold water to someone in need, I would ask, "Have you entertained angels unaware of who they were?"

SENDING THE APOSTLES

We were ready to serve, sent by Jesus to testify of His mission, traveling two by two throughout Israel. We boldly preached repentance and cast out many devils. When we found someone who was sick—and there were many—we anointed them with oil, just as Jesus had taught us, and they were healed.

Shortly after we left, Jesus appointed seventy more men and ordained them, not as Apostles, but as the "Seventy." As with us, He sent them out two by two, but He sent these unnamed men to cities to prepare the way for Him. He then went about teaching and healing, just as He had sent us to do.

We went as we were instructed, but when we returned to Galilee, my first concern was to make sure Jesus was safe. I knew that John the Baptist remained in Herod's prison, and I felt a personal obligation to protect Jesus if it ever came to that.

I was excited to see Him again. Even now, my heart beats faster and my eyes fill with tears as I remember seeing Him after returning from teaching so many about Him.

After Jesus greeted us, He asked each of us to report what we had done. John began: "We saw a man casting out devils in your name and forbade him because he was not one of us."

Jesus tactfully corrected him, saying, "Forbid him not, for he who is not against us is for us." I found myself repeating in my mind the word "us." It was wonderful to hear Jesus refer to "us" as if we were all "one." Certainly, I was "one" with Him.

SERMON ON THE MOUNT

While Jesus talked to us, the multitude that gathered around Him grew even more, expanded by the crowds that had followed us back to Galilee. They had traveled from many cities and towns to see and hear Jesus. They came from all of Judea, including Jerusalem, and from the coast as far north as Tyre and Sidon, cities in what is now Lebanon.

Jesus walked among the multitudes, preaching about the kingdom of God and healing those who had come to be healed. I marveled at His compassion and love for those who surrounded Him. We tried to keep up with Him, but the crowd often closed around Him, and people reached out for Him, trying to touch Him or His robe. And as they touched Him, they were healed. Upon seeing these healings, the multitude pressed even closer.

I thought that there was a real danger that people might be trampled. I led the Apostles, and we encircled Jesus, escorting Him from the middle of the crowd at the edge of the valley, up on the side of the mountain. Now Jesus was safely able to heal each person, one at a time, which He did.

It was near midday before the crowd drew back. As they did, Jesus went a short distance down the side of the mountain to stand on a stone outcropping. He motioned for everyone in the multitude to come closer. He asked them all to be seated and listen. We stood a little lower on the mountain, between Him and the crowd, until most of them were seated and quiet. When Jesus sat down, we made our way to His side and sat around Him.

From His position on the hillside, Jesus was able to speak so all could hear. He proceeded to preach to the multitude, instructing them both in things He had taught before and in things He had not. The multitude was there to hear the Master's words, and they would not be disappointed. The sermon from the side of the mountain shall not be forgotten.

He started slowly, breaking the silence, saying, "Many of you came to the Son of Man to be healed and blessed. All who come are blessed. I shall tell you now how you are blessed:

"Blessed are the humble who come to the Son of Man. Theirs is the kingdom of God.

"Blessed are those that mourn who come to the Son of Man. They shall be comforted.

"Blessed are the meek who come to the Son of Man. They shall inherit the earth.

"Blessed are those who hunger and thirst after righteousness who come to the Son of Man. They shall be filled.

"Blessed are those who weep who come to the Son of Man. They shall laugh.

"Blessed are the merciful who come to the Son of Man. They shall obtain mercy.

"Blessed are the pure in heart who come to the Son of Man. They shall see God.

"Blessed are the peacemakers who come to the Son of Man. They shall be called the children of God.

"Blessed are those who are persecuted for their righteousness who come to the Son of Man. Theirs is the kingdom of heaven.

"Blessed are you when men shall revile you, hate you, persecute you, falsely speak all manner of evil against you, and cast you out of their society, all for the sake of the Son of Man.

"Rejoice in the day of your persecution and leap for exceeding joy, for great shall be your reward in heaven because their fathers persecuted the prophets in a like manner.

"All this have I said about those who come to me, but what of those who do not? What of those who reject the Son of Man? Woe unto all who are rich who reject the Son of Man because they have received their reward in their riches.

"Woe unto all whose stomachs are full and reject the Son of Man because they shall hunger. And woe unto all who laugh and reject the Son of Man because they shall mourn and weep.

"Woe unto you when all men speak well of you because thusly their fathers spoke of the false prophets. You cannot serve God and please men."

His discourse included and expanded on many of the things He had taught us earlier, both in Judea and in Galilee, but He repeated them because this congregation had never heard these important teachings. Many times He taught the same things to people in different places. He also answered questions that we had heard at different times in different places. Those who were listening were touched by His message. As I listened, I came to understand that for every blessing received for obedience, there was a corresponding curse for disobedience.

As Jesus stood, marking the end of His message, some of the crowd left. This gave us the opportunity to spend more time alone with the Master and hear Him privately. It was a good day, and I knew more was yet to come.

INSTRUCTIONS TO THE APOSTLES

No one ever mentioned to me a time when Jesus laughed, but I did see Him smile many, many times. After He finished instructing the multitude from the mount, He smiled and asked us to gather closer to Him as we had done so many times before. We gladly moved up the hill again and sat as near to Him as possible. By this time, the sky was turning dark blue as night was coming upon us. After we were seated, He sat down again, looked around at our travel-weary gathering, and smiled. I could feel His love for us, and it warmed my soul. Tears of joy blurred my vision as I looked into the gentle eyes of the Son of God. It was difficult to see, but I thought I saw tears in His eyes too. We built a fire and cooked a meal.

Afterward, Jesus spoke to us: "It was with the approval of my Father that I called you to be my Apostles. When I sent you out, I gave you His instructions for that mission. Now I must also tell you more of what lies ahead for you as Apostles."

Referring to the salt that had seasoned our food, Jesus said, "My chosen servants, you are the salt of the earth, but what if the salt becomes soiled and loses its savor? What good is it? It is good for nothing, certainly not for the land or even the dunghill. It is only to be cast out and tram-pled by men. Keep in your hearts what I have taught you. Keep yourself and what I have taught you unsoiled from the world. Beware of mixing or compromising what I have taught you with the philosophies of those whom you teach."

As the darkness surrounded us on that hillside, some of the Apostles retrieved candles from their provisions and set them on stones around us. It was an oft-repeated scene, Jesus talking to us privately at night, sometimes with candles and other times by firelight, just as He was doing when Nicodemus came to visit. I have very tender memories of those nighttime sessions.

After the candles were lit, Jesus referred to the light they provided and started one of His one-word parables, saying, "You are the Light of the world, taking my pure Light to the world. You have become as a city that is set on a hill, a city that cannot be hidden. Know now that everyone is watching everything you do. Men do not light a candle to put it under a bushel or under their bed. They put it on a candlestick so it will give light to all that are in the house. You are my candles. Let your light so shine before men that they may see your good works and glorify your Father which is in heaven."

We were aware that we were different men now. Many people knew us as Apostles of the Lord Jesus Christ, and they expected us to be more virtuous than average citizens and certainly more so than the Pharisees or the Sadducees. The faithful and those in search of the Light of Christ looked to us as examples. Others watched us in search of excuses to accuse Jesus of treason or blasphemy. Indeed, we were "on a hill" and out in the open, just as we were at that moment. We had to be careful in all we said and did because people were watching.

Then Jesus added, "For nothing you do is secret to God. All of your acts shall be made manifest. Nothing will be hidden, and all will be made known. Take care what you do because if you act in accordance with what you know is right, the knowledge you have will be added upon. If you do not act in accordance with what you know is right, what knowledge you have will be taken from you."

Jesus paused from His teaching and asked us if our experiences did not confirm what He had taught. We all agreed. We had been watched all during our travels and our teaching.

Then Jesus invited us to share our experiences as missionaries. We all started to speak at once, overflowing with stories that we each wanted to tell Him. He started with Judas and ended with me, giving each of us His total attention during our individual interviews. From my earlier experience, I knew that He already knew all of the things we did—our successes, our failures, and our trials. Yet He still gave us the opportunity to express ourselves to Him. My fellow Apostles and I relished this private time with the Son of God.

After we had each reported our missions, a question arose about the law of Moses and the traditional rules of religious observance that were so much a part of our people's way of life. Some said the old law was done away with, but others insisted it would always be in place.

Jesus answered, "Do not think that I came to destroy the law of Moses or anything the prophets have spoken. Here is a truth I want you to know: until heaven and earth pass, not one jot or one tittle shall pass from the law in any way until they are all fulfilled. The law and prophets were in force until John, but since the time he preached the coming of the kingdom of God, every man is subject to it. I gave those commandments to the prophets, and they remain commandments.

"Whosoever among you breaks one of the least of the commandments and thereby teaches men to do so, that man shall be called the least in the kingdom of heaven. Whosoever shall keep the commandments and thereby teach men to do the same, that man shall be called great in the kingdom of heaven."

Jesus paused briefly before unfolding the law before us, giving us even more of the principles we should teach in the future: "There is more to observing the spirit of the law than ceremonial ritual. Unless you are more righteous than the Scribes and Pharisees, you shall not in any case enter into the kingdom of heaven. They observe the commandments outwardly, obeying the letter of the law only. You must first observe the commandments in your heart, and then your outward obedience will be lifted above the letter of the law to the spirit of the law.

"You know that the prophets taught, 'You shall not kill.' This is outward obedience only, and whoever kills shall be in danger of the judgment, but I tell you now that whoever is angry with his brother without cause shall be in danger of the judgment also, for it is what is in your heart that leads to sin. You know that whoever calls his brother 'worthless' shall be in danger of being called before the council to answer for this insult, but whosoever shall even call his brother a 'fool' shall be in danger of hellfire. Therefore, if you bring an offering to the altar and recall that your brother has a grievance against you, leave your offering before the altar, go to your brother, and be reconciled. Then return to place your offering on the altar.

"If you find yourself being called to court, and you are the one at fault, do what it takes to quickly settle with your adversary before you go to court. If not, you will be in the hands of the judge, and when the judgment is rendered, the judge may turn you over to the officers of the court, who will cast you into prison. If that happens, you will not be free until you have paid your debt to the last mite.

"You know that the prophets taught, 'You shall not commit adultery.' This also is outward obedience, but I tell you now that whoever even looks at a woman to lust after her has already committed adultery with her in her heart because that is where adultery begins, as it did with David of old.

"Consider this: it would be better to be blind than go to hell because of your eyes. Further, it would be better to have your hands cut off than go to hell because of the works of your hands."

Divorce was common in those days, but there were no courts for a divorce. A man could divorce his wife for any reason—or for no reason at all. There were formal divorces, where the husband gave his wife a document, or "bill of divorce," and there were less formal arrangements, where the husband simply put his wife out of the house or sent her away without a bill of divorce, or where the couple merely separated. Women were categorized as virgins, married, widowed, divorced, and undivorced. This last category included those who had been sent away without a bill of divorce.

Jesus warned us about the undivorced woman, saying, "It is said that 'Whosoever shall send away his wife, let him do so in writing, giving her a document showing they are divorced.' I tell you now that marriage is a covenant between a man and a woman, and whosoever shall send away his wife without a bill of divorce, except for fornication, causes her to commit adultery. Further, whosoever marries her who is undivorced also commits adultery.

"You have heard it said by them of old that 'You shall not break your oaths to the Lord, but keep them.' I tell you now that you should not swear oaths, not by heaven, because it is God's throne; not by earth, because it is His footstool; not by Jerusalem, because it is the city of the King; neither should you swear by your own head, because you do not have the power to make even one hair on your head black or white because it was created by God. Instead, let your communications be without oaths, but be 'yes' or 'no' because whatever is more than that is evil.

"You have heard it said, 'An eye for an eye, and a tooth for a tooth.' It has been taught that you are to love your neighbor and hate your enemies, to resist evil with evil, but I tell you who hear my voice, even more is expected of you because you are Apostles. Do not resist evil with evil, but love your enemies and do good to them who hate you. Bless them who curse you, and pray for them who scornfully use you. If a man strikes you on one cheek, turn your other cheek to him also. If any man sues you in court and takes away your coat, let him have your cloak also. If a man compels you to go a mile, go two miles with him. If someone asks for assistance or asks to borrow from you, don't turn them away. Do good things to them, asking and expecting nothing in return. In summary, be as merciful as your Father in Heaven.

"Do this and you will become what your Father in Heaven wants His children to become because He makes the sun rise on all of His children, the good and the evil. He makes the rain fall on all of His children, the just and the unjust. If you love only those who love you, what have you done that distinguishes you from a sinner? If you greet only your brothers with courtesy and concern, how are you different from the sinners of the world?"

Then Jesus gave us what I considered to be my ultimate challenge: "Become perfected, even as your Father in Heaven is perfected."

I immediately thought, "Isn't Jesus perfected?" I thought He was, but there was something I was not considering. I came to know that He would not be perfected until He was resurrected.

All of what we were hearing was new to us. We knew of the showy displays of pious righteousness put on by the Pharisees and the Sadducees. We also knew of their shadowy corruption and wickedness—no matter what image they presented to the public. They conspicuously lived the letter of the law in public, so everyone would see, but doing so did not make them righteous. I remembered also that the devils that possessed the man in Capernaum testified of Jesus, saying that He was the Son of God, so I knew that simply having a knowledge that Jesus is the Son of God was not enough. In my heart—in all of our hearts—we understood the difference. I realized that it wasn't just what we did or what we believed that qualified us as worthy servants of the Master; it took both, and they had to be bound together as one in our hearts. I felt pleased that I understood because I was not a learned man.

We heard every word and gained great understanding. Up to now, there were very few times when Jesus gave us so much undivided attention when we were the only ones to hear Him. Of course, we had heard many of His sermons, but they were usually given to crowds while we stood nearby. It seemed to me that He had never taught us and only us in such an extended discourse. This is truly what it was to be "taught at the feet of the Master."

He continued His instruction: "Take care that your acts of charity are done secretly. Do otherwise, and you will receive only the reward of those watching, not the reward of your Father in Heaven. When you give to the poor, do not sound a trumpet in the synagogues and streets, as is done by hypocrites. They shall receive the honor and glory of men, but that is the end of their reward. Instead, when you give to the poor, do it secretly so that your right hand doesn't know what your left hand is doing. Let your charity be in secret, and your Father in Heaven, who sees what you have done in secret, shall reward you openly."

I have observed that this teaching has been difficult to follow, especially for rich men. The rich take pride in having their generosity proclaimed to the world. Their names are put on public buildings and are proclaimed in public places in honor of their generosity. I know that it is a temptation to grant yourself such a legacy. Hear what Jesus counseled and let your Father in Heaven grant you His legacy; it is His reward you want.

INSTRUCTIONS ON PRAYER
AND FASTING

In my time, there was a Jewish tradition to offer "standing prayers" three times each day: early morning, afternoon, and evening. No matter where we were, we were supposed to face Jerusalem, cover our heads, and look downward as we prayed. For those of us who worshipped privately, we made it a habit to be in our homes or someplace private to offer those prayers. Others seemed to relish being in public places, on the streets, or where they knew they would be seen. Public displays of pious behavior bothered me, so I was delighted when Jesus taught us about prayer.

"When you pray, do not be as the hypocrites," Jesus said. "They love to pray, standing in the synagogues and on the corners of the streets so they can be seen of men. I tell you this truth; they have their reward—the honor of men— not the reward of their Father in Heaven. Instead, when you pray, go into a private room, shut the door, and pray to your Father in Heaven in secret. Again, your Father in Heaven, who sees what you have done in secret, shall reward you openly."

Then, seeking His specific instruction, I asked Jesus if He would teach us exactly how we were to pray. John told Him that John the Baptist had taught his disciples how to pray, but only he and Andrew were there. I asked Him to teach us.

He said, "When you pray, do not recite memorized prayers or incantations, repeating them over and over, as do the heathens. They mistakenly think their prayers are heard based on how many times they repeat them. Just remember, your Father in Heaven knows what you need even before you ask Him."

Jesus then knelt down, and we followed his lead, kneeling in a circle with Him at the head. Jesus said, "This is how to pray. 'Our Father in Heaven, whose name is Holy, Thy Kingdom come, Thy will be done on earth, as it is in heaven. Give us this day our daily bread. Forgive us our debts as we forgive our debtors. Lead us not into temptation, but deliver us from evil. For Thine is the Kingdom, and the power, and the glory forever. Amen.' "

After He prayed, we understood better. When we pray, we are talking to our Father in Heaven as if He were there listening, because He is. We acknowledge our total dependence on Him and His holiness and thank Him. Then we ask for the blessings we are worthy of, still acknowledging our dependence on Him. I heard Jesus speak to His Father. I was there. He was not praying to Himself.

Jesus then sat again on the stone outcropping and resumed His instructions. We all took our prior positions, and I asked, "Why is it important for us to forgive others?"

He explained, "If you will forgive men of their trespasses, your Heavenly Father will forgive you of yours, but if you do not forgive men of their trespasses, neither will your Father in Heaven forgive your trespasses."

I had asked the first question, so everyone waited for me to continue. I inquired about the need to fast. Jesus said, "Fasting is important to spiritually prepare you and your heart for prayer as an acknowledgment that you are dependent on your Father in Heaven for every blessing, including your daily bread. Moreover, when you fast, do not act as the hypocrites, who have sad faces to look as if they are suffering. They have their reward. But when you fast, wash your face and groom your hair so no one can tell you are fasting. Always remember that your Father in Heaven, who sees what you have done in secret, shall reward you openly.

"Do not lay up treasures for yourselves on earth where moths and rust will destroy and where thieves break in and steal, but lay up treasures for yourselves in heaven, where neither moths nor rust can destroy them and where thieves cannot break in and steal. Where your treasure is, there will be your heart also."

He went on, separating earthly from heavenly rewards, mortal from eternal blessings, differentiating what we could see now from what we had to look forward to, principles we had never heard before.

By this time, dawn was approaching, and the sky filled with the glow of the early morning light. Jesus had taught us through the night. Sleep had not been necessary. We were refreshed by the presence of the Son of God.

Jesus gestured toward the rising sun in the east and continued, "The light of the body is in the eyes. Therefore, if your eye is singly focused on the light you have received, your whole body shall be full of light. But if your eyes are focused on evil, your whole body shall be full of darkness. And in the absence of light, your darkness shall be even greater."

I have seen that light in people's countenances. I have also seen the darkness in their faces. I recognized the difference.

Counseled to Keep Focus
in Our Lives

Jesus paused to let us ponder His instructions. Even after a night-long session of learning, we were not weary of listening to Him speak. After a while, a question came to my mind. When we were sent out, we were told not to take even a spare set of shoes. I wanted to know if that would be the nature of our life from then on.

Jesus said, "I would have you understand that no man can serve two masters: he will either hate the one and love the other, or he will follow the one and reject the other. As Apostles, you cannot serve God full time and work for a living full time. Therefore, take no thought for your lives, what you shall eat, what you shall drink, nor what clothes you shall have to cover your body. Isn't your life more than what you eat and wear?"

As He spoke, a flock of sparrows landed on the ground near us, then quickly took flight again. Jesus gestured toward them and said, "Look at the birds of the air. They neither sow, reap, nor gather into barns, yet your Heavenly Father feeds them. Are you not so much better than they are?"

I have always considered myself an independent man, one that others depended on and not one that depended on others. Jesus had pointed out the foolishness of my image of self-reliance and independence. In my mind, I was as guilty of self-righteousness as the Pharisees. Jesus added to my humility, saying, "Which of you by thinking can add one cubit to your stature? If you cannot do this one small thing, why

worry about the rest?" I received His counsel and accepted
that I was not "my own man."

He then pointed to a small patch of wild lilies being
warmed by the rising sun and watered by the morning dew
and said, "And why worry about what to wear? Consider the
lilies of the field. They grow without making cloth or spin-
ning yarn. Even Solomon in all his glory was never arrayed in
the splendor of one of those flowers. Therefore, if God so generously dresses the grass of the field, which blooms today and
is burned tomorrow, how much better shall he dress you? Oh,
you of little faith! Do not worry yourselves, saying, 'What
shall we eat?' or, 'What shall we drink?' or, 'What shall we
wear?' All men, even the Gentiles, ask these questions. Your
Father in Heaven knows that you need all of these things, so
seek first the kingdom of God and His righteousness, and all
of these things will be provided for you. So don't waste today
worrying about tomorrow because tomorrow will take care
of itself."

Jesus paused as one of the Apostles pointed out that more
people were joining the crowd at the bottom of the mountain.
Jesus nodded His head, acknowledging the crowd, but said,
"We still have more to discuss."

As I looked at the crowd, I recognized one of them—a
scoundrel, I thought. I asked another question, "What of sinners? What are we . . . how are we . . . are we supposed to . . .
" I was having difficulty finding the right words to frame my
question.

Jesus said, "Do not become a judge or set the rules of
your judgment. Otherwise you'll be judged by the same stan-
dard with which you judge others, and the same condemnation you mete out shall be given you also. Forgive others and
you shall be forgiven. Why look for a speck of sawdust in your
brother's eye but ignore the wooden beam that is in your own
eye? Will you say to your brother, 'Let me remove that speck

of sawdust from your eye,' while a beam is in your own eye, you hypocrite? Remove the beam of wood from your own eye first, and then you shall see clearly to remove the speck from your brother's eye."

Jesus illustrated his point further by asking, "Can the blind lead the blind? Surely, they will both end up in the ditch. The disciple is not better than his master. His preparation is perfect. Only those who are so prepared shall be equal to the Master."

I understood. I was to judge wisely and righteously, as if it were through the eyes of Jesus, not my own. I would soon learn that it was not the good men but the sinners who were most in need of what we had to share. I was humbled at the realization that what seemed natural to me was not the right thing to do. Left to myself, I would avoid sinners, but we were charged to seek them out and teach them. Jesus caution us, saying, "Do not share that which is holy with dogs nor lay your pearls before swine, or they will mock and twist the sacred precepts you have shared with them and use them against you."

I understood. There is a difference between men that sin and evil men. Men with good hearts can do the wrong thing, out of either selfishness or ignorance. Men with evil hearts will not be changed by the truth. Instead, they will mock it. Because of the evil in their hearts, they will try to destroy everyone and everything that is righteous to ease their own guilt. Evil men wish to corrupt the righteous. We were free to share what we knew with those seeking truth, but we were instructed to withhold the truth from those who were evil. I worried that I would not be able to discern which was which.

Jesus continued His warning, saying, "Be cautious. Pray about what you are to do, when and where you are to do it, and for whom. Ask, and it shall be given you; seek, and you shall find; knock, and it shall be opened to you. Everyone that asks shall receive. He that seeks shall find, and to him that knocks, it shall be opened. I ask you, what man is there among you that if his son were to ask for bread would give him a stone? Or if he asks for a fish would give him a snake? Or if he asks for an egg would give him a scorpion? If you, being wicked by nature, know how to give good gifts to your children, how much more shall your Father in Heaven give good things to them that ask of Him?"

Just as I started to understand that following my natural tendencies would cause me not to do what Jesus wanted me to do, He confirmed my insights. Truly, I was learning from the Master. He taught in such a way that I agreed with His conclusion even before He presented it.

"Therefore, whatever you would have men do to you, do the same to them," He taught. "For this is what comprises the law and the prophets."

GOOD AND EVIL

When we were sent out as Apostles, we took the truth to many people. Of those claiming to seek the truth, only a small number recognized and accepted it. I never expected to baptize everyone, but there were times when the numbers were so low that I felt like a failure. I felt unworthy of my calling. But most of the time, I was uplifted by the joy of seeing those who followed Jesus, such as most of those gathering in the valley below us. Their numbers, their enthusiasm, and their love for Jesus filled my own heart, supplanting the darkness from those who rejected Him.

I knew that some people rejected our message because it required them to do hard things, make difficult choices, give up their sins, and change their lives. It seemed that I could not reach them no matter what I said or how hard I tried. I finally asked Jesus, "The multitudes that gather and follow are great in number, but they are very few compared to those we have taught. Are only these few going to be saved from their sins?"

"You can only enter heaven through the narrow gate, which is not the easy way. But wide is the gate and broad is the way that leads down to hell, and there are many who choose it. Because the gate that leads to eternal life is narrow, and the way is difficult, there will be but few that find it."

I had my answer. As a "fisher of men," my nets would gather only those seeking the Light. I was not a failure if I did not gather everyone. My job was to find those *seeking* the Light.

Sitting to my right was a fellow Apostle who asked about the many men that proclaimed themselves to be "prophets." It seemed that we encountered them often. He wanted to know how we could tell if a man was a false prophet.

Jesus answered using another of His parables: "Beware of false prophets, which come to you in sheep's clothing but are hungry wolves on the inside. You shall recognize them by their fruits. Do men gather grapes from a thorn bush or figs from a thistle? It follows that every good tree bears good fruit, but corrupt trees bear evil fruit. A good tree cannot bear evil fruit, neither can a corrupt tree bear good fruit. Every tree that does not bear good fruit is cut down and burned. Therefore, by their fruits, you shall know which are false prophets. A good man will bear good fruit from the goodness in his heart, and an evil man will bear evil fruit from the evil in his heart. His heart will betray itself by the fruit he bears."

I knew of predators who presented themselves as good men but who only sought to take advantage of their believers. The many false messiahs were easy to detect because they were not good men but pretenders, and their true motives eventually betrayed them.

The answer Jesus provided also reminded me of His comments about outward versus inward observance of the law. I knew that outward works were good only when they resulted from inward faith, but both were required, not just one or the other. The beauty of His teachings was in their simplicity and how they were all interrelated.

Jesus continued, "Not everyone that says to me, 'Lord, Lord,' shall enter into the kingdom of heaven. Only those that do the will of my Father in Heaven shall enter. Many will say to me in the day of their judgment, 'Lord, Lord, have we not prophesied in your name?' And, 'In your name have we not cast out devils?' And, 'In your name have we not done many wonderful works?' And I will respond to them, 'I never knew you. Depart from me you that do iniquity!' And I tell you now that those who do iniquity shall weep and gnash their teeth when they see Abraham, Isaac, and Jacob, and all the prophets in the kingdom of God because they will not be allowed in."

The future He painted was not pleasant. A flashing moment of self-doubt caused me to wonder if I would be one of those who would weep and gnash his teeth. I was less than perfect, but I was comforted because Jesus knew me personally and still asked me to serve. At that moment, I somehow felt that I would be with Him in the kingdom of God, and that was where I wanted to be.

Then Jesus tapped the boulder He was sitting on and said, "Therefore, whosoever hears my words and follows them is like a wise man who built his house upon a rock. When the rain descended, when the floods came, and when the winds blew and beat upon that house, it did not fall because it was built upon a rock." Then Jesus bent down and took a handful of sand, which He let fall through His fingers, saying, "Likewise, whoever hears my words but does not follow them is like a foolish man who built his house upon the sand. When the rain descended, when the floods came, and when the winds blew and beat upon that house, it fell, and great was its fall."

Jesus then stood, indicating that He had finished His remarks. We understood the counsel and instruction He had unfolded to us through the course of the night. He had certainly given us a "Sermon on the Mount." As the Master Teacher, He had a wonderful way with words; He used parables and symbolism so effectively that we completely understood His meanings. There were times when He used parables to mask the meaning from those in attendance who were not believers, to prevent them from understanding His teachings, but He never hid the meanings of His teachings from us; He knew our hearts. In fact, He was constantly helping us interpret His symbolism. Over time, I came to understand it more easily.

What caused me to marvel that day was not His speaking skills but that He presented new doctrine based upon His authority as the Son of God—as the God of the Old Testament. Unlike the scribes, He did not refer to the authority of ancient prophets or recite someone else's "interpretations" of the law or the prophets. Instead, He spoke by virtue of His own authority. When He spoke, He said, "I say to you . . ." and I heard Him.

I was there. I am Peter, disciple, Apostle, and witness of the Son of God.

THE CENTURION'S SERVANT

After our marvelous overnight experience with Jesus on the mountainside, we again returned to Capernaum, entering our city later in the day. We were met by a group of Jewish elders I recognized, who were waiting for Jesus, there to plead for His assistance. They told Jesus about a Roman centurion, the commander of approximately eighty soldiers, who lived in our city. He was a good man. His servant was lying in bed, apparently near death. This centurion loved his servant as if he were his own son. The centurion had heard stories of Jesus, and in his sincere desire to save his servant's life, he sent these Jewish elders to request Jesus to heal the poor servant.

The elders assured Jesus that the centurion was a worthy man. In fact, the centurion loved the Jews and had built a synagogue in Capernaum. They pleaded with Jesus to come immediately to the centurion's house. Acknowledging the great faith of this Roman centurion, Jesus said, "I will come and heal him."

As Jesus approached the centurion's house, the man's friends came out to greet Him. They brought word from the centurion, who said, "Lord, please do not trouble yourself. I am not worthy to have you come under my roof. I have sent these messengers to speak to you because I am not worthy to speak to you in person. I know that if you only say the word, my beloved servant shall be healed. I know you have the power to command, for I know of that power myself. I am a man sent here under Roman authority, having soldiers under me. When I say to one, 'Go!' he goes, and to another, 'Come!' he comes, and to my servant, 'Do this!' and he does it. I know you have the power to heal my servant."

Jesus turned from the friends of the centurion and spoke to the Jewish elders, saying, "I tell you all that I have not found such great faith, no, not anywhere in Israel, as in this Gentile. I tell you that many Gentiles shall come from the east and from the west, and they shall sit down with Abraham and Isaac and Jacob in the kingdom of heaven. But the children of the kingdom of Satan shall be cast out into outer darkness, and there shall be weeping and gnashing of teeth."

Jesus turned to the friends of the centurion, saying, "Return to the house of the centurion. According to his faith, it is done." When they went back into the house, they found that the servant who had been sick was healed.

I confess that I never lost the thrill of seeing Jesus perform miracles. As the day ended, we walked to our homes. Those of us not from Capernaum stayed in my home or the home of James and John. It had been two full, wonderful days and nights in my Galilee and my Capernaum.

RAISING THE DEAD IN NAIN

The following morning we journeyed from Capernaum, traveling south to the village of Nain, which was located about six miles southeast of Nazareth. As usual, Jesus was surrounded by the multitude, including several Pharisees, who followed Him wherever He went. As we arrived at the gates of Nain, we encountered an unusually large funeral procession leaving the city. When the body of a young man came into view, we saw that it was followed immediately by an older woman, clearly his mother. Jesus approached the procession and asked about the young man. Someone explained that the young man was the only son of the older woman, who was a widow.

Jesus had compassion on the widow and spoke to her, saying, "Weep not." She raised her head and looked at Him as if she did not understand. Rather than repeat Himself, He walked over to the bier, a wooden framework carrying the body, and put His hand on it. Those carrying the platform stopped, waiting to see what He would do. Jesus looked at the widow and then at the body of the young man. Jesus kept his hand on the bier and said firmly, "Young man, I say to you, arise!"

The young man sat up! He was alive! He spoke immediately, asking about his mother. Jesus reached out, took the young man by the hand, assisted him off the bier, and led him to his mother. Her face was white with shock. She was unable to speak, but she grabbed her son and held him close.

She sobbed and turned toward Jesus but could say nothing. Words were not necessary to convey her gratitude.

The first response from the funeral procession and the multitude that followed Jesus was also one of shock. Jesus had raised the dead! The Pharisees murmured, but one man said, "A great prophet is risen up among us. God has visited His people." And word spread throughout Galilee and then to all of Judea.

DISCIPLES OF JOHN THE BAPTIST

Among the throng that followed Jesus to Nain were two men that had come to Galilee after visiting John the Baptist in prison. They approached Jesus and introduced themselves as disciples of John the Baptist. They told Jesus that they had visited John in prison and related stories they had heard of a man doing miracles in Galilee and asked John what they should do. John told them to go and find the man and determine if He was the Christ, the One of whom John had testified when he said, "Behold the Lamb of God."

John's disciples pleaded with Jesus, asking, "Are you the One that should come, or do we look for another?"

Jesus knew that they had followed Him, along with many in the multitude, from Capernaum to Nain, observing the many miracles that had taken place along the way. Jesus answered them, saying, "Return to John and tell him what you have seen and heard. Tell him that the blind receive their sight, the lame walk, lepers are cleansed, the deaf hear, the dead are raised, and that the poor have the gospel taught them."

As John's disciples prepared to leave, they bade farewell to a number of people in the crowd, friends that had previously been John's disciples. I was a bit surprised at the number of John's followers who were now following Jesus.

Jesus then turned and spoke to the multitude, saying, "John the Baptist is blessed because he is not offended by my words and my deeds. Blessed is whoever shall not be offended by my words and my deeds."

Then Jesus lovingly taught John's disciples, asking them, "When you went into the wilderness to see John, what were you looking for? Were you seeking someone that bends like a reed to every change in the wind of doctrine? What were you looking for? Were you seeking someone that wore fine, soft clothing? Behold, they that wear beautiful, soft clothing and have a life of ease are found in the courts of kings, not in the wilderness. What were you looking for? A prophet? Yes, that is what you sought." Then, lifting his open hands, He gestured toward Himself and added, "Now you have found more than a prophet!

"Hear and know this about John the Baptist," Jesus continued. "He is the one of whom it is written, 'Behold, I will send my messenger before me, and he shall prepare the way before me.' There is not a greater prophet—nor a greater man than John the Baptist among those born of women." Then, again lifting His hands, He continued, "Notwithstanding John's greatness, He that is the least important in the kingdom of men is greater than John."

It was clear to me that Jesus had been simultaneously addressing His remarks to the Pharisees among the crowd. He continued, pointing His comments to the Pharisees: "From the first day John the Baptist started preaching and baptizing until this very day, the kingdom of God has suffered violence, and violent men have taken that kingdom by force. They imprisoned John the Baptist, and they seek to take away my own life. This is all as the prophets and the law prophesied, even up until the day John began to baptize.

"If you had received John, you would know that he is the 'Elias' who was prophesied would prepare the way." Then, after a brief pause, Jesus said slowly and clearly, pronouncing every word individually, "He that has ears, let him hear!"

In the moments that followed, the believers humbly spoke of their simple faith. The Pharisees spoke words of comfort to themselves, bragging of their great righteousness. Of the multitude that heard Jesus testify of John the Baptist, it was the disciples and the publicans that acknowledged John as a prophet of God, and they respected the baptism he gave them. The Pharisees and the lawyers rejected John and ignored the counsel of Jesus because they had chosen not to be baptized by John the Baptist.

Jesus spoke bluntly of the Pharisees and the lawyers, asking, "To what shall I liken this generation? Who or what are they like?" He then referred to the funeral procession that had now become a gathering of celebration, saying, "I shall say that they are like children playing in the markets, first pretending they are at a funeral, then pretending they are at a wedding. They call to each other, saying, 'We mourned for you, but you have not wept.' Then they say, 'We played music for you, but you have not danced.' "

I was pleased that I understood what Jesus was saying. There was nothing He could do or say that would please this generation because they were playing games. I knew exactly what He meant and to whom He was talking.

Jesus spoke to the multitude, again gesturing toward the Pharisees. "When John the Baptist came, neither eating nor drinking, they said, 'He has a devil in him!' When the Son of Man came eating and drinking, they said, 'Behold a gluttonous man, a drunkard, and a friend to publicans and sinners.' There is nothing that pleases them because wisdom is reserved for the wise."

I smiled inwardly—perhaps openly. The wicked ones were not to be changed by the truth, testimony, or miracles. When the Pharisees disapproved of the miracles they had seen, they were further condemned; their response to miracles testified of their wickedness.

I marveled that so many people saw miracles—acts that could have been performed only by the power of God—but they chose to ignore the miracles, deny God's power, and reject His Son. They were never converted by miracles; instead, they were condemned by them. I took comfort in the few that rejoiced at the miracles they witnessed and believed in Jesus. I was one of them.

EATING WITH SIMON THE PHARISEE

As we traveled in Galilee, a certain Pharisee named Simon invited Jesus to dine with him. Jesus went to his home and sat down to eat. The meal was served in an inner courtyard within the Pharisee's house. I do not know if the Pharisee was surprised that Jesus accepted the invitation, but I was not shocked. Jesus freely gave His time and His company to those who asked.

The table where we ate was square, with flat platform-like "couches" adjacent to three of its four sides. The fourth side was left open, providing access to the servants. The table was about the same height as the couches, which were each covered by cushions. We climbed onto the couches with our heads toward the table. We then reclined on our left sides, on our left arms, leaving our right hands free. This setup was what the Romans called a "triclinium."

A certain woman in the city heard that Jesus was going to be at the Pharisee's home, so she came early to await Him. (Uninvited visitors often attended such gatherings.) I noticed the woman, but I took her for a servant or a member of the household. When Jesus took His place at the table, she moved to stand directly behind Him but said nothing. I started to pay attention to her when the whites of her eyes reddened with emotion and she began to weep. Silently, she stepped forward and knelt over Jesus, letting her tears bathe His feet. She tenderly dried them with her hair and then kissed them. When she finished, she opened an alabaster flask of ointment and carefully anointed His feet. I was touched at the reverence and love she felt for Jesus. I didn't recognize her, but I wondered what wonderful thing He had done for her. She kept her head bowed and said nothing but went about her task as if it were the greatest joy in her life.

The Pharisee, who also happened to be named Simon, saw what was happening and commented to his friends, "If this man were a prophet, he would know who and what manner of woman it is that touches Him. She is a sinner!"

Jesus waited for the Pharisee's friends to agree before he said, "Simon, I have something to tell you."

Simon responded with a single word, "Speak."

Jesus said, "There was a certain lender who had two borrowers. One owed him five hundred denarii, the other fifty. When they had no way to pay, he freely forgave them both. So tell me, which of them will love him the most?"

"I suppose the one forgiven for the most," he said.

Jesus answered, "You have judged rightly." He then gestured toward the weeping woman and said, "See this woman? When I entered your home, you gave me no water for my feet, but she has washed my feet with her tears and then wiped them with the hair of her head." After a pause, Jesus continued, "You did not greet me with a kiss, but this woman has not ceased to kiss my feet since I came in." After another pause, He added, "You did not anoint my head with oil, but this woman has anointed my feet with ointment. For that reason, I tell you that her sins, which are many, are forgiven because she loved much. Those forgiven of little love little."

Jesus turned and spoke directly to the weeping woman, saying, "Your sins are forgiven."

Simon and his guests murmured, saying, "Who is this that forgives sins also?"

Jesus ignored them and continued speaking to the

woman, saying, "Your faith has saved you. Go in peace."

The woman bit her lip but could not keep from smiling broadly at the Son of God. As she left the room, the tears streaming down her cheeks were tears of joy.

HEALING IN CAPERNAUM

We spent the night at the Pharisee's house and started our journey back to Capernaum early the next morning. When we arrived, we were informed that my mother-in-law was sick in bed with a fever. We quietly walked into her room, and Jesus approached her. He reached out, held her hand, and lifted her up. The fever left her as she stood. She thanked Him and excused herself to go work in the kitchen. She prepared supper and served it as if she had never been ill. Jesus performed that miracle without saying a word. My mother-in-law's faith in Jesus healed her.

Later in the evening, a small crowd came to my home and asked to see Jesus. He went out to meet them, and they asked Him if He would cast the devils out of some who were possessed and if He would heal several other people. Jesus took compassion on the people. In a scene like the one we had observed from Judea to Galilee, Jesus commanded the devils to leave. Just like before, the devils cried out, testifying of Jesus: "You are Christ, the Son of God." Again, Jesus silenced them so they could not speak.

Jesus then laid His hands on all that were sick and healed them. One of the Apostles observed that He had fulfilled the prophecy of Isaiah that said, "He took upon Himself our infirmities, and He bore our sicknesses." Others came that night, and Jesus continued healing the sick until after dark when everyone had gone. He did not weary in serving.

The next morning, Jesus said He wished to go to sea. We

walked down to the edge of the Sea of Galilee where some of our boats were anchored. As He waited on the shore for me to retrieve my boat, a crowd gathered around Him. Word had already spread that Jesus had returned to Capernaum, and many had apparently been awaiting Him. The story spread quickly that He had raised a dead man in Nain. Before I was able to retrieve my boat, the growing numbers of people pressed closer, practically pushing Him into the coarse black rocks on the seashore.

Jesus calmed them and then healed all of the sick. When He finished, He asked me to take Him aboard my boat and sail to the other side of the sea. There was room in my boat for about twenty people but not enough for everyone who wanted to accompany us.

Standing in my boat, Jesus listened to some of the disciples as they pleaded with Him to be invited aboard. A young scribe approached Jesus and said, "Lord, I will follow you wherever you go. Wherever you may be, I shall be there."

I wondered what Jesus would say. Here was a scribe, an expert in the law of Moses, and a member of the inner circle of the ruling Jews. He was inviting himself to be one of us. I didn't know if he came as a spy or if he were sincere. I knew that Jesus did not accept "volunteers" as Apostles. He only called those He wanted to serve with Him. I waited for Jesus to answer.

Instead of rejecting his offer, Jesus turned to the scribe and, knowing his heart, said, "Foxes have holes, and birds of the air have nests, but the Son of Man has no home to lay His head," suggesting to the scribe that his life as a disciple would require him to leave the comfort of his home and become an itinerant. The scribe turned away, saying nothing more; the cost of being a disciple was too high for him.

Another man pushed his way to the edge of the crowd and said, "I shall join you, but allow me first to go and take care of my father until he dies."

Again, Jesus did not reject his offer; instead, He responded with instructions and an invitation, "Let the town bury the dead. You are to go and preach the kingdom of God. Follow me."

As the man climbed into one of the boats, another disciple said, "Lord, I will follow you also, but first allow me to go and bid farewell to those who live in my house."

Jesus said to him, "No man who has put his hand to the plow and still looks back is fit for the kingdom of God."

I was not a farmer, but I traded with farmers, exchanging fish for their produce. I knew that any farmer who looked back as he plowed was considered a lazy man; he wasn't focused in getting the job done. In order for a farmer to look back, he had to stop the oxen and loosen their straps before looking around. If he didn't stop before he looked back, he was likely to pull the oxen off their course, causing crooked furrows. A hard worker was the one that attended to the plowing until the job was done. It was understood that anyone preoccupied with what he had already accomplished was not likely to take on difficult tasks and complete them. I thought of this often as I watched disciples arrive with enthusiasm, only to leave with disappointment because it was not easy to be a follower of Jesus. The cost was high. Satan made certain of it.

PEACE, BE STILL!

Several small boats joined us, each filled with disciples, including the man Jesus had invited to come with Him. When we set sail for the far shore, it was cloudy, but the winds were favorable, and the sailing went smoothly. After a while, Jesus took the opportunity to take a nap, and He rested comfortably on a "bed" of dry nets at the rear of my boat. As we drew nearer to the middle of the lake, a great storm arose, the winds blew hard, and the waves quickly swelled higher than the boat. The sea washed into the boat, threatening to sink it. Some of the disciples who were not fishermen or familiar with the fickle nature of the weather on the sea feared we might sink.

One of those disciples panicked and shouted, "Lord, save us. Don't you care that we are going to die?"

Jesus awoke, looked at the man, and said, "Why are you afraid? Oh, you of little faith." Then he rose and rebuked the winds and commanded the sea, simply saying, "Peace! Be still!" The heavy winds ceased immediately, and the sea was calmed. In shock, we surveyed the astonishing calmness of the sea. "Where is your faith?" Jesus asked. As I watched, I realized that I was one of those with "little faith." Once again, I felt unworthy of being in His presence.

The other boats came alongside my boat, with everyone asking what had happened to the raging storm. Only those in the boat with us saw and heard what Jesus had said. When the disciples in the other boats heard what He had done, there were some disciples who actually feared Jesus. They said, "What manner of man is this that even the wind and the sea obey him?" It was clear that they were unfamiliar with the Son of God; they did not know what manner of man He was.

ACROSS THE SEA OF GALILEE

I came to myself and directed everyone to continue the journey as if nothing remarkable had happened, sailing to the far side of the Sea of Galilee. We disembarked in a region of Gentiles called Gergesa, a city in the area known as Decapolis on the main road to Damascus.

Almost as soon as we set foot on dry land, we were approached by a naked man obviously possessed by the devil. He was not a large man, but he was filled with such a wild rage that we knew better than to get near him. Another man from the area came by and warned us to be careful. He said the naked man lived in the tombs, and most people traveled around this area to avoid him. He said that there were times in the past when the man had been captured and bound in ropes and chains, but he had always escaped. He said that the man had such great strength that he could break ropes. He told us that the man usually kept to himself, but when people encountered him, he was usually crying or cutting himself with sharp stones. The man was truly a pathetic sight—filthy and covered with scars and wounds.

Jesus had great compassion for this possessed man. He motioned for us to step away. We obeyed, leaving Jesus alone. Then He gazed at the man without speaking. The man had been watching us, and when he saw Jesus standing by Himself, he started running toward Jesus. I instantly reached for my sword. No lunatic was going to harm my Lord. Jesus gestured for me to remain where I was. The naked man ran up to Jesus and fell on the ground before Him. I couldn't tell if the man had tripped or if he had thrown himself at the feet of Jesus.

The man raised his head and asked Jesus, "What have we to do with you, Jesus, the Son of God? I plead with you not to torment us before the time appointed for our eternal punishment."

Without pausing, Jesus commanded the evil spirits, saying, "Come out of this man, unclean spirits!"

Jesus paused briefly, then did something I had never seen Him do before—He spoke to the evil spirits, asking, "What is your name?"

The spirits answered defiantly, as if their great number gave them strength, "Our name is Legion because we are many."

At that time, a Roman legion included at least 5,120 soldiers, plus auxiliary support troops. By saying "legion," the evil spirits meant that they numbered in the thousands. As we soon saw, thousands of evil spirits were present.

Knowing that they were all about to be evicted from the mortal tabernacle of this wretched man, those thousands of spirits pleaded with Jesus saying, "If you cast us out, don't send us away into the abyss, but allow us to go into that herd of pigs on the mountainside and enter their bodies." A short distance away, on the side of the mountain, we could see a large herd of pigs.

Jesus commanded them, saying, "Go!" and the evil spirits left the man and entered the herd of pigs. As soon as they did, all of the pigs, around two thousand of them, stampeded down the mountainside and into the sea, where they were all drowned. The Gentiles herding the pigs grew angry and afraid.

I figured that Jesus had caused the pigs to drown themselves, which caused me to ponder what I had observed. I concluded that while possessed by an evil spirit, a man was not in control of himself and that men suffer greatly from evil spirits. I had learned that the servants of Satan were great in number. They did not have bodies of their own, and they greatly envied those who did. They entered into a man to have a mortal body, but they even preferred bodies of pigs to none at all. When they were not in a mortal body, they existed in a place they called "the abyss." I did not understand all of these things, but I found them interesting. These evil spirits knew and recognized Jesus as the Son of God. Also the servants of Satan already knew what their eternal punishment was to be, and they knew it would be one of torment. In some ways, they knew more than we did!

I knew that many of the Pharisees and the Sadducees had witnessed the miracles Jesus performed in Jerusalem and Judea, and their response was to want Him killed. I had just heard evil spirits, all of whom were destined for eternal punishment, address Jesus as the Son of God and plead with Him to do things only the Son of God could do. Yet the Pharisees and Sadducees, people who proclaimed themselves to be spiritual leaders of Israel, would not acknowledge the Son of God. I tried to understand. Clearly, witnessing miracles did not change a man's heart. Instead, miracles sealed the fate of unbelievers, cursing them for their unbelief.

I also observed that the act of acknowledging Jesus as the Son of God and testifying of Him meant nothing. Beware, those who say that all they need to do is acknowledge Jesus as the Son of God. The devil also knows Jesus to be the Son of God. It takes more than that to avoid eternal damnation.

While I was pondering the implications of what had taken place, the trembling, swine-herding Gentiles ran into the city to tell everyone what had happened. They told the people the story of Jesus, the naked man, and of course, the pigs. They wanted to make sure everyone knew it was not their fault that two thousand pigs had drowned in the sea. The whole city was less interested in the pigs than they were in the possessed man. They came out to see for themselves that the naked man was now clothed and was no longer possessed. I saw that the Gentiles were afraid of Jesus. A delegation approached Jesus and asked Him to leave their city and go back where He came from. I wondered if their demand may have had more to do with the pigs than the possessed man.

I probably need to explain something about pigs. Swine were considered "unclean" animals in our time, and we were forbidden to eat their meat or even to touch them. That Gentiles were raising them was a deliberate insult to our culture. I found it to be quite satisfying when the herd was destroyed, and I suspected the Gentiles were afraid Jesus might cause all of their pigs to drown.

After the Gentiles asked Jesus to leave, the once-possessed man asked Jesus if he could return with Him to the other side of the sea to be with Him. Jesus said, "Instead of coming with me, go home to your friends. Tell them what the Son of Man has done for you and how He had compassion on you."

Obediently, the man left us and returned to his home. He told his family and the people of the Ten Cities what great things Jesus had done for him. The people marveled at what had happened.

That was our marvelous experience on the eastern seashore of Galilee, after which we crossed the sea and returned to Galilee. At the time, I wished that more people could have been there. What they could have learned!

I learned that unbelievers are not converted by miracles, but I was converted by personal revelation from the Holy Ghost. Such revelation is the rock upon which God built His Church.

HEALING THE PARALYZED MAN

When we arrived back in Capernaum, Jesus once again rested in my home. I always did my best to make Him comfortable, and my family made sure He was taken care of. It was a great honor to have the Son of God under our roof. His mother, brothers, and sisters lived in Capernaum, but He chose to live in my home. He was in Capernaum so much that people came to refer to it as His city.

At the same time, I knew that Jesus still considered Nazareth to be His home, but He was not accepted there. In Capernaum, He was loved and honored, especially in my home. The people of Capernaum came to expect that if I were at my home, Jesus would be there too—and they were right; I went wherever Jesus did. Because of that, whenever I was home, word quickly spread and crowds gathered. They came to see Jesus, to hear Him teach, and to be healed by Him.

Some days, the crowds were so numerous that there was no way anyone could even approach my door, never mind be able to enter and hear Jesus speak. Those who gathered were not just those seeking to be healed, but Pharisees, scribes, and rabbis from Galilee, Judea, and Jerusalem. They came to hear Him speak and to watch what He did. Jesus welcomed them all, but oftentimes there was not enough room in my home for all who gathered.

One day, like many days, my home was surrounded by people when four men arrived carrying a paralyzed man, bearing him on a kind of cot. Because of the crowds, they were unable to gain entrance to my home. In fact, they couldn't even get close to the door. Their love for this man was so great that they would not give up. These men climbed the stairs to the top of my home, removed a section of roofing material, and used ropes to lower the paralyzed man down by his cot, setting him on the floor directly in front of Jesus.

Of course, the Pharisees and the scribes were infuriated that such a thing would happen while they were discussing the law with Jesus. There was a great commotion, and they demanded that the men pull their paralyzed friend up and leave at once. Jesus smiled, stood up, and motioned for silence. He gestured toward the ceiling and said, "These are men of great faith." Then He turned and spoke to the paralyzed man, saying, "My son, your sins are forgiven you."

I only thought I had seen the Pharisees and scribes upset before, but now they were offended. The Pharisees at the back of the room spoke among themselves, accusing Jesus of blasphemy, knowing that only God can forgive a man of his sins.

I don't know if Jesus heard them or not, but either way, He knew the wickedness of their hearts. He knew that they were there in search of something with which to accuse Him. Jesus faced and challenged them, asking, "Why are you thinking such evil in your hearts? Do you think it is easier to say, 'Your sins are forgiven you,' or to say to a paralyzed man, 'Arise and walk'?"

By asking this question, He had prepared the way to demonstrate who He was and by what authority He acted. Without pausing for their response, Jesus continued, "So that you may know that the Son of Man has power on earth to forgive sins," He paused, turned back to the paralyzed man, and commanded him, "pick up your bed and carry it back to your home."

There was absolute silence in the room. For a second, the paralyzed man did nothing, as if he wondered to whom Jesus had spoken. Then a smile filled his face. He wiggled his fingers and then his toes. He reached up and rubbed his face with his hands. He had tears in his eyes as he sat up on his bed. He looked up at Jesus and then slowly stood up. There was still silence in the room. He turned around, lifted his bed, and obediently placed it on his back. The silence was broken when the man said, "Glory be to God because I am healed!"

Someone on my roof shouted for joy—it was one of the four men who brought the paralyzed man to my home. Before long, it seemed like everyone was cheering. One of the men standing near the door went outside and told everyone what had just taken place. By the time the healed man reached the door, everyone was waiting to see him walk. Some of these people knew him from before he was paralyzed. Several of his friends had waited outside to see if he would be healed. As he stepped to the doorway of my home, they stood back to make room for him to walk. Tears flowed down their cheeks as he greeted them. As he carried his bed out of my home, they cheered and rushed forward to embrace him. He was healed!

One of his friends shouted, "Glory be to God!" Someone else said, "We have never seen anything like this. Never before have we seen this power given to anyone!" They were amazed and afraid at the same time. The man, carrying his bed, walked with his friends back to his home to celebrate with his family.

I saw Jesus perform many miracles, but only a few are recorded. He performed miracles for the faithful, not the skeptical. Every time it happened, I rejoiced with those who were healed and also for their faith in Jesus. The many miracles I saw did not give me my faith, but they certainly confirmed it.

MATTHEW CALLED AGAIN

The healing of the paralyzed man proved what Jesus had been teaching that day in my home. Nothing else was necessary to demonstrate that Jesus was the Son of God. The wicked Pharisees and scribes were still disturbed at His power and that He forgave the paralyzed man. Everyone else was in awe.

Jesus left my home, and we walked with Him down to the seashore. The size of the crowd at my home had grown so large that we were unable to hear Jesus. Unlike our last experience on the seashore, the multitude followed Him at a respectful distance. He found a good site at the seashore and taught them again. They listened quietly, absorbing every word.

After He finished teaching, He asked them to ponder what they had heard and witnessed. We then walked back into Capernaum. As we passed the office of the tax collector, Jesus saw Matthew the son of Alphaeus—the man who was known as Levi before He was called to follow Jesus as one of His Apostles.

Like the other Apostles, Matthew, after being ordained and instructed, returned to his home to continue making a living. Matthew was back at work as a tax collector, an office he had held since purchasing it from the Romans. When Jesus saw Matthew sitting in his office, He approached him and said, "Follow me." It was all Matthew needed to hear to leave his post and join with us again. He simply got up and followed Jesus, leaving his work in the hands of his assistant.

As we walked together though Capernaum that after-noon, Jesus taught the crowd that followed Him and others He encountered in the city, some at their homes, some at work, and some working along the rocky seashore. After a while, Jesus took Matthew aside spoke to him privately, and then Matthew left us. I asked Jesus if there was anything I could help with, and He told me that we would be attending a feast at Matthew's house that evening. I almost thought I saw a special sparkle in His eye. We both knew that the scribes and Pharisees would be indignant about Jesus's association with a publican, a tax collector.

That evening was a feast indeed. It wasn't just the food, but it was a feast of people too. Matthew's large house was filled with Apostles, disciples, and many people that had fol-lowed us all day long. At the request of Jesus, Matthew had invited many of his publican associates to join us. In our soci-ety, publicans were considered to be unacceptable company for reputable people. Anyone associating with a publican was considered a sinner, and a gathering that included publicans was referred to as a group of "publicans and sinners."

As expected, the Pharisees and scribes were greatly trou-bled at who was hosting the feast and the presence of other invited publicans. The Pharisees asked us, "Why does your Master eat and drink with publicans and sinners?" They intentionally spoke loudly so Jesus would hear.

Jesus answered them directly, saying, "They who are whole have no need of a physician, but they who are sick cer-tainly do. Take your time and go figure out what that means." Then He quoted Hosea, "I desire mercy and not sacrifice. I am not here to call the righteous, but sinners to repentance."

It was still a feast, and we all enjoyed the fine food that was prepared for us. Also included among those at the feast were followers of John the Baptist. Anyone who knew John

ARNOLD S. GRUNDVIG, JR.

knew that he was one who lived a life of plainness—he ate locusts and honey, wore crude clothing, and fasted often. The followers of John the Baptist were troubled that the followers of Jesus were often feasting while they were often fasting. Encouraged by the Pharisees, John the Baptist's followers asked Jesus, "We fast often, and the Pharisees fast often, but we see your disciples eat and drink at every feast, and we never see them fast. Why is that?"

"Do the children of the bride chamber fast while the Bridegroom is eating with them?" He asked. "As long as they have the Bridegroom eating with them, they cannot fast." I don't know that they understood. Jesus was the Bridegroom. Many did not realize or accept who He was, but I did. Jesus continued, "But the day will come when the Bridegroom shall be taken from them, and then they shall fast." I would like to say that I understood that too, but in truth I did not fully understand, at least not then.

Jesus then taught the Pharisees about His knowledge of the law of Moses, rejecting their convoluted interpretations. He was there to restore the truth and fulfill prophecy, not to correct their foolish, man-made traditions. Jesus started a rapid series of parables, saying, "No man sews a patch of new cloth over a tear in an old garment, because that which is used to patch the tear will make the tear worse. Neither do men put new wine into old bottles because the bottles will break, and the wine will run out, so both the wine and the bottle are lost, but they put new wine into new bottles, and both are preserved. Finally, no man having drunk old wine straightaway wants new wine; for he says, 'The old is better.' "

Jesus went about Galilee in all the cities and villages near Capernaum, teaching in the synagogues, preaching the gospel of the kingdom of God, and healing every sickness and infirmity of all of the people brought to Him. As He traveled, multitudes sought Him out, and He was moved with compassion toward them. He told us that they were as sheep, fainting, being scattered, having no shepherd. They were in search of a Master, and the Master was now among them. Jesus told us, "The harvest truly is plenteous, but the laborers are few. Pray therefore that the Lord of the harvest will send laborers into this harvest."

THE DAUGHTER OF JAIRUS AND
THREE OTHER MIRACLES

There is a certain day, a day I like to remember often, when Jesus was teaching near the seashore in Capernaum. I watched a man named Jairus work his way to the front of the crowd around Jesus. Many in the crowd were unaware that Jairus was the ruler of the Capernaum synagogue and a member of the Council, the local version of the Sanhedrin. He obviously had something on his mind, and I expected him to launch an attack on Jesus, but that didn't happen. Instead, Jairus immediately knelt and worshipped the Lord. Then he pleaded, "My twelve-year-old daughter—my only daughter—lies in her bed dying, but if you will come and lay your hands on her, she will live."

Jesus acted like He was expecting Jairus and agreed to go with him. He rose from the rock where He was sitting and followed Jairus through Capernaum, along with the crowd that had surrounded Him. Because many knew where Jairus lived, a number of them walked ahead of us slowing our progress. The crowd pressed in to be closer to Jesus, wishing to see Jesus heal the daughter of Jairus. I never got used to such chaos—such large crowds.

It was during this commotion that Jesus suddenly stopped and asked, "Who touched my clothes?"

Being a bit confused about why it was important, I asked, "Master, the multitude is thronging around and pressing in upon you, and you ask, 'Who touched me?' " My question was not one of mockery but of curiosity. Certainly He had been touched before—many, many times—so why would it concern Him now? I did not know that it would be an opportunity for Him to teach.

Jesus scanned the crowd and said, "Someone has touched me. I perceive that power has gone out of me."

The slow progress of the multitude had stopped entirely, everyone waiting for someone else to speak. After only a few seconds, the crowd behind us parted, and a trembling woman came forward. She wept as she knelt before Jesus. In a shaky voice, she said, "I touched you. I am the one that did it. For the past twelve years I have endured constant bleeding. I have spent all that I had and have suffered many things at the hands of many physicians, and it's only gotten worse. I have been unclean, an outcast, for twelve years now. I knew in my heart that if I could just touch the hem of your garment I would be made whole. When I touched your garment, the bleeding ceased, and I felt in my body that I was healed of my plague. I knew my suffering had ended." She then bowed her head as if ashamed of her faith. Tears fell from her eyes onto the dust of the ground.

Jesus said, "Daughter, lift up your head and take heart. It wasn't my garment but your faith that made you whole. Go in peace, knowing you are freed from your plague." I know He could have ignored the woman's belief that she was healed by His garment, but He stopped to address her misdirected belief. I have observed that many superstitious people become so centered on man-made images, icons, statues, and artifacts in search of miracles that they put them ahead of God, treating them with the reverence they should reserve only for God. In short, they worship idols, not God. He didn't want the woman, or those in the crowd, to put their faith in His garment.

The woman stood, wiped her tears, and thanked Jesus repeatedly, then quietly disappeared back into the crowd behind us. Jesus smiled after her, and someone in the crowd asked, "What about Jairus?" Without answering, Jesus turned back toward the house of Jairus. As we started walking, one of Jairus's servants arrived and declared, "Your daughter has died. Why trouble the Master any further?"

With a look of desperation on his face, Jairus turned to face Jesus. Jesus had compassion for the ruler and said, "Do not be afraid, only believe, and your daughter shall be made whole."

It was not many minutes until we arrived at the house of Jairus, but the traditional mourning had already begun. Minstrels were playing flutes, and people were weeping and wailing over the death of the girl. They had been there awaiting her death.

Jesus asked me, James, and John, along with Jairus and his wife, to accompany Him. Before Jesus stepped into the house, He stopped to speak to those who were mourning, saying, "Why are you making such ado and weeping? Make way because the maid is not dead. She's only sleeping." Some in the multitude laughed scornfully.

The crowd parted, allowing Jesus and the rest of us to enter the house and walk into the bedroom where the girl lay. Jesus took her lifeless hand and said, "Talitha, kumi!" which is Aramaic for "Maiden, arise!" The girl immediately arose and walked to the astonishment of everyone present. Jesus told her parents to give her something to eat, and they obeyed.

As the girl ate the meat, Jesus said, "Tell no one what has happened here." And as usual, word of the girl being raised from the dead quickly spread throughout Galilee. When we left the house of Jairus, the multitude followed as Jesus walked through the city back to my home.

Apparently, two blind men had been among the crowd, and with the assistance of their friends, they had gone ahead of us to my home to wait for Jesus to arrive. Guided by their friends, the blind men approached Jesus, saying, "Son of David, please have mercy on us and heal our blindness."

Jesus asked, "Do you believe that I am able to heal you?"

They answered Him, saying simply, "Yes, Lord."

Jesus then touched their eyes and said, "According to your faith, it shall be." And their eyes were opened, and both of them could see. As they marveled, Jesus said, "See that no man knows of this."

As was often the case when He performed miracles, Jesus did two things. First, He pointed out that it was their faith that healed them. As usual, it was wisdom on His part to confirm the faith of the believers and to discourage the foolish superstitions that are so quickly invented by men. It is in the very nature of man to find a relationship between cause and effect, but it is easy to assign the wrong cause, which then results in superstition. Second, as was often the case when Jesus performed a miracle, those who were healed told everyone, and it added to His fame in Galilee.

Grateful for the knowledge I have, I testify as a disciple, an Apostle, and as a personal witness that Jesus is the Son of God, the Messiah. He is the Christ.

DOING MIRACLES IN JERUSALEM
AT PASSOVER

A few days later, we made the journey to Jerusalem to participate in the annual Passover, making it the spring of AD 30. We approached the city from the northeast, near the sheep market, passing by the Pool of Bethesda. Great numbers of people were on the five porticos of the pool, waiting to be healed. (In addition to the porticos on each side of the pool, one ran through its middle.)

Because the pool was used to wash lambs for the paschal sacrifice, tradition held that the pool had the power to heal. At times, air from the spring that fed the pool would bubble to the surface, so a superstition grew that the water was "troubled by an angel." The superstition then grew to be that whoever first stepped into the water after it was "troubled" would be healed.

During Passover, many people who were blind, lame, with crippled or withered limbs, or suffered from all manner of illnesses gathered around the pool. People waited for the waters to be "troubled" so they could be the first into the pool and be healed.

Among those in this intensely pathetic scene was a man who had been unable to walk for thirty-eight years. Jesus knew of his suffering and asked him, "Will you be made whole?"

Not knowing why a stranger had asked this, the man pleaded with Jesus, saying, "Sir, I have no one to assist me when the water is troubled. So while I am trying to get myself into the pool, someone else always steps into the water before me."

Great hopelessness was in his voice, but he did not know that he was speaking to the Son of God. Jesus had compassion for the man and commanded him, "Rise, take up your bed, and walk!" Immediately, the man was healed. Then he picked up his bed and walked. He quickly drew the attention of everyone around the pool because he had been healed without entering the water. Jesus then continued on His way and was lost from the man's view in the large crowd.

Because it was the Sabbath of the feast, all the laws of the Sabbath applied, forbidding men to do any work. When the Pharisees and Sadducees saw the man carrying his bed, they reminded him of the law, saying, "Isn't it illegal for you to carry your bed on the Sabbath?"

"He that made me whole said, 'Take up your bed and walk,' " the man replied.

Hoping that it was Jesus who had healed the man, the Pharisees and Sadducees excitedly asked him, "Who was it that told you this?" We knew that spies for the Pharisees and Sadducees had followed Jesus almost everywhere and reported back to Jerusalem Certainly, they were expecting Him to attend Passover and wanted something to use against Him.

But the healed man did not know the identity of the man that had healed him, leaving the Pharisees and Sadducees with no way to accuse Jesus of authorizing the man to break the Sabbath. I marveled that they were able to ignore the fact that a man was healed and able to carry his bed for the first time in thirty-eight years. How was it that they could focus on him supposedly breaking the Sabbath in light of such a miracle?

Later that day, Jesus saw the healed man standing in the temple, smiled, and said to him, "Look at yourself. You are healed!" Then Jesus cautioned him. "Sin no more, lest an even worse thing come upon you."

Only Jesus and the healed man knew what sin Jesus had referred to. The man humbly thanked Jesus for the miracle of being healed. Afterward, he asked among those in the temple who it was that had spoken to him and was informed that His name was Jesus of Nazareth. Thinking he was honoring Jesus, the man sought out the Pharisees and Sadducees and reported to them that if they wanted to speak to the man that made him whole they should seek Jesus of Nazareth.

Of course, this is exactly what the wicked men of the Sanhedrin were hoping for: an excuse to persecute Jesus for violating the Sabbath. I wondered if those same Pharisees and Sadducees would have accused an angel of violating the Sabbath if the crippled man had been the first in the "troubled" waters, been healed on the Sabbath, and then been instructed to carry his bed away as a witness of the miracle.

The Pharisees and Sadducees promptly accused Jesus of violating the Sabbath. Jesus boldly testified, "This is how my Father works, therefore it is how I work."

His words incensed the Pharisees and Sadducees. In their minds, saying He was equal to God was nothing short of blasphemy. Once again, they ignored His healing power and where more bent on killing Him than before.

I came to know that because of their corrupt hearts, the Pharisees and Sadducees would always seek to kill Jesus. Or, more accurately, because of their cowardice, they would seek to have someone else kill Him. The evil in them angered me, and I looked forward to defending Jesus if I could. I knew that He was the Son of God and could escape anyone He wished, but if they attempted to harm Him in any way, I was prepared to do whatever it might take to defend Him. My sword was always at hand.

Standing in the temple with the other Apostles and

watching these evil men confront Jesus, I carefully controlled my anger. I waited in silence to see what Jesus would do, what He would say, or whether He would simply leave the presence of those wicked Jews. I knew that He did not fear them. I knew that if He wanted to, He could withdraw and escape, just as He had done in Nazareth. At the same time, it occurred to me that He may have intentionally provoked this confrontation for some wise purpose. I didn't know, so I said nothing as I watched and waited.

Then I saw a confident and peaceful look on Jesus's face as He testified more powerfully and eloquently than ever before. He referred to Himself in the third person, as was the tradition in those times, speaking plainly. He used no parables, no allegories—just simple words that the Pharisees and Sadducees could not misunderstand. There were no cloaked meanings in His message.

"I testify to you that the Son can do nothing of Himself, only what He sees the Father do," He said emphatically. "So whatever the Father does, the Son does likewise. Because the Father loves the Son, He shows Him all things that He Himself does and will yet show the Son works that are even greater than what you have seen so that you may yet marvel even more."

Their faces paled and their nostrils flared, but the Pharisees and Sadducees were speechless at His boldness.

Jesus continued, defining Himself and His power. "Just as the Father raises up the dead and causes them to live, the Son causes whom He will to raise from the dead and live." It was a powerful testimony of His power, reminding the Jewish leadership of what He had done. I was certain that they had heard the stories of Jesus raising the dead. I could see them wince as He spoke. His words were authoritative. His demeanor was as if He were the King, and they were His lowly servants. No one dared say a word as long as He continued speaking. "The

Father judges no man but has given the judgment of all men to the Son so that men should honor the Son, even as they honor the Father. He that does not honor the Son does not honor the Father who sent Him," He warned.

The Pharisees and Sadducees were shaken by the power of His authority. I was relieved to hear Him testify plainly who He was. His words stirred my heart. Then He gave them a promise. "He that hears my word and believes on Him that sent me shall have everlasting life and shall not come into condemnation but shall pass from death to eternal life." Jesus paused while they murmured among themselves, then added, "The hour which has long been coming is now here—the hour when the dead shall hear the voice of the Son of God. And they that listen shall live.

"As the Father has the power of life in Himself, He has given the Son the power of life in Himself." I gained a new understanding as He spoke. I knew that Jesus had power over the life and death of others because I had seen Him raise the dead. Now I understood that He had power over His own life and death. That meant that no one could take His life unless He allowed them. My understanding of what it meant to be the Son of God was growing, and I felt a profound reverence for Jesus.

"The Father has given the Son the authority to execute judgment because He is the Son of Man," Jesus continued. "Do not marvel at this! The hour is here in which all that are in their graves shall hear His voice. They that have done good shall come forth to the resurrection of life, and they that have done evil shall come forth to the resurrection of damnation."

The Sadducees in the crowd cringed when Jesus referred to the resurrection. They rejected the concept of eternal souls, and they had just heard Jesus promising it to everyone, both good and evil. I admit, I was pleased at their discomfort. Sadly, the Sadducees believed that our souls are some kind of amorphous "substance" that was separated from God, came to earth in mortal form, and would return to God from where it came, to be reabsorbed.

The Pharisees and Sadducees spoke among themselves, greatly pleased to witness what they considered as Jesus repeatedly committing blasphemy, but Jesus was not finished. "I can do nothing of myself. As I hear, I judge, and my judgment is just because I do not seek to accomplish my own will, but the will of the Father, who sent me.

"When I bear witness of myself, my witness alone is not enough to carry the weight of truth, but there is another that bears witness of me, and I know that the witness he bears is true. You know that witness too because it is John the Baptist who bore witness of the truth. You both sent people and went yourselves to hear his witness." Then, gesturing toward the lights burning in the temple, Jesus added, "John was a burning light, even a shining light, and for a season, you were willing to rejoice in his light."

The faithful disciples of John the Baptist gathered closer to hear what Jesus might say about John. He continued addressing the Pharisees and Sadducees directly. "John's witness was not that of an ordinary man—he was a prophet." Then, gesturing around the room, Jesus declared, "You called him so!" Addressing the Pharisees and Sadducees again, He continued, "As a prophet, what he spoke was from God, so do not deny it."

Jesus paused for the rumblings of the Pharisees and Sadducees to die down before He continued. "Now I tell you these things that you might be saved. There is an even greater witness of me than John, which is the works the Father has given me to finish, the same works that I do and have done. These works bear witness of me, and they bear witness that the Father sent me to do them. Finally, there is yet another that bears witness of me, but you have neither heard His voice nor have you seen His shape. His word is not in your hearts because you do not believe me, and I am the One He sent!"

Instead of whining that a man had carried his bed on the Sabbath, the Pharisees and Sadducees should have been marveling at the many wonderful works that testified who Jesus was. They were stung by His words.

"Search the scriptures," Jesus said. "What is in them makes you think you shall have eternal life. The scriptures that testify of me are what has given you that hope, but you refuse to hear me that you might have eternal life.

"I receive no honor from learned men such as yourselves. I know your hearts, and you do not have the love of God in you. I come in my Father's name, but you do not receive me. If another came in his own name, you would receive him and honor him. You offer each other titles, calling yourselves rabbis, Pharisees, Sadducees, and scribes, honoring your great knowledge of the law, but you do not understand that law nor do you honor the One sent by God. How can you claim to be believers of what you do not understand?"

The Pharisees and Sadducees went pale from the shock of His pointed remarks, and Jesus added the final blow to His condemnation: "Do not think that I will be the one to accuse you to the Father. The one that will accuse you will be someone you trust, even Moses. If you had believed Moses, you would have believed me because he wrote of me. If you do not believe the words Moses wrote, how shall you believe the words I speak?"

This last comment seemed to take the oxygen out of the air the Pharisees and Sadducees were breathing. After all, hadn't they had gone around quoting Moses as though he were a personal friend and they had just spoken to him moments before?

I had never before heard Jesus speak with such power and authority when addressing anyone, anywhere. He had clearly declared these Jewish leaders to be the enemies of truth—the enemies of God. He had disgraced them in the very areas they claimed to be superior, the law and the prophets. I forced myself not to smile, but I admit that might not have been successful.

Jesus remained in Jerusalem only long enough to observe the Passover before we left for Galilee. Personally, I found our time in Jerusalem to be a satisfying experience. I take great pleasure when the truth makes people uncomfortable. It gives them the opportunity to be enlightened and to change their ways accordingly, if they have the smallest bit of truth within them. Unfortunately, the Pharisees and Sadducees were so enamored with their corrupt traditions and creeds that eternal truths had no effect on them.

To the Pharisees and Sadducees, the most extreme observances of the Sabbath came to overshadow the basic tenants of virtuous behavior. The positive demonstrations of faith, hope, and charity were ignored in favor of how many steps a person could walk before violating the Sabbath. Each person has to choose to believe either in the traditions and creeds of man or in the uncorrupted truth.

Jesus said that no man had heard His Father's voice nor had seen His Father's shape. I know it to be true. Jesus is not His own Father, but Jesus was Jehovah, or the great "I Am," the One that had been seen by the prophets of the Old Testament.

It was then that I began to understand that Jesus was the God of the Old Testament, and He continually made it clear that He was the Son of God—that is, He has a Father, who is God. Jesus and His Father are two separate, individual beings who are both called God.

I testify, just as Jesus did, that Moses wrote that Jesus and His Father were both there, in "the Beginning" when Moses recorded what God instructed him to write: "*God* said, 'Let *us* make man in *our* image, after *our* likeness.' " The plural forms, "us" and "we," are obvious. In addition, the Hebrew word for "God" used in that verse is "Elohim," the plural form of the Hebrew word for God, the singular of which is "Eloah."

And finally, I know that the Old Testament stands on its own as truth, word for word, given to Moses by Jehovah. The word of God takes precedence over the creeds of men, no matter who offers them.

When the Pharisees and Sadducees were offended by the truth, Jesus did not alter or soften it to accommodate their false beliefs; He made no shameful effort to be politically correct. Instead, He spoke the truth plainly. I may be criticized for being crude and blunt, but do not criticize the words of the Son of God. Repent and be converted to the truth.

When we arrived in Galilee, it felt good to be out of Jerusalem. The Pharisees and the Sadducees wanted Jesus dead. He rejected their traditions and called them to repentance. I wondered if He could ever be so totally rejected at any other time in history, in any other place, by any other people.

THE PHARISEES FOLLOW
JESUS TO GALILEE

B ack in Galilee, we followed Jesus from village to village as He peacefully preached the gospel and taught the glad tidings of the kingdom of God. Several Pharisees from Jerusalem also continued to follow along merely to spy on Him.

A group of faithful women were numbered among the followers, women who had each been healed of their infirmities or had evil spirits cast out of them. One of those women was known as Mary Magdalene, a virtuous follower of Jesus, devoted to Him because He had cast seven evil spirits out of her.

The women that followed Jesus generously gave of their funds, providing us with food, clothing, and money. Two of the other women were named Susanna and Joanna. Joanna was the wife of Chuza, who was the servant of Herod Antipas the tetrarch, the son of Herod the Great.

One Sabbath day, as Jesus finished teaching and preaching to a multitude, we crossed through a field of grain. We were hungry and took the opportunity to pluck a few heads of fresh, raw grain to eat. We did not eat the heads of grain directly, but rolled them between our hands, rubbing the individual kernels off the shaft, removing the chaff. Then we blew the debris from our hands, leaving only the nutritional kernels of grain.

The traditions of my time allowed us to eat from any grain field as long as we did not gather it and carry it away. The problem that arose was not that we ate the grain but that we rubbed it between our hands on the Sabbath.

Under the elaborate, convoluted logic of the Pharisees, it was not a violation of the Sabbath to pick grain and eat it, but the necessary act of rubbing the chaff from the kernels of grain was forbidden. It seemed they deemed this act to be harvesting and winnowing, both of which were forbidden on the Sabbath. It was this kind of hair-splitting, ritualistic behavior that was the foundation of much of the Pharisaic law about the Sabbath. In theory, it was as silly as it sounds. In practice, it was often difficult not to violate one rule or another on any given day, especially the Sabbath. Of all their rules, laws governing the Sabbath were those the Pharisees militantly enforced.

When the Pharisees saw us rubbing the heads of grain in our hands, they grew accusatory toward Jesus. "Look, your disciples are doing that which is unlawful to do on the Sabbath day," they said with a tone of perverse pleasure in their voices.

"Have you not even read what David and those that were with him did when they were hungry?" He reasoned in return. "In the days of Abiathar the high priest, they entered the House of God and Ahimelech the priest gave them the twelve loaves of holy bread, the shewbread, which lay on the altar, and they ate the bread. Was it not lawful for only the priests to eat the bread and not lawful for David to eat it or any of those who were in the service of the Lord with him? Have you not read in the law that on Sabbath days, the priests in the temple profane the Sabbath by the work they do as they serve in the temple? Yet they are blameless?"

Without waiting for a reply, Jesus continued. "But I say to you that in this grain field is One which is greater than the temple, and for what those in this grain field do while in my service, they are blameless. If you had known what the prophet meant when he wrote, 'I desire mercy, not sacrifice,' you would not have condemned the guiltless. The Sabbath was made for man, not man for the Sabbath. Therefore, the Son of Man is Lord even over the Sabbath."

After He finished chastising them, Jesus continued to the synagogue to observe the Sabbath. Once inside the building, I spied a man whose right hand was withered and deformed. Jesus saw the man also and asked him to stand so everyone could see him. Thinking they could trick Jesus into doing or saying something else they might accuse Him of later, the Pharisees and scribes asked Jesus, "Is it lawful to heal on the Sabbath?"

Their question acknowledged His power, but they wanted to know if performing such a miracle would be lawful! I was amazed at their arrogance! Who were they to tell the Son of God what was lawful and what was not? He gave that law to Moses!

Jesus answered their question with questions of His own. "Is it lawful to do good on the Sabbath, or to do evil? To save a life, or to kill?" None of them answered. If they told the truth, it would take away their justification to accuse Him. If they did otherwise, they would be lying, and their evil would be exposed.

"What man is there among you that having a sheep that falls into a pit on the Sabbath will not lay hold of it and lift it out? How much greater is a man than a sheep? Therefore, it is lawful to do good on the Sabbath."

Jesus had told us before that the hardness of the Pharisees' hearts grieved Him, but I could see that He was angry with them too. He glanced around the synagogue at the Pharisees and the scribes, and then He looked at the man with the withered hand. His voice filled with compassion. "Stretch forth your hand," He requested tenderly. Obediently and faithfully, the man stretched out his right hand for all to see. As he did, his crippled hand was restored, becoming as strong and healthy as his left hand. The Pharisees and the scribes recoiled at Jesus's power and were silent.

I was there. I saw it. Jesus Christ is the Son of God.

The Pharisees Conspire to Murder Jesus

As I watched while the man's hand was healed by the divine power of Jesus, I felt another thrill that is difficult to describe. At that moment, I wanted to shout aloud as a testimony of Jesus, but my voice was stilled by the lump in my throat and the tears that filled my eyes.

The hearts of the Pharisees were filled not with any type of love, but with hate. They ignored the significance of the miracle, focusing instead on the fact that it violated one of their extreme definitions of the Sabbath. They left the synagogue to meet in a secret council to conspire to murder Jesus. Violating the Sabbath was unacceptable to them, but murder was not.

In their desperation, the Pharisees met with the Herodians, a political party that actually wanted Herod the tetrarch to remain in power. Such an alliance was unheard of in our society, somewhat like Jews forming a partnership with Samaritans. In fact, the Pharisees usually did anything they could to avoid contact with the Herodians, but now they were reduced to conspiring with them to take the life of Jesus. Jesus knew what business they were about, and He led us out of the synagogue and away from their city, returning to His city on the Sea of Galilee—my city, Capernaum.

As it was wherever He went, multitudes followed Him. They gathered to Galilee from Judea, Jerusalem, Idumea or Edom, Jordan, Tyre, and Sidon. Word of the miracles Jesus performed spread quickly and far. People came from all these places and more, all seeking to be healed. And He healed them all.

One day, as the multitudes grew around Him, it became apparent that they might soon crowd Jesus into the sea. As before, He had foreseen the problem and had asked me to have my boats standing by. He continued as long as it was safe for everyone, healing them from a diverse list of plagues and infirmities. Impatient to be healed, several people rushed forward to touch Him and His garments. That began to worry me. I feared that someone would get trampled or fall among the large rocks that form the shore of the sea.

When the crowd pushed forward without regard for safety, it was time to take Jesus aboard my boat and go out a short distance from the shore. I anchored quickly, and it was from there that Jesus taught for a time. Afterward, we sailed a short ways north until we came to a small dock, a convenient place to go ashore, and from there we walked back to my home.

BACK TO CAPERNAUM

By the time we arrived at my home, the crowds had already arrived from the seashore, anticipating Jesus's return. Before Jesus got a chance to address the crowd, certain people possessed of unclean spirits came forward. As they approached Jesus, they fell down before Him and cried, "Thou art the Son of God." They recognized Him, just as the naked man of Gergesa had done. As before, when evil spirits had testified of His divinity, Jesus commanded these to be silent. They obeyed. I marvel to note that evil spirits acknowledged Jesus as the Son of God and obeyed His command to be silent while the hierarchy of the Jews wanted to silence Him. Jesus promptly cast the evil spirits out, healing those who had been possessed.

Jesus exhorted all who were healed to tell no one, just as He had commanded others, but neither they nor the others ever obeyed. As usual, these men testified openly of Jesus while He went His way, quietly and confidently doing His work. He never proclaimed Himself upon entering a city or a synagogue, nor did He ever call multitudes to gather at His side to be healed, but His works spoke for Him, a beacon that directed people to Him. He took the time to speak to those who sought Him, one at a time, gently calming them, comforting them, and asking them if they would be healed. Jesus was meek and unassuming when dealing with believers.

I was never accused of being a meek man, but it was what

I needed to be. There was much yet for me to learn, and I was learning it from the Son of God.

As Jesus healed people that day, I felt that in our presence, the prophecy of Isaiah about the meekness of the Christ was fulfilled: "Behold my servant, whom I have chosen—my beloved, who brings delight to my soul. I will bless Him with my Spirit, and He shall bring forth to the Gentiles. He shall not cry, nor shall He lift up his voice, neither shall any man hear His voice in the streets. He shall be tender to the weakest of believers. He shall not break a bruised reed, nor shall he extinguish smoking flax, until He sends judgment to truth and victory. And the Gentiles shall trust in His name."

I watched as the prophecies of old were fulfilled!

CASTING OUT ANOTHER DEVIL

Later on, while we were still in my home, a man who was possessed by an evil spirit and was both blind and dumb was brought to Jesus. Previously, I had seen Jesus cast out evil spirits, make the blind to see, and the dumb to speak, but not all at once or for the same person. Jesus promptly cast the devil out of this man, gave him sight, and restored his speech. People in the crowd said in amazement, "Is not this the Son of David, the Messiah?"

Of course, when the Pharisees and scribes who were standing among the crowd in my home heard this comment, they completely ignored the miraculous healing they had just witnessed to offer a reason for the power of Jesus over Satan. They said, "This fellow cannot cast out devils but by the power of Beelzebub, the prince of devils."

Jesus heard them and knew both their thoughts and the wickedness in their hearts. He addressed their accusations, not by way of debate, but with calm, sound reasoning. "How can Satan cast out Satan?" He asked. Without waiting for their answer, Jesus continued. "Every kingdom divided against itself is brought to desolation, and every city or house that is divided against itself shall not stand. Therefore, if Satan is divided against himself, how then shall his kingdom stand? And if I cast out devils by Beelzebub, by whom then do your children cast out devils? Therefore, they shall be your judges.

"But if I cast out devils by the Spirit of God, then the kingdom of God has come to you because they that cast out

devils have that power given them by God and by none other."
His logic was clear. There were only two choices, and one was
illogical, which left only one possible explanation: Jesus was
the Son of God. Those who prided themselves on their flaw-
less logic were trapped by it. They had to acknowledge that it
was the Spirit of God that allowed Jesus to cast out devils. The
Pharisees and the scribes had no response.

Jesus provided an example. "How can one enter a strong
man's house and plunder his goods unless he binds the strong
man first? Only then can he plunder the strong man's house.
When an armed strong man guards his house, his goods are
safe. But when someone stronger than him comes to his house
and overcomes him, the stronger man will take all that the
first armed himself with along with the spoils of his conquest."
His reasoning left no doubt that Satan was His adversary, not
His colleague. Logically, He was fighting against Satan—not
collaborating with him.

"He that is not with me is against me. He that does not
gather with me, the same scatters abroad." The Pharisees and
the scribes were not "with" Jesus; in fact, they were against
Him, and He wanted them to know that He knew it. Jesus
warned the Pharisees, letting them know the consequences
of denying the power by which He performed the miracles
that had made Him famous throughout Galilee, Judea, and
Jerusalem.

"Wherefore, I tell you that all manner of sin and blasphemy shall be forgiven of those that receive me and repent,
but men that blaspheme against the Holy Ghost shall not be
forgiven," he warned. "And whosoever shall speak against the
Son of Man and repents shall be forgiven, but whosoever shall
speak against the Holy Ghost by which He overpowers Satan,
even if he later repents, shall not be forgiven, not in this world
nor in the world to come. Those that accuse me of having an
unclean spirit are in danger of eternal damnation.

"Every tree is known by his fruit," He continued. "Either the tree is good and his fruit is good, or the tree is corrupt and his fruit is corrupt. A good tree does not bring forth corrupt fruit, neither does a corrupt tree bring forth good fruit. Every tree is known by his fruit, for men do not gather figs from thorn bushes, nor do they gather grapes from bramble bushes."

Jesus paused briefly before trapping them with their own wickedness, "O, generation of vipers, how can you, being evil, speak good things? It is as if your heart were speaking. The words that come from your mouth come from your heart. A good man, from the good treasure of his heart, brings forth good words and good works. An evil man brings forth evil words and evil works from the evil treasure in his heart. I say to you that in the day of judgment, men will be accountable for every idle word they speak. By your words, you will be either justified or you will be condemned."

Upon hearing themselves condemned as vipers, some of the scribes and Pharisees challenged Jesus, saying, "Master, we want you to show us a sign from heaven."

Again, I found myself shaking my head in disbelief. Did they not witness Him healing many people of their infirmities, plagues, and illnesses? Did they not see Him raise the dead? Did they not see Him cast out devils? Were they blind and deaf or just stupid? I decided that they were not blind or deaf, but they were dead—spiritually dead. For a second, I wondered if it were possible to raise the spiritually dead. As I looked into their faces, I doubted it. Such a miracle would be rare.

The curious moved away from the scribes and Pharisees and gathered closer to Jesus to hear what He would do in response to their demand. "It is an evil and adulterous generation that seeks after a sign!" He said in condemnation. "This generation shall be given no sign but the sign of the prophet

Jonah. As Jonah was three days and three nights in the belly of the whale, so shall the Son of Man be three days and three nights in the heart of the earth. As Jonah was a sign to the Ninevites, so shall the Son of Man be a sign to this generation.

"This generation shall be judged against the men of Nineveh and condemned thereby because the men of Nineveh repented at the preaching of Jonah. "Yet, one greater than Jonah is here.

"This generation shall also be judged against the faith and acts of the Queen of Sheba and condemned thereby because she came from the uttermost parts of the earth to hear the wisdom of Solomon. Know that one greater than Solomon is here.

"When an unclean spirit is cast out of a man, that spirit wanders through dry places, seeking rest, but finds none. Then he says to himself, 'I will return to my house, from whence I was cast out.' But when he arrives, he finds it empty of evil, swept clean, and garnished with goodness. If the man does not keep himself free of evil, clean, and garnished with goodness, the unclean spirit shall gather seven additional spirits even more wicked than himself, and the eight spirits shall enter the man and dwell there. The man that repented but returned to evil shall be in a worse state than he was at the first. Even so, that is how it shall be with this wicked generation."

I watched. The Pharisees and scribes were resolute in their evil. There was nothing—no miracle, no truth—that would change them.

MARY COMES TO VISIT

Many were there that day to see Jesus. My home was filled to overflowing, and the crowds grew so large that people jammed into the doorway while others stood outside or tried to get in. There were scribes and Pharisees, disciples and Apostles, the casually curious and the sincerely interested, but there were others. The family of Jesus had arrived to visit with Jesus. They lived in Capernaum also, but Jesus kept his distance to protect them from the crowds who were always after Him. Because of the many people, His family was not able to enter my home to see Him. Someone near the door said, "Master, your mother and your brethren are outside. They wish to speak with you."

I didn't know what Jesus would do. A great many people had gathered to hear Him. Some had traveled great distances to see Him and be healed. I wondered if He would leave them to talk to His family or if He would continue teaching. I soon learned that Jesus was about His Father's business and was not to be distracted.

"Who is my mother, and who are my brethren?" he asked. He gestured around the courtyard of my home, saying, "Behold my mother and my brethren! For whosoever shall hear the word of God and do the will of my Father which is in heaven, the same is my brother, and my sister, and my mother."

A certain woman in the multitude, a mother herself, praised Mary. "Blessed is the womb that bare you and the breasts that suckled you."

Jesus looked at the woman and accepted her compliment on behalf of His beloved mother. "Yes, and blessed are they that hear the word of God and keep it." Jesus did not turn His family away that day, nor did He insult them or ignore them. He used their presence to teach that His family includes everyone that hears His word and obeys His commandments. I take great comfort in knowing that I am also His brother. Further, all those who have heard His word and have obeyed His commandments are also His brothers and sisters.

The family of Jesus waited patiently while He finished healing those that came to see Him. Jesus then invited His family into my home. We left them to be alone in one of the rooms. What they said was private and was not shared.

THE PARABLES

Jesus left my home to sit and teach by the seashore, where more people might hear Him. In order to keep the crowds from trampling one another, Jesus sat in one of my boats to teach those that listened from the shore.

That day, He taught His doctrine strictly through parables—something that He had not done before. Of course, He used parables often, but they were always sprinkled among His other stories and teachings. This day was different; He used parables to obscure the meaning of His words from those who were not spiritually able to receive it—primarily the Pharisees He had confounded earlier. He generally spoke to the Apostles in plainness, but not to the multitude listening that day.

That afternoon He shared the parable of the sower, which I now prefer to call the parable of the soils. I don't know if it became my favorite because it was the first of many or if I liked it most because of my own experiences. I have used it often in my teaching because it is so insightful.

"Now, a sower went out to sow," Jesus began. "When he sowed, some seeds fell by the wayside, where the soil was trodden down hard, and the fowls of the air came and devoured them. Some seeds fell on stony places, where the soil was shallow. Those seeds sprouted, but when the sun came up, the sprouts were scorched because they did not have enough soil to take root, and they withered away. Some seeds fell among thorns, and the thorns grew and choked the sprouts, so they yielded no fruit. But other seeds fell on good ground and yielded fruit, some thirty-fold, some sixty-fold, and some one hundred-fold. He who has ears to hear, let him hear."

After Jesus shared this simple parable, it was clear that few, if any, in the crowd understood His full meaning. Frankly, I wasn't confident that I totally understood it. As He continued to teach in parables, one right after another, I couldn't understand why Jesus was teaching that way.

If His goal was to illuminate the gospel, I feared his methods weren't working. Most of the people just didn't understand the symbolism. I knew He always had a good reason for doing what He did, so I did not interrupt. It was only after we had returned to my home, when only the Apostles and a few of His disciples were with Him, that we got the chance to ask Him.

"Why did you teach only in parables?" I asked.

"I taught this way because it is given to you to know the mysteries of the kingdom of heaven, but it is not given to the scribes, the Pharisees, the Sadducees, and the like. Because whoever has, to him shall be given, and he shall have even more abundance. But whoever has not, from him shall be taken even that which he has. Therefore, I speak to them in parables because they shall not understand the parables. Isaiah prophesied that those shall hear but not understand and see but not perceive. His words are fulfilled by these men.

"This people's hearts are calloused, their ears deaf, and their eyes closed. Otherwise, at any time, they would see with their eyes, hear with their ears, understand with their hearts and be converted.

"But blessed are your eyes because they see, and blessed are your ears because they hear. Many prophets, kings, and righteous men have desired to see what you have seen and have not seen them, to hear what you have heard and have not heard them."

As always, I knew how blessed we were to be in the presence of the Son of God. I am unable to communicate how I felt in my heart the many times I contemplated where I was and who I was with. Even to this day, it is beyond me to clearly express my love for Him.

Another disciple who was with us asked Jesus to explain the parable of the sower.

Before He did, Jesus asked the disciple, and all of us, really, "If you do not understand this parable, how will you understand any of my parables?

"The seed is the word of God," He explained patiently. "Those by the wayside are those who hear the word, but then the devil comes and takes it out of their hearts—otherwise they would believe the word and be saved. Those on the rocky places are those who, when they hear, receive the word with joy and believe and endure for a while. But, lacking soil for the word to take root in, they find reason to be offended and fall away when tribulation or persecution comes because of the word. They are those who find that other believers have weaknesses too, and this makes them doubt.

"Those that fell among thorns are those who are choked by the cares of the world, deceived by riches and the lusts and pleasures of this life. The seed bears fruit, but it does not ripen to maturity.

"Those that fell on good ground are they who have honest and good hearts and, upon hearing the word, keep it and patiently bring forth good fruit, some thirty-fold, some sixty-fold, and some a hundred-fold."

What a profound parable it was. Those with hard hearts had rejected the word of God without considering it. Such were the scribes, the Pharisees, and the Sadducees. The second group included those with inadequate commitment to follow Jesus, so they turned away after originally accepting the word of God. As Jesus said, they often made an excuse for their repudiation with a prideful claim of offense from the gospel or by the actions of someone else. The third group were those whose hearts were set so much on the things of the world that they became distracted by those things and the word of God languished in them and withered. It was only the valiant, those willing to make whatever sacrifices were necessary to follow the word of God, who shared the word of God with others.

I had taught many people in each of the groups, anguishing over many and rejoicing over few. Now I knew why— they were all given the same seed, but each received it differently. I had worried that it was my presentation, my personal weaknesses, or some fault of my own that had left so many rejecting the word of God. It wasn't me. It was them. It was my duty to teach them, to make sure they all had the opportunity to hear the word of God, but what they did with the message would either sanctify or condemn them.

I understood that Jesus was the Sower. It seemed to me that the Sower and the seeds were always the same, so I came to think of it as the parable of the soils. It was the soil, or the hearts of men, that made the difference in how they received the word of God. His explanation of the parable of the soils provided the foundation to understand them all.

Earlier that day, from my boat, Jesus taught other parables:

"The kingdom of heaven is like a man that went forth and sowed good wheat seed in his field, but during the night, his enemy came and sowed tares among the wheat and then went his way. When the wheat sprouts began to shoot forth from the ground, the tares sprouted also.

"So the servants of the householder came and said to him, 'Sir, did you not sow good seed in your field? Why are there tares?'

"He answered them, 'An enemy sowed them.'

"Then the servants asked, 'Would you have us pick the tares out of the field?' "

"But he said, 'No, lest while you pull the tares, you pull the wheat with them too. Let both grow together until the harvest, when it will be easy to tell the tares from the wheat. At harvest time, I will tell the reapers, "First, gather the tares and bind them to be burned, then gather the wheat into my barn." ' "

As the multitude pondered His words, I thought I knew exactly what He was talking about this time. He had spoken to us of the end-times before that day, and this was an end-times parable. Again, He explained the parable of the wheat after he sent the multitude away and we had returned to my home.

"He that sowed the good seed is the Son of Man; the field is the world; the good seeds are the children of the kingdom of God. But the tares are the children of the wicked one; the enemy that sowed them is the devil; the harvest is the end of the world; and the reapers are the angels. As the tares are gathered and burned in the fire, so shall it be at the end of this world. The Son of Man shall send forth His angels, and they shall gather out of His kingdom all things that are offensive and those who do iniquity and shall cast them into a furnace of fire. There shall be wailing and gnashing of teeth. Then shall the righteous shine forth as the sun in the kingdom of their Father. Who has ears to hear, let him hear."

Again, He spoke nothing but parables to the people that day, fulfilling that which was spoken by the prophet.

He spoke of the kingdom of heaven several times:

"The kingdom of heaven is like a grain of mustard seed, which a man sowed in his field. Mustard is the least of all seeds, but when it is grown it is the greatest among herbs. A mustard seed becomes a tree so that the birds of the air come and lodge in its branches.

"The kingdom of heaven is like leaven, which a woman took and kneaded into three measures of meal until it was all leavened.

"The kingdom of heaven is like a treasure hid in a field, which when a man finds it, he hides the treasure again, and for the joy thereof, he goes and sells all that he has and buys that field.

"The kingdom of heaven is like a merchant seeking goodly pearls who, when he had found one pearl of great price, went and sold all that he had and bought it.

"The kingdom of heaven is like a net that was cast into the sea and gathered of every kind, which when it was full, they drew it to shore. And they sat down and gathered the good into vessels but cast the bad away."

This parable He also explained later at my home: "So shall it be at the end of the world. The angels shall come forth and sever the wicked from among the just and shall cast the wicked into the furnace of fire, and there shall be wailing and gnashing of teeth."

When He finished speaking in parables, He sent the multitude their separate ways to consider what He had taught. We went ashore and returned to my home, where my wife and her mother had prepared a meal for us. It was while we were eating that He expounded the parables to us. After expounding on them, He shared more of them with us and then explained their meaning.

"The kingdom of God is like a man that casts seeds to be planted in the ground and then sleeps at night and arises each day. The seeds will sprout and grow, but the man does not know how because the earth brings forth the fruit by itself, first the blade, then the green seed head, and after that, the full head of mature wheat kernels or wheat berries. When the berries are ready, the man brings out his sickle and goes to work because it is time to harvest."

Jesus asked us, "Do you understand?"

We answered, "Yes, Lord."

"Every scribe instructed in the things of the kingdom of heaven is like a householder that brings forth from his treasure both new things and old things," he continued. I understood and treasured that understanding. Some of my treasure was new, such as those things that had been taught by Jesus. Some of my treasure was old, such as those things that had been taught by the prophets. To me, all knowledge of the gospel was a treasure.

As the night drew near, it became necessary to bring out the candles and light them in the courtyard. Jesus finished His instruction by referring to the candles. "Is a candle brought out to be lit and put under a bushel or under a bed and not to be set on a candlestick? Nothing is hidden from your knowledge that shall not be manifested. No truth will be kept secret but will be known abroad. If any man has ears to hear, let him hear. But pay attention to what you hear and with what measure you follow it, for you shall be measured by what you hear. And to you that hear, more shall be given. For he that hears, more shall be given to him; but he who does not listen, that which he had shall be taken from him."

BACK IN NAZARETH

Shortly after Jesus finished speaking His parables, He departed from Capernaum and traveled to Nazareth. This time, we were allowed to go with Him. Once again, He entered and taught in the synagogue of His hometown. Those in attendance that day were astonished by what He taught and the reputation He had garnered for the many miracles He had performed. They said, "Where does this man get such wisdom? Where does He get the power to do such mighty works? Is not this man the carpenter's son? Is not His mother named Mary? Are not His brothers James and Joseph and Simon and Judah? And are not His sisters living among us? Where then did this man obtain this power?"

They acknowledged the great wisdom and power Jesus exercised, yet they rejected Him because they knew Him as Joseph and Mary's son and they were acquainted with the rest of His family. Jesus, knowing of the weakness and foolishness within their hearts, said, "A prophet is not without honor, except in his own country, and in his own house."

He went to the villages near and around Nazareth and taught the people, but he could not do the many mighty works He had done elsewhere because of the lack of the people's faith. As He had said before, it is by faith that people are healed. Of all the people in the area around Nazareth, there were very few with such faith. He laid His hands on those few and healed them, but He expressed His disappointment at the general unbelief of the people.

JOHN THE BAPTIST

When I first heard that wicked King Herod had imprisoned John the Baptist in the Herodian Castle at Macherus, I was greatly concerned about the safety of Jesus. I knew that the Pharisees were conspiring with their enemies to have Jesus killed, so I kept my eyes and ears open to anything that might be a threat.

We learned that John was imprisoned for several months, possibly more than a year, before he was eventually beheaded. Herod's clever wife, Herodias, and her wicked daughter, Salome, had tricked Herod into beheading John. John's disciples took his body and buried it before they came to tell Jesus.

John had shamed Herod publicly by proclaiming that Herod had violated the law. In time, we learned from our friends in Jerusalem that after Herod ordered the beheading of John the Baptist, the tetrarch was stricken by guilt. He knew John the Baptist was an innocent man, and he had allowed himself to be manipulated by his wife and stepdaughter.

When Herod heard about the miracles being performed by Jesus, he was fearful that Jesus was in fact John the Baptist, risen from the dead. Later, when Herod heard that Jesus was baptizing and gathering followers, Herod grew even more fearful, and he wanted to see Jesus in person to assure himself that He was not John.

Some of those in Herod's court comforted him, assuring him that John the Baptist was dead and buried and that Jesus was Elias or some other Jewish prophet. When word came to King Herod that a number of men were preaching across Israel, casting out devils, and healing the sick, it troubled Herod even more. In his guilt, he complained that this was a great movement led by John the Baptist, raised from the dead, to punish him. We were told that his conscience tormented him relentlessly. He could not deny that he had murdered a prophet—a man he resentfully respected.

Jesus had sent us out to teach and baptize, but our travels and preaching came to an end when the disciples of John the Baptist sought Jesus to bring word that Herod had beheaded John. Through this increasingly fearful time, we, the disciples and the Apostles, gathered to be near Jesus. I felt the need to be with Him in case the conspiring Pharisees were moving in to murder Jesus too. When we found Jesus and reported the results of our missions, He acknowledged our service and thanked us for returning to be with Him.

I was pleased to be back at His side. I didn't know if I would be able to defend Him from Herod's soldiers, if he sent them, but I was resolved to protect Him from the Pharisees. I could not allow them to behead Jesus.

FIVE LOAVES AND TWO FISH

Jesus instructed us that we were to leave Capernaum and sail east along the northern shore of the Sea of Galilee. We set forth from the city in one of my ships, going along the coast until we came to a deserted place west of Bethsaida at the foot of a mountain. Jesus took the opportunity to rest during this time on the ship, but the crowds followed us, walking along the edge of the shore.

The crowds started arriving at the desert place in the evening. They gathered until it seemed to me that their numbers totaled in the thousands—perhaps as many as I had ever seen before, or more. Jesus stayed in my ship, saying little, remaining very somber. There must have been a great weight on His heart at the murder of John the Baptist, a prophet He respected deeply. Certainly, word of the death of John the Baptist had spread quickly among the gathered multitude. Everyone sought comfort—they wanted to see Jesus, hear Him, and feel of His spirit. I knew how they felt. Jesus was moved with compassion toward them, and he healed their sick for the rest of the day.

When the evening came, we walked with Jesus up the side of the mountain near the desert place. We spoke to Jesus privately, suggesting that He allow us to send the multitude away. There was nothing to eat where we were, but there was still time in the day that they could go to the nearby villages and buy food. We knew that it would soon be time for the Passover, and we wanted Jesus to be free to go to Jerusalem.

"They do not need to leave," Jesus said. "Give them something to eat."

"We would need something to feed them with before we could give it to them," Philip blurted. "Shall we buy bread for them?"

"Where could we buy bread for them to eat?" Jesus asked. We were in a desert. There was nowhere nearby for us to purchase bread. Jesus challenged Philip to offer a solution, knowing beforehand what He planned to do, but Philip didn't understand.

"We have two-hundred denarii in coins at hand, but that would not buy enough bread for each person to take even a little piece," Philip said.

My brother Andrew brought a young man forward. "What we have here is a lad with five barley loaves and two small fish," Andrew said. "But what good are they among so many people?"

May I repeat how much I love Jesus? Sometimes it fills my soul to overflowing.

"Bring the loaves and fish to me," Jesus said. Then He commanded the multitude to sit down on the grass in groups of fifty. When they were seated and quiet, He stopped and looked up into Heaven. He blessed the loaves and the fish, broke the loaves into pieces, and gave them to us. We put them into our bags and walked among the multitude, distributing pieces of bread and fish, each person receiving as much as they wanted.

The multitude numbered about five thousand, plus women and children. They all ate until they were satisfied. When they were finished, Jesus directed some of the disciples to take baskets and gather what was left from among the multitude. They filled twelve baskets with pieces of bread and with fish!

When the multitude saw the miracle that Jesus did, they

were comforted, saying among themselves, "It is true that He is the prophet that was to come into the world. He is the Messiah!"

Jesus told us that He perceived evil in the hearts of the people—they wished to force Him to be their king. He said that they wanted Him to feed them always. He immediately instructed us to return to our ship, telling us to sail back to Capernaum. As we headed toward the ship, Jesus sent the multitudes away and went further up onto the mountain to be alone to pray. When the night came, He was still alone on the mountain.

I was certain that the beheading of John the Baptist was a heavy burden for Jesus. He was more somber than usual. I knew that He needed to be alone to communicate with His Father in Heaven.

That knowledge comforted me. We had seen and heard Jesus pray many times. His prayers were as a Son speaking to His Father, similar to the way I spoke to my father when I was a younger man, asking for the guidance, advice, and comfort I needed. Once again, the Son of God would be on His knees, praying to His Father.

WALKING ON THE WATER

Our journey back to Capernaum was not uneventful. The westerly headwind on the Sea of Galilee that night was fierce, almost blowing us back to where we had started our journey. The sea was rough, tossing us back and forth. We seemed to slide—sometimes forward, sometimes backward—on slippery mountainsides of water. Finally we took the sails down and tried rowing across the sea, struggling against the force of the wind and the waves. We made very slow progress, probably less than three miles the whole of the night. As dawn approached, we were all exhausted. Some of the Apostles who were unfamiliar with the sea began to fear for their lives. I thought of trying to calm them, but I decided to stay silent.

When it was light enough that I could see across the water, I saw something impossible: a man was walking on the water toward my ship. I'd spent my life on the sea; I knew that what I saw could not be. Men cannot walk on water. Soon the others onboard my ship saw what I did.

"It is a spirit!" shouted one of the Apostles, panicked, as if he were certain we would all die.

"Do not fear!" We heard a voice call out to us from across the waves. "Be of good cheer for it is I."

I recognized His voice and then His face as He came closer to our boat. Still, I was not certain that it was not a spirit appearing as Jesus to deceive us. "Lord," I called back, "if it's you, bid me to walk on the water to you."

Sure enough, Jesus answered my request simply, saying, "Come!" I stepped out and down from the boat, and I walked on the water toward Jesus. I walked on the water!

Remember, the water was not still. The wind had not died down, and the waves were still rolling around me. I went up and down with the water. I looked around, and for only a second, I forgot that I was in the Master's hands. I grew fearful of the waves and started to sink into the rolling sea. In panic, I cried out to Jesus, saying, "Lord, save me!"

Jesus stepped closer, caught my hand, and, gripping my wrist with His powerful hand, he lifted me back up. He looked into my eyes and chided me with a smile, saying, "O, you of little faith. Why did you doubt?"

I could not answer, but I knew exactly why I started sinking into the water. I turned my attention from my faith in Jesus to the adversities of the moment. I learned my lesson. It took only a second, but the effect undermined my faith as though I had forgotten Jesus entirely. When He caught me by the hand, my faith was refreshed, and I walked on the water again. To those who doubt, I would tell you that by faith I walked on water; but I first had to exercise faith to step out of the safety of the boat.

After He lifted me up, we walked back to the boat and stepped into it together. As soon as we did, the wind ceased—immediately! Seemingly forgetting the miracles He had performed, including the feeding of the five thousand with just a few loaves and fishes, everyone in the boat stood in total amazement at the scene. They knelt before Jesus and someone spoke—I think it was John. "It is true!" he said in a near whisper. "You are the Son of God!" Certainly, some of the Apostles may not have fully understood what the title meant before that event.

Ashore at Gennesaret

As the waves were calmed and the night sky lightened even more, we turned our attention to the horizon and saw that we were near a rocky shore not far south of Capernaum, at a village called Gennesaret. Jesus had taken us there—not by sail, nor by oar, but by His power, the power He had as the Son of God.

When we disembarked, a small crowd immediately surrounded us. Because we were only a couple of miles from Capernaum, those at Gennesaret either knew Jesus or had heard of Him. Word of His presence spread quickly, and the multitude grew even larger, drawing people from the town and the surrounding villages. People came carrying their diseased loved ones, either on stretchers or in their beds. I then understood why we had come. It was too far for these people to carry their loved ones to Capernaum, but now that Jesus had come to their village, they were desirous that He heal all of their sick family and friends.

The people had heard that all they had to do was touch the hem of His garment and they would be made whole. Jesus spent most of the day walking through Gennesaret and the surrounding villages. Wherever He went, believers pressed in on Him, touched His robe, and were made perfectly whole.

THE BREAD OF LIFE

We departed in my boat from the village of Gennesaret and sailed northeast along the shore of the sea back toward Capernaum. I was pleased that the trip was so much easier than the one the night before. We were nearly exhausted from lack of sleep and a full day of walking with Jesus. When we came ashore at Capernaum, we went directly to my home and ate a satisfying meal. I watched Jesus during supper, observing that He did not appear as weary as I felt. It must have been regenerating for Him to visit with His Father on the mountain the night before. It seemed to me that He was no longer preoccupied with the murder of John the Baptist. We all went to bed early that night without entertaining anyone.

In the morning, a group of people arrived from the desert place near Bethsaida, the mountainside where the five thousand had been fed. They had come to Capernaum in search of Jesus. One of the men explained that they had heard that Jesus often stayed at Capernaum. He said that they observed only one boat at Bethsaida at the time Jesus blessed the bread and fish. When we, the Apostles, left in it and Jesus was not with us, they concluded that Jesus was still on the mountain. He explained that they waited for Him to come down the next morning. When He still did not come down, they went up the mountain to look for Him. When they could not find Him, they decided to come to Capernaum. They were going to walk, but when a boat came by on its way to Tiberias, they took passage on it.

I directed them to the synagogue, where they found Jesus teaching. "Master," they asked, "when did you come here?"

"You seek me, not because you saw miracles, but because you ate the fish and the loaves of bread and you were filled," he told them.

Then He went on to instruct them. "Labor not for meat that will spoil, but for meat that will endure unto everlasting life. It is this meat that the Son of Man will give you. For it is Him that God the Father has sealed and marked as His own."

They came seeking Jesus because they wanted more fish and bread. "What shall we do that we might be able to do the works of God?" they asked. It was clear that they did not immediately understand His use of symbolism. They wanted Jesus to tell them how they could do what He had done.

"This is the work of God that you should do: believe on Him whom God has sent," He answered simply.

Of course, there were also Pharisees, Sadducees, and scribes in the synagogue that day. Their response was to challenge Jesus, comparing Him to Moses. "What sign will you show us so that we will believe you?" they asked Him. "What miracle will you work? It is written that our fathers ate manna, bread from heaven in the desert, given them daily by Moses for forty years. You gave these people but one meal of barley loaves and fish. Was not Moses greater?"

"It was not Moses that gave your fathers bread from heaven!" Jesus exclaimed, pointing out their error. "My Father gives you the True Bread from heaven. For the Bread of God is He that has come down from heaven and gives life to the world."

Again, only a small part of the multitude seemed able to comprehend and accept His words. They pleaded with Jesus, "Lord, give us this bread forever."

Jesus taught these people to feed not their stomachs, but

their hungry souls. He spoke with confidence, tenderly saying, "I am the Bread of Life. He that comes to me shall never hunger. He that believes on me shall never thirst." Turning from this small group of believers, He addressed the disbelievers in the crowd, including the Pharisees and the Sadducees, saying, "You have seen me also, but you do not believe."

Then, turning back to the small number of believers, He said, "All that the Father has for me shall come to me. Likewise, I will keep him that comes to me and will in no wise cast him out. For I came down from heaven—not to do my will, but the will of Him that sent me. And, this is the will of my Father who sent me, that I shall not lose any of those that He has given me; I shall raise them up at the last day. And this is the will of Him that sent me: that everyone who sees the Son and believes on Him shall have everlasting life because I will raise him up on the last day."

The Pharisees, Sadducees, and scribes murmured because Jesus testified that he had come down from heaven. "Is this not Jesus, the son of Joseph, whose father and mother we know?" they asked, mocking. "How is it that He can say, 'I came down from heaven'?"

Jesus ignored them and addressed the believers again. "Murmur not among yourselves," He said. "No man can come to me, unless my Father, who sent me, draw that man to me. And I will raise him up to me at the last day." It was a word of warning. The Pharisees and Sadducees were not drawn to Jesus by the Father, but they came so they might trap Him in His words.

"It is written in the prophets, 'They shall all be taught of God,' " He said. "Therefore, every man will be taught, but only those who learn from the Father will come to me. Not all men can see the Father; only a man of God can see the Father."

Jesus said that His Father would teach us. He then explained that His Father would not teach us face to face.

In other words, it would be by personal revelation that the Father would reveal to each of us that Jesus is His Son. My friend John described it well when he said, "The testimony of Jesus is the spirit of prophecy."

Jesus continued His comments to the believers, speaking the words which would be the basis upon which the Pharisees and Sadducees would later accuse Him in the Sanhedrin. "He who believes on me has everlasting life because I am the Bread of Life."

Jesus addressed the Pharisees and Sadducees again, expanding on their comparison of Him to Moses. "Your fathers ate manna in the wilderness, and they are dead," He said. Then, motioning toward Himself, He said, "This is the Bread that comes down from heaven, that a man may eat thereof and not die. I am the living Bread, which came down from heaven. If any man eats of this Bread, he shall live forever. And the Bread that I will give is my flesh, which I will give for the life of the world."

The Jews spoke among themselves, saying, "How can this man give us His 'flesh' to eat?"

Jesus, offering more symbolism, responded, "In truth, except you eat the flesh of the Son of Man and drink His blood, you have no life in you! Whoso eats my flesh and drinks my blood has eternal life, and I will raise him up at the last day. For my flesh is meat indeed, and my blood is drink indeed. He that eats my flesh and drinks my blood dwells in me and I in him. As the living Father sent me, and as I live by the Father, he that eats of me shall live by me.

"This is that Bread that came down from heaven," he concluded. "Your fathers ate manna, and they are dead, but he who eats of this Bread shall live forever."

There were believers present, true disciples of Jesus, who said, "This is hard to comprehend. Who can understand these sayings?"

I didn't interrupt, but I understood the power of His symbolic wording. The words Jesus used, particularly with regard to his own flesh and blood, may have sounded like He was advocating some type of primitive cannibalistic ritual, but His symbolism was a beautiful and simple metaphor of His life and sacrifice.

Jesus lived His life as an example to us. First, by following His example and obeying His commandments, we take His life into ours, and we metaphorically consume His mortal life or flesh. Second, by changing our ways—that is, by repenting of our sins—we take advantage of His Atonement and metaphorically consume the blood He would soon shed in the Garden of Gethsemane and on the cross. It is by repenting that we consume the body He sacrificed. Even I, the crude fisherman, understood. I knew that the Jews did too.

Later, as we left the synagogue, Jesus overheard some of those who had followed Him from Bethsaida as they murmured, bothered that He had identified Himself as the Son of God. Jesus found a place to sit and talk with them not far from the synagogue.

"Does this offend you?" He asked. "And what if you shall see the Son of Man ascend up to heaven where He was before? It is your Spirit that gives you life, not your body. The flesh profits you nothing. The words that I speak to you are spiritual nourishment, and they give you life."

Jesus paused and looked around at those who had followed Him out of the synagogue. "There are some here that do not believe." Jesus knew which ones were disbelievers and which one of His Apostles would betray Him. "That is why I warned you that no man can come to me except it is given to him by my Father."

Those that came that day to make Jesus their king, who wanted Him to feed them bread and fish, all left and followed Jesus no longer. The disbelievers left us alone. Jesus turned to us, His Apostles, and asked, "Will you also go away?"

At first, I was deeply saddened. Jesus knew the hearts of the disbelievers, so He must have known my heart. I would never leave Him. I would die for Him. I stood and said for all to hear, "Lord, to whom shall we go? You have the words of eternal life. We believe and are certain that you are the Messiah, the Christ, the Son of the Living God." I wanted all to know that I knew who He was, for I was His witness.

Jesus then spoke words that echoed in my ears over and over, "Have I not chosen you twelve, and yet one of you is a devil?"

My stomach hurt, and I wondered if He were talking about me. It was not until later that I understood. He was talking then about Judas Iscariot, the son of Simon, because he was the one among the twelve that would betray Jesus.

Jesus was weary; I could see it in His face. My heart was heavy too. After all, I am an ordinary man.

After that day in the synagogue, Jesus walked in Galilee, but He would not walk again with those Pharisees and Sadducees because we received information from Nicodemus that they were plotting a strategy to kill Him. I could only see the wickedness in their eyes and their countenances, but I knew that Jesus knew their hearts. I could also see that their wickedness was a burden for Him.

I struggled to understand how anyone could see and listen to Jesus and still not believe Him. Their lack of faith did not try my faith, but it angered me that they were a burden and a distraction for Jesus. If they did not believe Him, why not just go away and leave Him alone? But they wouldn't be content until they insulted Him, confronted Him, and saw Him killed. They had wicked hearts that would not be converted.

I wondered how Jesus would deal with their plot. I myself didn't know what to do. I had a lot of ideas, impulses really. None of them were peaceful. What should an ordinary citizen do when those that govern are evil? How should he act when wicked men rule? I waited for Jesus to instruct me. In all the world, only His wisdom gave me peace of mind.

DEFILED BY THE TRADITIONS
OF MAN

After we entered my home, Jesus rested again, then we gathered later for a meal. He looked refreshed, which eased my worry for Him. About that time, we were joined by certain disciples and, of course, a different group of scribes and Pharisees, this time they were from Jerusalem, sent to watch and accuse Jesus. They were not spies because their mission was not secret. We knew who they were and why they were there.

I was weary of the wickedness of the scribes and Pharisees and did not want them in my home, but Jesus forbade me to cast them out, so I obeyed. I decided He must have something to say to them. I wondered if He would confront them and reveal their conspiracy, thereby frustrating their attempt to murder Him. The situation was very tense, and I was not at peace in their presence.

Almost immediately, the scribes and Pharisees found something to complain about, saying, "Why do your disciples transgress the traditions of the elders? For they eat bread and they have not washed their hands."

One of the countless traditions of the Pharisees dictated eating with dirty or defiled hands as unlawful. In addition, Jews maintained the tradition of only eating from cups, pots, brass vessels, and tables that were washed. They considered the violation of this man-made law to be a sin as serious as murder.

"Isaiah prophesied well of you hypocrites, as it is written,

'This people honors me with their lips, but their hearts are far from me," Jesus observed. "They worship me in vain, teaching for doctrine the commandments of men.' "

After setting the foundation with a quote from Isaiah, Jesus continued, "You have laid aside the commandments of God to hold onto the traditions of men, such as washing pots and cups. These are the kinds of things you do, rejecting the commandments of God, so that you may keep your own traditions. Why do you transgress the commandments of God by your traditions?"

I am not ashamed of Jesus, nor am I ashamed of what He taught, because I know that He is the Son of God. Just as Jesus spoke bluntly to the scribes and the Pharisees, I testify that His commandments are from God.

Jewish law commanded us not to worship idols. Instead, Jesus instructed us to pray to His Father. We are commanded to repent and do good works to earn our salvation. We are instructed that the honor of holding the holy priesthood and serving Him is not something we take upon ourselves, but it is only for those who are called of God, as was Aaron.

Jesus told the scribes and Pharisees that they "have laid aside the commandments of God to hold onto the traditions of men." As with the scribes and Pharisees, the traditions of man will not get anyone into heaven.

"Moses received the commandments of God, which said, 'Honor your father and mother,' and, 'Whoso curses his father or mother shall surely die.'

"But you say that whosoever shall say to his father or mother, 'My possessions are Corban, gifts dedicated to the temple. It is because of my generosity to the temple that you are thereby blessed.' Such a person does not honor his father or his mother when he believes he is free of any obligation to do more. Thus, you have devalued the commandments of God by your 'tradition.' You have done many such things."

Jesus invited those who were standing behind the scribes and Pharisees to come closer. "Hearken to me, every one of you," he said. "Hear and understand. It is not what goes into a man's mouth that defiles him, but that which comes out of his mouth. If any man has ears to hear, let him hear."

Jesus stood, left the open courtyard of my home, and retired to his room, leaving the scribes and Pharisees to themselves to contemplate the foolish traditions that they had elevated to be greater than the commandments of God. I knew it would lead to more trouble. I was pleased when the scribes and Pharisees left my home.

Some who considered themselves to be disciples asked me for permission to talk to Jesus privately. "Do you know how offended the Pharisees were after you talked to them?" they asked.

"Every plant that my Heavenly Father has not planted shall be uprooted," he answered. "Leave the Pharisees to themselves. They are the blind leading the blind, and if the blind lead the blind, they both shall fall into the ditch."

Those so-called disciples left my home, probably to report back to the Pharisees. I was happy to have them gone. When we were alone, I asked Jesus for a better understanding of His words.

"Are you still without understanding?" He chided gently. "Do you not yet understand that whatever enters in the mouth and goes into the belly is purged as are all meats and is cast into the sewer? But those things that proceed out of the mouth come from the heart and defile men. Out of their hearts proceed evil thoughts, adulteries, fornications, murders, thefts, covetousness, wickedness, deceit, lasciviousness, an eye to do evil, blasphemy, pride, and foolishness. All of these things come from within. They are what defile a man. Eating with unwashed hands does not defile a man."

His message was clear.

I'll admit that because I was an Israelite, tradition was an integral part of who I was. I freely admit that I was like many men. I believed and acted certain ways because of our traditions, not because of religious beliefs. That is why I can speak bluntly about the traditions others follow. I do not justify them or excuse myself; I only seek to explain how we came to be bound by traditions instead of commandments.

I might suggest that something about man makes us look for outward ways of expressing our inner beliefs, and thus traditions are born. Other times we create false beliefs to explain the unknown or to calm our fears. In time, traditions and false beliefs grow to become more important than the commandments themselves. Traditions are not commandments. False beliefs are not the truth. Let him who has ears hear. The commandments of God are to be obeyed, not the traditions of men.

THE FAITH OF A
CANAANITE WOMAN

The next morning, Jesus informed us that we were going to leave Capernaum for a time. As we journeyed, He explained that in order to frustrate the conspiracy to murder Him, we would be going to several distant places where the Pharisees and the Sadducees would not think to look for Him. We went some distance north and west until we came to the seacoast near the regions of Tyre and Sidon, a place we had never traveled before. When we came to the house of a disciple, Jesus rested. He was able to remain anonymous for only a short time, however, because wherever Jesus was, word spread quickly.

Late one afternoon, a Canaanite woman from the region known as Syria-Phoenicia came to the door of the disciple's house in search of Jesus. At that hour, no one was inside except Jesus, who was resting out of her view. Not knowing if anyone was home, she politely waited outside. After a while, hoping the Lord might be inside, she pleaded loudly through the door, saying, "Have mercy on me, O Lord, Son of David. My daughter is grievously vexed. Please cast out the devil that is in her."

Jesus remained in the house and left her alone outside. Concluding that no one was home, the woman gave up, left the house, and found us sitting nearby, resting from the heat of the day. She related where she had been and pleaded with us to heal her daughter. We returned to the disciple's house to talk to Jesus. I asked Him to heal the woman's daughter and then send her away. I explained to Him that when He did not respond to her appeal, she came to us and wanted our help. I assured Him that if He wasn't going to bless her daughter, we would not do so against His wishes. He had healed so many people, so many times, in so many places, I did not understand why this Canaanite woman was different.

Jesus explained simply, "I was not sent to anyone except the lost sheep of the house of Israel."

I did not fully appreciate His meaning until much later when He sent us on missions to teach first the Jews and then the Gentiles, in that order.

While we were talking, the Canaanite woman returned to the house, found us together, and knelt on the ground in front of Jesus. This time she pleaded tearfully, "Lord, Please help me and cast the devil out of my daughter."

Jesus answered, saying, "Let the children of Israel first be filled, for it is not proper to take bread meant for the children and cast it to the dogs."

"Yes, Lord, it is true," the woman agreed, but she was unwilling to leave as long as her daughter was possessed. "Still, the dogs under the table are happy to eat the children's crumbs."

Jesus smiled at her thoughtfully and said, "O woman, your words show how great your faith is." He paused briefly, then added, "It is as you have asked. The devil is gone out of your daughter." And when she returned to her house, she found her daughter resting on her bed. The devil had gone out of her when Jesus had spoken the words.

Back to Galilee to Feed the Four Thousand

Once the word spread that Jesus was in Tyre and Sidon, it was time to leave. We traveled to the east, then to the far side of the Sea of Galilee, making our way through the area known as Decapolis. Jesus went up onto a mountain and sat down to teach the multitude that gathered around Him. I was pleased that there were no Pharisees or anyone sent by the Sanhedrin in the crowd.

Before long, a great number of people drew unto Jesus, bringing the lame, the blind, the dumb, the maimed, and others with a number of afflictions. As they came to the hillside, they placed the afflicted ones at Jesus's feet, and over the next three days, He healed them, one by one.

One of those brought to Jesus was deaf and tongue-tied, causing him great difficulty in speaking. Those who brought him pleaded with Jesus, asking, "Please touch him so he will be healed."

Jesus took the man aside, away from the multitude, but still within in plain view so everyone could see what was to happen. Jesus then did something He'd never done before: He put His fingers in the man's ears. Then He spit on his fingers and touched the man's tongue. Jesus paused briefly, looked up toward heaven, and said loudly enough for everyone to hear, "Eph'phatha," which means, "be opened" in Aramaic.

The man could immediately both hear and speak. His tongue was loosed, and he spoke plainly so that we understood him. I counted four miracles at once. Not only could he hear and speak, he could also understand the words he was hearing—words he had never before heard—and he could speak those words clearly.

Jesus turned to the multitude and charged them that they should tell no man, but as was always the case, the more He told them to say nothing, the more they told the story. They were astonished beyond measure, saying, "He does everything well. He makes both the deaf to hear and the dumb to speak." The multitude glorified the God of Israel that day.

Jesus called us closer to Him and said, "I feel compassion for the multitude because they have stayed with me now for three days, and they have nothing left to eat. Some have traveled a good distance to be here, and I will not send them away hungry, lest they faint along the way."

I thought I understood, but I asked the obvious question to receive His instructions: "Where will we find enough bread here in the wilderness to feed such a great multitude?"

Jesus answered as I hoped He would, by asking the Twelve, "How many loaves do you have?"

We quickly gathered up what we had, and I answered, "We have seven loaves and a few small fish."

Jesus stood and commanded the multitude to sit down. He took the basket containing the loaves and prayed, giving thanks, and then He broke the bread. He handed the bread back to us, and we separated it among several baskets. We gave Him a second basket with the fish, and again He prayed, giving thanks and blessing the fish. We took fish and put them into our baskets.

We walked among the multitude, offering bread and fish to all. Everyone ate, and they were all filled. We all ate and were filled also. When we were finished, Jesus directed us to gather up the excess food. We filled seven baskets with the leftover fish. That day in my sight, there were four thousand men plus women and children, including a large number of

Gentiles, who were miraculously fed by seven loaves and a few small fish. After they were all fed, Jesus instructed them to return to their homes as we departed.

I was there, and I saw what everyone else did, but I think few appreciated the man who was both healed and taught. Somehow, Jesus gave the man the knowledge to understand and speak a language that he had never heard. Sometimes we don't recognize the miracles around us.

SEEKERS AFTER A SIGN

As the multitude dispersed, we entered ships and crossed the Sea of Galilee to the coasts of Magdala, near a place that some referred to as Dalmanutha. Shortly after we disembarked, a congregation of Pharisees and Sadducees arrived at the rocky seashore. They had been searching for Jesus. They tempted Him, saying, "Show us a sign from heaven!"

"When you see a cloud rise out from the west, straightway you say, 'It is going to rain,' and so it is," He countered. "And when you feel the south wind blow, you say, 'It is going to be hot.' And it comes to pass.

"And when it is evening, you say, 'It will be fair weather because the sky is red.' And in the morning, 'It will be foul weather today because the sky is red and clouds are dark.' Oh, you hypocrites! You can discern the face of the sky, but can you not discern the signs of the times? Why is it that you cannot judge for yourselves what is right?"

The Pharisees and the Sadducees were profound religious enemies, even to the point of engaging in a bloody civil war. They had fundamentally different and conflicting beliefs. Logically, they could not both be right. The only alternatives were that one of them was right or both were wrong. Because the Sadducees did not believe in resurrection, I knew they were wrong. Because the Pharisees had ignored the spirit of the law, replacing it with man-made traditions, I knew they were not right either. The Samaritans were wrong to reject whatever part of the truth that offended them. The Pagans were wrong because instead of worshipping God, they worshipped idols, praying to wooden, stone, and metal statues along with dead ancestors, and they used magic talismans, icons, and artifacts.

Some say God is blue, others insist He is green, or red with stripes, or even covered with dots. Each church has defined God differently, but He exists independent of what they believe. Because they differ in their beliefs, there are still two choices, either they are all wrong or only one is right.

In their wicked conspiracy, the Pharisees and the Sadducees had formed an alliance to trap Jesus. Because they were both in error, they wanted to remove the One that exposed that error. They repeated their demand for a sign.

Jesus sighed deeply before He spoke, sounding weary of the wickedness of the rulers of the Jews. He looked at them and asked, "Why does this generation seek after a sign?" They did not answer, so He continued, "It is a wicked and an adulterous generation that seeks after a sign. There shall be no sign given to this generation but the sign of the prophet Jonas."

I did not know then as I do now that the three days and three nights Jonas spent in the belly of the whale were symbolic of the three days and three nights Jesus would spend in the grave. The Jews did not understand then, just as they did not understand earlier, when He said the same thing to a group of them in my home. They looked to each other for understanding but found none. Jesus left them and entered the boat and departed with us, this time to the northeast side of the Sea of Galilee on our way to Bethsaida.

As we traveled, one of the Apostles discovered that in our haste to depart, no one had purchased bread when we were ashore. We had less than one loaf of bread among us all. Jesus warned us, saying, "Take heed and beware of the 'leaven' of the Pharisees and of the Sadducees and of Herod."

Some of the Apostles misunderstood, thinking that He

was warning them not to buy bread from the Jews. They feared that He was chastening them because of their poor planning.

Jesus knew their thoughts and said, "Oh, you of little faith. How is it you debate among yourselves because you have brought no bread? Do you not yet understand? Have you hardened your hearts? Have you eyes, but do not see? Have you ears, but do not hear? Do you not remember when I broke five loaves among five thousand? How many baskets of fragments did you gather?"

"We gathered twelve," I answered.

"And when I broke seven loaves among the four thousand, how many baskets of fragments did you gather?" He asked.

"We gathered seven baskets," I answered. I knew what Jesus was saying. After feeding the five thousand, I knew what He was going to do when the four thousand were hungry. Feeding twelve Apostles was insignificant compared to feeding thousands—if a miracle of any size can be considered insignificant.

I knew that not all of my follow Apostles truly appreciated who Jesus was; at least, they were not as comfortable with the knowledge as I was. It would take time. Even as I had tried to tell them in my way, they were slow to learn.

Jesus then asked us, "How is it that you do not understand that I wasn't speaking about bread when I warned you to beware of the 'leaven' of the Pharisees and the Sadducees? Their 'leaven' is hypocrisy!"

He often used symbolism, which we were only able to understand after thoroughly pondering His words. I felt pleased that I understood this time. Jesus expressed His concern that my brethren were not as quick to understand. It would be a while yet before we understood everything, for we were as children.

THE BLIND MAN OF BETHSAIDA

We sailed uneventfully to Bethsaida, our fourth destination in less than a month. As we disembarked and entered the town, a small group of people came forward from the crowd awaiting the arrival of Jesus. They brought a blind man toward Jesus and asked Him to touch the man.

Jesus took the blind man by the hand and led him back out of the center of the town, away from the multitude. When Jesus stopped, the man quickly knelt on the ground in front of Him. Then Jesus did something unfamiliar: He leaned over the man and carefully spit on each of the man's eyes. Then He laid His hands on the man and blessed him. When He finished, He asked, "Can you see anything?"

Looking around, he said, "I see men as trees, walking."

His description was equally amusing and pitiable. That he saw men as trees was humorous but that his blindness made it difficult for him to interpret what he saw was sad. Jesus laid His hands on the man again and blessed him. "What do you see now?" He asked the man. This time, the man said he saw every man clearly.

I knew that not only did he see clearly, but he now also understood what he saw. There were two miracles that day. In addition to healing, Jesus blessed the man with learning, to understand what he saw. I think He did it in two steps to demonstrate that there were two miracles.

Jesus told the man to return to his home without going back into Bethsaida and to tell no one in town what had happened, as He had with others. But the joy at being healed always seemed to prevent anyone from obeying His charge. If anything, it encouraged them to testify of the miracle.

MY TESTIMONY, MY REBUKE

After leaving Bethsaida, we walked about twenty-five miles north toward Caesarea Philippi, a wicked city located at the southwest base of Mount Hermon. The city of Caesarea Philippi was populated by pagans who worshipped Pan and Baal. As was His custom, Jesus knelt and prayed as we approached the city, even though we did not actually go into it.

Caesarea Philippi lay at the base of the rocky cliffs of Mount Hermon, where precious water flowed from a deep cave. Local pagans referred to the cave as the "Gates of Hades" because they believed it was the entrance to the underworld, where their dead resided. The stream flowing from the cave was the primary source of the River Jordan.

We stopped on the side of a nearby mountain to overlook Caesarea Philippi and Mount Hermon. We gathered around Jesus as He talked about the gods worshipped by the pagans, observing the several statues set into niches in the cliff around the cave entrance. After listing their gods, Jesus asked, "Who do men say that I, the Son of Man, am?"

No one had ever asked me if Jesus was one of the pagan gods, but each of us had heard many things. We told Him, "Some say you are John the Baptist, some Elias, and others Jeremiah or one of the prophets risen from the dead."

Sadly, I do not remember anyone asking me if Jesus were the Messiah. They believed more in tradition than in prophecy. Certainly, He was not what they expected in the Messiah; that may be why so many rejected Him.

Jesus then asked a question that stirred my heart: "But who do you say I am?"

I had answered this question many times before, but not to Jesus, so I could not let a second pass without answering. My heart burned, my eyes filled with tears, and I stood to boldly testify of the Messiah to the Messiah. My voice cracked with emotion as I said, "You are the Christ, the Son of the Living God!"

There are not words to express the joy I felt in saying those words to Jesus, testifying that I knew who He was. I am Peter, disciple, Apostle, and witness of the Son of God!

Then came the moment I cherish above all others. Jesus accepted my testimony and confirmed it. Calling me by my given name, Jesus said, "You are blessed, Simon Bar-Jonah, because flesh and blood have not revealed it to you, but my Father, which is in heaven."

I made no effort to control the tears that overflowed my eyes and ran down my cheeks. I was not ashamed of the emotion I displayed. It was love, pure love.

Many times I have experienced an overwhelming feeling of love, something that is very difficult to describe. The first time I met Jesus, I felt a loving Spirit that immediately confirmed to my heart that He was the Son of God. I experienced that confirmation many, many times thereafter. Sometimes it was when Jesus spoke, sometimes it was when He prayed, sometimes it was when He blessed or healed people. Other times, it was when I pondered what I had experienced. God spoke to my heart with a still, small voice—the tender, loving power of the Holy Ghost—confirming that Jesus was the Son of God. I had experienced it many times, but just one time would have been adequate for me to testify confidently that Jesus is the Christ.

When Jesus said, "Flesh and blood have not revealed it to you, but my Father, which is in heaven," I understood His meaning. Words that He had spoken earlier flooded into my mind: "No man can come to me except the Father, which sent me, draw him to me." I understood because it was by His Father that I was drawn to Jesus. My testimony of the divinity of Jesus was not based on anything anyone else said, nor upon His own words, or even upon witnessing His miracles, but upon personal revelation from His Father. I knew many people who saw the same miracles and heard the words I did, but they did not believe.

Yes, I knew the power of personal revelation because I had experienced it so many times. It was more compelling than any mortal experience. Nothing compares to the peace that comes from the quiet whisperings of the Spirit of God.

Jesus looked into my eyes and smiled. I can still see His face at that moment—it is burned into my memory. I felt His love.

Immediately after His last statement, He added, "To you I say, you are Peter, and upon this rock I will build my Church, and the 'Gates of Hades' shall not prevail against it."

He called me a "rock" as part of one of His single-word allegories, and then he referred to personal revelation as the rock upon which He would build His Church. I do not believe there is any opposition that can compromise the absolute conviction that derives from direct, personal revelation from God by the Holy Ghost. To deny such revelation is to commit the unforgivable sin. I knew that nothing, not even death, as represented by the nearby Gates of Hades, would overpower my knowledge that Jesus is the Son of God.

I shake my head in disbelief that anyone would suggest that Jesus would build His Church upon me, a mere mortal, when revelation received from God is the rock-solid foundation of pure testimony. Can any Christian doubt that the only man upon which the Church of Jesus Christ would be built would be the only perfect being, Jesus Christ Himself, and not a crude fisherman with so many faults and failings? Let all men quickly repent and believe in Jesus Christ, the Son of God.

Jesus was known for His skillful use of single-word allegories, just as others were known to misinterpret their meanings. I sorrow when anyone chooses to misinterpret the words of Jesus to extract only what they wish to find.

After His promise to build His Church on the foundation of revelation from His Father, Jesus promised that He would yet give us, the Apostles, the keys of the kingdom of heaven, so that whatsoever we would bind on earth would be bound in heaven, and whatsoever we would loose on earth would be loosed in heaven.

When He told us what He planned on doing, we did not understand. As with other things, He would teach us a little at a time. I remembered the words of Isaiah, "Whom shall he teach knowledge? And whom shall he make to understand doctrine? Those weaned from the milk, those drawn from the breasts. He gave precept upon precept, precept upon precept; line upon line, line upon line; here a little, there a little. For with stammering lips and another tongue he speaks to this people."

Yet those that did not accept His precepts and lines also reminded me again of Isaiah, "But the word of the Lord was given unto them precept upon precept, precept upon precept; line upon line, line upon line; here a little, there a little; that they might go, and fall backward, and be broken, and snared, and taken." His words were a snare for the Pharisees and the Sadducees, words that trapped them in their wickedness and lies.

Jesus also said He would build His Church. That an individual may not have found His Church does not mean it does not exist. This is His Church, one built on Apostles, revelation from God, and priesthood authority with those that hold the keys to bind on earth and in heaven, and that teaches that Jesus is the Son of God.

When Jesus finished His teaching, He commanded us to no longer testify that He was the Christ, the Messiah. He explained that from this time forward, we were not to openly testify of Him as we had heretofore done. The time had come that He would change what He was doing also, and He wanted us to follow this instruction. We spoke freely among ourselves and with the faithful, but we were careful not to proclaim Him as the Messiah to others.

Without symbolism or allegory, He solemnly told us that the conspiracy to kill Him would be fulfilled. He said that He would be killed and then be raised up again after three days. He was going to be killed! There was no misunderstanding what the future held for Him. He told us that He must go to Jerusalem and that there He would suffer many things of the elders, the chief priests, and the scribes.

At that time, my ears rang. My mind spun. I was numb with disbelief. "Being raised up" did not enter into my mind, but being killed echoed loudly in my thoughts. I could not believe what I was hearing! It could not be! I wondered what my life would hold without Him. Without thinking, I grabbed His arm and shouted, "No! This shall not be!"

I knew I was wrong to say it, but I spoke before my mind could control my words, and they hung in the air like black clouds over us.

As much as He loved me, Jesus rebuked me, saying, "Peter, get Thee behind me, tempter. You are a rock that I stumble over because you hold only to mortal life, which is dear to men, and not to eternal life, which is dear to God."

Selfishly, I did not want Him to die, not for any reason. With another of His single-word allegories, He called me a rock, but this time I was an obstacle in His way.

My heart was broken. I was not worthy even to be called a rock. I was dust under His feet.

Turning to my fellow Apostles, Jesus said, "If any will

come after me, let him deny himself, and take up his cross each day and follow me."

I did not yet fully understand His reference to the cross. None of us really did. I did understand, however, that I had been following Him long enough that I never wanted to be parted from Him—ever. I was deeply hurt, not by Jesus, but by my own selfishness.

I often wondered what I would do if the Jews tried to kill Him and I was there. Certainly my passion would not allow anyone to harm Him. From the time I met Jesus, I had resolved to protect Him at the cost of my own life, so what would I do if I saw a man lift his hand against Jesus? Could I stand by and let it happen? My hand had been on the hilt of my sword many times as the Jews crowded Him. I had never drawn my sword, but I was always ready. I had envisioned myself defending Him and dying at His feet, if necessary.

Jesus continued, "For whosoever will save his life shall lose it. And whosoever will lose his life for my sake, and the sake of the gospel, shall find it."

I would willingly lose my life for Him, but His words offered no consolation. I was still reeling from the thought of Jesus being killed by the Jews. Could I let them do it? How would it happen? It would be a privilege to lose my life for Him. He is the Son of God. I am nothing except when I am in His service.

Then He asked us, "What is a man profited if he gains the whole world but loses his soul? Or, what shall a man take in exchange for his soul?

"For the Son of Man shall come in His own glory," He cautioned, "and in the glory of His Father, and that of His angels, and then He shall reward every man according to his works. Whosoever shall be ashamed of me and of my words in this adulterous and sinful generation, the Son of Man shall be ashamed of that man when He comes with the glory of His

Father and the glory of the holy angels."

I was not ashamed of Him, nor was I ashamed of His words. I was not an adulterer, nor was I a wicked man. I was a man with many weaknesses, yet in spite of those weaknesses, I was willing to die in His defense. He mattered; I did not.

Jesus then said something that I did not understand: "Here is the truth I want you to know. There are some standing here which shall not taste of death till they see the Son of Man and His Kingdom come with power."

Some of us would live to see Jesus return in His glory? Would I be one of them? Would it be very long? I didn't dare to ask, especially after my embarrassing outburst just seconds earlier. I would keep quiet and remain at His side and see what happened. My hand trembled. My ears continued to ring. What would I do?

THE TRANSFIGURATION

We were taught there for six days when Jesus took me, along with James and John, the sons of Zebedee, to a high part of Mount Hermon. We were far away from the Pharisees, the Sadducees, and anyone else seeking to kill Jesus. High on Mount Hermon, we were certain to be alone.

Jesus comforted me with the assurance that His love for me had not diminished, in spite of my foolish emotional outburst. He knew that it was my love for Him that triggered my selfish desire to never be parted from Him. I had yet to learn how to submit my will to His without asking questions. Whether I was to die with Him or for Him, or to live until He returned in His glory, it should not matter. I had resolved to do whatever He asked. After making that resolution, my heart felt as if I had never sinned. I was at peace.

When we arrived at the place Jesus designed to go, we rested, and then Jesus knelt and prayed again to His Father. As He did, James, John, and I were overcome with an overwhelming weariness that caused us first to sit on the ground and then to fall asleep. I fought to stay awake, but I couldn't. I don't know how long I slept, but when I awoke and sat up, I saw that Jesus had been changed, or transfigured. His countenance was brighter than the noonday sun. So bright was His face that I could not see His features. His clothing glistened as if the cloth was made of some kind of translucent gemstone that was brightly lit from within. There was no fuller who could ever make cloth this white.

No sound or music, no lightning, nothing detectable by physical senses accompanied this sacred scene. Instead, there was a tender spirit of peace and love that could not be seen, only felt. No such spiritual experience can be adequately expressed or understood except by those who have had a similar experience.

There we were, entirely focused on the awesome sight of the Son of God as we had never seen any man. We sat in stunned silence. I'm not one to be without words on many occasions, but I was mute, almost not believing the sight before me. When I stood, I realized that we were no longer alone with Him. I saw two others appear from behind His blazing glory, each with the same wonderfully bright appearance. Because of the gleam of their countenance, I could not see their faces, but when Jesus addressed them, I recognized His voice. He called them Moses and Elijah.

I thought of Moses as the greatest prophet in our Jewish history: it was he who led the children of Israel out of Egypt. He wrote what Jehovah instructed him, compiling the books of Genesis, Exodus, Leviticus, Numbers, and Deuteronomy. He wrote what we called the law of Moses, which was the foundation of everything the house of Israel believed. He is the one the Pharisees and the Sadducees quoted. I was in his presence, along with Elijah and Jesus—no ordinary day for me.

Elijah was and is an important part of my people's tradition, for it was Elijah who was prophesied to come in preparation of the coming of the Messiah. The Greek name for Elijah was Elias, and Elias was so imbued with meaning in our time that it became more than a name; Elias was considered a title referring to anyone who came in advance to prepare the way or to restore.

As I watched, it was as if I already knew Moses and Elijah because I had read of them and had heard stories of them from my youth. But there they were, standing in front of us, in the presence of the Son of God! Along with James and John, I felt like we were children in the midst of our elders, invited to observe a very personal, sacred occasion, where Moses and Elijah were the guests of the Son of God.

My secret wish for Jesus not to die was not encouraged by the conversation He had with Moses and Elijah. They talked of His forthcoming departure, a departure that He would accomplish from Jerusalem. When they used the word departure, I understood them to mean His "death."

How He would accomplish His own death was beyond my grasp. I knew that the Son of God could not be killed—that no one had the power to take His life—so it seemed to me that He would have to allow them to take His life.

As I quietly listened, I wondered if there was something we were expected to say or do. I wanted to hear more about His departure, even to ask them questions. Instead, I just stood in astonishment of the scene. We were in the presence of glorious beings as they spoke with one another as if they were old friends. The tone of their conversation was somber, discussing what I later came to comprehend as the most important event in history.

As they paused, apparently finished with their discussion, I forced myself to speak, to offer my respect for being allowed to be in their presence. Referring to James, John, and myself, I said, "Master, it is good that we are here. Please let us build three tabernacles, one for you, one for Moses, and one for Elijah."

Tabernacles were a tradition, a small bowery built for private prayers. I didn't know if what I was offering was appropriate or not, but I wanted to do something, anything to show respect. My mouth ran ahead of my thoughts—something I was known for doing. I had no idea if Moses and Elijah were there to stay, if they were going to be with Jesus when He departed, but I hoped to encourage them to stay so I could hear more of their message.

As I spoke, a brightly lit cloud surrounded us, and I, along with James and John, became afraid to say anything or even move. As we stood there, something marvelous happened. We heard a deep, powerful male voice thunder from within the cloud, saying, "This is my beloved Son, in whom I am well pleased. Hear ye Him."

In absolute fear, we fell to the earth with our faces to the ground and our eyes tightly closed. We did not dare look for fear we would see God and die. God had just instructed us to listen to Jesus instead of Moses or Elijah. Jesus was the One designated to speak for His Father.

There is a tradition among my people that Moses is our prophet, as is Elijah or any Elias, of course. At that moment, God plainly told us that Jesus was His Son, and we were to put the words of Jesus ahead of our traditional prophets. This was a pivotal time in history. No longer would we turn to the prophets in search of information about the Messiah, but to Jesus Himself. He was the Messiah, and He spoke for Himself. I'll admit that it was a complex thought for a simple fisherman like me, but I figured it out.

After hearing that voice, we remained kneeling with our faces down to the ground. Jesus bent over us and gently touched each of us, saying, "Arise, and do not be afraid."

When we sat up and looked around, the cloud was gone and so were Moses and Elijah. We were again alone with Jesus. Where they went, or how, I do not know.

We stood and meekly faced Jesus. His countenance still glowed, but not nearly as brightly as before. Before, I felt weak in the knees and my hands had trembled, but now I felt refreshed and strong. The world seemed brighter to me. It seemed to me that the ground was softer; the trees, flowers, and grass seemed more beautiful and more full of color. The sky was a deeper blue. I was warmed inside and out. Even the air seemed sweet.

Jesus led the way as we started the long journey down the mountainside. For some distance, we said nothing as we wound our way down the steep, rocky pathway. Even the dust stirring at our feet seemed to rejoice in the day.

As we stopped to rest, Jesus broke the silence. He spoke softly, instructing us, "Tell no man of the vision you have seen, not until the Son of Man has risen from the dead."

We told no one, not even our fellow Apostles. We discussed it among ourselves, but we did not yet comprehend what rising from the dead meant.

ELIJAH OR ELIAS?

During our long journey down from the mountain, my curiosity got the best of me, which, of course, was not unusual. I was confused about the prophecies regarding Elijah.

The scribes often quoted Malachi, saying that Elijah (or Elias) must come before the Messiah. We had just seen Elijah, and I wanted to know if this was the coming of Elijah we were looking forward to. What confused me was that the Messiah had already come, but Elijah was supposed to come before Him.

Jesus answered, "Elias truly must come first so that he can restore all things. Further, the same things that were written to happen to the Son of God are to happen to Elias. Elias is to suffer many things and not be acknowledged of men."

I understood, but only in part. Elias was to restore all things. I obviously knew what restore meant, but I did not know what needed to be restored. I also knew that Elias was to come to prepare the way for His coming. But Jesus was already here.

I also didn't understand whether the Elijah we saw was the coming of Elias we were awaiting. Certainly, I hadn't met or heard of anyone that looked anything like the Elijah we had just seen on the mountain, nor had anyone referred to themselves as an Elias; yet the Messiah had already come.

I did know, however, that I had His answer and that I had to figure out the meaning for myself. That was often the way Jesus taught us. As I pondered His meaning, I thought of when Andrew and John talked to John the Baptist on the other side of the River Jordan near Bethabara, when he told them he was "preparing the way."

Certainly John had prepared the way for the Messiah. I concluded that John the Baptist may have been an Elias also. I did not know at the time that the Angel Gabriel had told Zacharias that his son, John the Baptist, would prepare the way for the Messiah by the spirit and power of Elias. I remembered very well hearing that John the Baptist had announced the arrival of Jesus, calling Him "the Lamb of God." Yes, John was an Elias, but I wasn't sure he was the Elias that Malachi said was to come before the Messiah.

I knew that there were times when Jesus told us only what He wanted us to know and nothing more. Sometimes He wanted us to ponder His words and figure things out on our own. I had learned to memorize His words and ponder them carefully.

Jesus certainly knew my thoughts. He said, "I say to you that Elias has already come, and they did not recognize him, but they have done to him as they wished. Likewise, so shall the Son of Man suffer by them."

I understood. Jesus was referring to John the Baptist. They killed him, and they would kill Jesus too!

As we continued our way down the mountainside, I wondered if the Elias we saw on the high mountain had actually been John the Baptist. I had never seen him, so I wouldn't recognize him. John, my fellow Apostle, had seen him, but the brilliant shining of Elijah's countenance made it impossible to see his face. I asked John if he recognized his voice, but he could not say for certain because it had been some time since he had heard it.

I didn't ask Jesus about it; instead, I silently concluded that it was John the Baptist who was there with Moses to visit the Son of God. At least, I hoped it was. But even as I thought it through, I knew I was wrong. John the Baptist had a mission—to prepare the way for Jesus and to baptize Him—and his mission was over. I knew that the mission of Elijah was yet to be. As quoted in Malachi, I knew that Elijah would be "sent before the coming of the great and dreadful day of the Lord."

I concluded that the mission of John the Baptist had been fulfilled, but the mission of Elijah was yet to be, so it had to be the prophet Elijah who was on the mountaintop. Jesus had told me just what I needed. I'll admit that I was pleased with myself that I understood. I wanted to ask Jesus to confirm my conclusion, but He never mentioned it again, and I knew better than to ask.

We had walked a long way down, but it was getting dark, and it was still a long walk to the bottom of the mountain where we would meet the rest of the Apostles. We stayed the night on the side of the mountain, building a fire and cooking supper with the provisions we carried.

Most of my evening was spent in quiet contemplation of what we had experienced. I had seen Moses and Elijah and had heard the commanding voice of God. I wondered why we were allowed to observe this meeting. I concluded that I was being prepared for something myself and would have to wait and see what it was.

HEALING A POSSESSED BOY

When we arrived at the bottom of the mountain, it was late the next morning, and a number of disciples, the other Apostles, and the usual multitude were all awaiting Jesus. His countenance continued to glow, and the people were greatly amazed at His appearance.

Jesus was immediately surrounded by the multitude. Among them was a man who had brought his possessed son for Jesus to heal. Some scribes had followed the believers and were doing their best to incite the crowd, taunting the disciples and the Apostles to heal the boy themselves. In their arrogance, the scribes seemed pleased that no one had been able to cast the demon out of the possessed boy. As we approached the multitude, some of the people recognized Jesus, and they ran to Him, welcoming Him warmly.

Jesus confronted the scribes, asking, "What are you demanding of them?"

The scribes dared not answer, but the father of the possessed boy came forward, leaving his son behind with his family. The father knelt in front of Jesus and begged for a blessing, saying, "Master, I plead with you to have mercy on my son, my only child. Please look at him, and you will see that he is insane and greatly tormented. He often throws himself into the fire and into the water. He is possessed by a spirit that does not speak, but it takes him here and there, causes him to claw his skin, gnash his teeth, and foam at the mouth. My son cries in pain, and his body is covered with bruises. I brought him to your disciples, but they could not cure him.

Jesus scanned the multitude and looked into the faces of the Apostles and back at the scribes. Finally, He addressed the scribes, saying, "Oh, faithless and perverse generation, how long shall I be with you? How long shall I suffer you?"

Jesus then turned to look into the eyes of the father kneeling before Him and said, "Bring your son here."

Before the father could get to his feet, his son was brought forward from the crowd. The boy resisted being taken toward Jesus, dragging his feet and stirring up dust. The spirit that possessed the boy made him claw his skin and growl. Then he threw himself to the ground where he wallowed in the dirt and foamed at the mouth.

Jesus knelt and looked at the boy. His skin was covered with scars, scabs, and bruises. Open wounds were bleeding. His suffering was obvious. Jesus rose and turned to the father, and for the benefit of those watching, asked, "How long has it been since this came upon him?"

The father looked at the boy, then back to Jesus before he answered, saying, "Since he was a child." Then grimacing as if remembering what the boy had suffered, he added, "If you can do anything, please have compassion on us and help us."

Jesus comforted the father, saying, "If you can believe, all things are possible to him that believes."

The father, with tears flowing down his cheeks, exclaimed, "Master, I believe!" Then, he added, "Help my unbelief."

The father had testified of his belief, then seemed to realize that the level of his faith was not perfect. I looked into my own heart and understood his plea.

People at the rear of the crowd pushed forward, crowding around Jesus in hopes of seeing Him perform another miracle. Taking no notice of their curiosity, Jesus rebuked the foul spirit, saying, "Thou deaf and dumb spirit, I charge you: Come out of the boy and enter him no more!"

Breaking his silence, the evil spirit in the boy cried out and caused the boy to claw himself once more. Then it left the boy, never to return. Exhausted, the boy lay on the ground as if he were dead. Someone in the crowd exclaimed, "Look, the boy has died!" Several people joined in, saying, "He is dead!"

The father of the boy stood paralyzed with fright. He looked at Jesus, then back at his son lying on the ground. The man's eyes widened, afraid the crowd might be right. Jesus said nothing but knelt down and took the boy by the hand. The boy opened his eyes to look into the loving face of Jesus, the Son of God. Jesus helped the boy rise, and he stood. Still silent, Jesus led the boy to his father.

A great cheer was heard among the multitude as the father and the rest of his family surrounded the boy. Tears of joy filled the family's eyes as they touched and hugged the boy. The boy's mother looked back at Jesus and whispered "Thank you," before turning and hugging her son again.

We joined Jesus as He walked away. None of us said a word; no words were needed. He left the area to travel toward Galilee, keeping His plans to Himself but following a circuitous route.

That night we stayed at the home of one of the disciples who had tried to cast the devil out of the boy. He asked Jesus, "Why could we not cast him out?"

Jesus answered, not by way of a stinging rebuke, but by way of an encouraging challenge: "It was because of your unbelief. Here is a truth I shall tell you: if you have faith as tiny as a grain of mustard seed, ye shall say unto this mountain, 'Remove hence to yonder place!' and it shall be removed. With faith, nothing shall be impossible to you!"

Then He added, "Nevertheless, this kind of evil spirit cannot be called forth, except by prayer and fasting."

After Jesus spoke to the disciples, I followed the father's example and asked Him, "Lord, increase our faith."

Jesus answered, "If you had the faith of a mustard seed, you might say to this sycamore tree, 'Be plucked up by the root and be planted in the sea,' and it would obey you."

There were times in my life when I called on the authority of God to perform miracles, but there were also times when I was not as prepared or as worthy as I should have been. Sometimes I had to clear my mind before I was ready. Sometimes I had to clear my conscience too. His words were gentle instruction, not searing condemnation.

Jesus continued teaching, this time with another parable, saying, "Which of you having a servant plowing or feeding cattle will say to him when he has come in from the field, 'Go and sit down to meat'? Instead, you would rather say to him, 'Now prepare that I may have my supper. Dress yourself and serve me until I have eaten and drunk; then afterward, you shall eat and drink.'

"I ask you, does he thank that servant because he did the things that he was commanded to do? I think not. So, likewise for you, when you have done all the things that you are commanded to do, say to yourselves, 'We are unprofitable servants. We have done only that which was our duty to do.' "

I was certainly an unprofitable servant. No matter what I would do, it seemed that I ended up doing no more than what He had asked. I needed to do more—I wanted to do more—but I didn't know what it would be. I knew that if I listened, I would learn. I trusted Jesus.

PROPHECY OF HIS DEATH AND RESURRECTION

While we were making our way back to Galilee and Capernaum, we talked privately. I was curious about the mighty power of God, the power of His priesthood. The power to move a mountain was more than I could expect to receive. I was amazed at the divine power Jesus had and wondered if I had the faith of a mustard seed. I hold His teaching sacred, as with any personal guidance from Jesus.

As we traveled, Jesus chose to prepare us for His death in Jerusalem, instructing how it would come to pass. He said, "Let these words sink into your hearts. Listen to them. The Son of Man shall be betrayed into the hands of men, they shall kill Him, and on the third day, He shall be raised again."

Even then, none of us understood what "being raised" meant. We clearly understood what He meant when He said He would be killed, so it seemed that "being killed" was all we heard.

I have come to know that our lack of understanding was not that we were not listening. We heard him clearly, but somehow He cloaked the meaning of His words from our understanding for a time.

I came to know that we heard them and let them sink into our hearts so we would be able to recall them at a later time. In the meantime, in our sorrow, we did not ask Jesus to explain. I am not sure I wanted to know how He would be killed; I did not want to think about it. I did not want Him to die.

Our journeys to Capernaum were always pleasant, but this trip was very somber. We walked along, mostly quiet, in contemplation of what He had told us. All I could think of was that He was going to be killed. Nothing else mattered. It was hot, dusty, and dry, but I was not thirsty. My comfort didn't matter either.

Tribute Coin in the
Mouth of a Fish

We continued on our journey through Galilee until we arrived in Capernaum, where we stayed again at my home, privileged to have the Son of God as my guest. Many came to Capernaum in search of Jesus to ask Him to heal them. Unfortunately, like a spider waiting for its prey, the Pharisees and the Sadducees were among those that were lying in wait, still looking for ways to mock and accuse Jesus. We had left Galilee and traveled to the northern regions to get away from them.

When we first arrived at Capernaum, those that collected the tribute money for the temple were waiting for me. These men were not the Pharisees or the Sadducees who would twist any comment into another accusation against Jesus. They were good-hearted men, as far as I knew. By commandment, everyone twenty years old and over was expected to pay an annual offering of half a shekel as an "atonement offering." The money was to be used to support the temple.

Rabbis often declared themselves exempt from this tax, so the collectors of tribute money wanted to know if Jesus was exempt. They asked me, not Jesus, "Does your Master not pay tribute?" First, they asked because Jesus was beloved and honored by many of the citizens of Capernaum and throughout Galilee, and they were being careful not to offer an insult. Second, they asked me because Jesus was a guest in my home, and, following tradition, they asked me to speak on His behalf.

Instead of unconsciously answering "yes," or testifying

of His identity as the Son of God, I obediently followed His instructions to not testify of His divinity. My only alternative, then, was to act as if Jesus were an ordinary man.

I left the tribute collectors outside my home and went inside to get some money for them. Jesus met me and told me not to pay them with my money. Jesus took the time to teach me, asking, "What do you think, Simon? From whom do the kings of earth take tribute—from their children or from strangers?"

"From strangers," I answered.

"Then," He asked, "are the children free of the obligation to pay tribute?"

I knew the answer. No king would require tribute from his children, just as God would not require tribute from His Son.

I assure you that I apologized for my mistake. I had no fear or hesitation to testify of Jesus, but I was being obedient to His instructions. He knew my heart.

Jesus continued His explanation without reproof: "Notwithstanding that I am the Son of Man, lest we offend them, go to the sea, cast in a hook, and pull in the first fish that comes up. When you open his mouth, you will find a piece of money. Take that coin and give it to them for me and for you."

He made the point that while the payment was for both of us, the payment was made for different reasons. Jesus was exempt because He was the Son of God. I was not exempt.

As I went to the sea, I pondered why Jesus chose this way to come up with a coin; yet He told me what to do, and I obeyed. Certainly He knew that I had money readily available to pay the tribute, but He didn't want me to use it. And if I didn't have money, I could have caught some fish and sold them. There was a reason He had me get the coin this way. I concluded that it was His way to emphasize the point we had just discussed, which is that He is the Son of God and He knows everything. I believe the simplest answer is usually the right answer.

WHO IS THE GREATEST
IN THE KINGDOM?

As we walked through Galilee the next morning, some of the Apostles debated among themselves what it would be like in the kingdom of heaven. Eventually, their musings turned to speculation about which of them would be the greatest there.

The discussion was not one of who was better; instead, it was more of an intellectual debate over whether one Apostle would be considered greater because of what he accomplished or what position he held. They were concerned about doing all they could to impress God with their faithfulness to His Son, Jesus. Some took one position to be the most important, such as teaching many people, while others took another, such as healing the sick. Before long, there were more opinions than I thought possible among my brethren.

I didn't know what actually triggered the debate, but I suspected that it might have been because Jesus invited only James, John, and me to accompany Him to Mount Hermon. The rest of the Apostles had no idea what happened on the mountain, but they were very sensitive to the fact that they were excluded.

As we rested in my home in Capernaum, a couple of the Apostles began to discuss what might be the most important contribution we might make. They wanted to talk about it among themselves, but they didn't want to involve Jesus in their debate. He knew what was going on anyway and decided to intervene. He asked the two, "What was it that you were debating among yourselves along the way?"

They were embarrassed and stumbled around the subject because the question had nothing to do with getting His work done. Who did the most important thing or who had the most important position were not important matters. We each did our part, and that was what counted. At least, that was how I saw it. It was as pointless as the silly argument over how many angels can dance on the head of a pin. Nobody can dance on the head of a pin. It didn't suit the followers of the Son of God to ask stupid questions.

I could give each Apostle credit for having good hearts and say that their dispute was harmless, but I won't. I think they were ashamed that Jesus was aware of their silly thoughts.

Rather than let it pass, Jesus taught them an important lesson. He sat down and summoned us all into the courtyard around Him. "If any man desires to be first," He began, "he should be last of all, and servant to all."

He called to one of the children—my son—wandering around my home and asked him to come to Him. Jesus took him in His arms. "Except you be converted and become as little children, you shall not enter the kingdom of heaven. Whoever shall humble himself as this little child, he that is the least among you, the same is the greatest in the kingdom of heaven. And whosoever receives one such little child in my name shall receive me, and whosoever shall receive me, shall receive not just me, but Him that sent me. But, whoso shall offend one of these little ones, which believe in me, it would be better for him to have a millstone hanged about his neck and be drowned in the depths of the sea. For I say to you that in heaven, their angels always behold the face of my Father which is in heaven."

His message was clear. Children were blameless—without sin before God. Teaching differently is contrary to the teachings of the Son of God. No child is punished for his parent's sins or for Adam's sins or for anyone else's sins.

There were often times when I felt like a small child in the presence of Jesus. I wished nothing more than to do what He wanted me to do, to become what He wanted me to become. I recognized these feelings from when I was a child and wanted nothing more than to please my father, just as Jesus had described. I completely understood Him; He was talking directly to my heart.

That morning, Jesus again taught us privately during a time of peace and tenderness. It is difficult to explain what it is like to sit and listen to the Son of God when He can speak freely, without fear of having His words twisted. His presence comforted me. His words warmed me. I was at peace again.

I share my experiences in hopes that others can experience what I did. This effort is not about me or for my benefit; rather, it is about Jesus for the benefit of others. I want to share the truths Jesus taught us.

STUMBLING BLOCKS SHALL COME

As the day passed, visitors came into my home as they always did, seeking comfort and uplifting from the Master. When the crowds were small enough, they were able to fit into my home. As my wife and mother-in-law prepared our meal, one man worked his way through the crowd toward Jesus. As he pushed his way to the front of the crowd, he stumbled and fell on the floor in front of Jesus. He looked up, his face flushed with embarrassment.

Jesus said, "Woe unto the world because of stumbling blocks! For it must needs be that stumbling blocks, or offenses, will come to people, but woe to that man by whom the offense comes! Wherefore, if your hand or your foot is your stumbling block, cut it off. It is better for you to go through your life crippled or disabled than to have two hands and two feet and be cast into everlasting fire, where their worm never dies, and the fire is never quenched. If your eye is your stumbling block, pluck it out and cast it away. It is better for you to go through life with one eye than to have two eyes and then be cast into hellfire."

As my wife carried a dish of salt to one of the tables, Jesus added, "Every one of you shall be seasoned with fire, and every one of your sacrifices shall season you as with salt. Salt is good, but if it loses its saltiness, what shall you use for seasoning? Have salt in yourselves, and have peace one with another."

I understood His instructions to mean that the Apostles

were to stop arguing over who is the greatest and continue with their work. Jesus remained somber as He paused and gazed into my son's face. I wondered what He knew about the boy's future. I was certain He always knew more than He told us. Sometimes I think it is best not to know what the future holds.

PARABLES OF THE LOST SHEEP
AND THE LOST COIN

Jesus continued to teach us and the visitors that crowded around Him. "For the Son of Man is come to save that which was lost," He said. "What do you think of this? What man among you, if he has a hundred sheep and one of them has gone astray, does not leave the ninety-nine and go into the wilderness or the mountains to seek the one that has gone astray until he finds it?

"And, if he finds that sheep, he will lay that sheep on his shoulders and rejoice more over that sheep than over the ninety-nine that did not go astray. He will even call his friends and neighbors, saying, 'Rejoice with me because I have found my sheep that was lost.' There shall likewise be joy in heaven over one sinner that repents, more than over ninety-nine just persons who need no repentance."

Jesus paused, touched my son's head, then added, "Even so, it is not the will of your Father in Heaven that even one of these little ones should perish, no, not even one."

My son scampered away to play with the other children in the house. Jesus watched him with a look of sadness on his face, then closed His eyes briefly before continuing His teaching.

This time, Jesus addressed a woman in the crowd. "Or what woman having ten pieces of silver, if she loses one piece, does not light a candle, sweep the house, and seek diligently until she finds it?" He asked. "And when she does find it, she calls her friends and her neighbors together, saying, 'Rejoice with me because I have found the piece which I had lost.'

Likewise, I say to you, there is joy in the presence of the angels of God over the one sinner that repents."

THE PRODIGAL SON

The courtyard remained quiet and attentive, encouraging Jesus to continue His teaching. Jesus began another parable. "A certain man had two sons. The younger of them said to his father, 'Father, give me the portion of your goods that is my inheritance.' So the man divided his possessions between his two sons. Not many days after, the younger son gathered up what was given him and took a journey into a far country, and there he wasted it all with riotous living.

"When he had spent his fortune, a mighty famine arose in the land, but he had nothing left. He took a job working for a citizen in that country and was sent to the fields to feed the pigs, the lowliest and most demeaning of jobs for a Jew. He was so hungry, he was prepared to fill his own belly with the husks the pigs were eating, because no one would give him anything.

"When he finally realized how far he had fallen, the younger son asked himself, 'How many of my father's hired servants have bread enough and to spare—and here I am perishing with hunger! I will leave here and go to my father and say to him, "Father, I have sinned against heaven and before you and am no longer worthy to be called your son. Make me as one of your hired servants." '

"And he left that country and returned to his father. But when he was yet a great way off, his father saw him, and his father's heart was filled with compassion, and he hugged his son's neck and kissed him. And the son said, 'Father, I have sinned against heaven and in your sight and am no longer worthy to be called your son.'

"But the father said to his servants, 'Bring forth the best robe and put it on him; and put a ring on his hand and shoes on his feet. And bring the fatted calf here, and kill it. Let us celebrate because this, my son, was dead and is alive again. He was lost and is found.' And they began to be merry.

"Now, the father's elder son was in the field, and as he approached the house, he heard music and dancing. He called to one of the servants and asked what was going on. And the servant said, 'Your brother has come home, and your father has killed the fatted calf because he has received your brother home safe and sound.'

"And the elder brother was angry and would not enter

the house, so his father came out and asked him what was the matter.

"And the brother answered his father, saying, 'Look at me. For many years I have served you, and I have never at any time transgressed your commandments. Yet you never gave me so much as a young goat, that I might make merry with my friends. But as soon as your sinful son comes home, even after he threw away his money living with harlots, you kill the fatted calf for him.'

"And the man said, 'Son, you are always with me and will ever be, and all that I have is yours. It was right that we should make merry and be glad because your brother was dead and is alive again; he was lost and now is found.' "

Finally, Jesus finished, and I savored what He had taught, resting my head in my hands and pondering His words. I delight in the memory of those sweet moments. There is hope for all of us, even me.

A Meal in Capernaum

That evening, we enjoyed the supper my family had pre-pared. Again, instead of chairs, we reclined on couches patterned after the Roman tradition.

There were several tables in my home, which allowed for guests—invited and uninvited—to join us. Some of the guests were men considered to be heathens, or sinners, along with the despised tax collectors or publicans. The Pharisees and scribes observed all that was happening—all who were accepted at the tables in my home—and spoke among them-selves, saying, "This man receives sinners, and He eats with them!"

Jesus did not respond to them but continued to teach us instead. "Moreover, if your brother shall trespass against you, go and tell him his fault when the two of you are alone," He instructed. "If he listens to you, you have gained a brother, but if he will not listen, take one or two witnesses with you so that in the mouth of two or three witnesses every word shall be established. If he refuses to listen to them, only then tell it to the Church, and if he refuses to listen to the Church, treat him as you would treat a heathen or a tax collector."

Jesus never sent either heathens or tax collectors away, and He would not allow me to send the Pharisees or the scribes away. Instead, He accepted them all into His company and treated them all with courtesy. I was to treat everyone courteously, even the Pharisees and the scribes.

The Pharisees and scribes departed my home, apparently

not wishing to be in the company of sinners and publicans. I have observed that everyone brings happiness—some when they arrive, some when they leave. The Pharisees and scribes were in the latter group; at least, that was my opinion. And I am not reluctant to admit that I was not often without an opinion.

How Much Forgiveness
Is Required?

After supper, we moved to the courtyard, where there was more room, and enjoyed a gentle breeze that blew in from the sea. Jesus sat calmly, surrounded by the Apostles and those who had listened to Him most of the afternoon and evening. The night surrounded us, separating us from the rest of the world.

He had spoken much about repentance but not about forgiveness. I personally wanted to hear what He would say about our responsibility to forgive those who trespassed against us, so I confidently asked Him, "Lord, how many times shall my brother sin against me and I forgive him? Seven times?"

I was confident that my suggestion of seven times was generous. It was our tradition, supported by the prophets, that we were only required to forgive someone three times.

Jesus answered me, saying, "I say to you, not seven times, but seventy times seven times! Take heed of this warning. If your brother trespasses against you, rebuke him; but if he repents, forgive him. And if he trespasses against you seven times in a day, and seven times in a day he comes to you and says, 'I repent,' you shall forgive him."

Seventy times seven was a huge number, which told me I was not supposed to count how many times I had forgiven someone; I should just do it. It seemed like a lot to ask. I was not one to be wronged by someone without remembering. Forgiveness did not come easily to me. Patience was not a virtue I was born with. Like my other weaknesses, I would have to work on it.

Jesus knew my heart and expanded on His instruction, giving another powerful parable, a clear and instructive story. He said, "The kingdom of heaven is likened to a certain king, which did an accounting of what was owed him by his servants. And when he began to reconcile what was owed, one servant, who owed him ten thousand talents—approximately tens of millions of modern American dollars—was brought to him. Because the servant had nothing to pay his debt, the king ordered him to be sold into bondage, along with his wife, his children, and all that the servant owned, with the proceeds going toward the servant's debt. The servant fell down and pleaded with the king, saying, 'Lord, have patience with me, and I will pay all that I owe you.'

"And the king was moved with compassion. He let the servant go and forgave him the debt. But that same servant went out and found one of his fellow servants, who owed the first servant one hundred denarii, which is less than the amount of cash some people carry in their pockets. The man laid his hands on his fellow servant, grabbed him by the throat, and said, 'Pay me what you owe!' And his fellow servant fell down at his feet and pleaded with him, saying, 'Have patience with me, and I will pay all that I owe you.' But the first servant would not agree, and he cast his fellow servant into prison until he could pay the debt.

"When the other servants saw what the man had done, they were very distressed and came to the king and told him all that had happened.

"Then the king called the servant to his presence and said, 'Oh, you wicked servant. I forgave all that you owed me because you pleaded with me to do so. Should you not have had compassion on your fellow servant, even as I had pity on you?' And the king was angry and delivered the man to the jailers until he could pay all that was due the king."

I silently pondered the wickedness of not being merciful while being the beneficiary of mercy, feeling a great pain from my own wickedness. My heart ached; I was not a merciful man.

Then Jesus finished, saying, "So likewise shall my Heavenly Father do unto you if in your own hearts you do not forgive every one of their trespasses against you."

His words were for me. My throat was tight. I was not comfortable with who I was. I went to bed, but I couldn't sleep. Guilt is not a soft pillow, and Jesus's words rang in my ears until I finally realized that He knew everything about me. He had always known me, including my weaknesses. I thought of myself as a worthy servant, but I was not. Yet He had called me to be one of His Apostles. I found consolation in knowing that He was teaching me, patiently and lovingly, as a father would teach his child. My guilt was replaced with a personal resolution to become what Jesus asked. At that, I finally found peace, and I slept for what was left of the night.

THE KEYS TO BIND ON EARTH
AND IN HEAVEN

In the morning when I saw Jesus, He smiled at me with a knowing smile that always warmed and comforted me. He put His hand on my shoulder but said nothing. I felt His love. He certainly knew that I had struggled during the night.

After we ate breakfast, Jesus called for the rest of the Apostles to gather again in my home. We were alone with Him, not for instruction, but to be given the keys of His priesthood, the keys of authority. Starting with me, He laid His hands on each of our heads and bestowed upon us the keys of heaven as He had promised.

As Jesus blessed each of us, He said, "Verily, I say unto you, whatsoever you shall bind on earth shall be bound in heaven, and whatsoever you shall loose on earth shall be loosed in heaven. Whosoever sins you remit on earth shall be remitted in heaven, and whosoever sins you retain shall be retained in heaven."

He gave us priesthood authority—the authority to bind on earth and in heaven—that was not elsewhere found on the earth because it could only come from Him. Having priesthood authority and the keys to administer it, given by God, ordained under the hand of the Son of God, was an awesome responsibility. To me, it emphasized my need to act with a greater level of dignity and to be more forgiving, as I had resolved the night before. I was bearing the vessel of the Lord Jesus Christ with powerful priesthood keys. I could no longer be comfortable with the weaknesses that I had enjoyed for so many years.

No man takes this honor unto himself but he that is called of God, as Aaron was and as we were. The Church of Jesus Christ is led by men who hold His holy priesthood with the keys to bind on earth and in heaven.

Jesus then gave us more instructions, repeating some of the things He said earlier. "Again I tell you that if two of you shall agree on earth as touching any thing that you shall ask, it shall be done for them by my Father which is in heaven. For where two or three are gathered together in my name, there am I in the midst of them."

Jesus asked if we understood the nature of the power He had given us. I volunteered that none of us truly understood enough to ask anything meaningful, but I knew that in time, we would learn.

Afterward, John told of his experience with a man who did not have priesthood keys, nor was he called by Jesus. He said, "Master, we saw one casting out devils in your name, and he was not one of those who follow us, so we forbade him because he was not one of our followers."

"Forbid him not," Jesus counseled, "for there is no man that shall do a miracle in my name that can speak evil of me without consequence. For he that is not against us is with us. Further, whosoever shall give you a cup of water to drink in my name, because you belong to Christ, I tell you this truth, he shall not lose his reward."

Faith is powerful. Faith in the Son of God is adequate to be blessed by miracles and to bless others, even to perform miracles in His name. I also knew, as John pointed out, that having faith in Christ was not the same as having His priesthood keys.

When a man without priesthood authority organizes a church to teach his version of beliefs, it is an expression of his faith and his belief in Jesus, but if he has no priesthood keys, what he has built is the man's own church.

Those seeking the Church of Jesus Christ will find it organized by the priesthood keys given by the Son of God. It is not by observing the traditions of men, nor by honoring the various beliefs of men, but by living the commandments of God that men are saved. It is not by faith, but by those holding the keys of His priesthood that what is bound on earth is bound in heaven.

As I reflected on what Jesus said, I realized that this was one of the few times Jesus referred to Himself and the Apostles as "us." He had always made a point of distinguishing Himself from the rest of us, such as when He referred to "my Father and your Father," or when He provided the coin to pay the temple tax for Him and for me. This was not meant to be demeaning, but I understood that His relationship with His Father in Heaven was different from my relationship with His Father. Yet, when He referred to those holding the keys of His holy priesthood, He said "us" because we had received priesthood keys from Him. I felt comforted to be included as "us."

Preparing for the Feast of the Tabernacles

The summer ended and autumn came, and the Feast of the Tabernacles was at hand. Jesus announced that it was time to return to Jerusalem. He told us earlier that He would go to Jerusalem, where He would be killed. I wondered if this would be the time. My heart ached at the thought, and I did not ask. I am not sure I truly wanted to know, but I was going to the Feast with Him.

The Feast of the Tabernacles was the final holiday of the Jewish year, and one of the most important. It was observed in remembrance of the Israelites' exodus from Egypt. It was more than just another Jewish tradition but a commandment that we all observed by living for seven days in small, hand-built booths called tabernacles like the ones I offered to build on Mount Hermon for Jesus, Moses, and Elijah.

The brothers of Jesus lived in Capernaum, and they came to my home, asking Jesus if He would travel with them to Jerusalem for the Feast. They challenged Him to go, saying, "Leave here and go into Judea so that your disciples there may also see the works you do. No man does works in secret if He is seeking to be known openly." It sounded to me like they were taunting Him. They did not believe that their brother was the Messiah. They proved my suspicion when they said, "If you can do these things, show yourself to the world."

I took their words as an insult, but Jesus knew their hearts and treated them not as disbelievers, but as His brothers who were not yet convinced that He could be the Messiah.

He was patient with them, and I was there to observe and learn. He answered His brothers using the same words He said to His mother when He performed His first miracle: "My time is not yet come." In other words, it was not yet time for Him to go. He then added, "But any time is acceptable for you."

Rather than chastise them for their lack of belief, Jesus tried to explain things to them. "The world cannot hate you for what you say, but it hates me because I testify against the world that their works are evil. You can go up unto the Feast now, but I will not yet go up to the Feast because the time is not right for me to go." I noted that He carefully did not refer to His status as the Son of God as being the difference between them; instead, he referred to His testifying of the wickedness of the world as the thing that set Him apart. To me, both what He said and didn't say had meaning. Jesus remained in Capernaum, and His brothers departed for Judea.

We stayed with Jesus until He finished His instructions to us, and then we prepared to go with Him to see what awaited Him in Judea. He designed to go to Jerusalem, traveling along the eastern coast of Judea beyond Jordan. Before we departed, He sent several of the Apostles before Him to prepare the way. When the Apostles arrived in a certain village in Samaria, not all the citizens agreed to receive Jesus. They were unhappy that He would not be staying in Samaria but traveling on to Jerusalem to the land and the enemies of the Samaritans.

My friends James and John were not very happy with the Samaritans either. They promptly returned to Capernaum and petitioned Jesus, "Lord, please allow us to command fire to come down from heaven and consume them, even as Elias did!"

Jesus smiled at their boldness yet gently rebuked them. "You do not know the kind of spirit that possesses you," He said. "The Son of Man did not come to destroy men's lives but to save them." Jesus then sent them into another village to prepare the way. I marveled at His patience with us.

The Seventy Appointed, Charged, and Sent

When the last pair of Apostles returned from Samaria, Jesus invited all of us to travel with Him to Jerusalem. He talked about the work yet to be done and acknowledged that there was more than could ever be accomplished by the Twelve. He then repeated an expression that He used in Samaria when He met the woman at the well. The harvest truly is great, but the laborers are few," He said. "Pray therefore that the Lord of the harvest will send forth laborers into His harvest."

We knew that we needed help at times, but we also knew that it was not our place to ask Him to appoint more Apostles. But like He instructed, we did ask Him for help, and He provided it, but He didn't name more Apostles. Instead, He appointed seventy additional men, which we came to refer to as the Seventy. By "appointed," I mean that He gave them authority to do specific things, just as He had given us specific authority to bind on earth and in heaven. The Seventy were sent forth as emissaries of Jesus, going before Him. He sent them out, two by two, into every city and place where He would be going. They were similar to the Apostles in that they had authority to represent Him, but they did not have the "keys" Jesus had given us.

He laid His hands on them and gave them the specific authority they needed to act on His behalf. Then He said to them, as he had to us, "Go your way, knowing that I send you forth as lambs among wolves."

I noted that these men did not take any authority upon themselves but were faithful disciples. Jesus clearly taught us that anyone could do good works in His name, but those who would act on His behalf must receive the authority to do so from Him or from those to whom He had delegated it.

Jesus gave them detailed instructions how they were to travel, what they were to take and not take, who to speak to, and what to say. "Carry neither purse nor wallet, nor spare shoes," He said. "And do not stop to speak to your friends along the way. And into whatsoever house you enter, first say, 'Peace be unto this house,' " which was the traditional greeting, dating from the time of King David.

"If the head of the house is a man of peace, your blessing of peace shall rest upon that house," He continued. "If not, your blessing of peace shall return again to you. Remain in that house, eating and drinking what they provide, because you will receive what you earn. Do not go from house to house in search of better accommodations or food.

"Into whatever city you enter that receives you, eat such things as are set before you. Take the opportunity to heal the sick in the cities you enter, saying, 'The kingdom of God has come here unto you.' But whatsoever city you enter and they receive you not, go your way out into the streets of that city and say, 'We wipe off even the very dust of your city that cleaves to us, and we do it as testimony against you.' And I tell you that at the Day of Judgment, it shall be more tolerable for Sodom than for that city."

I was surprised that He sent them not to Galilee, nor to Judea, but to Samaria. This was the first time He had sent His emissaries to teach and bless individuals other than Jews. I watched and understood that it was time to take the kingdom of God to others.

JESUS REBUKES THE
CITIES OF GALILEE

After the Seventy departed for Samaria, we again had time alone with Jesus. One of the Apostles asked Him about the Seventy going to Samaria, wondering if He wanted us to go there after we returned from Jerusalem or if we were to continue in Galilee. Our question caused Him to pause before He responded. When He spoke, I could see a great sadness in His face. He told us that Galilee is where many of his mighty works had been done, but Galilee did not repent.

He spoke of the cities of Galilee, saying, "Woe unto you, Chorazin! Woe unto you, Bethsaida! If the mighty works that were done in you had been done in Tyre or Sidon, they would have repented long ago in sackcloth and ashes (the traditional outward expression of repentance or extreme sorrow). But I say to you, it shall be more tolerable for Tyre and Sidon at the Day of Judgment than for you. And you, Capernaum, which is exalted unto heaven, you shall be thrust down to hell, because if the mighty works which have been done in you had been done in Sodom, it would have remained until this day. But I say to you that it shall be more tolerable for the land of Sodom at the Day of Judgment than for you."

"He that hears you, hears me," He told us Apostles. "And he that despises you, despises me. And he that despises me, despises Him that sent me."

In my mind, it sounded like Jesus was saying His farewell to Galilee. He had pronounced a curse on those cities because they had heard His voice and had seen His miracles but had not repented. He lived among them, He taught them, and He healed them, but it was not enough. There was a message for me too. Knowing what you should be doing, but not doing it, is wrong. I comforted myself in that I was always trying to be a better man.

After He spoke about the unrepentant cities of Galilee, He asked us to accompany Him to Jerusalem to attend the Feast of Tabernacles. We traveled discretely, taking a round-about route. We departed Galilee and came near to the coasts of Judea on the eastern side of the Jordan River valley into the land called Perea. As always, as soon as Jesus was recognized, He was surrounded by great multitudes, and as always, He taught them and healed them.

Meanwhile, we learned that the Jews at the Feast searched the crowds entering Jerusalem, seeking Jesus and asking, "Where is He?" Much quiet discussion and secret murmuring occurred among the people concerning Jesus. Some said that He was a good man, but others claimed He deceived the people. In any case, no man spoke openly of Jesus for fear of the Jewish leaders, who were watching for Him, awaiting Him. Jesus would arrive when He was ready, on His own timetable, when it was "His time."

THE SEVENTY RETURN

As we traveled toward Jerusalem, the Seventy started meeting up with us. Before long, most of them had joined us. With expressions of joy and amazement, they reported to Jesus, saying, "Lord, through your name, even the devils are subject to us!"

Jesus then did something He had not done before: He gathered us and told us something of the events that took place in the beginning—the time before our mortality. "I oversaw the fall of Satan from heaven, which was as lightning," He said. "Know that in my service, I have similarly given you the power to tread on serpents and scorpions and to be above the power of the enemy. Nothing shall by any means hurt you. Notwithstanding this knowledge, do not rejoice that evil spirits are subject to you, but rejoice instead because your names are written in heaven."

I noticed a change in His face: the pain that showed when He spoke of Galilee earlier was gone. In its place was a look of peace. I had seen it before, especially when He was expressing His love. It was comforting to see Him at peace.

Then Jesus knelt, and we knelt with Him. He offered a prayer to His Father in Heaven, uttering a prayer about us. "I thank Thee, O Father, Lord of Heaven and Earth," He said, "that Thou hast hid these things from the wise and prudent but revealed them unto those who are even as babes because it was good in thy sight."

He said this and much more to His Father in Heaven.

We heard Him say sacred things, and we kept them sacred.

After He arose, He referred to the words of His prayer, saying, "All things are delivered unto me by my Father. No man knows the Son except the Father. Nor does anyone know the Father except the Son and to whomsoever the Son will reveal it."

Jesus referred to revelation from His Father as the foundation of knowledge of the Son. I knew what He meant because, as I have expressed before, my testimony of the Messiah was based on revelation from His Father.

Jesus then offered peace. "Come unto me, all that labor and are heavy laden, and I will give you rest," He promised. "Take my yoke upon you and learn of me because I am meek and lowly in heart, and you shall find rest for your souls. For my yoke is easy and my burden is light."

I have delighted many times in these words. The burden of what people did and did not do weighed heavily on me at times. I have anguished over their pains and their sorrows through sleepless nights, but I've always found rest in my thoughts of Jesus Christ, the Son of God. I knew that I only found rest in my knowledge of Him and the peace that knowledge gave. I would that all men may share in that peace. That is why I so freely testify that Jesus is the Son of God. Find peace in Him.

TEN LEPERS HEALED

As we made progress toward Jerusalem, we passed into Samaria again. As we entered a certain village, we were met by ten lepers, who stood some distance away. They shouted while we were still a ways from them, saying, "Jesus, Master, have mercy on us."

Jesus walked closer to them, and when He could see their faces clearly, He said, "Go and show yourselves to the priests." His instructions were necessary because according to the law of Moses, a priest needed to pronounce them clean before they could rejoin the community.

As the lepers walked away, the ten were immediately cleansed of their leprosy. Only one of them, a Samaritan, turned around when he saw that he was healed. With a loud voice, he glorified God. Then he fell on his face and thanked Jesus.

Jesus accepted the healed man's thanks and asked, "Were there not ten cleansed? But where are the other nine? The nine did not return and give glory to God, except this stranger?

"Arise," He said to the man as we departed. "Go your way. Your faith has made you whole."

He used the same words He had spoken to the woman that had an issue of blood for twelve years, the one that was healed by touching His robe.

THE PARABLE OF THE
GOOD SAMARITAN

We continued our journey through Samaria and into Judea. I was surprised that we had been well received by any Samaritans. I marveled that Jesus was so beloved, respected, and honored in Samaria. When we arrived in Jerusalem, Jesus did not immediately go to the temple to attend the Feast of the Tabernacles. Instead, He sat down and taught those who had come to find Him.

As Jesus taught, a certain lawyer stood and tested His knowledge of the law, asking, "Master, what shall I do to inherit eternal life?"

Jesus answered his question with another question: "What is written in the law, and how do you read it?"

"You shall love the Lord your God will all your heart, and with all your soul, and with all your strength, and with all your mind," the lawyer responded. "And you shall love your neighbor as yourself."

"You have answered right," Jesus confirmed. "Do this and you shall live."

The lawyer looked for a way out of the obligation, asking, "And who is my neighbor?"

Knowing that the lawyer was seeking a loophole, Jesus told a story. Having just come from Samaria, the story was about a Samaritan. "A certain man journeyed down from Jerusalem to Jericho, and fell among thieves, which stripped him of his clothes, wounded him, and left him half dead. By chance, there came down that way a certain priest, and when he saw him, he crossed to the other side of the road and passed by. Likewise a Levite, when he came upon the man and looked at him, passed by on the other side of the road. But a certain Samaritan, as he journeyed on the road, came upon the man also, and when he saw him, he had compassion on him. He went to him, bound his wounds, anointed him with oil, gave him wine, set him on his own animal, and took him to an inn, where he took care of him. In the morning, when he departed, he took out two denarii, gave them to the innkeeper, and said to him, 'When I return, I will repay you however much more you spend on him.' "

As Jesus finished the story, the lawyer looked at Him, as if waiting for Jesus to make His point. Instead, Jesus asked the lawyer, "Now, which of these three do you think was neighbor to him that fell among the thieves?"

The lawyer could not utter the word "Samaritan," so he said, "He that showed mercy on him."

Jesus looked away from the lawyer, gestured toward the roadway, and said, "Go and do likewise."

MARY AND MARTHA

That afternoon, we continued our journey into Judea, arriving at the village called Bethany. A woman named Martha received Jesus and the rest of us into her home, treating us as if we were old friends.

Martha had a sister named Mary, who sat at the feet of Jesus and listened to Him as He spoke. It was obvious to me that Martha and Mary knew Jesus well. They treated Him like family, welcoming Him with a familiarity and concern usually reserved for someone you care for deeply.

While Mary sat and listened to Jesus speak, Martha busied herself in preparing and serving us, to the point of being preoccupied. Finally, Martha came into the room and asked Jesus, "Lord, do you not care that my sister has left me to serve everyone by myself? Tell her to come and help me."

Jesus answered, saying, "Martha, Martha, you worry and trouble yourself about many things when but one thing is needful. Mary has chosen to do a good thing, which shall not be taken from her."

I understood what He meant. As a fisherman, I am a practical man—a man that does what needs to be done. Yet I learned to pause from my "doing" and to sit and listen, just as Mary did.

Mary and Martha fed Jesus and the rest of us, and then Jesus excused Himself to go about His work in the villages around Bethany teaching and healing.

INSTRUCTED IN PRAYER

I had seen and heard Jesus pray many times before we entered each city or village. That day, as he finished praying in advance of entering a Judean village near Bethany, one of the disciples who followed along with us asked Him, "Lord, teach us to pray as John the Baptist taught his disciples to pray."

Jesus repeated the instructions He had privately given to the Apostles following the sermon He had given on the mountain, with a perfect example of how to pray to our Father in Heaven.

This time, however, He added a parable, saying, "Who of you would go to a friend at midnight and say to him, 'Friend, lend me three loaves of bread because a friend of mine has come to me as he journeyed and I have no food to set before him.?

"Your friend would answer from within his home and say, 'Don't bother me. The door is shut, and my family is all in bed. I cannot get up and give you food.'

"I say to you that although he would not give you what you need simply because you are his friend, he would do it if you persist in pleading for his assistance."

I was not a patient man, and when someone asked me for help, I either helped him immediately or he didn't get my help at all. If I didn't help and he kept asking, it only aggravated me. I gained a new perspective. God sometimes measures our sincerity by the effort we put out. That explains why my prayers have not always been answered when I expected. Sometimes I prayed casually. I never saw Jesus pray that way.

The message was for me as much as anyone, perhaps more for me than most.

As we walked, a man caught up to us and asked, "Master, please tell my brother to divide our inheritance with me."

Jesus stopped. "Sir, who made me a judge or a divider over you?" He asked. Then He offered the man some personal advice: "Take heed and beware of covetousness, because a man's life does not consist of the abundance of things he possesses."

Turning from the man, Jesus addressed the rest of those following Him, offering another parable: "The ground of a certain rich man brought forth plentifully, and he asked himself, 'What shall I do because I do not have enough room to store all my fruits?' Then he answered himself, saying, 'This is what I will do: I will pull down my existing barn and build bigger ones. And there I will gather all of my fruits and goods.' Then I will say to my soul, 'Soul, you have many goods laid up for many years. Take it easy, eat, drink, and be merry.' But God said to him, 'You fool, this night your soul shall be required of you. Who now will own these things that you have grown, harvested and stored?' So, he that lays up treasure for himself is not rich toward God."

Later in the day, a group of people arrived to tell Jesus that the soldiers of Pilate, the procurator, had killed certain Galileans. They were killed as they made sacrifices, and their spilled blood had mingled with the blood of their sacrifices at the base of the altar.

I knew what the "message bearers" were suggesting. It was a tradition held among our people that when someone suffered a tragedy, they were being punished for some evil or wrongdoing in their life. The Jews believed that suffering was caused either by the individual or his parents. Whenever someone was killed, it was simply understood that "they deserved it."

Jesus took the opportunity to teach us otherwise. Just

prior to this, in an area called Siloam, located in the southern part of Jerusalem, eighteen men that were working on a tower for the Romans were killed when the structure collapsed. In those days, anyone working for the Romans was considered a traitor of sorts. Their death was considered to be justice for their treason.

Jesus asked them about the murders at the altar, saying, "Do you suppose that these Galileans were the worst sinners of all Galileans because they suffered such things? I tell you, no. But except you repent, you shall all likewise perish. What of those eighteen men who were killed when the tower in Siloam fell upon them? Do you think they were the worst sinners of all those who dwell in Jerusalem? Again, I tell you, no. But except you repent, you shall all likewise perish."

Those were harsh words of warning, but I don't know how many listened. Clearly, Jesus wanted us to know that we were all sinners, but we were not all subject to tragedy or illness. Again, the truth freed us from the bondage of another foolish man-made tradition.

From what I saw, at least some of those following us in Judea were more curious than interested. They had heard stories of Jesus and wanted to see Him and what He would say and do. Still, I saw what I'd call "true belief" in some faces, and Jesus taught them, repeating principles He had taught others.

He then gave another parable, this time about a fig tree. "A certain man had a fig tree planted in his vineyard, and he came and sought the fruit thereon and found none. Then he said to the keeper of the vineyard, 'Behold, I have come seeking fruit on this tree for three years now and found none. Cut down. Why let it take space in the vineyard?' And the keeper answered, saying, 'Lord, let it alone this year also, until after I dig about it and dung it.' And the man said, 'If it bears fruit, that is well, but if not, then you shall cut it down.' "

It was not until later that I came to understand that the keeper of the vineyard was Jesus and that the vineyard was the house of Israel. He would spend three years nourishing His vineyard, but it would bear no fruit and would be cut down.

HEALING ON THE SABBATH

Jesus was teaching in the synagogue on the Sabbath in a village near Jerusalem when He saw a woman who had suffered with an infirmity for eighteen years. Her body was bent so that she could not straighten herself. Jesus called her to His side and said, "Woman, you are freed from your infirmity." Immediately, she stood straight and glorified God.

The rabbi of the synagogue was indignant because Jesus had healed the woman on the Sabbath day. In his arrogance, he announced to the people in the synagogue, "There are six days in which men ought to work. Therefore, come and be healed in those days, but not on the Sabbath!"

"You hypocrite!" Jesus rebuked. "Does not each one of you free your ox or ass from its stall and lead him away to be watered on the Sabbath? And ought not this woman, a daughter of Abraham, whom Satan has bound for eighteen years, be freed from this bond on the Sabbath?"

Those in the synagogue responded in one of two ways. Those who were His adversaries were shamed to silence. The rest of the people rejoiced for the glorious things He did.

Jesus took the opportunity to teach those who followed Him, repeating much of what He had taught earlier to the various multitudes at different places. Jesus taught many of His stories and parables over and over as He spoke to different audiences who had the same needs, the same questions. This day, He repeated His parables of the mustard seed and the leaven.

In the days that followed, Jesus continued His journey toward Jerusalem, teaching in the cities and villages as He progressed. As He came to the east side of the Mount of Olives, or Mount of Olivet, certain Pharisees approached Jesus, saying, "Get out of here and leave Judea, or Herod will kill you."

Ordinarily, I didn't trust Pharisees, but Nicodemus was among them, so I knew they were among the few that were different. Jesus replied, "Go and tell that fox these words: 'Watch, as I cast out devils and as I perform cures today and tomorrow. Tell him that on the third day, I shall be perfected.' Nevertheless, I must continue walking today, tomorrow, and the following day. For it cannot be that a prophet will be killed outside of Jerusalem."

Late in the day, as we crossed the Mount of Olives, Jerusalem came into view, and Jesus stopped to look over the city. For a while, He just gazed at the sight with tears flowing freely down His cheeks. Finally, He said, "Oh, Jerusalem, Jerusalem, which kills the prophets and stones them that are sent to you. How often would I have gathered your children together as a hen gathers her brood under her wings, but you would not be gathered! Behold, your house is left desolate to you. You shall not see me until the time comes when you shall say, 'Blessed is He that comes in the name of the Lord.' "

We stayed that night on the side of the Mount of Olives, overlooking the city of Jerusalem. Jesus did not teach us but just sat, gazing quietly upon the city. His sadness was a burden to me and the other Apostles.

IN JERUSALEM

The next morning, we walked down the western side of the Mount of Olives into Jerusalem, where the Feast of the Tabernacles had been in progress for a few days. Jesus went directly to the temple, where He sat down and taught the people. The Jews—the Pharisees and the Sadducees—listened and marveled, saying, "How does this man know so much, having never been taught?"

Certainly Jesus had not attended their schools, but He was Jehovah. Jesus knew well the words Moses had written because they were the words Jesus had given him. In reality, when Moses quoted Jehovah, he was quoting Jesus.

"My doctrine is not mine but is His that sent me," He explained. "If any man shall do His will, he shall know whether the doctrine is of God or whether I speak of myself. He that speaks for himself seeks his own glory. He that seeks the glory of Him that sent Him is true and righteous."

Then, after pausing only long enough for them to absorb what He said, Jesus continued: "Did not Moses give you the law? And yet, none of you keep that law. It was written, 'Thou shall not kill.' Why do you go about to kill me?"

Shocked at His boldness, but not denying His accusation, the Pharisees and Sadducees countered by attacking Him personally: "You are possessed by a devil! Who is going about to kill you?"

Rather than answer their ridiculous denial, Jesus continued. Referring to His healing of the man at the Pool of

Bethesda on the Sabbath, He said, "I have done but one work in Jerusalem, and you all marvel."

He then taught those of the Sanhedrin, saying, "Moses is the one that gave you circumcision, not because it was from Moses, but of the Father, and you circumcise a man on the Sabbath day. If a man is circumcised on the Sabbath, the law of Moses is not broken, but you are angry with me because I healed a man on the Sabbath of the Passover? Judge not for the sake of appearance, but judge a righteous judgment."

Then one of the men openly acknowledged the conspiracy to kill Jesus: "Is not this the One they seek to kill? But look, He speaks boldly, yet they say nothing to Him. Do the Pharisees and the Sadducees know for a fact that this is the very Christ? How is it that we know where this man is from, but when the Christ comes, no man will know where He is from?"

Jesus cried out to those in the temple. "You both know me and you know where I came from," He proclaimed. "And you know that I have not come of myself. He that sent me is true—He who you do not know, but I know Him because I am from Him, and He has sent me."

I believe the Jews wanted to arrest Jesus, but no one laid a hand on Him. His "hour" had not yet come. Many of the people who believed in Jesus challenged the Jews, saying, "When Christ comes, will He do more miracles than the ones this man has done?"

Spies from the Sanhedrin ran to tell the Pharisees what the people were saying about Jesus, so the Pharisees and the Sadducees sent officers of the Sanhedrin to arrest Him.

Jesus spoke to the multitude, "For only a little while longer will I be with you, and then I shall go to Him that sent me. You shall seek me, but you shall not find me because you cannot come where I will be."

The Jews spoke among themselves, saying, "Where will

He go that we shall not find him? Will He go to the dispersed among the Gentiles and teach the Gentiles? What does He mean?"

It seemed to me that they were worried He would go into hiding and that they would not be able to find Him. If they couldn't find Him, it would frustrate their conspiracy to kill Him, just as He had done by His travels in recent weeks.

On the last day of the Feast of the Tabernacles, there was a ritual of carrying a golden vessel of water from the Pool of Siloam, or "Shiloh" in Hebrew, to commemorate when Moses struck the rock twice and water flowed from it. The ritual acknowledged that God had provided the needed water when the thirsty children of Israel had nothing to drink.

Jesus used this event as an opportunity to teach an object lesson. He stood among the people and cried loudly, "If any man thirst, let him come unto me and drink. He that believes on me, as the scriptures say, 'Out of His belly shall flow rivers of living water.' "

I knew that Jesus was referring to the quenching effect of the Spirit, which testifies to anyone who would but seek it. I would note that the Holy Ghost was not yet given to man because Jesus was still with us and was not yet glorified.

When people heard these words, they said, "Truly, this man is a prophet." Others said, "This is the Christ." But some asked, "Shall Christ come out of Galilee? Does not the scripture say that Christ comes of the seed of David and out of the town of Bethlehem, where David was?"

Because Jesus was raised in Nazareth, He was known only as Jesus of Nazareth, and everyone assumed that Nazareth was His birthplace. I could have spoken to correct their ignorance, but seeing that Jesus did not, I kept quiet. I knew better than to interrupt Jesus. I also knew He could handle the Pharisees. Still, I kept my hand on my sword hilt, ready to defend Jesus if necessary; there were many Pharisees but only one Son of God.

A dispute arose among the people whether Jesus was the Christ. While they were debating, officers of the Sanhedrin came to arrest Jesus, but none of them dared lay hands on Him. Nicodemus told us later that when the officers returned to the chief priests, the Pharisees asked, "Why have you not brought Him?"

The officers of the Sanhedrin answered them, "Never has a man spoken like this man speaks."

The Pharisees asked them, "Are you deceived also? Have any of the Jews or have any of the Pharisees believed Him? The people who do not know the law are cursed."

Nicodemus asked the Sanhedrin, "Does our law judge any man before it hears him and knows what he does?"

Caught in their obvious plot to unjustly condemn Jesus, the Pharisees focused their venom on Nicodemus. "Are you also from Galilee? Search the scriptures and look, but you will not find a prophet who came from Galilee." They ignored Elijah and Hosea, both from Galilee, and comforted themselves with the prophecy of Micah, that the Messiah would come from Bethlehem. Then, caught in their manifest guilt and lies, every man returned to his home.

In the House of
a Chief Pharisee

The Sabbath afternoon brought something very unusual. Jesus was invited by one of the chief Pharisees to eat at his house. I concluded that the Pharisee invited Jesus to his house so he could study Him. I did not trust the Pharisee, but Jesus courteously accepted the invitation.

When we arrived at the Pharisee's house, there were several rooms on several levels, each with multiple tables. Jesus ate at the table with the Pharisee in the uppermost room. We, the Apostles, were directed to a different table in the same room.

In our time, houses were built to accommodate the uneven terrain. In fact, most homes were on several levels. In addition, rooms were added as needs demanded, or in some cases, as space became available in an adjoining dwelling.

By tradition, it was not the size of a room that determined its importance, but its elevation. The higher the room, the more important it was. The most important guests were always hosted in the uppermost room. Guests of lesser importance were invited to lower rooms, reserved for those with the lowest social standing—at least in the eyes of the host. Being invited to dine in the uppermost room was not an honor one took upon himself. It was the exclusive right of the host to determine who sat where.

As Jesus talked and ate in the uppermost room, a man was brought before Him, a man with dropsy, a condition that caused his ankles and feet to swell greatly with accumulated fluid. It was obvious that the man was in great pain and found it difficult to walk. Jesus observed the man and his condition but said nothing. He was waiting for the host to say something. I was certain that the man had been brought to the Pharisee's house on the Sabbath to test Jesus because it had only been a week since He had healed the woman in the synagogue. Turning to the lawyers and Pharisees, Jesus tested them by asking, "Is it lawful to heal on the Sabbath day?"

The lawyers and Pharisees held their peace, unable to answer without acknowledging that it was lawful to heal. Perhaps the harder thing for them to do was acknowledge that Jesus possessed the power to heal. In the silence that followed, I knew they were waiting to see what Jesus would do. He rose from the table and went to the man with dropsy. Without fanfare or ceremony, He healed the man and sent him on his way. No commentary or argument followed. Jesus returned to His place at the table and asked those around him: "Which of you shall have an ass or an ox that has fallen into a pit and will not straightway pull him out on the Sabbath day?"

He had asked that question before and would ask it again of other Pharisees. Observance of the Sabbath had come to be ruled by a long list of complicated rules that were vigorously enforced by the Pharisees. The distorted letter of the law had overridden the spirit of the law, and ritual had replaced religion.

Our host, one of the chief Pharisees, invited Jesus to speak. I looked forward to hearing what He might say. Would He teach them or rebuke them? What would He say to this group that was conspiring to kill Him?

Jesus started by talking about etiquette. It sounded harmless enough, but it was a parable, overflowing with meaning. How I love the wisdom of the Son of God!

Jesus observed that as each invited guest arrived at the house of the Pharisee, they had chosen the most important place available. He reminded them of the teaching of Solomon. "When you are invited to a wedding, do not choose the most important seat in the uppermost room lest you take the place of a more honored guest than you, a man that may not have arrived yet. By so doing, you put the host in the position of shaming you by asking you to move, saying, 'Give this man your place,' and you have to relocate to a lower room to whatever seat is left.

"Instead, when you are invited, go and sit down in the lowest room. Then, when the host sees you, he may say to you, 'My friend, come up to the table of my most honored guests.' Those sitting with you shall have respect for you. For whosoever honors himself shall be humiliated, but he that humbles himself shall be honored."

Then Jesus spoke directly to the host: "When you prepare to host a dinner or a supper, do not invite your friends or your brothers, neither your kinsmen, nor your rich neighbors, lest they return the invitation. Instead, when you prepare a feast, invite the poor, the maimed, the lame, and the blind because they certainly cannot repay your generosity. Your compensation will be given you at the resurrection of the just."

It was only at that point that everyone realized that this etiquette lesson was a parable. Jesus was a gracious guest, not offending His host, the Pharisee, but teaching him, if he would only listen. Someone was listening. One of the guests at the table with Jesus spoke up and said, "Blessed is he that shall eat bread in the kingdom of God."

Jesus responded to that man's remarks with another parable: "A certain man prepared a great feast and invited many people. He sent his servant at suppertime to courteously remind his guests that they were invited and the time had arrived. The servant was told to say, 'Come, because all things are now ready.' And all of those who were invited made excuses about why they could not come.

"The first invited guest told the servant, 'I have bought a piece of ground, and I need to go see it. I pray that you will have me excused.'

"Another invited guest said, 'I have bought a yoke of five oxen, and I need to test their strength. I pray that you will have me excused.'

"And another invited guest said, 'I have just married a wife, and therefore I cannot come.'

"So the servant returned to his lord and gave the invited guests' excuses. The master of the house became angry and told his servant, 'Go out quickly into the streets and lanes of the city, and bring the poor, the maimed, the lame, and the blind into my house.'

"The servant obeyed and went into the streets, inviting people to the feast. He returned to the master of the house and said, 'Lord, it is done as you commanded, but there is still room.'

"The master of the house said, 'Then go out into the highways and hedged pathways and urge others to come, that my house may be filled, because I'll tell you something for certain: none of those men who were invited shall taste of my supper.' "

Jesus said what needed to be said to the Pharisee and his guests without making His host uncomfortable. His meaning was clear to me, but I wasn't sure the Pharisee saw himself as one of the invited guests that had conspired to reject the Master's invitation.

I understood that Jesus wasn't contrasting the Pharisees to the rest of the house of Israel. He contrasted the house of Israel from the Gentiles. When He invited all of the house of Israel, they did not come, but all reject His invitation. In time, the Apostles would be sent to invite the Gentiles to Him, and there no longer would be room for the house of Israel. It was certain that they would not taste of His feast.

COUNT THE COST

After the dinner, the chief Pharisee invited everyone to the courtyard, where a great multitude of believers were waiting to hear Jesus teach. As before, much of what Jesus said was similar to things He had taught earlier in different settings, including His sermon on the mountain. He did not teach different things to different people. The chief Pharisee sat and listened without interrupting.

Jesus taught the believers about the cost of being a disciple. Few seemed to understand that the cost of following Jesus was so high. He looked around at the crowd and said, "If any man come to me and is not willing to forsake his father, mother, wife, children, brothers, sisters—even his own life—he cannot be my disciple. Whosoever does not bear this cross and come after me cannot be my disciple."

We had done this. We, the Apostles, had forsaken our lives to be disciples. Without intending to boast or complain, I knew that I had left my family, my fishing business, and all that was my life to follow Christ. I was fortunate that my family knew and loved Jesus as I did. Some of my fellow Apostles had lost everything because their families were not like mine. And yet, like me, my fellow Apostles would have gladly given their lives to serve the Son of God. Certainly we knew that there was a cost to being His disciple. We were willing to pay that cost. But this was not true of everyone.

Murmurings arose among the multitude. I could tell that not everyone comprehended the cost of following Christ.

Some were only excited at the opportunity to be with Him and hear His words. Jesus cautioned them to consider the steep cost of discipleship before leaving their families. If they were to follow Jesus, they needed to be prepared to not look back with regret.

Jesus taught them with another story. "Which of you, intending to build a tower, does not sit down first and count the cost to know whether you have sufficient to finish it? If not, after you have laid the foundation, you will find yourself unable to finish it, and all will see what you have done and mock you, saying, 'This man began to build but was unable to finish.'

"Or, what king, preparing to make war against another king, does not sit down first and consult whether he is able with his ten thousand to do battle with the king that comes against him with twenty thousand? Or sends ambassadors to the other king while he is yet a great ways off, desiring to know the conditions necessary to make peace? So likewise, whosoever of you that does not forsake all that he has cannot be my disciple."

I mention another cost that Jesus did not include: when you choose to be a disciple of Christ, you choose to have His enemies—His adversaries—as your own.

THE PARABLE OF THE
UNRIGHTEOUS STEWARD

Surrounded by the wealth of the chief Pharisee, Jesus shared another parable that evening, saying, "There was a certain rich man who had a steward. Someone went to the rich man and accused the steward of wasting the rich man's goods. The rich man sent word to his steward, asking him, 'How is it that I hear these things about you? Prepare an accounting of your stewardship, because you may no longer be my steward.'

"Then the steward asked himself, 'What shall I do? For my lord has taken away my stewardship. I cannot make my living digging, and I am ashamed to beg. I am resolved as to what I shall do. When I am fired from my stewardship, I will be received into the houses of those who owe my lord.'

"So the steward called every one of his lord's debtors to him and said to the first, 'How much do you owe my lord?' And the first debtor said, 'One hundred measures of oil.' And the steward said, 'Take your bill, sit down quickly, and write fifty.' Then the steward said to another, 'And how much do you owe?' And he said, 'One hundred measures of wheat.' And the steward said, 'Take your bill and write eighty.' "

Jesus then commended the unjust steward for his clever wisdom in preparing for his inevitable future, explaining, "This wicked generation of children of the world is wiser than the children of light in making preparations for their future."

Jesus instructed us to learn how to be responsible for what little we have in this world in order to be prepared for receiving greater responsibilities in the world to come. "Make yourself familiar with the duties of wealth as the unrighteous do so that when your mortal tabernacle fails, and you die, you will receive an everlasting tabernacle," He taught.

"Know that he who is faithful in the lesser things is faithful in great things. He that is unjust in the lesser things is unjust in great things. Therefore, if you have not been faithful in the duties of wealth in this world of unrighteousness, who would trust you with true riches? And, if you have not been faithful in that which belongs to another man, who will give you that which is your own?"

Jesus instructed us to manage our resources wisely, but he still cautioned us, saying, "But no servant can serve two masters because he will either hate the one and love the other or else he will hold to one and despise the other. You cannot serve both God and wealth."

Jesus carefully crafted this parable, making it instructive without offending His wealthy host. He let His disciples know that they were often shortsighted as they looked to the future. He used the unjust steward as an example of how even wicked people in the world take responsibility for their future. Wealth serves the wise man, not the other way around.

When I became a disciple of Jesus, I did not expect Him to feed and clothe me. I gave up my life as a fisherman, but my business continued to provide for my family. I did not know if I would die serving Jesus or if I would ever be a fisherman again, but it was still my responsibility to provide for myself and my family and to prepare for my future. It was not the responsibility of Jesus or of His Church. Unlike some disciples, I knew better than to believe that Jesus should feed and provide for us all, just as He had fed the five thousand and the four thousand.

The Pharisees and Another Parable

Several Pharisees, men known to be self-righteous, who publicly proclaimed their knowledge of the scriptures, were among the guests too. They had derided Jesus and mocked Him openly. The house of Israel held these men in high regard, but their outward piousness hid their inner wickedness. They boasted of their great learning, especially compared to a poor Galilean who had never attended their schools. Jesus turned toward them and said, "You are ones who stand justified before men, but God knows your hearts. What is highly esteemed among men is an abomination in the sight of God.

"There was a certain rich man who was clothed in purple and fine linen and ate sumptuously every day. There was also a certain beggar named Lazarus, who was covered with sores. His only desire was to be fed with the crumbs that fell from the rich man's table, so he was laid at the rich man's gate. While lying there, the dogs came and licked Lazarus' sores.

"When Lazarus died, he was carried by the angels into Abraham's bosom. The rich man died also and was buried in the earth. Looking up from hell in his tormented state, the rich man saw Abraham far off and Lazarus in his bosom. And he cried, saying, 'Father Abraham, have mercy on me and send Lazarus, that he may dip the tip of his finger in water and cool my tongue because I am tormented in this flame.' But Abraham said, 'Son, remember that you received good things in your lifetime while Lazarus received evil things, but now he is comforted and you are tormented. Besides, between you and us there is a great gulf fixed so that no one can pass from here to there, neither can anyone who would come from there to here.'

"Then the rich man said, 'I pray therefore, Father Abraham, that you would send Lazarus to my father's house, where I have five brothers, that he may testify unto them lest they also come into this place of torment.'

"Abraham replied, saying, 'They have Moses, and they have the prophets. Let them hear them.'

"The rich main said, 'No, they will not, Father Abraham, but if one went to them from the dead, they will repent.'

"Abraham replied, saying, 'If they do not listen to Moses and the prophets, they will not be persuaded by one that rose from the dead either.' "

Jesus used many parables, but I'd never heard Him give a name to any of the characters, at least I didn't remember any. I wondered why Jesus chose to call this one Lazarus, which was the name of His dear friend living in Bethany.

While I did not understand the name, I did understand several truths. First, after death, good people go to Father Abraham's bosom, where they are comforted and are at peace. Second, evil people go to hell, which is down from Abraham's bosom, where they suffer torment. Third, the good and evil dead are separated by a fixed great gulf. Fourth, paradise and hell are close enough that people can see one another in the other realms.

After dining with the Pharisee and his guests, we returned to the side of the Mount of Olives for the night.

WHEN WILL THE KINGDOM
OF GOD COME?

The next morning, a delegation of Pharisees met us as we prepared to leave the Mount of Olives. I figured they were sent to question what Jesus had taught the night before about Lazarus and the rich man. Instead they demanded, "When shall the kingdom of God come?"

Jesus answered, "Israel will not see the kingdom of God when it comes. Neither shall anyone say, 'Look, it is here!' or 'Look, it is there!' For behold, the kingdom of God is already within Israel."

The Pharisees did not understand that Jesus referred to Himself and His Church because He was among them and had organized His Church. We were also forbidden to tell them what they did not know.

Do not be as the Pharisees of old and reject the invitation to the great feast Jesus has prepared for you.

After the Pharisees left, Jesus spoke privately to us, the Apostles, saying, "The days will come, when you shall desire to see one of the days of the Son of Man, and you shall not be able see it. And there will be those who shall say to you, 'Look here' or 'Look there,' but do not go after them or follow them. For as the lightning bolt that lightens from one part under heaven and shines into another part under heaven to be seen of all, so shall the Son of Man also be in His day.

"As it was in the days of Noah, so shall it also be in the days of the Son of Man. In the days of Noah, they ate, drank, married wives, and were given in marriage until the very day

Noah entered into the ark and the flood came and destroyed them all. Likewise was it in the days of Lot: they also ate and drank, bought and sold, planted and built. But the same day Lot went out of Sodom, it rained fire and brimstone from heaven and destroyed all of them in Sodom. Thus it shall be when the Son of Man shall be revealed to the world.

"In that day, he that happens to be on the housetop and has his valuables in his house, let him not come down to take it away. And he that is working in the field, let him likewise not return to his house. Remember Lot's wife. Whosoever shall seek to save his life shall lose it, and whosoever shall lose his life shall preserve it. I tell you that in that night, there shall be two men in one bed. One shall be taken and the other left. Two women shall be grinding together. One shall be taken and the other shall be left. Two men shall be working in the field. One shall be taken and the other left."

I asked him, "Where, Lord? Where shall they be taken?"

Jesus answered, saying, "Wherever the body is. That is where the eagles shall be gathered."

I understood that they would be taken from the body of Israel, meaning Jerusalem. The eagles, the house of Israel, would gather to Jerusalem, where they would die. In time, this season of great death and destruction at Jerusalem would be wrought by the hands of the Roman army. As Jesus spoke, a great sadness came over His countenance.

Jesus continued to teach us as we prepared to go down into Jerusalem, using parables to guard the truth from the ears of those who would not hear. That day His subject was prayer. "In a certain city, there was a judge who did not fear God, nor did he care for man. And there was a widow in that city, and she came unto the judge saying, 'Avenge me of my adversary.' And for a while he would not, but afterward, he said within himself, 'Though I do not fear God, nor do I have any regard for man, but because this widow troubles me,

I will avenge her, lest by her continually coming to me she make me weary.' "

And Jesus said, "Hear what the unjust judge said and ask yourself, 'Shall God not avenge His own elect, which cry unto Him day and night, though He bear with them a long time?' I tell you that He will avenge them speedily. Nevertheless, when the Son of Man comes, shall He find faith on earth?"

To those that wonder if it is enough to approach God in prayer one time and be done, I would say, pray as much as it takes. God hears and answers your prayers, but He answers them in His time, when He knows it to be best. Persevere— do not weary in your prayers.

THE ADULTEROUS WOMAN

After Jesus knelt and prayed to His Father in Heaven, we were ready to enter Jerusalem. It was still early in the morning when He came down from the mount and went into the temple as part of the Feast of the Tabernacles. As Jesus sat, everyone in the temple gathered close to hear Him speak.

As He taught, the scribes and Pharisees brought a woman forward who had been taken in adultery, clearly trying to set another trap for Him. They pulled her into the middle of those surrounding Jesus, pushed her to the dirty floor, and asked, "Master, this woman was taken in the very act of adultery. In the law, Moses commanded us that such should be stoned, but what do you say?"

I knew that the scribes and Pharisees wanted to catch Him in saying something they could use to accuse Him or, even worse, something to justify their conspiracy to kill Him. In reality, the Jews had not actually stoned anyone for some time. Certainly the law and the facts were clear. It was the law that the woman be stoned, but the law could not be enforced because the Romans had recently barred the Jews from executing anyone. As I relate this experience, I wonder why they did not comply with the whole law and bring the man forward too. After all, he would have been "taken in the very act of adultery" with her. Knowing the Pharisees, my opinion is they were too cowardly to confront a man but not a woman.

The strategy of the Pharisees was shrewd. If Jesus agreed that the woman should be stoned, He would be violating the

Roman law, and they could accuse Him before the Romans. If He said that she should not be stoned, they could accuse Him of violating the law of Moses. They figured they had cleverly maneuvered Jesus into a trap. However, they did not know that they were dealing with the Son of God. He saw their plan and was not trapped by their sophistry.

At first, instead of answering the scribes and Pharisees, Jesus acted as though He had not heard them. He stooped down and wrote in the dust of the floor with his finger.

This did not stop the scribes and the Pharisees, or the "accusers," as I prefer to call them. They were confident in their cleverness, but needing something with which to accuse Jesus, they repeated their question. Jesus stood up and looked around, making eye contact with each of the woman's accusers. With wisdom only found in the Son of God, Jesus said, "He among you that is without sin, let him be the first to cast a stone at her." Then Jesus knelt down and wrote in the dust again.

Jesus knew the law too, and that was also part of the law. The accusers were required to cast the first stones. The trap they set had ensnared only themselves. If they did stone her, they would be violating Roman law, but if they didn't, they would be violating the law of Moses. Upon being confronted with this heart-stopping challenge, the accusers departed, one by one, until they were all gone, leaving the accused woman still lying on the dusty floor of the temple.

The other Pharisees not among the accusers remained at the rear of the crowd, talking among themselves. After a minute, Jesus stood, looked around, and said, "Woman, where are your accusers? Has no man condemned you?"

The woman, obviously filled with relief at her good fortune, stood up, smiled from behind her tears, and said, "No man, Lord."

Jesus looked into her eyes and challenged her to change

her ways, saying, "Neither do I condemn you. Go, and sin no more."

In a battle of wits, the Pharisees had lost. Even the Pharisees standing at the rear of the crowd knew that under the law of Moses, only actual witnesses could testify against the woman. Jesus could not condemn the woman because He was not a witness. He didn't condone what she had done. He simply told her to repent, just as I would expect Him to do.

THE LIGHT OF THE WORLD

After the humiliated Pharisees retreated, Jesus was able to address those who came to hear Him. We were in the treasury of the temple, just off the Court of the Women, where Jesus spoke to them. The hall was filled with large lamps used to light the rooms during the daily celebrations of the Feast of the Tabernacles. Jesus gestured toward the lamps and said, "I am the Light of the World. He that follows me shall not walk in darkness but shall have the Light of Life."

The remaining Pharisees objected to what Jesus declared, saying, "You are bearing witness of yourself, and your witness is not true."

Jesus countered their objection. "Though I bear witness of myself, my witness is true because I know where I came from, and I know where I am going," He proclaimed. "You cannot say where I came from, and you cannot say where I am going. You judge according to the flesh, but I judge no man. And yet, if I did judge, my judgment would be true. I am not alone in my judgment because it is of me and of my Father that sent me.

"It is written in your law that the testimony of two men is true. I am one that bears witness of myself, and the Father that sent me is the second that bears witness of me."

The Pharisees continued their contemptuous interrogation of Jesus, asking, "Where is your Father?"

Jesus was very controlled in His response: "You neither know me nor do you know my Father. If you had known me, you would have known my Father also."

That didn't mean Jesus was His own Father. He is so much like His Father in word and deed that to know Jesus is to know His Father, or as He later put it, "I and my Father are one."

The Pharisees flushed with rage at His response, immediately trying to arrest Jesus and take Him before the Sanhedrin to accuse Him. Again, not one of them was able to lay his hands on Jesus because His "hour" had not yet come.

As He turned to walk away, Jesus said to them, "I shall go my way, and you shall seek me, and you shall die in your sins. Where I go, you cannot come."

Upon hearing this, one of the Pharisees raved to the multitude, "Is He going to kill Himself because He said, 'Where I go, you cannot come'?"

The Jews believed that anyone who committed suicide would automatically go to hell. Using that logic, they suggested that Jesus meant He would kill himself so He would go where they could not. Part of their belief included the tradition that hell was located beneath the surface of the earth, a place they did not want to go.

Jesus turned back to the Pharisees, addressing their suggestion that He was going to hell, "You are from beneath the earth. I am from above. You are of this world. I am not of this world. I said that you shall die in your sins because you do not believe that I am He."

In shock at His pointed condemnation, the Pharisees breathlessly demanded, "Who are you?"

Jesus answered, "I am as I told you from the beginning. I have many things to say and to judge of you, but know that I speak to the world only those things that I have heard of Him that sent me, because He is true."

The Pharisees still did not understand that He was speaking of His Father.

"When you have lifted up the Son of Man," He

continued, "then you shall know that I am He and that I do nothing of myself. The things I speak of are only what my Father has taught me. He that sent me is with me. The Father has not left me on my own because I always do the things that please Him."

As Jesus spoke, there were many that believed His words. Jesus addressed them, saying, "If you continue in my word, you are my disciples indeed, and you shall know the truth, and the truth shall make you free."

Freedom was a matter of pride for the Pharisees. Their claim to be free ignored the reality that for the last century, Israel had been under the absolute dominion of the Romans, who even controlled the enforcement of Jewish law.

In response to Jesus, the angry Pharisees ignored the bondage of the Hebrews in Egypt and the subsequent captivity under Babylon. They shouted, "We are Abraham's seed! And we were never in bondage to any man! How can you say, 'You shall be made free'?"

Jesus answered them softly: "This is the truth I tell you. Whosoever commits sin is the servant of sin, but the servant cannot live in the master's house except as a visitor. But the Son of the Master lives in the Master's house forever. If the Son therefore makes you free, you shall be free indeed. Yes, I know that you are Abraham's seed, but you are not his children. You seek to kill me because my word has no place in you. Know now that I do what I have seen while with my Father, while you do what you have seen with your father."

At that, one of the Pharisees, shrieked, "Abraham is our father!"

Jesus responded, "If you were Abraham's children, you would do the works of Abraham, but even now you seek to kill a man, a man who has told you the truth, which truth I heard from God, but Abraham did not do the things you do. In fact, you do the deeds of your father."

Jesus had just insulted their ancestors by accusing them of not being descended of Abraham, making them sons of some foreign man and not descended from Israelite fathers. Anyone could have predicted their next outburst, "We are not children born of fornication! We have one father, who is God!"

Jesus countered, "If God were your father, you would love me, for I came forth from God. I did not come of myself, but from Him that sent me. Why do you not understand my words? Because you cannot stand to hear my words! One thing is certain: your father is the devil, and you are his children. You follow the lusts of your father because that is what you do. He was a murderer from the beginning and does not live in the truth because there is no truth in him. When he speaks a lie, he speaks his own lie, because he is a liar, the father of lies. Because I tell the truth, you do not believe me. Which of you can find me guilty of sin? And if I tell the truth, why do you not believe me? He that is of God hears God's words, but because you are not of God, you do not hear God's words!"

Having no other response, the Pharisees were reduced to name calling, "So, when we say you are a Samaritan and are possessed by a devil, are we not right?"

Calling Jesus a Samaritan was intended to disown Jesus as a fellow Jew. Jesus answered them calmly, "I am not possessed by a devil. I honor my Father, and you dishonor me. And, while I do not seek glory for myself, there is one that seeks glory for himself and judges. I tell you another truth: if a man follows what I say, he shall never see death."

The Pharisees said, "Now we know that you are possessed! Abraham is dead, and also the prophets. Yet you say, "If a man follows what I say, he shall never taste death.' Are you greater than our father, Abraham, and the prophets, who are dead? Who made you who you are?"

"If I were to honor myself, my honor would be nothing," Jesus answered. "It is my Father that honors me. You say that my Father is your God, yet you have not known Him, but I know Him. If I should say that I do not know Him, I would be a liar, like you. But I do know Him, and I follow what He says. Your father, Abraham, rejoiced to see my day; he saw it and was glad."

The Pharisees countered, again twisting His words: "You are not yet fifty years old, and you say that you have seen Abraham?"

Jesus responded with something that inflamed them with unquenchable anger. Using the same language as Jehovah of the books of Moses, Jesus said, "I say to you that before Abraham was, I Am."

Recoiling at Jesus using the words "I Am," the Pharisees picked up construction rubble, intending to stone Jesus for blasphemy. But suddenly they could not see Him, and He walked out of that part of the temple, passing directly through the midst of them. They searched for Him but could not see Him.

THE BLIND MAN HEALED
ON THE SABBATH

On the Sabbath day, we left the temple as the lights for the Feast of the Tabernacles were being extinguished. As we did, we passed a beggar who had been blind from birth. I asked Jesus, "Master, who sinned, this man or his parents, that he was born blind?"

"Neither this man nor his parents sinned," He answered, "but he is blind so the works of God may be manifested in him this day. I must do the works of Him who sent me while it is yet day, for the night is coming when no man can work. As long as I am in the world, I am the Light of the world."

Even as He spoke, He knelt down, spit on the ground, made a ball of clay with the spittle and dirt, then anointed the eyes of the blind man with the clay. When He finished, Jesus spoke to the blind man, saying, "Go and wash in the pool of Siloam."

The blind man obeyed immediately, going to Siloam, washing himself and gaining his sight. He returned to the temple, no longer blind. The man's neighbors, who had known him when he was blind, said, "Is this not the same man who sat and begged?" Some answered, "This is he." Others said, "He looks like him," but they had doubts until the man testified, "I am he!"

When he assured them that he was the one who had been blind, they asked, "How were your eyes opened?"

"A man who is called Jesus made clay, anointed my eyes,

and said, 'Go to the pool of Siloam and wash.' And, I went and washed, and I received my sight."

The Pharisees, still trying to find Jesus to stone Him, asked the man, "Where is He?"

"I do not know," the man answered.

They took the man who was blind to the other Pharisees of the Sanhedrin and explained what had happened—that a blind man had been healed on the Sabbath. The Pharisees were delighted that Jesus had violated the Sabbath by making the clay and healing the blind man. This would be the third healing on the Sabbath within a few weeks. Not willing to lose this opportunity to accuse Jesus, the Pharisees asked the man to repeat how he had received his sight. He said, "Jesus put clay on my eyes, I washed, and now I see."

The lawyers agreed among themselves: "This man is not of God because He does not observe the Sabbath day."

And other Pharisees, led by Nicodemus, asked them, "How can a man who is a sinner do such miracles?" This question created a difference of opinion among them. Nicodemus asked the man that was blind, "What do you have to say about Jesus? Did He open your eyes?"

"He is a prophet!" the man proclaimed.

The rest of the Pharisees did not believe what the man said, even when he insisted that he had been blind and had received his sight at the hands of Jesus. Trapped by Nicodemus's question about what kind of man it took to perform miracles, the lawyers conferred among themselves, insisting there must be another explanation. They concluded that the man must not have been blind in the first place. To validate their desperate conclusion, they summoned the parents of the man to be interrogated.

Nicodemus, the Pharisee who related this story to us, prepared the man and his parents on how to answer the questions to protect themselves from being expelled from the synagogue for telling the truth. Nicodemus warned them that the Pharisees decided that anyone who testified that Jesus was the Messiah would be expelled from the synagogue.

The Pharisees asked the man's parents, "Is this your son, whom you say was born blind?"

And his parents answered carefully, saying, "We know that this is our son, and we know that he was born blind."

And the Pharisees asked, "How then, does he now see?"

The parents, following Nicodemus's advice, answered, "We do not know by what means he sees, nor do we know who has opened his eyes. He is of age. Ask him. He can speak for himself."

The Pharisees, unable to deny the power of God manifested by Jesus by healing the blind man, called the man back before their tribunal. They issued their irrelevant legal judgment, ignoring the divine power of Jesus, saying, "Give God the praise. We know that this man called Jesus is a sinner."

The healed man carefully restated what he knew: "Whether He is a sinner, I do not know. One thing I do know is that whereas I was blind, I can now see."

Still perplexed that Jesus had made a blind man see, they asked, "What did He do to you? How did He open your eyes?"

The man said boldly, "I told you already, and you did not listen! Why would you hear it again? Do you wish to become his disciples?"

The man was impatient with their interrogation and his foolhardy comeback shook them. They were not used to being addressed so defiantly, especially by someone who was clearly not a master of the law. They reviled the man, "You are His disciple, but we are Moses's disciples! We know that God spoke to Moses, but as for this fellow, we do not know where He gets His power."

The man's growing confidence seemed to bloom out of his new ability to see, as did his knowledge that Jesus was the one who had restored his vision. "It is something to marvel about, that you do not know where He gets His power, and yet He has opened my eyes," the man continued with confidence. "Let's reason this out, shall we? Now, we all know that God does not hear the pleas of sinners, but if any man worships God and does His will, He will hear him. Since the world began, has it ever been heard that any man has opened the eyes of one that was born blind? If this man were not of God, He could do nothing!"

The man's pure logic and testimony could not be countered, and it shamed the Pharisees' legal arguments. They were outdone by a man who lacked their elite legal training.

Once again, the Pharisees reviled the man, saying, "You were altogether born in your sins, yet you dare to teach us?" And they expelled him from the synagogue.

Nicodemus sent word to us that the man had been expelled, which meant they barred him from returning to the synagogue. The man knew where Jesus had found him earlier, so he returned there, hoping to see Jesus. Word of his situation had reached us by then.

Jesus approached the man and asked, "Do you believe in the Son of God?"

I should note that this was one of the few times Jesus referred to Himself as the Son of God, preferring to use the title of Son of Man in most public utterances.

"Who is He, Lord, that I might believe in Him?" the man answered.

Jesus responded, "You have both seen Him and talked to Him, and it is He who is talking to you now."

I wish everyone could have seen the man's face when he heard those wonderful words from Jesus. I was reminded of the Samaritan woman at the well. The man knelt in front of Jesus and smiled up at Him; tears flowed freely down his cheeks. He said simply, "Lord, I believe."

The multitude believed also. Jesus turned to them and commented on the miracle that had just happened, saying, "By wisdom I came into this world, so that they who cannot see might see, and they who do see might be made blind."

By this time, the Pharisees following the man had arrived. "Are we then blind also?" they asked Jesus.

"If you were blind, you would have no sin. But as you now testify, 'We see,' therefore, your sins remain."

They had practically asked Him to accuse them of something. They were sinners, and Jesus did not soften the truth. The Pharisees spoke angrily among themselves as we left the temple, Jesus leading us out of Jerusalem to the Mount of Olives. I felt relieved. There was nothing about the Pharisees I liked, unless it was leaving their presence.

As I looked behind us, I saw the Pharisees following only a short distance below. They were relentless. I put my hand on the hilt of the sword that hung from my hip.

THE PARABLE OF
THE GOOD SHEPHERD

We walked with Jesus up the side of the Mount of Olives to one of His favorite spots, where we could look over the city and the area around Jerusalem. The Pharisees followed behind, close enough that they would be able to overhear some of what was said, but not close enough to be part of our group.

Nearby, shepherds tended their flocks. Each shepherd had what were called sheepfolds—enclosures where the sheep were kept at night. The sides of the enclosure may be made of bushes, rocks, or man-made structures. Each sheepfold had a single narrow doorway of sorts.

As He often did, Jesus chose something at hand to use as a basis for a parable from which He would teach. This time He chose the sheepfolds. Jesus turned toward the Pharisees and spoke loudly so they would hear, saying, "He that does not enter the sheepfold by the door,] but climbs up some other way, is a thief and a robber. But He that enters by the door is the Shepherd of the sheep, and the porter opens the door to the Shepherd. The sheep hear the Shepherd's voice when He calls His sheep by name, and then He leads His sheep out of the sheepfold. When He brings forth His sheep, He goes before them, and the sheep follow Him, for they know His voice. The sheep will not follow a stranger, but will flee from him because they do not know the voices of strangers."

When Jesus finished the parable, He watched the Pharisees to see their response, but none of them understood what

He meant. "I am the door to the sheep," Jesus proclaimed. "All that came before me are thieves and robbers, but the sheep did not hear them. I am the door. If any man enters in by me, he shall be saved and shall go in and out and shall find pasture. The thief comes only to steal, to kill, and to destroy. I have come that the sheep might have life and that they might have it more abundantly. I am the Good Shepherd. The Good Shepherd gives His life for the sheep.

"He that is a hireling and not the shepherd, whose sheep are not his, sees the wolf coming and leaves the sheep and flees, and the wolf catches the sheep and scatters them. The hireling flees because he is a hireling and doesn't care for the sheep."

Beware of those who claim to be a shepherd by their own authority. If they are not authorized by Jesus Christ, they do not have His authority. They are hirelings, preaching to get gain, and only acting as if they were shepherds to receive money. As Jesus said, He is "the door."

Jesus continued, repeating His identity to the Pharisees: "I am the Good Shepherd, and I know my sheep, and I am known by my sheep, just as the Father knows me; even so, I know the Father, and I lay down my life for the sheep."

Then Jesus added something that I did not understand at the time. "I have other sheep, which are not of this fold. I must bring them also, and they shall hear my voice, and there shall be one fold and one Shepherd.

"Therefore, my Father loves me because I lay down my life in order that I might take it up again." Then He pointed to the most senior Pharisee. "No man takes it from me, but I have the power to lay it down, and I have power to take it up again. This is a commandment that I received from my Father."

The Pharisees were divided among themselves about what Jesus meant by this parable. Many mocked Him, saying,

"He has a devil!" Or, "He is mad!" Or, "Why listen to Him?" Other Pharisees, led by Nicodemus, said, "These are not the words of one that has a devil. Can a devil open the eyes of the blind?"

I marveled at Nicodemus. I wondered if he were putting his livelihood, and even his life, at risk by defending Jesus, no matter how careful he worded his remarks. I wondered what would be the consequences of his pointed defense of Jesus. I quietly respected him because he was different from his fellow Pharisees. Perhaps I have done him a disservice by saying that the Pharisees were "his fellows."

THE SUBJECT OF DIVORCE

As we walked together, some of the conspiring Pharisees came forward to test Jesus, asking, "Is it lawful for a man to send his wife away for every cause?"

At that time, divorce was the subject of endless debate. The liberal philosophy of Hillel was strongly opposed by the conservative argument of Shammai. By taking a position one way or another, either condoning divorce as Hillel or condemning it as Shammai, the Pharisees hoped to turn one of the groups against Jesus. At least, that was the way I saw it.

Instead of falling into their trap, Jesus answered them with a question, asking, "What did Moses command you?"

The Pharisee that had challenged Jesus stumbled over his words. "Moses allowed us to write a bill of divorce and to send her away."

Jesus continued, "Have you not read that He which made them in the beginning made them 'male and female'? For this cause shall a man leave his father and mother and shall cleave to his wife, and the two shall be one flesh. Therefore they are not two, but one flesh. What God has joined together, do not let man put asunder."

The Pharisees challenged Jesus, getting to the cause of the debate that had divided them, "Then why did Moses command to give a bill of divorce to send her away?"

"Because of the hardness of your hearts," Jesus answered, "Moses allowed you to divorce your wives and send them away, but it was not so from the beginning. Whosoever shall divorce his wife by sending her away—except for fornication—to marry another, commits adultery, and whoever marries her which is thus divorced commits adultery."

That group of Pharisees left us, frustrated that they could not trap Jesus in His words. I grew suspicious of the true motives of any who came seeking Jesus.

Later on, as we sat around the night's fire, we asked Jesus to expand on what He had told the Pharisees.

"Whosoever sends his wife away to marry another, commits adultery," He taught us. "And if a woman sends her husband away to marry another, she commits adultery also."

One of the disciples asked, "If this is the case for both a man and his wife, then is it good to not marry?"

I knew that lifelong celibacy was not right, but Jesus cleared up the question by explaining to whom marriage applies. "Not all men are subject to this teaching, but only those to whom it is given," He clarified. "To some it is not given. Who are they? There are some eunuchs, who were so from their mother's womb; there are also some eunuchs, made so by men; and finally, there are eunuchs, who made themselves so, thinking they were doing it for the sake of the kingdom of heaven. These are they who are unable, but let him who is not a eunuch take a wife."

I was married; so James, John, and my brother Andrew. We were not eunuchs. Marriage between a man and a woman is ordained of God, and forbidding a man to marry departs from the faith.

Further, unions between a man and a man or a woman and a woman are not ordained of God. Though they may be sanctioned by men who suppose they are greater than God, such unions are an abomination.

SUFFER THE LITTLE CHILDREN

We traveled eastward from Judea into the region of Perea, and when the evening came, crowds gathered to hear Jesus teach. Many parents brought their little children to Him, asking Jesus to lay His hands on them and bless them. I remained wary of people trying to trick Jesus into saying or doing something that could be used against Him. I love children, but I had discouraged some of the parents from approaching Jesus, trying to protect Him from those who would try to deceive Him.

As I quickly learned, this very much displeased Jesus. "Allow the little children to come to me, and do not forbid them because of such is the kingdom of heaven," He said. "Whosoever shall not receive the kingdom of God as a little child does, shall not enter therein." Then He took each child into His arms, laid his hands on them, and blessed them, one at a time.

I looked into the eyes of the parents of these children, and I saw pure faith and great joy as Jesus blessed their children. The eyes of many of the parents were filled with tears. As Jesus said, "of such is the kingdom of heaven." The kingdom of heaven is not filled with sinners.

THE RICH YOUNG MAN

As Jesus departed from the multitude that had brought their children, a young man dressed in fine robes came running toward us. I was walking next to Jesus and was prepared to defend Him if necessary. The young man ran up to Jesus and knelt in front of Him. At first, I wondered if someone was chasing the young man, but no one appeared. The young man was nearly out of breath when he looked up to Jesus and said, "Wonderful Master, what good thing shall I do that I may inherit eternal life?"

With Pharisees looking on and listening, Jesus asked him, "Why do you call me 'wonderful'? There is but One who is wonderful, and that is God." The response was intended for the ears of those Pharisees, suggesting that the young man was acknowledging Jesus as God. Then Jesus answered the young man's question, saying, "But if you would gain eternal life, keep the commandments."

"Which?" the young man asked.

Jesus cocked His head to the side and answered with a subtle smile. "You know the commandments: do not commit adultery, do not murder, do not steal, do not bear false witness, do not defraud anyone, honor your father and your mother, love your neighbor as yourself."

The young man looked up and said, "Master, all these commandments I have kept from my youth up. What do I yet lack?"

Jesus looked down into the young man's eyes, touched

him gently on his shoulder, and said, "If you would be perfect, there is but one thing you lack. Go your way, sell whatsoever you have, and give the proceeds to the poor, and you shall have treasure in heaven. Then come back, take up your cross, and follow me."

When the young man heard His words, his demeanor changed, tears filled his eyes, and he became quite sorrowful. He arose and left grieving because he had great riches. He had failed the test.

Jesus looked around and then spoke to us, saying, "It is only with great difficulty that a rich man can enter into the kingdom of heaven. Again, I tell you, it is easier for a heavy rope to go through the eye of a needle than for a rich man to enter into the kingdom of God."

That was something we were amazed to hear. If a young man, without sin, one that had obeyed the commandments all of his life, could not enter into the kingdom of heaven, we didn't know who could enter it. Our question was simple: "Then who can be saved?"

Jesus comforted us, saying, "My sons, know that it is hard for those that put their trust in riches to enter into the kingdom of God! With men it is impossible, but with God, all things are possible."

Riches were not going to be a problem for me. I had neither silver nor gold, but I knew that the Pharisees and Sadducees valued silver and gold above the Messiah. Nicodemus told us that the Pharisees were conspiring to murder Jesus because He was a threat to their corrupt ways.

THE TWELVE AS JUDGES OF
THE TRIBES OF ISRAEL

After Jesus told us how hard it was for a rich man to enter the kingdom of God, I needed to ask Him about our standing in His eyes. "Behold, we have forsaken all and followed you, just as you counseled that young man," I said. "What shall there be for us as a result?"

Jesus answered with a response that has both comforted and discomforted me many times. "You that have followed me during my trials, in the restoration, when the Son of Man shall sit on His throne of glory, I have appointed to you a kingdom, just as my Father has appointed to me. You shall eat and drink at my table and sit upon twelve thrones, judging the twelve tribes of Israel. And everyone that has forsaken homes, brothers, sisters, mothers, wives, or children, and has been persecuted for my name's sake, shall receive back a hundredfold at that time and shall inherit eternal life in the world to come, because with God all things are possible to them. But know that many that are first shall be last, and the last shall be first."

We sought peace and were told that we would be at His side, eating and drinking at His table. That was all I needed to know. Sitting on a throne and judging the twelve tribes of Israel concerned me, but knowing that I would be at His side was enough.

Jesus then shared another parable to provide additional comfort to us. "For the kingdom of heaven is likened to a man that is a householder, who went out early in the morning to hire laborers for his vineyard. When he had agreed with the laborers for a denarius a day, he sent them into his vineyard.

Later, about nine o'clock in the morning, he went out and saw others standing idly in the marketplace. He said to them, 'Go to the vineyard also, and I will give you whatever is right.' And they went their way. Again, he went out about noon, and again at three o'clock in the afternoon, and did likewise. Finally, he went out about five o'clock in the afternoon and found others standing idly. He said, 'Why do you stand here idle all day long?' And they said to him, 'Because no man has hired us.' And he said to them, 'Go into the vineyard also, and you shall receive whatever is right.'

"So when the evening came, the lord of the vineyard told his steward, 'Call the laborers and give them their wages, beginning from the last to the first.' And when they came that were hired about the eleventh hour, each laborer received a denarius, but when those that were hired first came to be paid, they expected to receive more, but each laborer received a denarius. And when they received their pay, they murmured, saying, 'Those who came to the vineyard last have worked only one hour, and you have made them our equal in pay even though we worked during the heat of the day.'

"And the lord of the house said, 'Friend, I have done you no wrong. Did you not agree to work for a denarius? Take your pay and go your way. I will give to the last the same as you received. Is it unlawful for me to do what I will with my money? Why are you giving me such an evil look? Is it because I am charitable?' "

Jesus finished His parable, saying, "So the last shall be first, and the first shall be last because many are called to the labor, but few are chosen."

At the time, I did not realize that one of the first who would be last was Judas, the traitor who was to betray Jesus.

Jesus continued to teach all who would listen in the land of Perea, and those who heard and followed Jesus without delay all received the same compensation or reward.

THE FEAST OF DEDICATION

The winter came, and Jesus returned to Jerusalem for the Feast of Dedication. Like the Feast of the Tabernacles, this celebration lasted eight days.

As Jesus walked into the temple, in the area known as Solomon's Porch, the Pharisees immediately approached Him in another attempt to entrap Him with their questions. They asked, "How long will you keep us in doubt? If you are the Messiah, tell us plainly."

At first, I wondered if the words of Nicodemus had some of them doubting their decision to kill Him. Certainly Jesus had not hidden His identity. They had clearly heard what He said to them before they tried to stone Him the last time He was in Jerusalem. My loathing for the Pharisees was difficult to control. I was not patient with fools.

"I have told you, and you did not believe my testimony," Jesus answered. "I do works in my Father's name, and my works testify of me, but you do not believe because you are not my sheep, just as I said to you before.

"My sheep hear my voice, and I know them, and they follow me. And I give them eternal life, and they shall never perish, neither shall any man pluck them out of my hand. My Father, which gave them to me, is greater than all, and no man is able to pluck them out of my Father's hand. I and my Father are one."

His last six words clearly incensed the Pharisees. Saying that He was one with the Father, perceiving that He defined

Himself as a peer equal to His Father, which would make Him God, was considered blasphemy.

In their anger, the Pharisees again picked up stones from the rubble of the construction of the temple to stone Jesus. Without panic or fear, Jesus asked them, "I have shown you many good works from my Father. For which of those works do you stone me?"

The Pharisees answered, "We do not stone you for a good work but for blasphemy, because you, being a man, make yourself God."

"Is it not written in your law, 'I have said, "You are Gods"'? If those to whom the word of God came He called Gods, and scripture cannot be broken, how can you say to Him whom the Father has sanctified and sent into the world, 'You blaspheme!' because I said, 'I am the Son of God'? If I am not doing the works of my Father, do not believe me, but if I am doing them, even if you do not believe me, believe the works I do, so that you may know and believe that the Father is in me and I in Him."

As the Pharisees again sought to capture Jesus to accuse Him before the Sanhedrin, He escaped out of their midst untouched. Truly, "His time" had not yet come.

It was becoming clear to me why Jesus had commanded us to no longer testify that He was the Christ. He was protecting us from the persecution of the wicked Jews. It was also clear to me that they would not give up until they had taken Him and accused Him before the Sanhedrin.

After Jesus removed Himself from the temple grounds, He left Jerusalem and returned beyond Jordan to Bethabara, the place where John had first baptized. We all stayed there for several weeks.

Many believers came in search of Jesus. They told us that John the Baptist had not done miracles but that he had prophesied of Jesus, and all of the things he had spoken about Jesus were true. Many who came believed in Jesus. I was pleased to have believers surround Him, especially while the Sanhedrin was plotting to silence Him.

On Our Way to Jerusalem

While we were in Perea, north of Jericho, Mary and Martha sent for Jesus because their brother, Lazarus, was very sick. Their message pleaded with Jesus to come to Bethany and bless Lazarus, saying, "Lord, behold our brother, whom you love, is sick."

Jesus knew and loved Mary, Martha, and their brother, Lazarus. He sent a message back to them, saying, "Lazarus is not sick so that he will die, but his sickness is for the glory of God, that the Son of God might be glorified thereby."

I noticed that He referred to Himself as the Son of God, not as the Son of Man. I knew that it was true, but I was not allowed to testify of it.

I also knew that Jesus cared deeply for Mary, Martha, and Lazarus, so I was surprised when He did not immediately begin the journey to Bethany. Clearly Jesus had something different in mind than just healing Lazarus, but I had no idea what it was. Instead of leaving promptly, He stayed two more days in Perea. Only then did He say to us, "Let us return to Judea."

On our way to Jerusalem, Jesus took the Apostles aside and, referring to Himself in the third person, confided in us, "Behold, we are now going up to Jerusalem, where the Son of Man will be betrayed to the chief priests and to the scribes, and they will condemn Him to death. They will deliver Him to the Gentiles to mock, and to scourge, and to spit upon, and to crucify Him. And the third day He shall rise again."

My mind reeled, and my ears rang at the thought. The time had come! This would be His last journey to Jerusalem. He was going there to be scourged and crucified! Just before His Transfiguration and shortly afterward in Galilee, He had told us that He was going to be killed. Now He let us know how and where He would die. I was sickened as I contemplated Jesus being scourged and crucified.

"But not yet," Jesus assured us, indicating that Jerusalem was the place where He would be crucified, but it was not yet "His time." My arms and legs were still weak, my head began to ache, and I still felt sick. Then I forced myself to straighten up. I was not a weakling! I would not act like one.

Some of the disciples were afraid of what was going to happen, thinking it might happen to them too.

I was not afraid of suffering and dying alongside Jesus, but I had seen crucifixions, and I was sickened that He would suffer such a painful, humiliating death. I resolved that if it happened that I were crucified next to Jesus, I would face it as an honor to be next to Him in death and with Him in the eternities. Could a disciple ask for a greater privilege?

THE GREATEST CALL

Before we left for Bethany, the mother of James and John, the wife of Zebedee, came forward and knelt before Jesus. She was a true disciple who loved Jesus and followed Him. She asked Him, "Will you grant the desire of a mother's heart?"

Jesus asked, "What is it you desire of me?"

Knowing that Jesus had told the Apostles that they would be with Him in His kingdom, she said, "Grant that these, my two sons, may sit—one on your right hand and one your left hand—in your kingdom."

"You do not know what you ask," He responded. Then, turning to her sons James and John, He asked, "Are you able to drink of the cup that I shall drink and to be baptized with the baptism with which I shall be baptized?"

Without a true understanding, they said, "We are able." I knew these men. In their hearts, they were willing to pay whatever price was asked to be with Jesus in the eternities; they were good men. I believed they were willing to die with Him. That made three of us.

"You shall indeed drink of the cup that I drink of and be baptized with the baptism that I am baptized with, but who shall sit on my right hand and on my left is not mine to give. It is my Father's, and it shall be given to them for whom it is prepared by my Father."

And when the rest of the Apostles heard their request, we were somewhat indignant, a bit upset at James and John because they asked to be above us. Jesus called us together and said, "You know that the kings of the Gentiles exercise dominion over the Gentiles and are called benefactors. Those who exercise authority are given honors by men, but it shall not be so among you. Whosoever will be great among you, let him be your minister, and whosoever will be chief among you, let him be your servant. Be as the Son of Man, who did not come to be ministered to, but to minister, and to give His life as ransom for many. I ask you, which is greater in the world, he that sits at meat or he that serves? Is it not he that sits at meat? Yet I am among you as the One that serves."

There was no question. He served us all, blessed us all, taught us all, and comforted us all. At the same time, He was the greatest of all men but not so honored by the world. I tried to follow His example in service, but it was difficult to love everyone. I certainly didn't know how He could love the Pharisees and the Sadducees.

I was starting to comprehend that the value of my life was based on what I did to help others, especially to help them know Jesus and follow His commandments. I came to understand that the greatness of a man is not measured by the honors men bestowed upon him, but by how many people he helped in his life. Jesus helped all of us in ways we could not help ourselves, but no honors were granted Him.

THE BLIND MAN HEALED

As we came nearer to Jericho, another multitude joined us and started following Jesus. Near the wayside, just outside the city, there was a blind beggar named Bartimaeus. As the noisy multitude approached, he asked of anyone that would answer, "What is going on? Who is this?" Someone toward the front of the crowd told him that it was Jesus of Nazareth who was coming into Jericho. Bartimaeus knew of Jesus, and when he heard Him passing by, Bartimaeus cried loudly, "Have mercy on me, O Lord Jesus, Son of David."

Those near Bartimaeus rebuked him because they thought he should not be yelling at Jesus. At this, he repeated his plea even louder, shouting, "Have mercy on me, O Lord, Son of David."

Jesus stopped the procession and stood still to hear what Bartimaeus had to say. Jesus took compassion on him and instructed me to bring Bartimaeus closer. I crossed over the road to the blind man and said, "Be of good cheer and rise. The Master asks for you." Bartimaeus removed his jacket and stood slowly. Then he walked stiffly with me as I guided him to Jesus.

When we stood in front of Jesus, the Lord asked Bartimaeus, "What would you have me do to you?"

He answered without hesitation: "Lord, I would that I might receive my sight."

Jesus touched the blind man's eyes, and immediately he received sight. Then Jesus said, "Go your way. Your faith has made you whole." Rather than return to his home, Bartimaeus joined the multitude and followed Jesus. The multitude gave praise to God when they saw the miracle Jesus performed.

I expected when we entered Jericho that we would pass directly through the city, but I soon learned otherwise. The chief tax collector of the city was a rich man of rather short stature. His name was Zacchaeus, and he wanted to meet Jesus. The multitude was so tightly crowded around Jesus, and Zacchaeus was so small, that he could neither get close to nor see the Lord.

Zacchaeus watched as the crowd passed by. Figuring which direction Jesus would be walking next, Zacchaeus ran ahead and climbed into a sycamore tree so he would have the privilege of seeing Jesus when He passed by.

As he hoped, Jesus took the route toward him. When Jesus arrived at the tree, He looked up and saw the short publican watching from the tree. Jesus called out to him, saying, "Zacchaeus, hurry and come down from that tree because I must stay at your house today."

Zacchaeus joyfully obeyed. He hastily climbed down from the tree and excitedly received Jesus into his home. When some of those following Jesus saw Him enter the publican's house, they murmured, saying that Jesus was the guest of a sinner.

Zacchaeus stood respectfully at the dinner and said to Jesus, "Lord, please know that I give half of my goods to the poor, and if I have taken anything from any man by false accusation, I have restored it to him fourfold.

Jesus accepted his repentance. "This day, salvation has come to this house because you also are a son of Abraham, and the Son of Man has come to find and save that which was lost," He told Zacchaeus.

The Pharisees were greatly displeased.

PARABLE OF THE MINAS,
OR "POUNDS"

That evening, when we were alone in the house of Zacchaeus, Jesus privately instructed us, the twelve Apostles. Later, as I looked back, I realized that he was spending even more time teaching us, taking every chance to prepare us for the time when He would be no longer be with us. At the time, my mind was more focused on the fact that He would be crucified, and my heart still ached at the thought. Sometimes I got lost in my thoughts, something I had never done before. I was a man of action, not a man given to much pondering. I forced myself to pay attention to what was happening, to be aware of the Pharisees and their spies, and to listen to every word Jesus spoke.

I came to know that He used parables so we could remember His instructions easier and let their meanings unfold in our minds as we remembered them. And whether He was talking about Living Water at Jacob's well, about the Good Shepherd near a sheepfold, about the Bread of Life after feeding five thousand, or about the Light of the World standing in the temple during the Festival of Lights, He relied on what was around us to teach us.

Jesus explained that because we were leaving Jericho and because those in Jerusalem expected the kingdom of God to immediately appear upon His arrival, we needed to be prepared for what was actually going to happen. He shared another parable relating to our political history.

At that moment, we were within view of the magnificent

palace built by Archelaus, one of the wicked sons of Herod the Great. After Herod suffered a painful death in his summer palace in Jericho in 4 BC, Archelaus went to Rome to plead with Emperor Augustus that he be the one to receive the kingdom of his father, instead of one of his brothers. Archelaus was hated by the Jews because of his merciless acts of cruelty. Prior to departing for Rome, Archelaus had mercilessly massacred three thousand Jews who had congregated in rebellion at the temple on the eve of Passover. A congregation of Pharisees also went to Rome, but they went to plead with Augustus, asking that he not appoint Archelaus to succeed Herod as king. They asked to be ruled by the Sanhedrin, under the consent of the Roman Consul in Damascus. They even preferred the appointment of Antipas, Archelaus's brother.

Emperor Augustus compromised with Archelaus, giving him a portion of the kingdom, the diminished title of ethnarch, and a promise that he could earn the title of king if he ruled this smaller region well. Hearing that Archelaus would be their leader, the Jews revolted, and one of Herod's slaves started a fire that destroyed the palace at Jericho. The Roman army brutally crucified around two thousand Jews before the rebellion was finally suppressed. Archelaus proved to be a cruel despot and was allowed to rule only until AD 6, when Caesar Augustus deposed him and added his realm to the Roman province of Syria.

"A certain nobleman went into a far country to take upon himself a kingdom and thence to return to his home," Jesus began. "Before he left, he called ten of his servants and delivered a silver coin with a weight equal to a mina to each of them, saying, 'Use this and do business until I return.'

"But his citizens hated him and sent a message after him, saying, 'We will not have this man to reign over us.'

"And it came to pass that after he received the kingdom, he returned from the far country. Upon his arrival, he commanded the servants that had received money to be called to him to report how much money every man had gained by trading.

"The first man came to him, saying, 'Lord, I have increased your silver coin by ten coins.'

"The nobleman said, 'Well done. Because you have been faithful over a very little, you are granted authority over ten cities.'

"The second man came to him, saying, 'Lord, I have increased your silver coin by five coins.'

"The nobleman said likewise to him, 'You are granted authority over five cities.'

"Another man came to him, saying, 'Lord, behold, here is your silver coin, which I have kept wrapped in a napkin because I feared you, because I know you to be a harsh man without generosity, and you pick up what you did not lay down and reap what you did not sow.'

"The nobleman said, 'Wicked servant! I shall judge you out of your own mouth. You knew that I was a harsh man, without generosity, picking up what I did not lay down, and reaping what I did not sow. Why did you not give my money to a lender, that upon my return I might have at least collected interest when I received my money back?'

"The servant did not answer but hung his head in silence. The nobleman said to the servants that were standing by, 'Take the money from him and give it to him that increased ten coins.'

"But Lord, he already has ten coins,' his servants objected.

"The nobleman answered, 'I say to you that unto everyone that has gained from what he was given shall be given more. And everyone that has not gained from what he was given, even that which he was given shall be taken away from him. Now bring those forward who rebelled and declared themselves to be my enemies, those who would not have me reign over them.' They were brought forward, as commanded. Then the nobleman ordered solemnly, 'Slay them.' "

I thought the nobleman's order was severe, and I did not understand at first, but as I contemplated the parable, it became clear to me that the nobleman was not Archelaus, but Jesus. He was the one that would be leaving to a far land to receive the kingdom from His Father. Those around the nobleman that did not want Him to reign over them were those of the house of Israel, the wicked Jews who had rejected Jesus as the Messiah, and they would not receive what He only could offer them. I knew that not receiving eternal life would be their death. As history unfolded, the Jews were literally slain by the Romans.

I applied the principle to me, and I saw that the Apostles could also be considered His servants. Each of us received the same authority from Jesus. What we did with it, how we fulfilled our calling, would be up to us. Each of us would receive from Him based upon what we did with what He gave us. It unfolded clearly in my mind, and it seemed to me that I was getting better at understanding parables.

LAZARUS RESTORED TO LIFE

The next morning, Jesus said, "Let us return to Judea."
I was relieved that we would be visiting Lazarus, but I was concerned about being in Judea because that was where Jesus would be crucified. His words continued to echo in my ears. I knew that the cowardly Jews of Jerusalem would have to manipulate the Romans to execute Him for them. While I knew what the Jews were going to do, I didn't know how they would do it. Jesus had escaped them previously, so I knew the Jews would not be able to arrest Him unless He allowed it.

"Master, the Jews have only recently sought to stone you, and you are again returning to Jerusalem openly?" I asked.

"Are there not twelve hours of daylight?" Jesus answered. "If a man walks during the day, he won't stumble because he sees by the sunlight of this world, but if a man walks during the night, he will stumble because there is no sunlight in him."

His answer was obvious. Yes, if we traveled during the day, our journey would be safer, but His answer meant more than that. He had things yet to do and limited time to get them done.

As we left Jericho, Jesus said, "Our friend Lazarus sleeps, but I'm going to him so I may awaken him from his sleep."

"Lord, if he is sleeping, that will be a cure for him," I said, misunderstanding and thinking that Jesus was talking about actual sleep. But He was speaking symbolically of death.

Jesus replied bluntly, "Lazarus is dead, and I am pleased

for your sakes that I was not there so that you may believe. So let us go to Lazarus."

Lazarus was dead? When did that happen? If he had been dead very long, his body may have already begun to decompose, so what would Jesus do for him? If I were one of the believers, or if I wished to see a sign that Jesus had divine power, it might be realized in seeing Jesus raise Lazarus from the dead. On the other hand, I had no doubt that Jesus was the Son of God. He didn't need to prove anything to me.

Upon hearing that we were headed to Judea, where the wicked Jews were waiting to kill Jesus, Thomas, the twin, said, "Let us all go, that we may die with Jesus."

Thomas said what several of us were thinking, but I wasn't going to Jerusalem to die. I was going to be with Jesus, just as I had been with Him since I met Him. Whatever should happen, would happen. Still, Thomas spoke for all of us. Thomas was the first one to offer to die with Jesus. It was in all of our hearts, but it was Thomas who boldly spoke the words.

As we neared Bethany, word came that Lazarus had been in the grave for four days, which was significant. There was a tradition among Jews that someone was not certain to be dead until they had been dead more than three days. A dead body was certain to stink after three days, signaling that the person was certainly dead. Traditionally we held the funeral and entombed our loved ones the same day as their death. Then, in the days following the funeral, family members would return to the tomb to anoint and wrap the body. Because four days had passed, Lazarus's body had undoubtedly started to decompose.

Bethany was less than two miles east of Jerusalem, and a number of friends and family were there from Jerusalem, mourning with Mary and Martha. As a long-standing tradition, mourners brought food and drink and grieved with the family.

Word came to Martha that Jesus was on His way, so she left her home and rushed out to meet Him, leaving Mary with the mourners. Martha expressed both her disappointment and her great faith in Jesus, saying, "Lord, if you had been here, my brother would not have died, but I know that even now, whatsoever you will ask of God, He will give you."

"Your brother shall rise again," He told her.

Thinking Jesus was referring to resurrection as He had taught her previously, she said, "I know that he will rise again in the resurrection at the last day."

Jesus comforted her further, adding, "I am the Resurrection and the Life. He that believes in me, though he were dead, shall live, and whosoever lives and believes in me shall never die. Do you believe this?"

"Yes, Lord, I believe that you are the Christ, the Son of God, which was prophesied to come into the world," she answered in complete faith.

Jesus asked Martha to invite Mary to join them but to not tell anyone else in the home what He had said. She obediently excused herself and ran home. When she arrived, she found her sister lying on the bed resting; her grief had left her weary. She secretly spoke to Mary, saying, "The Master is here, and He is asking for you." Mary immediately arose, and they went to meet Jesus.

As Mary hastily left with Martha, the mourners followed behind her, saying, "She is going to the grave to weep." It was not curiosity, but courtesy that caused them to follow her. Part of our tradition was for mourners to accompany those grieving the loss of a loved one and weep with them. Family members were not left to weep alone.

The grieving sisters had only a short distance to walk to meet Jesus. When Mary found Him, she fell at His feet in total grief and, echoing Martha's words, said, "Lord, if you had been here, my brother would not have died." Certainly they had discussed this in the last few days.

When Jesus saw her weeping and that the Jews accompanying her were weeping also, I heard Him sigh deeply, then groan from within Himself. It was obvious to me that He was greatly troubled; the weight of their sadness burdened His heart. Jesus asked simply, "Where have you laid him?"

Mary and Martha said, "Come and see, Lord." Then they led the way to the place where the body of Lazarus was entombed.

As we walked together, Jesus wept quietly.

The mourners said, "Behold how He loved him!"

I knew Jesus. He was not weeping at the death of Lazarus but at the profound grief being suffered by His dear friends, Mary and Martha. I knew that He was feeling their anguish. He understood them as no mortal could because He is the Son of God.

Among the mourners were skeptics. One of them said, "This man who opened the eyes of the blind man, could He not have caused that Lazarus would have lived and not died?"

I watched Jesus walk with Mary and Martha, He grimaced and groaned within Himself as we reached the tomb. I knew that He was feeling their pain, but I also knew that the wickedness of the Jews was a great burden on Him.

The tomb was a cave, with a stone covering the doorway. Without delay or ceremony, Jesus simply directed some of the mourners, "Take the stone away."

Martha voiced the Jewish tradition, "Lord, by this time he stinks because he has been dead for four days."

Jesus looked into her bloodshot eyes, swollen from many tears, and reminded her, "Did I not say that if you would believe, you would see the glory of God?"

A couple of mourners moved the stone away from the tomb. Then, lifting His eyes toward Heaven in prayer, Jesus offered thanks to His Father, saying, "Father, I thank Thee that Thou hast heard me. I know that Thou always hear my prayers, both spoken and unspoken, but I speak these words aloud so the people standing nearby may hear and believe that Thou hast sent me."

And when Jesus had thus prayed, He cried with a loud voice, saying, "Lazarus! Come forth!"

We watched in amazement as Lazarus shuffled to the doorway of the grave, bound hand and foot with burial clothes and his face wrapped with a napkin. When Lazarus stopped at the doorway, Jesus said, "Loose him. Let him go."

At first, no one moved. Then Mary and Martha cautiously stepped forward and started to unwrap Lazarus. Everyone else stood quietly and watched. As soon as his face was visible, our old friend Lazarus was standing there, eyes open, looking quite healthy. Stunned silence was followed by shocked murmurings. Lazarus was alive!

This was the third time I saw Jesus raise someone from the dead. The first was the young man in the city of Nain. The second was the daughter of Jairus in Capernaum. I recognized that in all three cases, Jesus raised the dead in response to the profound grief of a family member. It spoke of His compassion.

As Lazarus came out of the grave, the parable Jesus told of Lazarus and the rich man came forcefully to my mind. In it, Jesus spoke of Lazarus being raised from the dead, the only time He had ever named a character in His parables. The point of the parable was that no one would be convinced to repent by seeing Lazarus raised from the dead. As I watched Lazarus being unwrapped, I knew it would be true. Some of those watching were skeptics and would never be convinced that Jesus was the Christ. They would think this was some kind of trick. I had come to know that miracles do not change people's hearts, but they do convict them of the wickedness in their hearts.

I have since learned that these individuals raised from the dead were simply restored to their mortal life. None were "resurrected" because they were not restored to an immortal body. Those who were restored to life were still mortal, and each of them would yet die once more.

THE SANHEDRIN'S
MURDER CONSPIRACY

Those that came to the house of Lazarus to mourn his death saw a miracle instead. And many of those, upon seeing the miracle, believed in Jesus. Of course, there were also spies at hand who rushed back to Jerusalem to report to the Pharisees that Jesus had performed another miracle.

In response, we heard that the Pharisees called a meeting of the Council of the Sanhedrin. Their leaders were mostly Sadducees, with Pharisees making up the general membership. A Sadducee presided over the Council, a man selected at the whim of the Roman Prefect to serve a one-year term. His name was Caiaphas, and his spies reported directly to him.

Members of the Sanhedrin had no doubt that Jesus had performed many miracles, including the raising of Lazarus. Instead of honoring His power to do miracles and wanting to know the source of that power, they viewed Jesus as a threat to their entrenched power and profitable corruption. They wanted the Messiah to be a political leader, not a spiritual one, especially not one that would question their corrupt ways—as Jesus had.

I kept thinking of the parable of the rich man and the beggar named Lazarus. The words Jesus attributed to Abraham echoed in my mind: "If they do not hear Moses and the prophets, they will not be persuaded by one man that rose from the dead either." Fulfilling what Jesus had taught, the Sanhedrin did not care to hear what Lazarus might have to say about Jesus after he was raised from the dead. Instead, they asked each other, "What shall we do? This man does many miracles. If we let Him alone, all men will believe in Him, and the Romans will come and take away both our place and our nation."

They wanted a messiah that would not interfere in religious matters. The Sanhedrin held the power to interpret and enforce the law, and they viewed themselves as essential to the survival of the house of Israel. If the common people were to follow Jesus and His teachings, no one would need them, and those in power would lose their positions—powerful positions that allowed them to amass great wealth. Jesus was more of a threat than the Romans; they had to deal with Him.

Caiaphas, the arrogant high priest selected and approved by the Romans, presided over their conspiracy. He spoke condescendingly to the Pharisees: "You know nothing at all! Nor have you contemplated that it is expedient for this council to decide that one man should die for the good of the people so that the whole nation does not perish."

He did not speak as an ordinary Sadducee, but as the high priest, the one that led them all. His words implemented the murder conspiracy. Jesus needed to die to preserve their power.

As Caiaphas uttered those words, he launched the plot to murder Jesus. From that day forward, the conspiracy to put Jesus to death gained momentum. Not only did the Jews ignore that Lazarus had been raised from the dead, but they also revolted against it, fulfilling the prophetic parable.

Secret words of warning came to us from Nicodemus. From that day forth, Jesus did not walk openly among the Jews. Instead, he left Judea and went into the country near the wilderness, into the city called Ephraim. We all remained there, out of the sight of the Sanhedrin, from winter until early spring.

Six Days before Passover

As the annual Passover approached, people started leaving their own countries to travel up to Jerusalem to purify themselves as part of the Passover. Religious enthusiasm filled Jerusalem, spreading throughout the region of Judea. Stories of Lazarus being raised from the dead were on everyone's lips. Many went to the temple looking for Jesus, wanting to know whether or not He was the Messiah. They asked one another, "What do you think? Will He come to the feast or not?"

As a result of the order by Caiaphas, a standing directive required that any man learning the location of Jesus must immediately report it to the Sanhedrin so Jesus could be arrested.

Just six days before Passover, Jesus returned to the home of Mary and Martha in Bethany. They had the honor of preparing and serving His supper. Of course, Lazarus was one of those who sat at the table with Jesus. Many Jews were there too, not just to see and hear Jesus, but also to see Lazarus, the man Jesus had raised from the dead.

As Martha served the supper, it was convenient for Mary to anoint the feet of Jesus as He ate. She took a pound of very costly ointment of spikenard and anointed His feet, then wiped them with her hair. The aroma of the expensive ointment filled the house.

None other than Judas Iscariot, the son of Simon, objected, saying, "Why was this ointment not sold for three hundred denarii and the money given to the poor?"

I knew that Judas was not concerned for the poor. While he did act as treasurer for the Apostles, keeping our funds in his bag, it was no secret that Judas was a thief. I also knew that Judas had no right to ask about the ointment because it belonged to Mary.

Jesus defended Mary, saying, "Let her alone. She has kept this ointment against the day of my burial. You will always have the poor with you, but you will not always have me with you."

His words went through my heart like a sword. Was Mary anointing Him in advance of His funeral? I watched, imagining her in a crypt anointing His lifeless body instead of at a meal among friends. My stomach was sickened at the thought. I closed my eyes and shook my head to end what I was seeing. I found that I could not eat.

Word soon got back to the Sanhedrin where Jesus was and what He was doing. The Sanhedrin viewed Jesus as a threat to their entrenched power, and they also viewed the living, breathing Lazarus as a threat. Their murderous conspiracy expanded to include the murder of Lazarus; his very life testified of Jesus and caused many to follow Him. The Sanhedrin watched as their influence was encroached upon by the son of a carpenter, the man I knew to be the Son of God.

FIVE DAYS BEFORE PASSOVER

On the fifth day before the Passover, Jesus left Bethany, crossing the Mount of Olives toward Jerusalem. Jesus rested on the hillside near Bethpage and sent two Apostles ahead. "Go into the village that lies ahead," He instructed, "and you will straightaway find a colt that no man has sat upon. The colt will be tied, and a foal will be with her. Untie them and bring them to me. If anyone says anything to you, tell them, 'The Lord has need of them,' and straightaway, he will send them.

Later I recognized that all this had been done in fulfillment of the prophecy spoken by the prophet Zechariah: "Rejoice greatly, O daughter of Zion; shout, O daughter of Jerusalem. Behold, thy King comes to Thee. He is just, He has salvation, and He is lowly, and will ride upon an ass. Along with the colt will be the foal of an ass."

The two Apostles went and did as Jesus commanded. They found the colt tied outside of a door in a place where two streets meet. They untied the colt and brought it. And, as He had prophesied, there were some who asked, 'What are you doing, untying that colt?' They responded as Jesus had commanded. As He had prophesied, they let the Apostles go their way. The Apostles then put their coats on the colt and helped Jesus to sit on the animal.

As Jesus rode around to the western side of the Mount of Olives, Jerusalem came into our view. Jesus stopped, halting our whole procession. Jesus dismounted from the colt and surveyed Jerusalem. I watched His face as He stood gazing at the city. I saw much sadness in His countenance; tears flowed down his cheeks. A lump gathered in my throat as I watched Him, and I wondered if He was seeing the future of Jerusalem.

Jesus wept as if in mourning for the dead, and then He prophesied, saying, "If only you would have known, at least on this day, the things that would bring you peace! But now they are hidden from your eyes. In the days that shall come upon you, your enemies shall build fortifications around you and surround you, keeping you in from every side. They shall lay siege and level you even to the ground and your children within you. They will not leave one stone upon another within your walls because you knew not the time of your visitation."

After a time of silence, Jesus remounted the colt and somberly continued His journey down the rocky slope into Jerusalem. Our procession traveled quietly, but the crowds that awaited Him would be exuberant to see Him.

I was surprised that word had spread so quickly that Jesus was entering Jerusalem. As He rode into the city, multitudes awaited Him, spreading their clothes along the way—a tradition reserved only for kings. They had cut branches from palm trees and placed them on the ground in front of Him. When they saw Him, they cried, "Hosanna to the Son of David. Blessed is the King of Israel that comes in the name of the Lord. Hosanna in the highest!"

I think it was a bittersweet moment for Jesus. His heart was heavy with the doom that He had just prophesied was awaiting the city. At that singular moment, however, He was being treated like the King He was. I remember that day as the one time He was most honored by the most people. As He entered the gates of the city, all of Jerusalem was moved, asking, "Who is this?"

The multitude following Jesus answered enthusiastically,

saying, "This is Jesus, the prophet of Nazareth of Galilee." Yes, there were both Galileans and people from Nazareth in the multitude, and they were all proud that Jesus was from Galilee. They were even proud that He was from Nazareth, the area often mocked. Some of those in the multitude had been there when He called Lazarus out of his grave, raising him from the dead. These believers, all of which had heard of the miracle of Lazarus, testified loudly and boldly of Jesus.

The Pharisees were there—watching, waiting, and plotting. Nicodemus observed with a delightful note of sarcasm to a fellow Pharisee, "Do you see that you do not prevail over Jesus? Behold, the world follows Him!" We reveled in the impotence of the wicked Jews as they tried to quiet believers in the Son of God. It was a small moment, but it spoke of things to come.

In obvious frustration, one of the Pharisees called to Jesus, saying, "Master, rebuke your disciples!" They demanded that He silence those who were testifying of Him. *Why would He do that?* I asked myself.

In response to the irritated Pharisees, Jesus testified, "I tell you that if these people should hold their peace, the stones would immediately cry out."

I knew the truth of His statement. There was a certain feeling of electricity in the air that could not be stopped by mortal man, and the Son of God would not do it. It was a day like no other. I testify that there will be another day when He will be honored as the Son of God, but that day will not be seen until He returns.

Jesus continued His triumphal entry into Jerusalem, heading to the temple. Once there, He dismounted and entered the sacred edifice.

Philip, among those at the rear of the procession, was approached by certain Greeks who had come to observe the feast and to worship. They came to Philip and said, "Sir, we would like to see Jesus." Because they were not Jewish, they were only allowed to enter the temple as far as the Court of the Gentiles. Philip told the Greeks to be patient and left them outside. He found my brother Andrew, and both of them went into the temple to be with Jesus.

JESUS SPEAKING IN THE TEMPLE

From the moment Jesus arrived at the temple, the multitudes swarmed around Him, pleading with Him to speak. Like everyone else, I wanted to hear what He would have to say. Never had He been surrounded by such fanfare and so many joyful believers. Stories of Jesus raising Lazarus from the dead were whispered. Believers pointed toward Jesus, telling their friends, "He is the prophet that raised Lazarus!" The crowd honored and praised Jesus, and now they waited for Him to speak.

Jesus gathered the Apostles around Him and sat in the midst of us. Then He said, "The hour has come that the Son of Man should be glorified."

I can testify that on that day, He was glorified by all who came. No Pharisees, Sadducees, scribes, or any manner of wickedness could prevail over the Son of God. What was prophesied since the beginning could not be stopped by the wickedness of evil men.

Jesus continued speaking to us. "A kernel of wheat lives alone until it falls to the ground and dies, but only when it dies and is buried can it bring forth much fruit. So He that loves his life shall lose it; and he that hates his mortal life shall have eternal life. If any man would serve me, let him follow me. Where I am, my servant shall also be. Know that if any man will serve me, my Father will honor him."

Jesus paused to let His words sink in, so His listeners would understand what was required of them if they chose to follow Him. His symbolism was clear.

I am a simple fisherman, and I chose to serve Jesus—not for the eternal life He spoke of, but for the honor of serving the Son of God. I bore witness of Him before, I do so again, and I will always do so. Jesus is the Christ, the Son of God.

Jesus spoke again. This time His voice was different, a bit quieter, almost meek—but not fearful. He said, "Now my soul is troubled about what lies ahead. Shall I say, 'Father, save me from this hour'? I cannot do that. What lies ahead is the reason I came to this hour."

Jesus looked around at all of us, His Apostles surrounding Him in the temple. He gazed into our faces, one at a time. Then He stood, looked upward, lifted His open palms, and uttered four words, surrendering His will to God, "Father, glorify thy name!"

Then came a deep, booming voice from heaven, the magnificent voice of God, which filled the temple, saying, "I have both glorified it and will glorify it again!" Those who were standing in the temple that day, those who had the privilege of hearing the voice of God, said that the voice thundered. Others said, "An angel spoke to Him." God had testified of His Son!

In the silence that followed, Jesus spoke, "This voice did not come for my sake, but for your sakes. Now is the time of judgment of this world. Now is the time that the Prince of this world shall be cast out. And if I, the Son of Man, am lifted up from the earth, I will draw all unto me."

I know now that Jesus was referring to the death He would suffer when lifted up on the cross. Those that did not know He was to be crucified said, "We have been taught out of the law that Christ lives forever. How is it you say, 'The Son of Man must be lifted up'? Who is this Son of Man?"

They were entangled in tradition, looking for the messiah created in the minds of their fathers, not the Messiah of the

I AM PETER

law of Moses. The prophet spoke only of His Kingdom and His throne being established forever.

Being in the temple, where lamps were set to light the darkness, Jesus did as He often did and incorporated His surroundings into His allegory. "Yet a little while longer is the Light with you. Walk while you have the Light, lest darkness come upon you, for he that walks in darkness does not know where he is going. While you have Light, believe in the Light so you may be children of the Light."

Jesus paused, knowing that they doubted Him to be the Messiah because He was not what they expected. He warned them, saying, "He that believes in me does not believe in me but in Him that sent me. And he that sees me sees Him that sent me. I have come as a Light into the world that whosoever believes me should not live in darkness.

"If any man hear my words and believe not, I do not judge him, for I came not to judge the world but to save it. He that rejects me and receives not my words has one that will judge him, which is the word that I have spoken. The same shall judge him on the last day, for I have not spoken of myself but as I was told by my Father, which sent me. He gave me a commandment about what I should say and what I should speak. And I know that His commandment is life everlasting. Therefore, whatsoever I speak, I speak as the Father spoke to me."

After Jesus finished speaking, He left the temple, but no one could follow or find Him because He hid himself.

What I witnessed next I could not believe. Even though He had performed so many miracles, even though they had heard the voice of God, the people did not believe in Him. These were the same people who were there when Lazarus rose from the grave. They were the ones that lay their clothes on the ground in front of Him and cut palm fronds to place in the way He traveled. They rejected Him because He was

321

not the kind of messiah they wanted. Will all mankind be like the Jews of Jerusalem?

The rejection by the Jews fulfilled the words of Isaiah that say, "Lord, who has believed our report? And to whom has the arm of the Lord been revealed?" Therefore they could not believe because, as Isaiah said, "He has blinded their eyes and hardened their hearts that they should not see with their eyes nor understand with their hearts and be converted that I should heal them." Isaiah truly foresaw the glory of Jesus and prophesied of Him.

Among those listening in the temple that day were those from the Sanhedrin, and many of them, in addition to Nicodemus, believed in Jesus. However, they dared not express their belief because the other Pharisees would have them barred from the synagogue. These men remained silent because they loved the praise of men more than the praise of God.

After Jesus left the temple, He returned to the hillside above Jerusalem. He looked over the city again and prayed. We joined Him as He concluded His prayer, and we continued our journey back to Bethany.

THE PRIESTS AND THE PARABLES

When we arrived at the temple, the chief priests and elders of the people were again awaiting Jesus. They had conspired during the night to interrogate Him and use His words to trap Him, giving them cause to arrest Him and accuse Him before the Sanhedrin.

Knowing that no man was allowed to take priesthood authority upon himself, they asked, "By what authority do you do the things you do? Who gave you this authority?"

Jesus looked them over and then responded quietly, "I will also ask you one question, which if you answer me, I will likewise answer by what authority I do these things. By what authority did John baptize? Was it from heaven or of men?" He paused to hear their answer, and when they did not respond, He added, "Answer me!"

The chief priests and elders quickly huddled together to consider His question. They concluded that they dared not answer Him. They said, "If we say, 'From heaven,' He will say to us, 'Why do you not then believe him?' But if we say, 'Of men,' we are afraid of what the people will do, for they all esteem John as a prophet indeed." So they answered Jesus, saying, "We cannot tell you."

Jesus answered them, saying, "Neither will I tell you by what authority I do these things."

The chief priests and elders were outwitted and frustrated. Jesus posed another question: "What do you think of this? A man had two sons, and he came to the first and said,

'Son, go work today in my vineyard.' The son answered, 'I will not,' but afterward he repented and went to work. And he man came to his second son and said likewise. And he answered, saying, 'I go, sir,' but then did not go. Which of the two did the will of his father?"

The chief priests and elders said, "The first son."

They gave the only answer they could, but it condemned them. The first son, the one who went to work after disobeying his father, represented all repentant sinners. The second son, the one who promised to obey his father but did not, represented the self-righteous, pious chief priests and elders. They condemned themselves, and I smiled.

Jesus said to them, "The publicans and the harlots go into the kingdom of God before you because John came to you in the way of righteousness, but you did not believe him. The publicans and harlots believed him, but after you saw him, you did not repent and believe him."

The Jews said nothing because nothing would remove the sting of His pointed condemnation.

THE PARABLE OF THE
WICKED HUSBANDMEN

Jesus continued to convict the Pharisees and Sadducees, saying, "Hear another parable. There was a certain householder who planted a vineyard. He hedged around it, dug a winepress in it, and built a tower. Then he let it out to husbandmen and went into a far country. And when the time to harvest the fruit drew near, the lord of the vineyard sent his servants to the husbandmen, that they might receive the fruits of his vineyard.

"The husbandmen received the lord's servants shamefully. They beat the first one and sent him away empty-handed. He sent a second, and they stoned him, wounded him in the head, and sent him away, also empty handed. He sent a third, and they killed him. Then the lord of the vineyard sent more servants than the first time, and the husbandmen did the same to them—beating, stoning, and killing them.

"Last of all, the lord sent his son saying, 'They will reverence my son,' but when the husbandmen saw the son, they said among themselves, 'This is the heir. Come, let us kill him and seize his inheritance.' And they caught the lord's son and cast him out of the vineyard and slew him." Then Jesus asked them, "When the lord of the vineyard comes, what will he do to those husbandmen?"

They offered, "He will miserably destroy those wicked men and will let out his vineyard to other husbandmen, which shall render to him the fruits in their season." Then one chief priest gasped, "God forbid!" realizing that they were the husbandmen spoken of.

As soon as they pronounced the doom of the husbandmen, it was clear that they understood that they had pronounced their own punishment. I knew it, and they knew it.

Jesus did not let up. I figured that He wanted them to know what they were doing and to whom they were doing it, to leave them no doubt about their guilt.

Referring to the psalms, Jesus announced Himself as the Messiah, asking, "Did you never read in the scriptures, 'The Stone which the builders rejected is the cornerstone. This is the Lord's doing, and it is marvelous in our eyes'? Therefore, the kingdom of God shall be taken from you and given to a nation bringing forth the fruits thereof. And whosoever shall fall on this stone shall be broken, but on whomsoever it shall fall, it will grind him to powder."

This was the third parable in a row Jesus used to identify Himself as the Son of God and to identify the wicked chief priests and scribes for what they were. There was no mistaking His message. They knew He spoke of them, and they wanted to arrest Him, but they feared the multitude surrounding Jesus. The multitudes did not accept Him as their Messiah, but they did love Him and accept Him as a prophet.

Again, the chief priests and scribes left Jesus and went their way. We learned that they met elsewhere and conspired to send spies pretending to be just men. They were to watch Jesus and listen for words they might use to accuse Him so they might arrest Him and deliver Him into the power and authority of the Roman Prefect. That was their strategy.

THE PARABLE OF THE ROYAL
MARRIAGE FEAST AND OTHERS

Jesus continued to speak to the multitude in the temple, teaching them about their legacy and their inheritance through another parable, similar to one He used before, saying, "The kingdom of heaven is likened unto a certain king who prepared a celebration for his son's wedding. The king sent forth his servants to call those who had already been invited to the wedding, but they did not want to come. The king sent his servants a second time, saying, 'Remind them that I invited them earlier, and now they are asked to come. Behold, I have prepared the dinner. My oxen and my fatlings are killed, and all things are ready. Tell them that now is the time to come to the wedding.'

"But they scoffed at the wedding and went their separate ways, one to his farm and another to his merchandise. And the rest that were asked to come took the king's servants, treated them poorly, and killed them. When the king heard of this, he was angry and sent his armies to destroy those that had murdered his servants; and their city was burned also.

"Then the king said to his servants, 'The wedding is ready, but those who were invited are not worthy to attend. Therefore, go into the highways, and as many people as you shall find, invite them to the wedding.'

"So those servants went out into the highways and gathered together as many as they found, both bad and good, and the wedding was furnished with guests. When the king came in to see the guests, he saw a man there who had not dressed to attend the wedding, and he said to him, 'Friend, why did you come here not being dressed for a wedding?' And the man had no answer. Then the king said to his servants, 'Bind him hand and foot, take him away, and cast him into outer darkness, where there is weeping and gnashing of teeth. For many are called but few are chosen.' "

I understood that in the parable, the man who did not dress to meet the king meant that he had not shed his sins and put on the garments of worthiness. As a result, he was unprepared to meet the king. I recognized the subtlety of the parable. I knew that coming to Christ requires preparation by obeying His commandments, not just casually acknowledging Him as the Son of God without doing more.

The members of house of Israel were those who were invited and were awaiting the time when the feast was ready. When the wedding celebration was announced, they did not come, or they killed the messengers—the prophets that invited them to come to the king. As prophesied, they were to be destroyed and their city was to be burned.

Render unto Caesar

While Jesus taught in the temple, much went on among the chief priests and the scribes. The same Jews who were unmasked by three parables furiously conspired to murder Jesus. The Pharisees counseled with the Herodians, their hated political enemies, and combined forces with them to send spies to trick Jesus. Their plan was to ask Jesus a clever question that would require Him to voice disrespect for either the Mosaic law or the Roman law. The cunning conspirators were to pose as believers struggling to resolve the conflicts between Mosaic and Roman laws. They figured that no matter how Jesus answered, they would have something to accuse Him of.

The deceivers began by attempting to flatter Jesus, pretending to be disciples and saying, "Master, we know that you are true and that you teach the way of God in truth. We know that you do not care what men think of you. We also know that you do not treat men differently because of title or rank. Therefore, tell us what you think: is it lawful to give tribute to Caesar or not?"

But Jesus perceived their wicked conspiracy. "You hypocrites, why do you test me?" He asked them. They said nothing, clearly recognizing that their clever strategy had been unmasked. "Show me the tribute money," Jesus requested, and they handed Him a Roman denarius. Then He asked them, "Whose is this image? Whose name is written here?"

The conspirators answered in a word, "Caesar's."

Then Jesus handed the coin back to them and said, "Render therefore unto Caesar the things which are Caesar's and unto God the things that are God's."

When they heard these wise words from Jesus, they marveled aloud at His wisdom and went their way confounded.

THE SADDUCEES TRY TO
OUTWIT JESUS AGAIN

The same day that Jesus confounded the spies sent by the Pharisees and Herodians, the Sadducees came to Him with an elaborate tale of a woman with seven husbands, inquiring who she would be married to in the resurrection. The Sadducees did not believe in the resurrection, so their question was meaningless to them. They believed that man lived and died and there was nothing beyond that. They also believed in using any means to obtain all they could for themselves without fearing eternal consequences. I knew that they came with the same intention as the spies—to trick Jesus into saying something they could use to accuse Him. Yet I knew they could not and would not outwit Jesus.

"Master, Moses said that if a man dies, having no children, his brother shall marry his widow and raise up children to his brother," one of the Sadducees said. "Now there were seven brothers, and the first died after he married, having no children, leaving his wife to his brother. Likewise the second died, and the third, even down to the seventh brother. Finally, the widow of these seven brothers died. Here is the question. In the resurrection, who of the seven will be her husband, for they all took her as wife?"

Jesus answered their question and addressed their disbelief in the resurrection. "Your error is that you do not know the scriptures or the power of God," He told them. "The children of this world marry and are given in marriage while in this world, but those who shall be accounted worthy to obtain that world after the resurrection from the dead neither marry nor are given in marriage. They cannot die any more, but they are equal to the angels as children of God in heaven after they are resurrected."

In this case, the widow was married only to the first brother. Her "marriage" to the subsequent brothers was to fulfill an obligation of the original husband—a commandment. The logic of the Sadducees was based on the false assumption that each husband gained the same status as the first.

Jesus addressed the folly of their rejection of resurrection, saying, "As touching the resurrection of the dead, have you not read that which was said to Moses by God at the burning bush, which was written for you to read, saying, 'I am the God of Abraham and the God of Isaac and the God of Jacob'? He is not the God of the dead but of the living, for all are alive to Him! You, therefore, do greatly err."

When the multitude heard the wisdom of Jesus, they were clearly astonished at the power and clarity of His doctrine. The Sadducees, who were unshakable in their denial of the resurrection, had been shown the foolishness of their beliefs in a matter of seconds!

The Sadducees did refer to the accepted belief that men and women remain husband and wife following death, which is accurate, depending on how and by what authority they are married. If a man and woman vow to take each other as husband and wife until death, their vows are for mortality and their marriage terminates upon death. If a man and woman are bound on earth to be bound in heaven by the keys of the priesthood given to the Apostles, they will be bound as husband and wife in heaven.

When Jesus told them that marriages happen in this world—not the one to come—some mistakenly took Him to mean there are no families in the eternities, which was not accurate. In fact, Jesus specifically gave the Apostles the keys of the priesthood so that whatsoever we would bind on earth would be bound in heaven. But being bound as families must be done on earth because, as He said, "after the resurrection from the dead, children of this world neither marry nor are given in marriage."

The First and Greatest Commandment

When the Pharisees heard that Jesus had confounded the Sadducees, they both gathered together to conspire to kill Him. In a second round of conceit to somehow outwit Jesus, they sent a lawyer to ask Jesus a question to test Him, trying to find something else with which to accuse Him.

The lawyer asked Jesus, "Master, which is the first and greatest commandment in the law?"

Jesus responded with the answer known to every Jew: "The first of all the commandments is, 'Hear, O Israel: The Lord our God is one Lord. And you shall love the Lord thy God with all your heart, and with all your soul, and with all your mind, and with all your strength.' This is the first commandment. And the second is like unto it: 'You shall love your neighbor as yourself.' There is no other commandment greater than these. On these two commandments hang all the law and the prophets."

The lawyer agreed with Jesus. "Master, you have well spoken the truth because there is one God and no other but Him," the lawyer said. "And to love Him with all your heart, with all your soul, and with all your strength, and to love your neighbor as yourself, is worth more than all burnt offerings and sacrifices."

"You are not far from the kingdom of God," Jesus responded. His words had two meanings. First, He confirmed that the lawyer was close to the truth, becoming part of the kingdom of God, and second, He referred to Himself physically. In other words, the lawyer was standing in close proximity to the Savior. The double meaning was lost on the scribe, but once again the Pharisees were confounded.

While the Pharisees were thus gathered together, listening to the conversation between Jesus and the lawyer, Jesus turned to them. "What do you think of the Christ? Whose Son is He?" He asked.

"The Son of David," they answered.

"Then how does David, by the Holy Ghost, call Christ 'Lord' in the Book of Psalms? He said, 'The Lord said unto my Lord, "Sit Thou on my right hand, till I make my enemies your footstool." ' If David calls Christ 'Lord,' how then is Christ the Son of David?"

None of the Pharisees would answer because to do so would acknowledge that the Christ, the Messiah, would be a direct descendant of David, which Jesus was.

From that day on, none of them dared ask Jesus any more of their questions. They had learned that His wisdom was greater than their most cunning conspiracies, having been silenced time after time. The common man heard what Jesus said to them, however, and their hearts were lifted. They understood that with priesthood authority, they could be bound together, husband to wife and wife to husband, in the kingdom of God.

THE WIDOW'S MITE

Three days before Passover, we sat with Jesus on the stairs near the wall of the Court of the Women, watching the events at the temple treasury. The treasury contained thirteen chests, each with a receptacle that looked like a ram's horn, designed to funnel coins into the chest. Each container was labeled to indicate how the money would be used. Many who gave money were rich and made a pompous show of their generosity. It was a competition to see who could be the most conspicuous in their charity.

I could see sorrow in Jesus's face as He observed these pretentious men. Those who gave with great displays of piety received the reward they sought: the honors of men. Now and then, someone would come forward, quietly put their coins into one of the boxes, and silently withdraw, keeping their head bowed, shamed that they could not give as much as the wealthy. In my opinion, these humble people were giving for the right reason, no matter the amount.

As we watched, a certain poor widow came meekly out of the crowd. She selected a chest for her contribution and threw two mites, or leptons as they were known, into the ram's horn. Mites were the smallest coin in our monetary system. They were of such minimal economic value that her gift appeared to be insignificant in comparison.

Addressing that reality, Jesus gave a spiritual perspective to her contribution.

He called us close to His side and said, "This is a truth I

would have you know: this poor widow has cast more in than anyone else who has cast into the treasury. They all give in of their abundance, but she, in her extreme poverty, cast in all that she had to live on."

HYPOCRISY AND THE PRETENDERS

Without being interrupted by the scribes and Pharisees who were watching nearby, Jesus taught us about obedience to the law.

He said, "The scribes and the Pharisees sit with authority in the 'Moses seat.' Therefore, observe and do all that they instruct you to observe and do, but do not follow the examples they set in their own works because they do not do as they teach. They are pretenders—hypocrites—preaching one thing but doing another."

I needed to hear this. I had wondered about obedience to the law when it was both interpreted and administered by wicked men. I sometimes thought of it as "their" law, not God's law. I confess that at times, I obeyed their law reluctantly, and at other times I took a certain pleasure in not obeying their law. I resolved to obey their law, in spite of the scribes and Pharisees, simply because Jesus told me to, but that was the only reason. I did everything I could to obey Jesus in all things.

Then one of the lawyers, who had been listening in, stepped forward and whined, "Master, by saying this, you bring shame on us also."

Jesus turned to the lawyer. "You create heavy requirements, which are extremely difficult to bear, and lay them upon men's shoulders," He said bluntly, "but you do not lift one finger to help those you have thus burdened."

The Jews traditionally classified certain commandments as

being either light or heavy, depending on the effort required to comply with them or the consequences of compliance.

Jesus went on to condemn the way the scribes and the Pharisees ignored the heavy requirements of their interpretation of the law in favor of observing the light ones. He said, "You are blind guides. You strain out a gnat, but you swallow a camel!"

There have always been self-proclaimed masters of the law, who focus on outward observance of lesser laws while ignoring the greatest commandment "to love the Lord thy God with all our heart, and all our soul, and with all our mind, and with all our strength." What is in our hearts qualifies us for the kingdom of God because that is where love resides.

Gesturing toward the lawyer, Jesus continued His indictment. "They do their works to be seen of men. They make their phylacteries bigger than necessary to be seen of men. They enlarge the fringes of their garments to be seen of men. They love to sit in the uppermost rooms at feasts to be seen of men. They love to sit in the chief seats in the synagogues to be seen of men. And they love to receive greetings in the markets to be called of men, 'Rabbi, Rabbi.' All these things they do to be seen of men."

Jesus commented on their ostentatious use of titles among their peers, referring to each other as masters of the law, or rabbis, as a tribute to the study they had put into the law. I had marveled several times that the so-called established theocratic leadership of Israel placed more value on training in the law than it did on its observation, the service of others, or the living of a righteous life. In fact, the Jews honored rabbis over the actual priests and the priesthood.

Jesus knew it too. He said, "But do not be called 'Rabbi,' for only one is your Master, even Christ. You are all brothers.

And do not call any man upon the earth 'Father,' for only one is your Father, even your Father which is in heaven. Neither be called 'Master,' for only one is your Master, even Christ. But he that is greatest among you shall be your servant. Whosoever shall exalt himself shall be humiliated, and he that shall humble himself shall be exalted."

Jesus continued His attack, turning to the lawyers and Pharisees. "Woe unto you, scribes and Pharisees. You are hypocrites! You shut up the kingdom of heaven against men, and you neither enter yourselves, nor allow those who would enter to do so. Woe unto you, scribes and Pharisees, you hypocrites! You devour widows' houses, and at the same time, as a pretense of virtue, you offer long prayers. As a consequence, you shall receive even greater damnation."

He pointed out that the arbitrary rules and regulations in their law confused and misled those who desired to be obedient. In their wickedness, they had perverted the law and applied it unjustly to seize other people's possessions, including the homes of widows, which they then used to enrich themselves.

I was continuously bothered by the way the rulers of the Jews had become wealthy as they held positions of power. It was no secret to anyone. In my opinion, they disgracefully sought these positions for power and greed, not for spiritual improvement.

As Jesus spoke, the scribes and Pharisees sought for a strategy to provoke Him into saying something they might use to accuse Him.

While some of the lawyers and Pharisees still tried to recover their composure after being condemned in such precise critical language, Jesus continued His attack on their wickedness, saying, "Woe unto you, lawyers and Pharisees, you hypocrites! You will travel both sea and land to convert one proselyte, but when you have baptized one, you make him into double the child of hell you are."

I had no doubt in my mind that Jesus was saying what needed to be said. He was neither subtle nor gentle. He used no allegory, but He pierced their hearts with sharp darts.

Jesus addressed the fact that the Pharisees had created loopholes in their law to excuse someone from an oath if they had sworn "by the temple" or "by the altar of the temple." At the same time, the Pharisees granted no forgiveness if someone swore an oath "by the gold" in the temple or "by the gold" on the altar of the temple. I remembered that following the sermon on the mountain, Jesus had forbidden oaths of all kinds.

My heart raced as Jesus said, "Woe unto you blind guides who say, 'Whomsoever shall swear by the temple, know that it is nothing!' I tell you that whomsoever shall swear by the gold of the temple, he is a debtor. You blind fools! Which is greater, the gold in the temple or the temple that sanctifies the gold therein? And to those who say, 'Whomsoever shall swear by the altar, know that it is nothing.' I tell you that whomsoever shall swear by the gift that is upon the altar, he is guilty. You are blind fools! Which is greater, the gift on the altar or the altar that sanctifies the gift thereon?

"Whosoever shall swear 'by the altar,' swears by it and all things thereon. And whoso shall swear 'by the temple,' swears by it and all things therein. And whoso shall swear 'by heaven,' swears by the throne of God and by Him that sits thereon."

Jesus both instructed and condemned. We were the ones being instructed; the scribes and the Pharisees were the ones being condemned. They left the area quietly, a silence I enjoyed.

As I saw their backs, I shuddered at what their fate might be. They honored gold more than the temple and the altars of the temple. They would perish, and they would not take their gold with them. Instead, their rejection of Jesus would follow them into the eternities. They thought of themselves as wise, learned, and powerful, but just as Jesus said, they were "blind fools."

IN THE HOUSE OF A PHARISEE

After Jesus spoke, a certain Pharisee asked Jesus to come to his house to dine with him. Jesus entered the Pharisee's house and immediately sat down without following the traditional ritual of washing His hands. Everyone noticed it because it violated one of the most stringent rules in their law. Knowing Jesus, I figured He had a reason for deliberately violating their law. This particular rule was considered at least as heavy as murder. I concluded that Jesus was probably provoking the Pharisee to make a comment. Sure enough, the Pharisee saw and asked why Jesus had not first washed His hands for dinner.

"Now, you Pharisees clean the outside of the cup and the platter, but the inward part is left filled with plunder and wickedness," He said. "You are fools! Did not the one that made the outside dirty make the inside dirty also? First cleanse the inside of the cup and platter, and the outside shall be cleaned in the process. Instead of doing as you do, you should obediently give alms from what you own, and behold, you shall also be cleansed on the inside."

"But woe unto you, scribes and Pharisees! For you tithe of your mint, anise, cumin, and all manner of your herbs, but you have abandoned the heavy matters of the law: judgment, mercy, faith, and the love of God. These are what you ought to do, and you will not leave the other undone either. Woe unto you, lawyers and Pharisees. You are hypocrites! You are the same as unmarked graves. Men walk upon them and are not aware of the corruption under their feet.

"Woe unto you, scribes and Pharisees. You are hypocrites! You are like whitewashed sepulchers, which indeed appear beautiful on the outside, but on the inside they are filled with dead bones and rotting flesh. Even so, you also appear righteous on the outside, but on the inside you are filled with hypocrisy and iniquity."

Jesus continued His harsh indictment of the wickedness of the lawyers and Pharisees, saying, "Woe unto you! You build the tombs of the prophets and garnish the sepulchers of the righteous dead, and yet it was your fathers who killed the prophets. Then you say, 'If we had been alive in the days of our fathers, we would not have participated in spilling the blood of the prophets.' By so saying, you testify that you are the children of them that killed the prophets. You are living up to your fathers' legacy as serpents because you are a generation of vipers! How can you escape the damnation of hell?

"Wherefore, behold, I shall send prophets, Apostles, wise men, and righteous scribes, and you shall kill and crucify them, and some of them you shall scourge in your synagogues and drive them from city to city, so that upon you shall come all the righteous blood shed from the foundation of the world, from the blood of righteous Abel to the blood of Zecharias, son of Barachias, whom you killed between the temple and the altar. All of these things shall be required of this generation!"

Jesus testified that He was the One that sent the prophets and that He was Jehovah of the Old Testament. As usual, the scribes and lawyers rejected His testimony, focusing instead on the rest of His story. I can safely say that most people claim to accept dead prophets, but they reject living prophets. This is the hypocrisy Jesus was talking about. Living and dead prophets serve the same God. Rejecting living or dead prophets is the same as rejecting God. There are those who say there are no prophets, which suggests they do not believe in God because, as one of His prophets said, "Surely, the Lord God will do nothing unless He reveals His secret to His servants the prophets."

As the lawyers and Pharisees contemplated the curse He had pronounced on them, Jesus finished His monologue with a parable. He addressed those who assured everyone of their righteousness while despising those they considered lower than them. "Two men went up into the temple to pray, the one a Pharisee, the other a publican," Jesus taught. "The Pharisee stood and prayed thus with himself, 'God, I thank Thee that I am not as other men—extortionists, unjust, adulterers, or even as this publican. I fast twice each week, and I give tithes of all that I possess.' The publican, standing away from everyone else in the temple, would not so much as lift his eyes unto heaven, but smote upon his breast saying, 'God, be merciful to me, a sinner.' The publican returned to his house justified, rather than the Pharisee. Everyone that exalts himself shall be humiliated, and he that humbles himself shall be exalted."

I understood the humility of the publican. I had a lot to be humble about. I was an Apostle of the Son of God, and still, I was a weak man. In my heart I often wished those who sought to harm Jesus would fall under my sword or be swallowed up by the earth in a great earthquake. Paying tithes was easy compared to controlling the things in my heart.

Then, in private, Jesus spoke to us, repeating an earlier warning: "Beware of the lawyers, which desire to walk about in long robes and love greetings in the markets and sitting in the chief seats in the synagogues and the uppermost rooms at feasts. Beware of those who devour widows' houses and, for a show, make long prayers: they shall receive even greater damnation."

Those were His last words to us about lawyers and Pharisees, and it didn't take a lot for me to be warned about Pharisees; I had never trusted them. We left the house of the

Pharisee and returned to the temple. When not surrounded by Pharisees and scribes, Jesus sometimes found peace in the temple. I hoped He would do so again. His heart seemed heavy.

JESUS PROPHESIES ABOUT AND
LAMENTS OVER JERUSALEM

That day, Jesus walked along the parapets on the edge of the Temple Mount, pausing to look out over Jerusalem. He said nothing as He surveyed the city, looking at the byways and along the rooftops. I don't know what He was foreseeing or what He was thinking, but His mood was somber, and a great sadness was apparent in His countenance. I felt a knot in my stomach again as I watched His pain.

He also gazed keenly at the temple, sometimes turning away and then looking back again. I stared at the temple, wondering what He was seeing. Nearly fifty years had passed since Herod started the project to rebuild and expand the temple and the Temple Mount. Debris and rubble from ongoing construction and finishing touches cluttered the courtyards, accumulating over several years.

"Master, look at the excellent stone, the priceless adornments, and the kind of buildings here," one of the Apostles said, interrupting His thoughts. "What shall happen to them?"

"See these great buildings around us?" He asked in response, breaking his silence at last. "Verily I say to you, the day will come when there shall not be so much as one stone left upon another. They shall all be scattered."

He was prophesying the destruction of the temple! His voice was quiet, sad, and weary, and I could do nothing. I just watched Him. I remained silent, but I felt His sadness.

We quietly followed Him as He left the Temple Mount,

or Mount Zion, as it was sometimes called, and walked part-way up the eastern side of the Mount of Olives. He gestured for us to sit where we could look across the Kidron Valley and see the city.

Jesus stood and said, "O Jerusalem, Jerusalem, you that kill the prophets and stone them who are sent to you; how often would I have gathered your children together, even as a hen gathers her brood of chicks under her wings, but you would not be gathered! Behold, your house is left unto you—desolate." Then, with tears in His eyes, He continued. "I say unto you, you shall not see me again until the time comes when you shall say, 'Blessed is He that comes in the name of the Lord.'"

I was saddened by His pronouncement, even if I only understood part of it. I did notice, however, that up to now, Jesus had always referred to the temple as the house of His Father or His house. At that moment, He disowned the temple, calling it "your house." How despondent He seemed. I ached inside for my Master.

Signs of the Second Coming

As the sun began to set, Jesus dismissed eight of the Apostles and sent them on to Bethany to stay the night. While he told them He would meet them again the next morning, He asked four of us to remain with Him on the Mount of Olives, including James and John, my brother Andrew, and myself. We followed Jesus along the rocky path further up the side of the mountain. As we walked, I silently contemplated the fact that we were another day closer to His death. The tightness in my chest and a lump in my throat made it difficult to breathe. The thought of His death became a burden I struggled to bear.

We came to a spot on the mountainside where Jesus had previously taught us privately, away from the Pharisees. Darkness was approaching, so when He stopped and sat down, I knew it was a signal that He wanted to have a discussion with us. The temperature dropped quickly as the sun went down, but there was no breeze, and the trees provided us with a generous supply of dead branches for a fire to give light and warmth. We sat close to hear Him speak, literally spending the night at the Master's feet.

We talked of many things during the night, but I shall mention only a few. Jesus wanted to prepare us for the time when He would not be here with us. I was the senior Apostle and was to take charge. It was a serious responsibility that I did not want to think about. Instead, I tried to focus on those who would harm Jesus.

As we talked, John asked Jesus to explain three things about His prophecies. "Tell us, when shall these things be?" John asked. "And what will be the sign of your coming, the sign when all these things shall be fulfilled?" It was a hard thing to ask.

Jesus started with a warning, saying, "Beware that you are not deceived by any man. The time draws near when many shall come in my name, saying, 'I am Christ,' and they shall deceive many people.

"And when you hear of wars and rumors of wars, do not be frightened, for all these things must come to pass, but the end shall not yet be. Nation shall rise against nation and kingdom against kingdom, and there shall be famines, and pestilences, and earthquakes in diverse places. There will be frightening sights and great signs from heaven. All of these are the beginning of sorrows for Jerusalem."

Jesus then prophesied about us individually, repeating his earlier counsel, "Be warned. They shall arrest you and deliver you up to their councils. You shall be beaten in the synagogues, and they shall kill you. You shall be hated by all nations, and you shall be brought before rulers and kings on account of my name as a testimony against me. And when they shall bind you and lead you and deliver you up, take no thought beforehand what you shall say, neither contemplate before you answer. Whatsoever shall come into your mind, say that; I will give your mouth wisdom by the Holy Ghost, wisdom that your adversaries shall not be able to dispute or resist."

When Thomas first volunteered to die with Jesus, some of the Apostles agreed with him. Jesus told us that we would not die with Him but that we would be killed. Dying with or for Jesus was not a problem, but what would happen to His Church following His death? How would it survive with the leaders killed by the Jews? I knew that faithful people, if there were any left after the wars, would still be faithful, but they did not hold His holy priesthood. Without His priesthood, they did not have His authority. Would they organize their own churches? Would they be true to His teaching or would they invent their own because they did not know better? Certainly there would be false prophets who would organize churches for personal gain, but what of the good people who sought leadership? I worried they would be deceived.

"And then many shall be estranged, and brother shall betray brother to death, and children shall rise up against parents, and shall hate one another, and put them to death, "He continued. "And you shall be betrayed both by parents and brothers, by family and friends. And friends and family shall cause some of you to be put to death. And you shall be hated for my name's sake, but there shall not be a hair of your head lost without my knowledge. Patiently master your own soul."

I heard two things. First, some of us would not be killed. Would we live to continue to lead His Church? Second, His last words were for me. He knew that I was prepared to fight and die for Him, to declare His word to everyone. I would testify that Jesus is the Son of God with my last breath, but it would take a submissiveness that I did not think I had within me to allow myself to be imprisoned. I was a proud man, unwilling to simply let others arrest me. I was troubled at my pride.

"And many false prophets shall rise and they shall deceive many people," He continued. "And because iniquity shall abound, the love of many for the gospel shall wax cold. But he that endures to the end shall be saved.

"And the gospel of the kingdom of God shall be brought to all the world for a witness to all nations. That is when the end of Judea shall come."

As He spoke, I imagined the missions we were to undertake, bringing the light of the gospel to every people.

"When you shall see Jerusalem surrounded by Roman armies, know that the desolation of Jerusalem is next," He said. "Therefore, when you see the abomination of desolation, which was spoken of by Daniel the prophet, stand in the holy place (whoever reads this, let him understand); then let those in Judea flee into the mountains. Flee from the midst of Judea and depart out of it.

"Let them who are in the countries around Judea stay out of Judea. Let him who is on the housetop not come down to enter his house and take anything out of it, neither let him who is in the field return to his house to take his clothes. When you see these things, flee from Judea because these will be the days of vengeance by the Romans, the days when all things which are written shall be fulfilled."

I tried to envision the great destruction and abomination that was to come upon the house of Israel. The knot in my stomach seemed to increase in size until I felt ill. The picture being painted by Jesus was difficult to contemplate.

Jesus continued His warning, "And woe unto them that are with child and to them that suckle their children in those days! Pray that your flight is not in the winter neither on the Sabbath, when travel is restricted, because there shall then be a great tribulation in Judea and upon this people such as has not existed from the beginning of the creation which God created, to this time, no, nor shall there ever be. They shall fall by the sword, and they shall be led away captive into all nations. Jerusalem shall be trodden down by the Gentiles until the times of the Gentiles shall be fulfilled. And except those days are shortened, no flesh should be saved but for the elect's sake, for those whom He has chosen, those days shall be shortened."

"Then if any man shall say to you, 'Look, here is Christ,' or 'There is Christ,' do not believe them!" He warned, speaking of the near future and the time when He would return. "For false Christs and false prophets shall arise, and they shall show great signs and wonders insomuch that they shall attempt to deceive the very elect."

Repeating an earlier comment, Jesus said, "Behold, I have told you before, if they shall say to you, 'Behold, He is in the desert,' do not go into the desert. Or if they shall say, 'Behold, He is in the secret chambers of the temple,' do not believe it. As the light of the morning comes out of the east and shines even to the west, so also shall be the coming of the Son of Man. For wherever the carcass is, there will the eagles gather together."

I understood His symbolism to mean that the "carcass" was Jerusalem and the "eagles" were the members of the house of Israel. The images He created suggested that the house of Israel would gather to Jerusalem and a season of great death would follow. I realized that Jesus was speaking of the near future of Israel while simultaneously prophesying about His Second Coming, as if the events would have similarities. I felt confused as I tried to unravel the double nature of His prophecy.

"Immediately after the tribulation of those days," He continued, "the sun shall be darkened, the moon shall not give her light, the stars shall fall from heaven, the powers of the heavens will shake, and the waves of the sea shall roar.

"And then shall the sign of the Son of Man appear in heaven. Men's hearts shall fail them for fear, looking for those things that shall come. And then shall all the tribes of the earth mourn, and they shall see the Son of Man coming in the clouds of heaven with power and with glory. When these things begin to come to pass, look up and lift your heads in joy, for your redemption draws near. He shall send His angels with the great sound of a trumpet, and they shall gather His elect from the four winds, from the uttermost parts of the earth to the uttermost parts of heaven."

There were to be many earthquakes and signs in the sky unlike anything seen before. Israel would come to live in fear of the trembling of the earth.

We heard His words, but we did not fully understand what the immediate future held for Israel or for us.

THE PARABLE OF THE FIG TREE

After a while, Jesus pointed toward the trees and offered the parable of the fig tree. "Behold the fig tree and all of the trees. When the branch is yet tender, it puts forth leaves, and you know that the summer is at hand. So likewise for you, when you see all these things come to pass, know that He is near, even at the door. This generation shall not pass away until all these things shall be fulfilled. Heaven and earth shall pass away, but my words shall not pass away." Jesus spoke the truth. What remains to be fulfilled is His return and the great persecutions which will precede it.

"Hear this also: no man but my Father—no, not the angels of heaven or even the Son—knows what day I shall come," He told us. "The coming of the Son of Man shall be just as it was during the days of Noah. For as in the days before the flood, there was much eating and drinking and marrying and giving in marriage, right up to the day Noah entered into the ark. They did not know about the flood until it came and took them all away. So shall the time of the coming of the Son of Man be.

"Two shall be in the field, the one taken and the other left. Two women shall be grinding at the mill, the one taken and the other left. Watch therefore, for you do not know what hour your Lord comes. Know this though: if the good man of the house had known in what hour the thief would come, he would have watched and would not have allowed his house to be broken into. Blessed are the servants whom the Lord will find watching when He comes. He shall dress Himself and arrange for them to sit down to meat, and He will come forth and serve them. It does not matter if He comes in the second or the third watch. If He finds them watching, blessed are those servants. Therefore, be ready, because the Son of Man will come in an hour you won't expect."

"Lord," I asked, "do you speak this parable for us alone or for everyone?"

"What I say to you, I say to all. Watch!"

I asked Him to explain the parable, and He did. "The Son of Man is taking a distant journey, leaving His house, giving authority to His servants, and giving to every man his work. Then He will command His porter—that faithful and wise servant whom his Lord has made ruler over His household—to watch. The porter will give them their portion of meat in due season. And blessed are the servants whom his Lord shall find doing as commanded when He comes. Watch therefore, for you do not know the hour the Master returns: at eventide, at midnight, at the cock crowing, or in the morning. I say to all, watch, lest He comes suddenly and finds you sleeping.

"He shall make that faithful servant ruler over all He has. But if an evil servant shall say in his heart, 'My Lord is delaying His coming' and shall beat his own servants and maidens, and eat and drink and be drunken, the Lord of that servant shall come in a day when the servant is not looking for Him and in an hour when he is not aware. The Lord shall cut him down and give him a reward equal to that of the hypocrites and unbelievers. The servant who knows his Lord's will but does not prepare accordingly shall be beaten with many stripes. He that does not know his Lord's will and does things worthy of being beaten shall be beaten too, but with only a few stripes. For him unto whom much is given, much is required. Of those men to whom much has been committed,

He will ask even more. There will be weeping and gnashing of teeth.

"And take heed to yourselves, lest at any time your hearts overflow with debauchery, drunkenness, and the cares of this life, causing you to be unprepared when the day comes. For it shall come as a snare upon everyone that dwells upon the face of the whole earth. Therefore, watch and pray always that you may be counted worthy to escape all the things that shall come to pass and be worthy to stand before the Son of Man."

THE PARABLE OF THE TEN VIRGINS

In the early morning before it was light, people traveled along the pathways toward Jerusalem. They lit their way with oil lamps and carried them at the end of a rod. All of the people went to the temple early in the morning in hopes of hearing Jesus. They were unaware that they were passing Him on the Mount of Olives as He taught us, four of His Apostles.

Observing the parade of people walking in the dark by the light of their lamps, Jesus told a new parable. "When the Son of Man comes, the kingdom of heaven shall be likened unto ten virgins, which took their lamps and went forth in the night to meet the bridegroom. Five of them were wise and five were foolish. They that were foolish had full lamps but took no oil with them; the wise took spare oil in vessels.

"When the bridegroom did not come when the ten virgins expected, they rested and napped. At midnight, when they least expected him, the word came, saying, 'Behold, the bridegroom is coming; go out to meet him.' Then all of the virgins arose and began to fill their lamps to join the wedding procession. The foolish virgins said to the wise, 'Give us some of your oil—our lamps have gone out.' But the wise virgins answered, saying, 'We can't, otherwise there wouldn't be enough for us. Go to the oil merchant and buy your own.'

"And while the five foolish virgins went to buy oil, the bridegroom came, and they that were ready went with him and entered the great hall where the wedding feast was being held, and the door was shut behind them. Once the door was shut, the five foolish virgins returned, saying, 'Lord, open the door for us.' But the bridegroom answered, 'I do not know you.' "

It was our tradition that as the bridegroom walked to the hall where the wedding feast was to be held, friends and family would join the procession. Each person held a rod with a lamp at the end, lighting the way, creating a delightful parade of lights in the darkness. Each light contributed to the joy of the procession. It was unacceptable to join the pageant without a lamp. The problem was in knowing when the bridegroom would come by. It was important to be ready with an adequate supply of oil, even if the bridegroom was delayed.

"Watch therefore," Jesus concluded, "for you know neither the day nor the hour wherein the Son of Man comes."

He offered a final comment, saying, "Let your loins be girded about, and let your lights be kept burning. Be men that wait for their Lord. When He returns from the wedding, when He comes and knocks, be ready to open the door to Him immediately.

I understood that He was talking to us, and I thought I understood what He wanted us to do. The concept He taught was simple: I had to prepare and act on my own as His senior Apostle, without relying on anyone except Jesus. Of all the things I heard Jesus teach, this was one concept already a part of who I was. I was fiercely independent, perhaps even a bit stubborn.

Parable of the Talents

Jesus continued teaching us with parables as the sun came up. It was now two days until Passover. We watched groups of people travel across the Mount of Olives toward Jerusalem. Between the groups of travelers, a lone man came by, carrying a bundle on his back. Although it was only morning, he already looked weary from his journey.

As we watched him pass by, Jesus offered the parable of the talents. "The kingdom of heaven is as a man traveling into a far country. He called his servants together and delivered his goods to them. To one, he gave five talents, to another two, and to another one, giving to every man according to his ability. Straightway, the man left on his journey.

"He that received five talents went and traded with them, making five more talents. And likewise, he that received two talents went and traded, and he also gained two talents. But he that received one talent dug a hole and hid his lord's money in the earth."

"After a long time, the lord of the servants returned and asked for an accounting. He that had received five talents came and brought five more talents, saying, 'Lord, you entrusted me with five talents. I have gained five talents more with them.' His lord said to him, 'Well done, my good and faithful servant. You have been faithful over a few things. I will make you ruler over many things. Enter into the joy of the lord.'

"He that had received two talents came and said, 'Lord,

you entrusted me with two talents. I have gained two talents more with them.' As before, His lord said to him, 'Well done, my good and faithful servant. You have been faithful over a few things. I will make you ruler over many things. Enter into the joy of the Lord.'

"Then he that had received one talent came and said, 'Lord, I knew that you are a strict man, reaping where you have not sown and gathering where you have not strewn seed. I was afraid of you and hid your talent in the earth. Look, here it is.'

"His lord answered, saying, 'You are a wicked and sloth-ful servant. You knew that I reaped where I had not sown and gathered where I had not strewn seed. You should have at least given my money to the money lender, and then at my coming, I would have received my money back with interest.' Then turning to his servants, the lord said, 'Therefore, take the talent from him and give it to the one that has ten tal-ents. For unto everyone that has, shall be given, and he shall have abundantly, but from him that has not, shall be taken even that which he has. And, take the unprofitable servant into outer darkness. There shall be weeping and gnashing of teeth.' "

Sometimes I felt like that unprofitable servant, for I was not sure I did enough with what I had been given. Some-times I feared that I was a slothful servant. I did not know what more I could do, but I was certain that I had not done enough. I always wanted to do more for the Lord.

Separating the Sheep
and the Goats

Jesus continued teaching as we watched people cross the Mount of Olives on their way down to Jerusalem. We saw a herd of sheep followed by a herd of goats, kept separate by their shepherds, as they worked their way toward the city.

"When the Son of Man comes in His glory, and all the angels are with Him, He shall sit upon the throne of His glory," Jesus said. "And all nations shall be gathered before Him. Then He shall separate them one from another, as a shepherd divides His sheep from his goats. He will set the sheep on His right hand and the goats on the left. Then the King shall say to those on His right, 'Come, blessed of my Father, and inherit the Kingdom, which was prepared for you from the foundation of the world.' "

Because of my own concerns, I asked Jesus who would be on His right hand. I needed to know if He considered me a sheep or a goat. I had to ask, but I wasn't sure I wanted to hear His answer. I looked at His face for a clue about what He might say, and I saw His countenance change noticeably. He had looked so somber, but the sadness disappeared, replaced by the look of peace and love that had always lifted my soul. He said, "You are my sheep. You are all my sheep." He was speaking to me and my fellow Apostles. He was also speaking to my heart.

I admit that tears came to my eyes. I did not want to be separated from Jesus in life, and I certainly did not wish to be separated from Him in the eternities. As relieved as I was,

I still had concerns that I could be the slothful servant He described earlier. I said nothing, but Jesus knew my thoughts. "You have served me well, my good and faithful servant," He assured me. Then, looking around at the rest of the Apostles, He said, "You have all served me well."

I trusted Him, but I thought of my own acts more as obedience than service. I always wanted to do more for Him, but the only thing I could do well was provide a place for Him to rest and to feed Him when He was hungry. It was my privilege, but I did not consider it to be service. I was reluctant to ask how I had served Him, but it didn't matter. He understood my need.

"For I was hungry, and you gave me meat," He explained. "I was thirsty, and you gave me drink. I was a stranger, and you took me in. I was naked, and you clothed me. I was sick, and you visited me. I was in prison, and you came unto me."

His explanation made me feel even worse. I had done none of those things for Him. Well, I had fed Him and given Him a place to sleep, but that was all. Besides, He fasted often, so He didn't eat that much. In fact, it was my wife and mother-in-law that fed Him, and I ate alongside Him.

But as always, He knew my thoughts. "Then shall the righteous answer Him, saying 'Lord, when did we see Thee hungry and feed Thee? Or thirsty, and give Thee drink? When did we see Thee as a stranger, and take Thee in? Or naked, and clothed Thee. Or when did we see Thee sick, or in prison, and came unto Thee?' And the King shall answer them saying, 'I tell you this truth, inasmuch as you have done it to the least of these my brethren, you have done it unto me.' Then shall He turn to those on the left hand and say, 'Depart from me, cursed, into the everlasting fire, which was prepared for the devil and his angels. For I was hungry, and you gave me no meat. I was thirsty, and you gave me no drink. I was a stranger, and you did not take me in; naked, and you did not clothe me; sick and in prison, and you did not visit me.'

"Then shall they answer him also, saying, 'Lord, when did we see you hungry, or thirsty, or a stranger, or naked, or sick, or in prison, and did not minister to you?"

"Then shall He answer them, saying, 'Inasmuch as you did it not to one of the least of these, you did it not to me.' And they shall go away into everlasting punishment, but the righteous shall go into eternal life."

Two Days before the Passover

After Jesus finished teaching, we prepared to go on to Bethany. He looked me in the eye, put his hand on my shoulder, and said soberly, "You know that the Feast of the Passover is in two days, and that is when the Son of Man is to be betrayed and crucified."

His blunt message made my ears ring, my stomach ache, and my body feel weak. I forced myself to stay silent. I had spoken out before and had said the wrong thing. At that moment, I knew what was going to happen and who was going to do it, but I could do nothing. How could a faithful servant do nothing? How could Peter, a man of action, do nothing? All I did was walk numbly along the rocky trail, my legs barely carrying my body. Even small stones seemed large. The dust tasted terrible. I felt sick. We walked over the Mount of Olives toward the village of Bethany.

We were later told by Nicodemus that at that very hour of the morning, the conspirators—the chief priests, scribes, and elders—were meeting in the palace of the high priest, Caiaphas, to plot how they would arrest Jesus through treachery and then kill Him. They decided not to take him on the day of the Passover Feast. "Not on the feast day, lest there be an uproar among the people."

Nicodemus and others among the conspirators knew that Jesus was a prophet, but they could not prevail over the wicked Jews.

Eating with Simon the Leper

As the sun rose, we arrived at the village of Bethany, joined by the rest of the Apostles. We spent the day resting and talking with Jesus at the home of Mary and Martha. That evening, we ate at the house of Simon the leper. There was not much said during the meal.

As we ate, a woman quietly entered the room and opened a flask of spikenard. I had seen this happen before, in the house of the Pharisee and in Bethany at the house of Mary and Martha, but instead of anointing His feet, this woman poured the contents of the flask onto Jesus's head. I thought of the psalmist.

As before, Judas was indignant that the spikenard was being used on Jesus and said, "What is the purpose of this waste? This ointment might have been sold for more than three hundred denarii, and the money given to the poor." Following Judas's lead, some of the others in the room complained about her.

Jesus heard their murmurings and said, "Why be troubled about this woman? She has done a good thing to me. You shall always have the poor with you, and whenever you wish, you may do good for them, but you shall not always have me with you. She poured her ointment on my body in advance of my burial."

The words stung. I could not contemplate His burial.

Jesus offered a tribute to the unnamed woman, saying, "Wherever in the world the gospel is preached, the story of what this woman has done will be told as a memorial to her."

 We never learned the name of this woman who anointed His body for burial, but I know her story will live on—whatever Jesus prophesied must surely come to pass.

JUDAS THE TRAITOR

In contrast to the love and generosity of the unnamed woman, to me the name of Judas will forever mean "traitor." After the woman anointed the head of Jesus, Judas, as we later learned, left Bethany and went to Jerusalem to join the conspiracy of the chief priests. Clearly, Satan had entered into the heart of Judas Iscariot, and he plotted with the chief priests and the temple captains about how he might betray Jesus into their hands.

Judas went to them to negotiate for the life of Jesus, saying, "What will you give me if I deliver Him to you?"

The chief priests were glad to hear what Judas had to offer. They formed a pact with him, promising to give him money if he would betray Jesus into their hands. They promised to pay him thirty pieces of silver, the price set by tradition as the value of a slave's life. From that time, Judas sought the opportunity to betray Jesus into their hands. His treachery had to take place away from the multitudes, so that those who loved Jesus could not protect Him, and in a place that would be convenient for the conspirators. The traitor did their bidding, selling the life of the Son of God for the price of a slave.

The Feast of Unleavened Bread

Tradition required that we eat a meal of unleavened bread the evening of the first day of the Passover. Leaven was removed from everyone's house in advance of that day, and it was unlawful to eat anything that contained leaven for the next eight days. It was also the time when representatives of each family went to the court of the temple, where the Passover lamb would be killed. Blood from each paschal lamb was sprinkled at the foot of the sacrificial altar by a priest. This sacrifice of an innocent lamb had been instituted as a prophecy of the day when the Lamb of God would be sacrificed.

I had been told the story of the birth of Jesus in Bethlehem. I knew that He had been born in the spring, at the time of lambing, when shepherds stayed with their flocks by night to protect newborn lambs from wolves. The Lamb of God was born with the other lambs of the house of Israel. Now He would be sacrificed along with the lambs of the house of Israel.

Jesus had told us that the hour would come when He would depart this world and go to His Father. His innocent blood would be spilled. It was His "hour," the one He had referred to so many times. Even as He prepared to be crucified, He spent time with His friends. He loved us to the end, we who were of this world. We were His, and He spent His final hours with us, instructing us and preparing us for what lay ahead. I was at His side during those hours—they are among the most cherished moments of my mortal life.

It seemed to me that some of the Apostles were more concerned with observing the Passover tradition than with the coming crucifixion of Jesus. I suppose they were busying themselves, trying not to think about it. I understood. I was never so confused as I was then. I had stood ready to defend Jesus to the death for three years, but now I knew that I must stand by and do nothing as He was killed. My heart was doing battle with my mind. My heart loved Him and would die for Him, but my mind knew that He had commanded me to let Him be crucified.

One of the Apostles turned to me for instructions. Without thinking, I heard myself ask Jesus, "What would you have us do for Passover?"

"Take John and go prepare for the Passover that we may eat together," He said.

Again, without thinking, I asked, "Where would you have us prepare?"

Usually it wasn't in me to need instructions, but I was still not thinking clearly. I was not one to get lost in my thoughts. I was a man that took charge; I got things done. I had always made arrangements for Him. I didn't need to be told what to do, but today was different. I was distracted.

He did not scold me for being in somewhat of a daze. Instead He said, "Go into the city, and you will find a certain man who will be carrying a pitcher of water. Follow him. When he enters his home, tell him that the Master says, 'My time is at hand. Where is the guest chamber of your house, where I shall eat the Passover with my disciples?' He will show you into a large upper room, which is already furnished and prepared. That is where you will make preparations for the Passover."

We obeyed immediately, knowing that it was appropriate for Jesus to eat in the upper room, the room reserved for honored guests. I also knew that it was usually a woman's job to carry water except for men hired to take care of a wealthy man's house. If we saw such a man, he would be a servant carrying water to his master's house. And it unfolded exactly as Jesus said it would. We found the large upper room, the room of the highest honor, to eat our Passover meal.

The setting of the sun marked the first day of Passover. Jesus sat down with us, the Twelve Apostles. He blessed the food, and we ate the Passover meal.

After supper, Jesus looked at us as if He were looking into our souls. We were reclining on the couches on three sides of the table, with our heads toward the table, so it was easy for Him to see each of us and look directly into our eyes.

Jesus said, "It is with great emotion that I have looked forward to eating this Passover with you before I suffer."

Jesus knew what the devil had put into the heart of Judas Iscariot and that the time had come for this despicable worm to betray Him. Jesus explained that His Father had given control of what would happen into His hands. He said that He was sent from God to accomplish what lay ahead and that He would return to His Father's presence afterward.

With the supper finished, Jesus rose and laid His garments aside, girdled Himself with a towel, and poured water into a bowl. He washed each Apostle's feet and wiped them dry on the towel with which He was girdled. When my turn came, I objected, saying, "Lord, do you wash my feet?"

Jesus answered, "You do not understand what I am doing, but you shall know hereafter."

I objected to Him performing a servant's task, saying, "You shall never wash my feet!"

"If I do not cleanse you, you will have no part with me," He explained without chastisement.

I responded in complete compliance, saying, "Lord, wash not only my feet, but my hands and my head."

"He that is washed needs only to have his feet washed but

is thereby clean throughout." Jesus finished washing my feet and said, "And now you are clean." Then He looked around and added, "But not all of you are clean." Jesus knew that Judas was preparing to betray Him.

After Jesus had finished washing our feet and put his garments back on, He asked us, "Do you know what I have done to you?"

We had no idea of the significance of what He had just done. He explained, "You call me 'Master' and 'Lord,' and you say rightly, for so I am. If I then, being your Lord and Master, have washed your feet, you also ought to wash one another's feet. For I have given you an example that you should follow. Do as I have done to you. The servant is not greater than his Lord, neither is He that is sent greater than He that sent Him. If you know these things, you will be happy if you do them."

Jesus put down the towel, then continued, "I tell you this truth, that one of you shall betray me."

His announcement compounded our great sadness and added a dose of anger to mine. If one of us was to betray Him, who was it? Knowing that I sometimes said things without thinking, I wondered if I would say or do something that would betray Jesus. I barely managed to utter, "Lord, is it I?" and each of my fellow Apostles repeated the question in turn. I was not the only one who was worried that he might somehow slip and say or do something that might betray His location.

Jesus held his peace until each Apostle had repeated the same question. Then Jesus said, "I speak not of all of you. I know whom I have chosen, but that the scriptures may be fulfilled, one of you that has eaten bread with me has lifted up his heel against me. I am telling you about it now, before it happens, so that when it comes to pass, you will see and believe that I am the Christ." Then Jesus added, "I tell you this truth also: he that receives whomever I send receives me, and he that receives me will receive Him that sent me."

When Jesus finished saying this, His countenance grew somber. He gazed at each of us, then He slowly repeated the words: "I tell you that one of you shall betray me."

I was confused at why He would repeat Himself. We all looked around at each other, not knowing which of us it was.

I looked across the table and motioned to John the beloved, who was leaning next to Jesus's chest. I beckoned to him saying, "Ask Him who it is."

Jesus responded to John's inquiry, speaking not to John, but to Judas, saying, "It is he to whom I shall give a morsel of food." Then Jesus dipped the bread into the sop and gave it to Judas Iscariot. He continued, speaking directly and quietly to Judas, "The Son of Man goes away, as it is written of Him to do, but woe to that man by whom the Son of Man is betrayed! It would have been better for that man if he had not been born."

Judas had been warned so that he would never be able to deny that he knew what he was doing and what the consequences were. Let no man defend him. Judas whispered to Jesus, asking weakly, "Master, is it I?"

Jesus answered him, again speaking for only him to hear, "It is as you have said."

John heard the whispered conversation but said nothing. He told me of it privately and later wrote it for others to know.

Judas realized that his part in the conspiracy was no longer a secret. Jesus knew that he was the traitor. He said nothing, but sat there, frozen. Jesus spoke to Him one more time, this time for everyone to hear, saying, "What you do, do quickly!"

Except for John, none of us understood what Jesus meant when He spoke those words to Judas. Some of us thought He was sending Judas on another financial errand. We thought that maybe he had gone to purchase food for the feast or that he had been sent to give money to the poor. All we knew was that after Judas received the sop, he went from the presence of Jesus and into the darkness of the night. I later realized that his exit from the presence of the Son of God into the darkness was more than symbolic.

After we had finished our meal, Jesus took a loaf of bread and blessed it. Then he broke it into pieces and gave it to us. He said solemnly, "Take and eat. This is my body, which is given for you. Do this in remembrance of me. I will not eat any more thereof until my life is fulfilled in the kingdom of God."

Next Jesus took a cup of wine and blessed it and gave it to us to pass around. As we each took a drink, He said, "Each of you drink of it because this is my blood of the New Testament, which is shed for many for the remission of sins."

The holy sacrament was thus instituted. From the time of Adam until that day, we observed the law of sacrifice, looking to the day when the Lamb of God would be sacrificed. We were now instructed to hereafter remember Him with the bread and wine, signifying His flesh and blood. As He had said, His blood was not shed for everyone but for the many who would repent and receive a remission of their sins.

"I will not drink henceforth of the fruit of the vine until that day when I drink it new with you in the kingdom of God."

FINAL INSTRUCTIONS
TO THE APOSTLES

After Jesus had given us His new sacrament, His demeanor seemed to lift. Later I concluded that the absence of Judas had removed a darkness from the room. There was a tangible, sweet, tender feeling there—a feeling we had experienced many times before.

Jesus said, "Now is the time that the Son of Man is glorified, and God is glorified in Him. If God is glorified in Him, God shall also glorify the Son of Man in Himself, and God is glorified in Him."

I did not understand what He meant, but turning to us, the remaining eleven Apostles, Jesus said, "Little children, I am with you yet a little while. You shall seek me, but as I said to the Jews, 'Where I go you cannot come.' And I now give you a new commandment, that you love one another, and that you also love one another as I have loved you. By this shall all men know that you are my disciples, if you have love one to another."

I knew that we had always been commanded to love one another, but now we were commanded to love one another as Jesus loved us. In that way, it was both a new commandment and an old commandment. His love was a whole level higher than one might usually show to another.

We were brothers, we Apostles. We did not know what the future held, but it was certain to be difficult. We would need to watch out for one another. Knowing that the Pharisees wanted to kill Jesus and that they would arrest, try, and kill us also, we would need each other's support to face these trials. It was going to be difficult. I was not afraid of the Jews, but I was afraid of the unknown. I was troubled not knowing what was going to happen, who would take us, when, and where. I wondered when I would be back with Jesus.

Jesus knew of my concern and said, "Let not your heart be troubled. You believe in God; believe in me also. In my Father's house are many mansions. If it were not so, I would have told you. I am going to prepare a place for you. And if I go and prepare a place for you, I will come again and receive you to myself, that where I am you may be also. You know where I am going, and now you know the way I am going."

"But Lord," Thomas interrupted, "we do not know where you are going, and how can we know the way?"

Jesus answered Thomas, saying, "I am the Way, the Truth, and the Life. No man comes unto the Father but by me. If you have known me, you should have known my Father also, and from henceforth, you know Him and have seen Him."

"Lord," Philip said, "show us the Father, and that will be sufficient for us."

"Have I been such a long time with you, and yet you do not know me, Philip?" He answered. "He that has seen me has seen the Father, so how can you say, 'Show us the Father?' Do you not believe that I am in the Father and the Father in me? The words I speak to you I speak not of myself but of the Father that dwells in me. I do His works. Believe me that I am in the Father and the Father in me. The works that I do He shall do also; and He shall do greater works than these because I go unto my Father. And whatever you shall ask in my name I will do so that the Father may be glorified in the Son. If you shall ask anything in my name, I will do it."

Jesus was telling us that, from a physical perspective, He looked exactly like His Father. He also spoke from a spiritual perspective, reminding us that He and His Father were in total spiritual unity—the same as if Jesus were part of His Father and vice versa. I had changed from being an ordinary man because of Him. In a spiritual sense, Jesus was in me, and I was better for it.

At this time, Jesus promised us a Second Comforter, saying, "If you love me, keep my commandments. I will pray to my Father, and He shall give you another Comforter, that He may abide with you forever, even the Spirit of Truth, whom the world cannot receive because it does not see Him, neither does it know Him. You know Him because He dwells with you and shall be in you.

I loved Jesus's symbolic language. He was the First Comforter, and the Holy Ghost was the Second Comforter. Just as the Spirit of Truth is in me, but I am not the Spirit of Truth, the Father is in the Son, but the Son is not the Father, nor is the Father the Son. They are separate beings.

"I will not leave you orphans," Jesus said. "I will come to you. In a little while, the world will see me no more, but you shall see me. Because I live, you shall live also. At that day, you shall know that I am in my Father, and you are in me, and I am in you.

"He that has my commandments, and keeps them, loves me; he that loves me shall be loved by my Father, and I will love him and will manifest myself to Him."

"Lord, how will you manifest yourself to us and not unto the world?" Judas Thaddeus Lebbeus, the Apostle, asked.

"If a man loves me, he will keep my commandments, and my Father will love him, and we will both come to him and abide with him. He that does not love me will not keep my commandments. Know that the commandments, which you hear, are not mine, but my Father's that sent me. These things I have spoken to you while with you. But the Comforter, which is the Holy Ghost, whom the Father will send in my name, shall teach you all things, and the Holy Ghost shall bring all things to your remembrance. Through the Holy Ghost, you shall remember all that I have said to you."

It was by the power of the Holy Ghost that we remembered everything Jesus said. He promised that it would happen, so it did. We later remembered and understood things Jesus told us, even the things we did not understand when He first spoke them.

"I leave peace with you," Jesus said, offering us comfort. "I give you my peace. I do not give you the peace the world gives. Do not let your heart be troubled, neither let it be afraid."

Jesus is the Prince of Peace spoken of by Isaiah. When He pronounces a blessing of peace on you, you feel it. Words are inadequate to communicate how I felt as He blessed us that day. The worry, the anxiety, the fear, and the concerns that had filled my mind disappeared. The knot that had been in my stomach since He told us He would be crucified was gone too. I was just as He said—I was no longer troubled. I was at peace.

"You have heard me say I am going away and will come again to you. If you love me, you will rejoice because I said I am going to the Father, for the Father is greater than I am. I told you this before it came to pass, so that when it does come to pass you will see and believe."

"Hereafter, I will not talk much with you because the prince of darkness, the prince of this world, is coming," He warned us. "He has no power over me, but he seeks to have power over you."

His words were sobering. I resolved to be more careful about what I said and did, so I would not subject myself to the will of the prince of darkness.

"So that the world may know that I love the Father, I shall do what the Father commanded me to do," He said, reminding us that what was to happen was the will of the

Father. "Arise, let us go from this room."

We moved from the upper room and the table where we had eaten together into another room, where Jesus sat and talked to us. Jesus thanked our host for the supper he had prepared and his courtesy in providing the upper room. Our host, in return, thanked Jesus for allowing him to provide the Passover to Him, having no idea how significant that supper was.

As we made ourselves more comfortable in the next room, Jesus continued to teach. We had done it this way for two years, and my heart holds fond memories of those talks. That was how it always was when He taught us. Those moments were gold to me.

Jesus continued to instruct, prepare, and assure us that we would not be alone after He was gone. He made a point of telling us how we would abide in Him and He would abide in us, applying the words He used earlier referring to Him and His Father.

"I am the True Vine, and my Father is the Husbandman," Jesus taught. "Every branch in me that does not bear fruit, He takes away. He purifies every branch that bears fruit, that it may bring forth even more fruit. You are now clean; know that by the words I have spoken to you. Abide in me, and I shall abide in you. As the branch cannot bear fruit by itself except it abide in the vine, no more can you bear fruit of yourself, except you abide in me. I am the Vine, and you are the branches. He that abides in me, and I in him, the same brings forth much fruit, but without me you can do nothing.

"If a man does not abide in me, he is cast forth as a broken branch and is withered, and men gather these withered branches and cast them into the fire, where they are burned. If you abide in me and my words abide in you, ask whatever you will, and it shall be done unto you. Herein is my Father glorified, that you bear much fruit, and in so doing you are my disciples.

"I have loved you as my Father has loved me. Continue in my love. If you keep my commandments, you shall abide in my love, even as I have kept my Father's commandments and I abide in His love. I have told you these things that my joy might remain in you, that your joy might be full.

"This is my commandment to you: love one another as I have loved you. Greater love has no man than this, that a man lay down his life for his friends. If you do whatever I command you, you are my friends. From now on, I do not call you servants, for the servant does not know what the master does, but I call you friends, for all of the things I have heard of my Father I make known to you. You have not chosen me, but I have chosen you. And I have ordained you that you should go forth and bring fruit and that your fruit should remain, that whatever you shall ask of the Father in my name, He may give it to you."

Until then, He had always directed us to pray to the Father, but He told us to pray to the Father in the name of the Son from then on. I understood that things would be different when Jesus was gone—the harsh reality was that Jesus was going to be crucified, and He was preparing us for afterward.

Jesus had many followers—people that heard about Him, sought Him out, and followed Him. All of them chose Him, but it was different for the Twelve Apostles, He had asked us to follow Him. He truly chose us. I had always known this, but hearing it then, in His own words, made it so much more real. I was an ordinary man; we were all ordinary men. I did not know why He chose me, but I accepted His choice and loved Him. He had given us His priesthood, and as my fellow Apostle Paul warned, that authority was not ours to take. It is always His to give.

"This is my commandment to you: love one another. If

the world shall hate you, know that it hated me first. If you were of the world, the world would love you as its own. But because you are not of the world, and because I have chosen you out of the world, the world hates you."

He paused as we contemplated His words. I considered it a privilege to be hated because Christ chose me, but I remained bewildered about why He had chosen ordinary men, even men like me, crude, uneducated, and of no particular social or economic standing.

It was not until later that I understood. He called men like me because we trusted in Him, not in ourselves, because we had no learning but what He gave us, and because we obeyed Him. He chose me *because* I was weak, not in spite of it. His wisdom is unlimited.

"Remember what I said: the servant is not greater than his Lord," He warned us. "If they have persecuted me, they will also persecute you. If they have kept my teachings, they will keep yours also, but all the things they shall do to you, they will do for my name's sake, because they do not know Him that sent me."

Then Jesus spoke of the wicked Jews who were plotting against Him: "If I had not come and spoken to them, they would have no sin, but now they have no excuse for it. He that hates me also hates my Father. If I had not come among them and done the works I did, which no other man could do, they would have no sin, but now they have both seen my works and hated me and my Father. This came to pass so that which is written in their law might be fulfilled; they hated me without cause.

"But when the Comforter has come—whom I will send unto you from the Father, even the Spirit of Truth, which proceeds from the Father—He shall testify of me. And you shall also bear witness of me because you have been with me from the beginning.

"I have spoken these things to you that you should not be surprised and stumble when they occur. Know that they shall bar you from the synagogues. Yes, the time is coming that whoever kills you will think they are serving God. They will do these things to you because they have not known the Father or me. Again, I have told you these things that when the time shall come, you will remember that I told you about them. I did not tell you these things at the beginning because I was with you. Now that I go to Him that sent me, none of you will need to ask me, 'Where are you going?'

"Because I have told you these things, your hearts are filled with sorrow. Nevertheless, I have told you the truth. It is for your benefit that I go away. If I do not go away, the Comforter will not come unto you. But if I depart, I will send Him to you. When He comes, He will convict the world of its sin and testify of my righteousness and of my judgments. They will be convicted of their sins because they do not believe in me. He will be the one to testify of my righteousness because I go to my Father, and they shall see me no more. He will testify of my judgment because the Prince of this World shall be judged for His works."

"I have many things yet to say to you, but you cannot bear them right now," Jesus said, mindful of our limitations. "Nevertheless, when the Spirit of Truth comes, He will guide you into all truth, for He shall not speak of Himself, but He shall speak whatever He shall hear, and He will show you things to come.

"He shall glorify me, for He shall receive of me and shall show it to you because all things that the Father has are mine. That is why I said that He shall take from that which is mine and shall show it to you."

I understood that He was referring to revelation. After all, He built His Church on the "rock of revelation."

"It is only a little while, and you shall not see me. And

after another little while, you shall see me, because I am going to the Father."

One of the Apostles whispered to another, asking, "What does He mean when He says, 'A little while, and you shall not see me. And after another little while, you shall see me because I am going to the Father'? I do not understand what He means."

Jesus saw that there was some confusion about His words, so He explained them to us. "I tell you this truth, you shall weep and lament, but the world shall rejoice."

He then compared His crucifixion and resurrection to the pain and joy of a woman giving birth, saying, "And you shall be sorrowful, but your sorrow shall be turned into joy. A woman, when she suffers the pain of childbirth is sorrowful because her hour is come, but as soon as she is delivered of her child, she no longer remembers her anguish because of the joy she feels that her child is born into the world. Likewise, you now feel sorrow, but I will see you again, and your heart shall rejoice, and no man will be able to take your joy from you.

"In that day, you shall ask nothing of me. But you shall ask of the Father in my name, and He will give it to you. Up to now, you have asked for nothing in my name. Ask now in my name and you shall receive that your joy may be full."

I listened, I heard, but I was yet to fully understand. I trusted Jesus and knew that what He said would come to pass.

WARNING TO THE APOSTLES

Jesus continued to teach us as we sat together. "I have taught you in proverbs, but the time is coming when I shall teach no more in proverbs. Instead, I shall show you plainly by the Father. At that day, you shall ask of Him in my name. I need not pray for you because the Father Himself loves you, for you have loved me and have believed that I came from God. I came forth from the Father into the world. Again, remember that I leave the world to go to the Father."

"Please speak plainly now, without proverb," we requested. "We have no doubt that you know all things, and we know no man could give you what you know, and by that, we believe that you came forth from God."

"Do you believe now?" He asked us. "Behold, the hour comes; in fact, it has now come that you shall be scattered, every man on his own, and you shall leave me alone. And yet, I am not alone because the Father is with me. I have told you these things that you might have peace in me. You shall have tribulation in the world, but be of good cheer because I have overcome the world.

"All of you shall stumble this night because of me, for it is written, 'I will smite the shepherd, and the sheep of the flock shall be scattered.' But after I am risen again, I will go before you into Galilee."

I was yet to understand those words. Or perhaps I was in denial about the possibility of stumbling or denying Jesus. My mind still swirled around Him being crucified.

ADVOCACY PRAYER

Jesus finished His final instructions and said it was time for prayer. We knelt and He lifted His eyes to heaven, saying, "Father, the hour has come. Glorify thy Son that thy Son may glorify Thee also. And Thou hast given Him power over all flesh that He should give eternal life to as many as Thou hast given Him. And this is life eternal, that they might know Thee, the only true God, and Jesus Christ, whom Thou has sent."

"I have glorified Thee on the earth: I have finished the work which Thou gave me to do. And now, O Father, glorify Thou me with Thine Own Self, with the glory which I had with Thee before the world was."

Jesus prayed to His Father for Himself. His prior prayers were for others—for their faith, their healing, and their acceptance of His word. Now we heard Him pray for what He needed. Through my tears, I prayed with Him.

Then I heard the Son of God pray for us. To me, these were the most tender words I ever heard Him utter: "I have manifested thy name unto the men whom Thou gave me out of the world. They were Thine and Thou gave them to me, and they have kept thy word. Now they know that all things Thou gave me are from Thee. I gave them the words which Thou gavest me, and they have received them, and they know for a certainty that I came from Thee, and they believe that Thou sent me.

"I pray for them, Father. I do not pray for the world, but

only them, which Thou gave me, for they are thine. And all that are mine are thine, and Thine are mine, and I am glorified in them. And now I am to be no more in the world. I come to Thee, but these remain in the world. Holy Father, keep through Thine own name those whom Thou has given me, that they may be one as we are one. While I was with them in the world, I kept them in thy name. Those that Thou gave me I have kept, and none of them is lost except the son of perdition, that the scripture might be fulfilled.

"And now I am coming to Thee, Father. These things I speak while here in the world, that these men might have joy, are fulfilled in themselves. I have given them thy word, and the world has hated them because they are not of the world even as I am not of the world. I do not pray that Thou should take them out of the world but that Thou should preserve them from the world. They are not of the world, even as I am not of the world. Sanctify them through thy word, which word is truth. As Thou sent me into the world, I sent them into the world. For their sakes, I sanctify myself that they also might be sanctified through the truth.

"I do not pray for these alone but also for them which shall believe on me through their word, that they may all be one, as thou, Father, are in me, and I in Thee, that they also may be one in us, that the world may believe that Thou sent me. And the glory which Thou gave me, I have given them, that they may be one even as we are one; I in them and Thou in me, that they may be made perfect in one, that the world may know that Thou sent me, and love them as Thou loves me.

"Father, I also ask that they whom Thou gave me will be with me where I am to be; that they may behold my glory, which Thou gave me, for Thou loved me before the foundation of the world. O righteous Father, the world has not known Thee, but I have known Thee, and these have known that Thou sent me. I have declared thy name to them and will declare it, that the love wherewith Thou has loved me may be in them, and I in them."

After He prayed, we sang a hymn and rose from our seats to leave the house of our host. I thought we might be going to the Mount of Olives. Jesus loved the Mount of Olives, and we always went there as we left Jerusalem.

SIMON, SIMON

As we prepared to leave the house, Jesus stopped me. "Simon, Simon," He said, "know that Satan has wanted you so he may sift you as wheat, but I have prayed for you, that your faith will not fail you. When you are converted, strengthen your brethren."

At first I did not understand what he meant by being converted. Certainly, I thought I was converted. I knew that Jesus was the Son of God. I was not converted to the idea that He need be crucified. I did not understand why it needed to happen. Yes, He told us it was part of His Father's plan, but I did not yet understand that plan. It would not be until later that I became converted. Then it would be my duty to strengthen my brethren who also did not understand the need for the crucifixion.

Because I did not yet understand His meaning, I assured Him that I could not be offended by anyone. In other words, no event or comment would cause me to stop doing what I knew was right.

"Even if all men shall be offended because of you, I will never be offended!" I vowed.

As we left the house, I asked Jesus privately, "Lord, where are you going?"

He knew what I was asking. "Where I am going, you cannot follow now," He told me, "but you shall follow me afterward."

"Lord, why can I not follow you now? I will lay down my life for your sake."

His prophetic response shook me. He said, "Will you lay down your life for my sake? I tell you this truth: this night, before the cock crows twice, you shall deny knowing me three times."

"I am ready to go with you, both to prison and to death, and if I should die with you, I will not deny knowing you," I said with sincere conviction. "As soon as I spoke, all of the Apostles said that they would die before denying Jesus.

I looked to Jesus for a response, but He said nothing. When He prophesied, nothing more needed to be said. Jesus did not argue with me.

As we walked through Jerusalem toward the Mount of Olives, Jesus asked us, "When I sent you without purse or scrip and shoes, did you do without anything?"

"Nothing," we answered.

"But now I tell you that he that has a purse, let him take it and likewise his money, and he that has no sword, let him sell one of his garments and buy one."

With this commandment, we were no longer to go out without purse or scrip. I did not understand, however, His reference to swords. He was referring to being prepared, but I thought He was talking about defending ourselves. I reached for my sword, something I always had ready, and another Apostle followed my example. We said, "Lord, look, here are two swords."

Jesus said, "That is enough. I tell you that the words which have been written about me, 'And He was numbered among the transgressors,' must be accomplished because the words written about me brought me to this end."

THE GARDEN OF GETHSEMANE

It was early in the evening when we left Jerusalem, passed through the Kidron Valley, and walked along the lower western slope of the Mount of Olives. I noticed a few men following along, but they did not join us. I suspected they were spies for the Sanhedrin. We walked until we arrived at a grove of olive trees, a place called Gethsemane. We had stopped just outside the grove and talked for a time before Jesus asked me, along with James and John, to accompany Him into the garden. Once inside, Jesus said, "Sit here while I go yonder and pray."

Even by the faint light of my lamp, I could tell that Jesus was very troubled, His thoughts weighing heavily on His mind. "My soul is deeply grieved, even to the point of death," He confided. "Stay here and watch over me. We obeyed and sat down to watch as He walked about a stone's throw further into Gethsemane.

I watched Jesus kneel down and place His face to the ground before He prayed, something I had never seen Him do before. He always knelt but never in such a submissive position. I listened as He prayed. "O my Father, if it be possible, let this cup pass from me, nevertheless not as I will, but as Thou will."

It was not long before my eyes grew very heavy, and I grew too tired to sit. James and John were similarly overwhelmed with tiredness. We all reclined on the ground, still trying to stay awake. But we could not keep our eyes open, and we soon fell asleep. I did not hear the rest of His prayer.

The next thing I knew, He was waking us up, saying, "What? Are you sleeping? Are you so weak that you could not stay awake with me one hour? Watch and pray that you do not give in to temptation." He paused for a moment. "The spirit indeed is willing, but the flesh is weak." Then He went a ways away to pray again.

At first I thought He was referring to the weakness of our flesh, but I soon concluded that He was talking about the weakness of His own flesh. He was struggling as He suffered greatly in the olive grove.

Once again, we listened as He knelt with His face to the ground and prayed, submitting Himself completely to the will of His Father, saying, "O my Father, if this cup may not pass away from me except I drink it, thy will be done."

After that, we fell asleep a second time—our eyes were too heavy to keep open. When He returned, He found us sleeping again. He woke us again, but we were still very sleepy. He left us again and prayed a third time. I watched Him as long as I could force myself to stay awake. He started His prayer by saying the same words as before.

This time, however, He was joined by an angel from heaven, who stood behind Him. I used my fingers to hold my eyelids open as the angel ministered to Jesus. I saw Jesus bow His face to the ground and pray again, seemingly even more earnestly than before. I did not understand everything I was seeing, but it looked like Jesus was in severe pain. His voice sounded like it was filled with agony, almost breaking with emotion. He struggled to pronounce the words of His prayer. His whole body appeared to tremble as if He were holding a great weight on His back.

Then I saw something that I have never seen before. The sweat that appeared on His brow was red. It looked to me like He was sweating blood! His sweat beaded up and fell to the ground as if He were bleeding from every pore. I saw it, but I did not understand it. I fought an overwhelming weariness that caused my eyes to burn and made me long for sleep. Tears filled my eyes as I saw the Son of God weep from unbearable pain and cry out in agony. I closed my eyes to pray for Jesus and was immediately overtaken by sleep.

When He had finished praying, Jesus came to us, and I heard Him say, "Sleep on now and take your rest." His voice was weary and ragged, evidencing the stress He had just gone through. We were so drowsy, we fell asleep immediately.

Looking back, I know that we had been present for one of the most important events in history. We had witnessed the beginning of His Atonement, where He took upon Himself the sins of all mankind and paid for them—for all of us.

After a time, He awakened us. I did not know how long we had slept, but it was certainly well after midnight. Jesus spoke, His voice weak and raspy, saying, "Behold, the hour is at hand. The Son of Man is betrayed into the hands of sinners. Arise and let us go. He that will betray me is at hand."

The sleepiness that had overtaken me was suddenly gone. I stood quickly, wide awake as Jesus gestured toward the path from Jerusalem. I could see a large procession carrying lamps and torches approaching us from the city, but I could not see who they were. The cowards were hiding their acts and their identities in the dark of the night. *It is time!* I said to myself. *They are coming!*

The same evil Pharisees, scribes, and Sadducees who had plotted to kill Jesus were coming to arrest Him, just as He he said. My hands began to sweat. I wondered what I should do. Should I do nothing as He commanded? I knew I was not supposed to stop them, but the pounding of my heart and the ringing in my ears seemed to drown out what I knew. Evil men were approaching.

The Betrayal

As they drew near, I recognized Judas leading the procession. Behind him, men carried lamps and torches. Some of them had swords, but most were armed with wooden staffs. Our two swords would be no match for their numbers. It was apparent that the Pharisees, chief priests, and lawyers had sent these evildoers to arrest Jesus in the dark of night so the people would not see what they did. We were later told that Judas had volunteered to betray Jesus by kissing Him. He had told them, "Whomever I shall kiss, He is the one you seek. Hold Him fast."

Judas knew of Gethsemane because we had met there many times before. He came forward and approached the Master. Despite His weariness, Jesus stood straight, cleared His throat, and addressed the traitor as if he were an honorable man, saying, "Friend, why have you come?"

Then the traitor continued his duplicity, saying, "Hail, Master," and he immediately kissed Jesus on the cheek, signaling that Jesus was the one they sought.

"Judas, do you betray the Son of Man with a kiss?" He asked Judas, who silently cowered back into the darkness of the night. Jesus addressed the gathering band. "Whom do you seek?" He asked.

"Jesus of Nazareth," called someone at the front.

Jesus reached for one of the lamps and held it up, revealing that His face and clothes were covered with blood, and spoke boldly, "I am He."

When they heard Him speak and saw His face, they stumbled backward, falling to the ground.

His voice was strong, even though he had just suffered greater pain than anything known to man. They crowd fearfully whispered among themselves, but no one came forward or spoke.

Jesus repeated His question, speaking loud enough for the whole mob to hear. "Whom do you seek?"

"Jesus of Nazareth," someone said weakly, as if he hoped it was someone other than this blood-covered man.

"I have told you that I am He," Jesus said boldy, pointing to Himself. "If you seek me, let these men go their way." Even now, He sought to protect us, His Apostles, thus fulfilling His prophecy, "Of them which Thou gave me, I have lost none."

One of the men stepped forward, put his hands on the Son of God, and tried to take hold of Him.

Immediately, my nostrils flared, and my muscles tensed. The man was Malchus, a sniveling lackey of the high priest Caiaphas. I had seen him before, slyly whispering to his evil master as they listened to Jesus in the temple. The look in the man's face as he held Jesus was smug and self-righteous. At that moment, he represented everything evil in Judea, even all of Israel.

I heard one of the Apostles ask, "Lord, shall we smite them with the sword?" But I did not need to ask. In a single move, my right hand drew my sword, and my body lunged forward. I meant to split the skull of this sleazy servant of evil, but as he recoiled in fear, I managed only to separate the coward from his right ear. I had been ready for this moment from our first journey through Samaria when I resolved to protect Jesus, but I had missed my mark!

I was only a fisherman, not a soldier, but the message I sent was clear. I was poised to impale anyone else that might step forward to touch Jesus. My heart continued to beat rapidly, and my ears rang more loudly than ever. I felt light-headed, but I was ready to disembowel as many as I could before they struck me down. I stood ready for an attack that did not come. The cowards stood there, frozen in shock, the wound on the right side of the servant's head bleeding heavily. His ear lay on the ground.

Jesus put His hand on mine, near the hilt of my sword, and gently pushed it down. He put His other hand on my shoulder, calming me. "Put your sword back into its place, for all they that take the sword shall perish by the sword," He said gently. "My Father has given me a cup. Shall I not drink it? Do you not think that I could ask my Father and He would immediately give me tens of thousands of angels? But if I do that, how shall the scriptures be fulfilled that say this must be?"

I saw tears in His eyes that matched the tears in mine.

Jesus turned, picked up the severed ear, touched it to the wound on the side of Malchus's head, and said, "Suffer no more." Malchus was immediately healed. He performed a miracle for the entire mob to see, and for a brief moment, I wondered if they would still try to arrest Him. But I should have known better. Evil people are not converted by miracles; they are condemned by them.

Still free from their grasp, Jesus turned from Malchus to address the chief priests, condemning them all. "Do you come out late into the night, carrying swords and wooden staffs, as if I were a thief?" He asked. "When I was with you during the day in the temple, you did not even lift your hand against me, but now you come in the night, carrying weapons. This hour of darkness is your hour, and you act with the power of darkness."

I just stood there, forcing myself to do nothing. No one else moved either. Finally, someone from the mob came forward and took hold of Jesus, quickly bound His hands with cords, and led Him away. I slowly put my sword away, clenched my fists at my side, and tightened my jaw. Tears of love changed to tears of anger, hot on my cheeks. In the darkness, my emotions were my secret.

Obedient to Jesus's command, I stepped back from the crowd, escaping into the dark of the night, the other Apostles following behind. We left before they tried to arrest us too. All of this was done so the words of the prophets would be fulfilled. None of us were lost.

It was soon apparent that our decision to escape the mob was timely. As they entered the city, a certain young man awoke from his sleep, and being curious to see what was going on, he joined the crowd following Jesus. Some of the younger men in the crowd tried to grab him, taking hold of his linen night clothing. The young man panicked and escaped by freeing himself from his clothing, running naked into the night. Had we not escaped when we did, we could have been arrested with Jesus.

Hidden by the darkness of the night, we secretly followed the procession back into Jerusalem, watching their path. The captain of the temple and the officers of the Sanhedrin took Jesus into the palace of Caiaphas the high priest.

In my heart, I wished for the tens of thousands of angels Jesus had mentioned. I knew it was not to be, but the image would not leave my mind.

I was not a coward, but I felt like one, hiding in the darkness to avoid arrest. I had been prepared to die for Him. Instead, He had forbidden me to defend Him. Still, what my heart wanted to do was cut off the arms of those holding Him and to loose His bindings. Obediently, I had done nothing. I was a man of action, not a spectator in life. My stomach churned inside me. My throat was tight, making it painful to swallow. Tears of anger came to my eyes. I began to feel cold.

THE PALACE OF CAIAPHAS

When the band of evildoers arrived at the palace of Caiaphas, the chief priests, along with the scribes and elders, were already assembled. The palace was well lit, and everyone was awaiting Jesus. I didn't know if it was late in the night or early in the morning, but they had planned well.

The door to the palace was locked, requiring us to obtain permission to enter. John, the son of Zebedee, reminded me that he was acquainted with Caiaphas, so he could get us in. As he approached the door, I observed sarcastically, "Being a member of the Sanhedrin certainly pays well." *Caiaphas is a sinfully rich man*, I thought. I waited at the bottom of the stairs while John spoke to the servant girl tending the door. He was quickly admitted and motioned for me to join him.

As I passed through the door, the servant girl looked at me quizzically, then exclaimed, "You were with Jesus of Nazareth!" Then she turned to the people in the room and said, "This man was also with Him!"

I needed to get into the palace to see what was going on, so without thinking, I said, "Woman, I don't know what you are talking about," and walked casually to the portico to warm myself by the fire like everyone else. As I stood alongside the servants and officers, I heard the cock crow. It was still dark, but the morning was approaching.

At first I warmed myself by the fire, trying to appear as disinterested in Jesus as possible, but I soon moved closer to watch. Jesus had commanded me not to protect Him, but that did not mean I had to abandon Him. I had lied my way into the palace of the high priest, but now that I was in, I didn't know what I would do. My mind reeled with conflicting thoughts. I had no answers. I was still cold.

As I watched, Annas, the former high priest and Caiaphas's father-in-law, interrogated Jesus. The rumor was that Annas was the power behind Caiaphas, and his presence at this meeting confirmed it. Caiaphas was the wicked high priest who had prophesied that it was expedient that one man should die for the good of the people.

Annas questioned Jesus about the Apostles. That was when I knew I must remain anonymous. I figured Annas already knew the answers to his questions; Judas had surely divulged everything he wished to know. I watched as Jesus stood silently. Then Annas asked Jesus about His doctrine, wanting to know what He taught. His tone was more accusatory than anything.

Instead of answering the questions illegally put forward by Annas, Jesus invoked the sophisticated laws that governed the Sanhedrin. By law, the council was not allowed to accuse anyone of anything, only to question witnesses. The law required them to hold open, public inquiries during the day and only within the confines of the Hall of Hewn Stones, the official quarters of the Sanhedrin.

Here we were in a private interrogation held behind locked doors at the palace of the head of the Sanhedrin, during the middle of the night! They were also forbidden to arrest or detain anyone that was accused, allowing the accused the freedom to find and question his own witnesses. Accusers were not allowed to bind, torture, or abuse anyone. If an accused man voluntarily confessed, his confession required the corroboration of two credible witnesses. They were violating so many of the Sanhedrin's rules, they could never claim that this proceeding was anything more than a Jewish Inquisition.

"I spoke openly for the world to hear," Jesus responded. "I always taught in the synagogue and in the temple, where the Jews always go to be taught. I have not taught in secret, so why do you ask me what I teach? Ask witnesses, those that heard me, what I said. Behold, they know what I said."

One of the officers of the court stepped forward and slapped Jesus on the face, saying, "How dare you speak to the high priest like that?"

Jesus stood solidly. If the anger in my heart at that moment could have been felt by that cowardly officer of the court, he would have burst into flames and fallen dead on the floor. My fists and jaw clenched involuntarily, but I did not reach for my sword. I confess that I thought about it, but I didn't do it. Without knowing who was watching, I had to be careful.

Jesus knew the law, and He had accurately pointed out their flagrant violation of that law. Their indignation betrayed their intent: Jesus was to be killed. They just had to find an excuse for their treachery. Jesus challenged them further, saying, "If I have spoken evil, address that evil. But if I have spoken well, why do you strike me?"

His challenge to their courage ended that phase of the inquisition. Annas apparently realized that he had been outwitted by an unlawfully bound prisoner. Unable to respond, he told the servants to have Jesus stand before Caiaphas, the high priest.

For the next hour, the chief priests, the elders, and all of the council solicited witnesses to come forward and testify falsely against Jesus in order to find a cause to put Him to death. Many testified, but the lies they offered did not coincide, which greatly frustrated the conspirators.

Finally, two false witnesses came forward to testify against Jesus, saying, "This man said, 'I am able to destroy the temple of God that was built by the hand of man and then rebuild it in three days, without the hand of man.' "

What precious Pharisaic rule does this false accusation break? I wondered in silence.

Caiaphas finally stood, and I knew that we were going to hear from the man who had been given "authority" by the Romans. He interrogated Jesus, asking, "Have you no answer to the charge that these witnesses have testified against you?"

Bound and detained illegally, Jesus did not respond. Caiaphas violated another of the laws, shouting, "I command you by the living God that you tell us whether you be the Christ, the Son of God!" According to Jewish law, no man could be compelled to testify against himself, but the corrupt Caiaphas was demanding it of Jesus.

Jesus lifted His head and responded, "It is as you have said. Hereafter you shall see the Son of Man sitting on the right hand of God and coming in the clouds of heaven."

Then Caiaphas tore his robe in a traditional melodramatic display of self-righteous indignation. "He has blasphemed!" he shouted, addressing the Sanhedrin. "What further need do we have of witnesses? Behold, you have now heard His blasphemy from His own mouth. What do you think of that?"

I thought my sword should cut off some more ears and maybe even remove a certain high priest's evil tongue. Still, I did nothing. I began to feel colder. Caiaphas had accused Jesus of sedition, but he found Him guilty of blasphemy.

"He is guilty of death." The Sanhedrin found the evidence it sought. Jesus bore testimony of who He was. They judged Him based on His own testimony and rejected Him. Every member of the Sanhedrin in attendance stood, signifying by unanimous vote that Jesus should die. I looked for Nicodemus, but he was not there. I concluded that he and those who had challenged the Sanhedrin earlier had not been invited to this illegal inquisition.

According to Jewish law, in the event of a unanimous

vote of the council, the trial was to be nullified. Of course, this was not a real trial, so the law was of no consequence to them.

Jesus stood there alone, His hands bound. His face and garments were still covered with the blood He had shed in the Garden of Gethsemane. His muscled arms and powerful chest were visible through His torn garments. With His arms tied, a couple of the cowardly servants of the council members stepped forward and spit in His face. They pushed Jesus around, trying to knock Him to the floor.

I stood frozen. I held my chin in my left hand while my right hand rested on the hilt of my sword, just below my left elbow. In a flash, I could have disemboweled these cowardly tormentors. If they had known how close I was and what was in my heart, they would certainly have soiled their garments. The muscles in my stomach shivered, but it was not from the cold. Unable to move, I stood there watching Jesus.

Jesus was too strong for them to dominate, so one of the "brave" ones came forward and put a hood over His eyes, giving the crowd the courage to slap His covered face. "Prophesy, Christ. Who is it that struck you?" they asked, full of sarcasm. In the cleverness of their mockery, they blasphemed against the Son of God.

Jesus ignored them as if they did not exist. He was stronger than I was. I was boiling inside. Here they were, mocking the Son of God, and I was watching from my corner as if I were nothing more than one of the curious spectators. Unable to move, I debated within myself what to do. My hand continued to rest on the hilt of my sword, but I did not grasp it. Obeying Jesus's commandment, I did nothing. I grew weary, and the coldness I'd been feeling continued to get worse. My legs shivered, but the coldness I felt was not from the temperature.

MORE DENIALS

After a while, one of the servants removed the blindfold from Jesus. I continued to watch in silence, still not knowing what to do. The increasing chill of the night caused me to refocus my attention. I tried to move closer to the warmth of the fire.

As I stood on the portico, warming myself along with everyone else, a young woman studied my face and told everyone around the fire, "This man was also with Jesus of Nazareth." A man standing by the fire wagged his finger in my face and said, "You are one of them. You are one of His disciples."

I shivered from the cold and denied Jesus a second time, saying, "I do not know the man. I am not one of them."

I tried to ignore the group as I moved even closer to the fire. I acted as if I were just another visitor in Jerusalem for the Passover. I felt colder than I should have. Maybe it was the lack of sleep. I had been there for over an hour, but it seemed longer, maybe because I was feeling so tired. How could I be so cold when I was boiling inside?

Another of the servants of Caiaphas came closer and studied me. He was apparently there when I sliced off the ear of his friend. "Didn't I see you at the Garden of Gethsemane?" Another quickly added, "Surely, you are one of them. Your accent betrays you as a Galilean."

I could not hide my accent. I was cold and tired, and now these servants were trying to line me up for their next inquisition. I cursed them and swore an oath, saying, "I don't know what you are talking about. I do not know the man!" No sooner had I pronounced the words than I heard the cock crow the second time.

I had just denied Jesus for the third time before the cock crowed twice, just as Jesus prophesied. His words echoed in my ears. I spun around and glanced at Jesus, who stood alone at the front of the hall. Did He know what I had just done? My sword still had the blood of Malchus on it, and I had just denied the Son of God three times! My gaze fixed on Jesus, knowing that He truly was the Son of God. I was nothing more than a crude fisherman, a fisherman that had denied knowing Him. Was I any better than Judas the traitor?

My mind reeled with the knowledge that I was not the valiant defender of the Messiah I had thought myself to be. As these thoughts filled me with guilt, Jesus turned His head and looked directly into my eyes. I could not withstand His gaze. I ran from the courtyard into the streets of the city. My eyes overflowed with bitter tears, and I sobbed like a child. I was a traitor too.

In the Morning

The morning came quickly, and I forced myself to return to the palace of Caiaphas. Jesus was still standing near the front of the hall. The chief priests and the elders had all returned to the hall and were talking among themselves about putting Jesus to death. When Caiaphas entered the hall, Jesus was standing quietly, awaiting their next confrontation. The eventual decision would be no surprise. The purpose of the inquisition was to find a way to kill Jesus. It did not pretend to be a legal trial.

As before, Caiaphas presided over the council of the elders, chief priests, and scribes. Jesus was led from the center of the hall to face Caiaphas. I wondered if the temporary delay was planned, taking into consideration the law requiring a recess before the mandatory second trial, a trial required by law to be held on a second day. The council did not fast and pray the prescribed day between trials, but they opened the illegal proceedings as if they were being held publicly in the official hall of the Sanhedrin and not in the palace of Caiaphas.

One of the council, who was apparently appointed to illegally interrogate Jesus, started his questioning by saying, "Are you the Messiah? Tell us!"

Jesus spoke slowly and deliberately, pointing out that they had already made their decision. "If I tell you, you will not believe me. If I ask you something, you will not answer me. No matter my answer, you will not loose the cords that bind me. Know only this: hereafter, the Son of Man shall sit on the right hand of the power of God."

Hoping Jesus had somehow confessed a sin, His accuser asked, "So are you saying that you are the Son of God?"

"It is as you have said."

"What need do we have of further witnesses?" His accusers asked. "We have heard His guilt from His own mouth!"

Jesus was right. No matter what He said, He would be judged guilty of something. *Jesus is only guilty of being the Son of God,* I thought.

As the sun began to warm the day, the Sadducees consulted with the rest of the council, then instructed the guards to make sure Jesus was bound tightly and to take Him to Pontius Pilate, the prefect.

I watched helplessly. My arms and legs were weak. I had not eaten, but I was not hungry. When I moved, I felt like I might stumble, but I forced myself to follow them.

JUDAS THE TRAITOR

As Jesus was led out of the hall, Judas heard that the Jews had condemned Jesus to die. Because of this puny man's betrayal, Jesus was going to be crucified. I knew it was too late for him to undo what he had done. But obviously racked by guilt, he had changed his mind. He came out of the darkness from where he had been watching the proceedings and slithered his way to the temple. He went into the chief priests and elders and returned their thirty pieces of silver. "I have sinned in that I have betrayed innocent blood," he confessed.

One of the chief priests handed the coins back to Judas and sneered, projecting their guilt on Judas, saying, "What is that to us? Your sins are on your head, not ours."

Judas the traitor stared at the thirty pieces of silver in his hand, threw them on the floor of the temple treasury, and ran out into the courtyard.

The chief priests picked up the pieces of silver but did not put them into the temple treasury. "It is unlawful to put this money into the treasury because it is blood money," they said. The chief priests counseled among themselves what to do with the blood money. Later we heard that they used the coins to purchase a potter's field, a field formerly used by a potter for its clay. They turned the depleted field into a cemetery to bury strangers. Because the field was bought with blood money, it was thereafter called the Field of Blood.

And thus it was that the prophecy of Zechariah was fulfilled; they took the thirty pieces of silver, the value they placed on the Lord, and gave it to the potter, as the Lord appointed.

Judas then went out and hanged himself from the upper branches of a tree. His dead body hung in the branches for days until the rope finally gave way, and his bloated carcass fell, apparently landing headfirst to the ground below. When his corpse hit the ground, his stomach burst open and his bowels gushed out. I felt that it was a proper end for such a putrid person.

PONTIUS PILATE

The Jews led Jesus from the hall, His arms bound, escorting Him in a procession of pious persecutors to the Roman praetorium, or "Hall of Judgment," where Pontius Pilate lived when he was in Jerusalem. Because it was Passover, the Jews refused to enter the praetorium. The commandment was to not eat leavened bread during the Passover, but as with most Pharisaic interpretations of the law, it had been exaggerated to the point that they were forbidden to even be in the same building as leaven, otherwise they would be considered unclean. At the same time, they had no problem plotting to murder an innocent man by making false accusations in an illegal inquisition. They stood outside the Hall and piously asked for Pontius Pilate to come out to meet them.

Pilate, knowing of their sanctions during Passover, tolerantly came out of the Hall. "What accusation do you bring against this man?" he asked.

Jesus stood before the prefect as the Jews laid out their accusations. "If He were not a malefactor," they began, "we would not have delivered Him up to be judged by you. We found this man to be perverting the nation and forbidding the payment of tribute to Caesar, saying that He Himself is the Messiah, a King."

I wondered where that accusation had come from. What they had found Him guilty of in the palace of Caiaphas was blasphemy, not sedition. The problem for the Jews was that there was no Roman law against blasphemy. In order to present a charge that the Romans might deal with, they had to accuse Jesus of encouraging rebellion against the Romans, a crime that the Romans punished by crucifixion. The accusers were clever liars.

For a moment, it seemed that Pilate was aggravated by the interruption and their accusations. He dismissed the validity of their charges, saying, "Take Him away and judge Him according to your law."

The Jews objected, saying, "It is not lawful for us to put a man to death." With the approval of Pilate, the Jews could have stoned Jesus, but the Jews knew that if they executed Jesus, everyone would know that the Sanhedrin was behind His death. The Jews could not have their involvement known because the people loved Jesus. The Jews needed to have the Romans crucify Jesus for them, fulfilling His prophecy about how He would die.

Pilate impatiently turned to Jesus and asked, "Are you the King of the Jews?"

Jesus answered the Prefect, saying, "It is as you have said."

Obviously emboldened by His response, the chief priests and elders concocted more accusations against Jesus.

Jesus acted as if they had not spoken. Their accusations were meaningless in their own law because they were without a single credible witness. He said nothing because if He did, it would give the Jews something else to accuse Him of.

Intrigued at His wisdom in remaining silent, Pilate wanted to prod Jesus into saying something. "Have you no answer?" Pilate asked. "Do you not hear how many things they testify against you?"

Jesus said nothing, and the wisdom of His continued silence caused Pilate to marvel greatly.

Pilate walked back into the Hall of Judgment as if He were finished with the affair, but he knew that he could not ignore the Jews' accusations. He had to do something.

For a moment, I thought it might be over and that Jesus might be freed, but Pilate stopped, turned around, and called Jesus to his side. Jesus walked forward, barefoot and bound, but with the majesty of a King unbeaten, unbowed by His captors. Pilate asked Him gently, with a tone of curious respect in his voice, "Are you the King of the Jews?"

Jesus responded with His own question, "Do you ask because you want to know if I am a King by your definition or by the definition of these Jews?"

"Am I a Jew?" Pilate fired back. "If you are their King, why did your own nation and the chief priests bring you to me? What have you done?"

Jesus responded with a respectful explanation, "My kingdom is not of this world. If my kindom were of this world, then my servants would fight so that I would not be delivered to the Jews—but my kingdom is not of this place."

Pilate asked Him a third time, "Are you a King then?"

Jesus answered Him as before. "It is as you say," He confirmed. "I am a King. To this end was I born, and for this cause I came into the world, that I should bear witness to the truth. Everyone that hears my voice hears the truth."

"What is truth?" Pilate asked the question rhetorically. I did not know if he expected anyone to answer. This time, instead of walking away, Pilate came out of the Hall of Judgment to speak to the Jews who were awaiting his judgment. Pilate spoke with finality, saying, "I find no fault in Him!"

This was not what the Jews wanted to hear. It angered them even more. "This man stirs up the people, teaching throughout all Jewry, starting from Galilee to this city."

Pilate's eyebrows arched, and he smiled briefly. He turned to Jesus and asked Jesus, "Are you a Galilean?" Clearly, he was pleased.

Pilate did not have jurisdiction over Galilee or Galileans, no matter where they happened to be. He was the prefect, or governor, over Judea, Samaria, and Idumea. The responsibility of dealing with those from Galilee and Perea belonged to Herod, the tetrarch. (Herod Antipas should not be confused with his equally wicked father, King Herod, even though Herod Antipas was sometimes mockingly called "king.")

Ordinarily, it would have been necessary to travel to Tiberius, which was located on the Sea of Galilee, to meet with Herod. As an "orthodox" Jew, Herod was in Jerusalem for the Passover, so Pilate was pleased to send them to see Herod. By so doing, Pilate did not have to face the consequences of alienating the Jews he was supposed to be governing.

HEROD HEARS THE CHARGES

When the Jews brought Jesus to Herod, the tetrarch was looking forward to meeting Him. Herod, a corrupt Jew and puppet of the Roman emperor, had overcome his earlier fear of Jesus. I had heard that when Herod first heard of Jesus, he was certain Jesus was John the Baptist, risen from the dead to punish the Herod for beheading him. The tetrarch had heard of the miracles Jesus performed, including healing the centurion's servant and the Roman nobleman's son in Capernaum. Both of these miracles had occurred in Galilee, the area over which Herod governed. In fact, Herod had hoped to meet Jesus for some time because he wished to see Jesus perform a miracle in person.

When Herod saw Jesus, he was quietly relieved to finally see for himself that Jesus was not John the Baptist. Herod questioned Jesus for some time, wanting to know all about Him. Instead of responding to his questions, Jesus stood mute.

Certainly, Jesus knew Herod to be a wicked Jew who could be manipulated into killing someone unjustly, as he had done with John the Baptist. Jesus also knew that Herod was a degenerate who had divorced his wife to marry his niece, a woman divorced from Herod's own brother.

Jesus remained silent, not allowing this murderer to hear the voice of the Son of God. In all of His dealings with wicked Jews, the only time Jesus ever called anyone a name was when He expressed His contempt for Herod by calling

Him a fox. Herod was a living example of how power can corrupt. Jesus also knew the law, which stated a man could not testify against himself. Like Pilate, Herod interpreted Jesus's refusal to speak as a sign of His wisdom.

As Jesus stood silently, the chief priests and scribes vehemently accused Him, repeating their absurdly false claims. Herod laughed and directed his soldiers to dress Jesus in one of his magnificent royal robes, mocking Jesus as "King of the Jews." Herod rubbed the stubble on his unshaven chin as he considered what to do. He smiled, then ordered Jesus to be returned to Pilate so the prefect could deal with Him.

By sending Jesus to Herod to be judged, Pilate had healed a rift that existed between the two men. When Pilate massacred Galileans in Jerusalem as they made sacrifices at the altar, he had unintentionally offended Herod. Sending Jesus to Herod was a way for Pilate to show his submission to the tetrarch and salve Herod's bruised ego. Returning Jesus to Pilate was Herod's way of accepting Pilate's apology.

Politically, Pilate feared Herod because Herod repeatedly assured everyone that he was a friend of Emperor Tiberius. Tiberius had become quite suspicious, almost paranoid, of politicians and his military because of the numerous attempts on his life and the unresolved death of his beloved son Drusus. Pilate knew it was not a good idea to do anything that might draw the attention of anyone in Rome, especially someone with the lethal reputation of Emperor Tiberius. So for political reasons, and to protect his very life, Pilate had to assure himself that Herod was not his enemy.

PILATE TRIES TO RELEASE JESUS

When Herod returned Jesus to Pilate, the prefect gave the impression that he was both pleased and concerned. He was now reconciled with Herod, but He still had to deal with Jesus, someone who had not committed an act worthy of death. The Jews insisted that Pilate execute Jesus, but he was smart enough to perceive that he was being manipulated. He mumbled and paced, worried about the consequences of granting their request. It was a power struggle that he did not want to lose because it would only serve to strengthen the Jews and weaken his control over them.

Pilate chose to reason with the Jews, calling the chief priests and the rulers of the people together. Pilate said, "You brought this man to me, accusing Him of leading the people astray, so I questioned Him thoroughly in your presence. You know that I found no fault in this man relating to the accusations you made. Then I sent you to Herod, and he also found that this man had done nothing worthy of death. Therefore, what I will do is chastise Him and release Him."

Pilate had arrived at what sounded like a satisfactory compromise. What he proposed was part of a Passover tradition that allowed the voice of the people to select a condemned prisoner to be released. He would whip Jesus severely for a crime He had not committed and then release Him. Pilate refused to be manipulated by the Jews. It threatened to reduce the fear he had tried so hard to create.

After being dismissed, the Jews left Pilate, knowing better

than to argue with the decision of the prefect after he had listened to all of their arguments, no matter how exaggerated or false they were. The Jews were fully aware that it would be within their power, not the prefect's, to select the prisoner to be released. Pilate, on the other hand, had been informed that many people loved Jesus, so he felt safe putting Jesus next to a murderer, thinking Jesus would be freed by the voice of the people. However, he underestimated the wickedness of the Jews. With only a short time to work their evil plan, the Jews needed to move quickly so their conspiracy would not fail.

Pilate carefully selected Barabbas as the least likely to be freed by the people, especially with Jesus as the alternative. Barabbas was a notorious insurrectionist who had committed murder and was awaiting execution for his crimes. Jesus had been accused of insurrection, but both Pilate and Herod found Him innocent of the charge.

If the Jews were truly concerned about punishing someone for sedition, Barabbas would be the one to die. Pilate shrewdly calculated that if the crowd voted for Barabbas to be freed, it could be viewed as an act of rebellion. The Jews had the choice of executing an innocent man or a guilty man, but it was clearly their choice.

In order to step them through the same reasoning and arrive at the same conclusion, Pilate called the chief priests and the leaders of the Jews back to his presence. This time, he told them who they would have to choose from. "Consider who you will have me release to you, Barabbas or Jesus, which is called Christ," he said, dismissing them once more. Pilate knew that the Jews envied the popularity of Jesus, but that was a minor thing to have Him executed for.

Within the hour, Pilate returned to the judgment seat in the Roman Hall of Judgment to hear the voice of the people. The crowd was growing noisy in anticipation of the annual spectacle. Before Pilate sat down, a messenger arrived, sent by

Pilate's wife. Her message to her husband was direct: "Have nothing to do with the death of that just man. I have suffered many things this day in a dream because of Him." It appeared that the Roman wife of the prefect was a believer.

As the crowd grew noisier, the chief priests and elders walked among them, reinforcing their conspiracy, saying, "Barabbas is the one to save. Crucify Jesus!"

By the time Pilate sat down, the Jews had agitated the crowd into a frenzied state. Pilate asked them, "Which of these two shall I release to you, Barabbas or Jesus, King of the Jews?"

The crowd chanted what they had been instructed by the chief priests and elders: "Barabbas! Barabbas! Barabbas!"

Obviously surprised, Pilate asked them, "Then what shall I do with Jesus, which is called Christ, King of the Jews?"

The crowd again chanted what they had been told to say, "Crucify Him!"

Clearly reluctant to accept what he was hearing, Pilate asked, "Why? What evil has He done?"

Prompted by the chief priests and the elders, the crowd chanted even louder than before, "Crucify Him!"

Acknowledging that his clever plan had failed, Pilate called for a pitcher of water. He decided to distance himself from the Jews and deal with those that followed Jesus. His career did not need another bloody uprising to quash. He observed the Hebrew ritual of ceremoniously washing his hands for everyone to see. He announced, "I am innocent of the blood of this just man." Then, gesturing around the crowd, Pilate said, "His blood is on you!"

"Let His blood be upon us and upon our children!" one of the wicked leaders cried. In this proclamation, the Jews invoked a curse that would fulfill many prophecies.

Clearly annoyed, Pilate promptly released Barabbas and sent Jesus to be scourged before He was crucified.

SCOURGED

The Roman soldiers took Jesus back into the common hall of the Praetorium, the prefect's palace, where a cohort of soldiers gathered to strip Him of His clothes and to scourge Him.

It is not in my heart to describe in great detail what the Roman soldiers did to Jesus when they scourged Him. I will only say that they beat His bare flesh with whips weighted with metal balls and pieces of bone. His skin was flayed, exposing muscle and bone. Many men were so weakened by scourging that they died of blood loss, shock, or infection. I shall not describe the torture or the pain further because it causes my heart to ache even to think of it. I will only say that the looks on the soldiers' faces betrayed the perverse joy they took in beating Jesus.

After the soldiers scourged Jesus, they again dressed Him in the deep scarlet, almost purple robe from Herod. Then a soldier weaved a crown of thorns and forced it onto His head. Another soldier put a heavy stick in His right hand, as if it were a royal scepter. Then they bowed on bent knee, mocking Him, saying, "Hail, King of the Jews." They spit on Him and took the stick from His hands and beat Him on the head with it.

After they finished their tormenting, the commander of the soldiers reported to Pilate that Jesus had been scourged and was ready to be crucified. Pilate called the leaders of the Jews into the Praetorium once more and made His final public pronouncement of innocence, solemnly declaring, "Behold, I bring Jesus in front of you, that you may know I find no fault in him."

Weakened and clearly in shock from being beaten nearly to death, Jesus was barely able to walk as He was led before the Jews. He entered the room dressed in Herod's robe, still wearing the crown of thorns, blood running down His face. Pilate confronted them with the result of their evil works, saying, "Behold, the Man!"

I whispered His name to myself as He lifted His head.

The bloodthirsty chief priests and elders saw the fulfillment of their cunning plan and callously cried out, "Crucify Him! Crucify Him!"

I could see controlled anger in Pilate's face. He was a harsh leader, a cruel man known for scourging and crucifying many people. Cruelty was an effective tool for dealing with opposition to Roman domination. The unjust execution of an innocent man with a large following was the kind of thing that could stir general rebellion and put Pilate's command at risk. Pilate was reputed to be a skilled politician, so he certainly considered the consequences of crucifying Jesus. Being manipulated into killing a man to protect the interests of corrupt Jews was not a good precedent. The Jews wanted it to look like the Romans killed Jesus, but that was a sham; it was the wicked leaders of the Jews. They used the Romans to shield themselves from the backlash of the followers of Jesus.

Pilate acted disgusted with the Jews. He dismissed them a final time, saying firmly, "You take Him and crucify Him—I find no fault in Him!" Everyone watched as the soldiers removed Jesus, taking Him back to the Hall of Judgment.

As Jesus disappeared from sight, the Jews countered Pilate's dismissal of His guilt, "We have laws, and by our laws, He ought to die because He put Himself forward as the Son of God."

That was the first time Pilate had heard anything about Jesus being the Messiah. Pilate knew the Jews were looking for a Messiah and that many of them believed the Messiah would lead a rebellion against the Romans. "This man is no threat to Rome," Pilate mumbled, then he turned and went into the Hall of Judgment, followed by the Jews. He turned to Jesus. "Where did you come from?" Pilate asked. "Who are you?"

Jesus said nothing.

Frustrated, Pilate pleaded, "Will you not speak to me? Do you not know that I have the power to crucify you and that I have the power to release you?"

Jesus lifted His weary, bloody head and said, "You have no power over me except what is given to you from above. Therefore, they that delivered me to you have the greater sin." Jesus did not relieve Pilate of the guilt he bore for allowing himself to be manipulated by the Jews, but Jesus placed the greater sin on the Jews because they were the ones that had falsely accused Him and manipulated Pilate.

Clearly, Pilate knew that his best option to keep the peace would be to release Jesus. The people accepted Jesus as the Jewish Messiah, and he was about to do something that was likely to incite an unnecessary rebellion. It would not be good for Pilate's political ambitions if the Emperor interpreted his failure to keep the peace as failure to govern.

Pilate turned to the Jews, who were waiting to hear the procurator's final order to crucify Jesus. When Pilate told the Jews that he wanted to release Jesus, the Jews cried out, "If you let this man go, you are not Caesar's friend. Any man that makes Himself a king speaks against Caesar."

The Jews had found Pilate's weak spot! Political realities were something he could never ignore. He was serving at the whim of Emperor Tiberius Julius Caesar, the "melancholy" Emperor. Tiberius had become openly suspicious of everyone, retreating from the murderous atmosphere of Rome to the relative safety of the island of Capri. Everyone also knew that when the Emperor left Rome, a cunning praetorian prefect named Sejanus had seized control of many of the Emperor's responsibilities. Pilate was also aware of rumors among his military friends that Sejanus was planning to overthrow and probably assassinate Tiberius.

Pilate's mind had to be racing over the fate of previous rebels from Galilee. Certainly he knew of Herod Archelaus, who had governed Galilee three decades earlier. Everyone knew of Judas of Galilee, who helped found the extremist Zealot sect and foment a violent rebellion. The Roman general Quirinius quashed the insurrection by crucifying thousands of Galileans, after which Archelaus himself was banished. Romans traditionally did not trust Galileans and would not tolerate any Jew whose actions provoked rebellion. Pilate simply could not release Jesus of Galilee without the Roman government taking notice, especially if these Jews went to Rome to report it.

There was no doubt in anyone's mind that Herod would do what was in his own best interest. If Herod sent a dispatch to Tiberius that Pilate had not publicly executed a rebel who aspired to be king, Herod would be perceived as defending the Emperor, and Pilate's life could end quickly. Pilate had to wonder if that was why Herod had sent Jesus back to him. Was it a ploy to eliminate him?

Pilate must have weighed his own life and career against the life of a Galilean that claimed to be the Jewish Messiah. There was no question what he had to do to preserve his own life and prosper his career. He ordered the soldiers to take Jesus back into the Hall of Judgment and then resumed his place in the judgment seat in the place called "the pavement," or *Gabbatha* in Hebrew.

It was still early morning on the day of the Passover, yet

Jesus had been in the hands of the Jews for several hours. In an obvious attempt to dissuade the Jews, Pilate again announced Jesus, saying, "Behold your King!"

Once again, the Jews joined in a chorus of evil, saying, "Away with Him! Away with Him! Crucify Him!"

Pilate, obviously still trying to dissuade the Jews from killing an innocent man and thereby stirring a rebellion, asked them, "Shall I crucify your King?"

Caiaphas spoke for the house of Israel, saying, "We have no king but Caesar." I recognized that in so doing, Caiaphas did two things. First, he blasphemed in that Jews were forbidden to recognize the authority of Rome over the authority of God. Second, he reminded Pilate again of his political vulnerability.

Pilate sighed, and his shoulders drooped in failure. He had potentially put his career at risk by intentionally infuriating the Jews, something that was unacceptable to Emperor Tiberius. It was intended that the Romans would tolerate the religions of those they dominated without interference, so long as those religions did not advocate rebellion. I remembered what had happened earlier, when Pilate ordered his soldiers into Jerusalem under cover of night carrying ensigns and images of Tiberius. When the Jews rebelled against this defilement of Jerusalem, Pilate threatened to massacre them. The Jews responded by offering themselves as a sacrifice, forcing Pilate to remove the offending images or create another bloody rebellion. No prefect's career would survive such a failure to govern.

The Jews knew that Pilate had only narrowly avoided a rebellion when he plundered the corban, or temple funds, to build an aqueduct. When the Pharisees gathered to protest that political blunder, Pilate's soldiers drew hidden weapons and massacred a great number of them. Pilate seemed to repeat offenses to the uncompromisingly rigid religious traditions of the Pharisees. He often found himself choosing between offending the Pharisees and the Sadducees or offending the Emperor. He walked a narrow path with lethal political risks on both sides.

After the Jews pointed out his political vulnerability, Pilate took a deep breath and called his soldiers to his side. He spoke to them in a quiet voice, giving them instructions. Pilate watched as they removed Herod's robe from Jesus, replacing it with His own blood-stained clothes, and then took Him away to be crucified.

The Jews had succeeded in their evil plan; Jesus would be crucified. They had hoped to hide behind the fiction that Pilate was the one who put Jesus to death, but the truth was obvious. Pilate lacked the courage to do what he knew was right, but it was the leaders of the Jews who used Pilate to murder Jesus. But in their brash effort to obtain the release of Barabbas, they had involved the public, so their conspiracy was no longer a secret.

THE CRUCIFIXION

As the Roman soldiers took Jesus through the city's gate to be crucified, they saw a man entering Jerusalem from Kyrene. I recognized the man as Simon, the father of Alexander and Rufus, disciples of Jesus. The soldiers took hold of Simon, put the crossbar intended for Jesus on his back, and forced him to carry it to the place of crucifixion, a place called Golgotha, meaning "the place of a skull."

The fact that the soldiers compelled Simon to carry the crossbar was extraordinary. Usually prisoners were forced to carry their own crossbars to the site of crucifixion. It is just my opinion, but I believe the soldiers were following Pilate's orders when they enlisted the first able man they encountered to carry the crossbar for Jesus. Pilate was a cruel man, a pagan and a Roman, but he was not without a certain kind of integrity. And, like me, he had no respect for the rulers of the Jews.

A great company of people followed Jesus to Golgotha, including crying women who lamented His imminent death. Jesus spoke to them, saying, "Daughters of Jerusalem, do not weep for me. Weep for yourselves and your children because the days are coming in which it shall be said, 'Blessed are the barren, the wombs that never bare, and the breasts that never gave milk.' They shall say to the mountains, 'Fall on us!' and to the hills, 'Cover us!' For I ask you, if they do this to me, what shall they do to you?"

It was still morning when they arrived at Golgotha. They offered Jesus a drink of sour wine mixed with myrrh, which was intended to dull His senses, cloud His mind, and reduce His pain. Dazed and in shock, Jesus accepted it, but when He tasted it, He refused to drink further.

Without ceremony, they stripped Jesus of His clothes and nailed His arms to the crossbar, hoisted it up, and then nailed His feet to the horizontal pole of the cross. I must be excused for not providing more detail or describing the tremendous pain this inflicted. I do not wish to dwell upon it.

Except for an involuntary cry of pain when each nail was driven into His body, Jesus was silent during the entire ordeal. As he hung there, with nails through His wrists and ankles, He lifted His head heavenward and prayed, saying, "Forgive them, Father, because they do not know what they are doing."

Two criminals were crucified on Calvary with Him—one to His right, the other to His left—fulfilling the scripture that prophesied, "He was numbered with the transgressors."

Crucifixions were intentionally located near heavy foot traffic so that everyone passing by could see them. It was intended to make a statement to anyone who might mistakenly think the consequence of crime or rebellion against Rome was minor. The Romans were brutally effective in their domination of a people.

To maximize the meaning of a crucifixion, a sign was also affixed to the cross, bearing the name of the individual being crucified and the nature of his or her crime. I gained a certain degree of respect for Pilate when I saw what he ordered to be written on the sign for Jesus:

"Jesus of Nazareth, The King of the Jews."

It was written in Hebrew, Greek, and Latin, so everyone could understand it. Jesus hung on the middle of three crosses, guarded by four Roman soldiers to prevent anyone from rescuing any of the condemned.

In my heart, I believe that Pilate feared that what he had ordered to be written was true. He was not mocking Jesus. I am convinced that Pilate respected Jesus and that he feared what Jesus said was true. Yes, Pilate's wife was apparently a believer, but I think that being in the presence of the Son of God and questioning Him was not without consequence to Pilate personally. His belief did not absolve Pilate of his guilt in crucifying Christ. Like many others, Pilate feared men more than he feared God. Still, I felt differently about this pagan Roman after He had Simon carry the crossbar and ordered the sign acknowledging who Jesus was.

Of course, the chief priests of the Jews were outraged at Pilate's sign. They went to Pilate and demanded the sign be changed to say, "He that said, I am the King of the Jews." Pilate dismissed them, saying, "I have written what I have written."

After the four soldiers removed Jesus's clothes and nailed Him to the cross, they divided His clothes among them. They found that His robe was a single piece of fabric, woven top to bottom without a seam, so they cast lots for it instead of tearing it. In so doing, another prophecy was fulfilled.

As Jesus hung on the cross, passersby mocked Him, shaking their heads, saying, "You that would destroy the temple and build it in three days, save yourself. If you are the Son of God, come down from the cross." I knew that it would not matter what miracle He performed; He healed the ear of Malchus, and still his captors were not deterred.

The wicked chief priests, scribes, and elders joined in the mockery, saying, "He saved others, but He cannot save Himself." And they challenged Him, saying, "King of Israel, come down from the cross, and we will believe." Others said, "He trusted in God; let God deliver Him now if He will have Him, because He said, 'I am the Son of God.'"

The centurion, perhaps a secret believer or just overcome by curiosity, offered Jesus some vinegar to relieve His thirst and then asked Him, "If you are the King of the Jews, save yourself." One of the thieves being crucified with Jesus mocked Him, adding, "If you are the Messiah, save us all."

Angered at the insult offered Jesus, the other thief said, "Do you not fear God, seeing that you are being crucified too? We are crucified as a just reward for our deeds, but this man did nothing wrong." Once again, I noticed the words of the prophets being fulfilled.

The thief that defended Jesus asked Him, "Lord, please remember me when you arrive in your kingdom."

Jesus answered Him, saying, "In truth, today you shall be with me in paradise."

I note that the word "paradise" has created confusion among believers. Being with Jesus after death did not imply that the man had gone to heaven; rather, they would be at the same place after death, nothing more.

From eleven o'clock to around two in the afternoon, the light left the sky until darkness covered the whole land. At about two, as His suffering neared its peak, Jesus cried aloud with words that once again fulfilled a prophecy, saying, "*Eli, Eli, lama sabachthani?*" which translated to, "My God! My God! Why have Thou forsaken me?"

Someone standing nearby misunderstood His words and said, "Behold, He calls for Elias." Someone else ran to get a sponge filled with vinegar and put it on a reed for Jesus to drink. One of those standing by mocked Him, shouting, "Let Him be! Let's see whether Elias will come and take Him down."

Most of us stood afar off, watching the crucifixion. My fellow Apostles urged me to stay with them. They knew that it was in my heart to slay the soldiers and remove Jesus from the cross to save His life, but I would be breaking His command-ment if I did. I could not speak, so I stood a silent watch.

My good friend John, the son of Zebedee, left us to escort the three Marys to the foot of the cross: Mary the mother of Jesus; Mary the wife of Cleophas; and Mary Magdalene, along with His mother's sister. As they approached, Jesus lifted His head to see. I observed but did not fully understand the deep compassion He felt for His mother. In an act of love that was typical of the Son of God, He looked at His mother, then nodded toward John, saying, "Woman, behold your son!" Then looking at John, He nodded toward Mary, saying, "Behold your mother!" Overcome with emotion, Mary bowed her head and wept. Thus the prophecy of Simeon was fulfilled. John put his arm around Mary and took her away. From that hour, she lived in John's home as a member of his family, treated with love and respect.

Although Mary had other sons, they were not yet converted. Jesus made John responsible for her because He did not want them taunting her, saying things that would add to her pain. Such was His love and respect for His mother.

When Mary had gone, Jesus, knowing that He was about to complete all things to which He had been born, said, "I am thirsty." The centurion soaked a sponge in a pitcher of vinegar that was sitting nearby, stuck it on a branch of hyssop, and lifted it to His mouth.

When Jesus received the vinegar, He said, "It is finished!" not referring to His life but to His life's work. Then He cried aloud, saying, "Father, into thy hands I commend my Spirit." He bowed His head and voluntarily "gave up the ghost," or rather, He gave up His life at His will.

After His last breath, an earthquake shook the earth, tearing rocks apart. It was as if the earth were mourning the death of its Creator, the Son of God. I later heard that at the same moment, the veil of the temple was torn in half, starting at the top and running to the bottom.

The tearing of the veil of the temple was a symbolic event. Each year on the Day of Atonement, one priest was to pass through that veil and enter the holiest part of the temple, a small room known as the Holy of Holies, where the Ark of the Covenant had rested in the desert tabernacle and then in Solomon's temple. It was in this room in the Tabernacle where Jehovah met with Moses, making it the holiest of holy places and a place considered to be in the presence of God.

On the Day of Atonement, the priest was to make an offering that symbolized the sacrifice and atonement of the Messiah. Beginning with the suffering Jesus endured in the Garden of Gethsemane and ending with Him giving up His life on the cross, Jesus had undergone the complete process of the Atonement. He had taken upon Himself the sins of the world and shed His blood as payment for those sins of which mankind repented. When He said, "It is finished!" He was not referring to His life but to this infinite Atonement.

At the moment He gave His life, all that the prophets had foreseen was fulfilled. Instead of looking forward and honoring Him by offering symbolic sacrifices, we were to look back and honor Him by partaking of His Sacrament. The tearing of the veil in the temple declared the ending of sacrifice. Further, it ended the limitation of only one man being allowed to enter the presence of God. Jesus's Atonement made it possible for all repentant men to enter His presence. Yes, the tearing of the veil of the temple was a significant symbolic event.

Those guarding Jesus had all heard of Him, and they knew that some had said that He was the Son of God. They had mocked Him on the cross, but when the earth trembled, they were afraid. The centurion glorified God, saying, "Truly, this was the Son of God." In all of the crucifixions they had observed, they had never seen a man capable of willing his own death.

All of the people who came to be with Jesus smote their breasts in the traditional expression of grief. Among them were the women that had followed Him from Galilee, including Mary Magdalene; Mary the mother of James and Joseph; and Salome, the wife of Zebedee. We watched His death from a distance, seeing these things unfold. And when it was over, the crowds began to leave Calvary.

With the approach of sundown and the beginning of the Sabbath, the Jews asked Pilate to break the legs of those being crucified, which greatly hastened death. They wanted to make sure Jesus was dead. They also wanted the bodies to be taken down and prepared for burial before nighttime, to prevent the land from being "defiled." The soldiers received their orders and broke the legs of the two thieves, but they found that Jesus was already dead, so they did not break His legs.

To prove that Jesus was dead, one of the soldiers desecrated His body by piercing His side with a spear. When he did, blood and water poured out of the wound. We saw it as proof that Jesus was dead. These events also fulfilled the scriptures that forbade the breaking of a bone of the sacrificial lamb and the scripture that says they shall look upon Him whom they pierced. And this is my testimony, which I give as a witness of His death.

After this was done, the rest of us withdrew and walked slowly back into Jerusalem, retreating to the same upper room where we had eaten the Passover. It was a private place, and we would be safe there. We did not know what else to do.

Grief filled our souls. Jesus was dead.

The Burial

When sundown approached, the Sabbath was about to begin. Word came to us that a rich Pharisee went to Pilate in secret to petition the prefect for the body of Jesus. He wanted to prepare it for burial. That man was Joseph of Arimathea, a city in Judea. He was one of the few honorable members of the Sanhedrin. Like Nicodemus, he feared retribution by the Jews, so he kept secret the fact that he was a disciple of Jesus. Joseph and Nicodemus had both dissented from the conspiracy to murder Jesus.

Pilate was surprised to hear that Jesus had died so quickly, so he called for the centurion and asked him how long Jesus had been dead. This centurion was with Jesus during the scourging and was there while Jesus was on the cross. He had been the one to exclaim, "This was the Son of God." I suspected that Pilate commanded him to watch over Jesus to protect Him from further torture by the Jews. The unnamed centurion confirmed that Jesus had died, just as Joseph said. Pilate ordered the centurion to remove the body of Jesus from the cross and deliver it to Joseph so he could prepare it for burial.

Nicodemus joined Joseph at the cross, and they took the body of Jesus down from Calvary to a tomb located in a garden. This tomb was new, one that Joseph had hewn out of rock for his own use. Nicodemus brought an expensive mixture of myrrh and aloe, about one hundred pounds in weight. Joseph and Nicodemus wrapped the body in new fine linen, applied it with the spices, and laid it in the new sepulcher. Mary Magdalene and Mary, the mother of James and Joseph sat in front of the tomb as Joseph and Nicodemus hurriedly prepared the body before the beginning of the Sabbath. When the men finished their task, they rolled a great stone over the doorway of the tomb and departed.

The women returned to their homes for the Passover Sabbath. They prepared spices and ointments to be used on the body, specifically the face, and then they rested, observing the law of the Sabbath.

The next day, on the Sabbath of the Passover, we heard that the chief priests and Pharisees came to Pilate, saying, "Sir, we remember what that deceiver said while He was yet alive: 'After three days I will rise again.' Order the sepulcher to be made secure until the third day, lest His disciples come by night and steal Him away and then say to the people, 'He is risen from the dead,' so the last deception be worse than the first."

Pilate conceded to their demands, saying, "I will provide you with guards to watch the tomb. Make the tomb as secure as you can, and then they will watch it." So the chief priests and the Pharisees went and secured the tomb, sealing the stone, and left the Roman guards to watch it. I note that in so doing, the chief priests and Pharisees violated the law of the Sabbath, but nothing would prevent these wicked men from attaining their evil goals.

AT THE TOMB

Mary Magdalene later told me that she waited patiently for the sun to rise on Sunday morning, when the weekly Sabbath ended. She walked to the tomb carrying the sweet spices that had been prepared to anoint the face of Jesus. Mary the mother of James and Joseph; Joanna, the wife of Chuza, Herod's steward; and Salome, the mother of the Apostles James and John accompanied her. On the way there, the four women asked one another, "Who shall roll the stone away from the sepulcher door for us?"

Before they arrived, there was a great earthquake, and an angel descended from heaven. He rolled back the stone and sat upon it. The Roman guards keeping watch on behalf of the Jews were very superstitious. Upon hearing that they were guarding the tomb of the Son of God, they became afraid of what might happen. When they saw the angel, with clothes as white as snow and with a countenance as bright as lightning, they shook from fright and fell to the ground as if they were dead.

When Mary Magdalene and the other women arrived, they saw the two soldiers lying on the ground. From outside the tomb, they could see an angel sitting inside, on the right side of the tomb. The women described him as being dressed in long, white, shining garments and having a countenance as bright as lightning. They bowed their faces to the earth in fear. The angel spoke to them, saying, "Fear not. I know that you seek Jesus of Nazareth, who was crucified." Then he uttered the wonderful words, "He is not here. He is risen." When the angel saw that the women did not believe him, he gestured for them to enter the tomb, saying, "Come, see the place where they laid the Lord."

The women looked into the tomb, where they saw a second angel, but the body of Jesus was not there. The second angel asked, "Why do you seek the living among the dead?"

The first angel said, "Go quickly! Now! Tell Peter and the other Apostles that Jesus is risen from the dead and that He is going to Galilee ahead of them. They shall see Him when they go there. Tell them to remember what He said to them in Galilee: 'The Son of man will be delivered into the hands of men, and they shall kill Him; and after He is killed, He shall rise the third day.'" Then the angel added, "This is what I was commanded to say." Mary told me that the women remembered what Jesus had said, but they did not understand because no one had been resurrected before.

The women departed the tomb quickly, and Mary Magdalene obediently followed the angel's instructions to find me and tell me what had happened. At the time, I was with the other Apostles in the upper room.

Mary Magdalene ran all the way to the upper room without stopping to speak to anyone, so she was nearly out of breath when she arrived. When she saw me, she cried out, "They have taken the Lord out of the sepulcher! We do not know where they have laid Him!"

In the meantime, the unconscious soldiers apparently recovered from their stupor, ran from the tomb in a panic, and reported to the chief priests that an angel had rolled the stone from the tomb and that it was empty! There was no body for them to guard!

When Mary told us of the angels, we did not believe her. We were sure someone had stolen the body of Jesus. Just then, Joanna, Mary, and Salome arrived to confirm her story.

Still skeptical, I immediately ran all the way to the tomb. Young John outran me. He stooped down and looked into the tomb, but he waited respectfully for me, the senior Apostle, to catch up. When I arrived, I rushed directly into the tomb, with John following behind. We found only the linens, folded and laid aside. The napkin that had been placed on His head was also folded and set aside. It was just as Mary Magdalene had said.

We did not know what to do. We had not yet understood what Jesus meant when He said He would rise from the dead. Like Mary, I was convinced that someone had stolen His body but was confused about why they left the wrappings. Our hearts were heavy as we sat in the empty sepulcher. After a time, we walked out into the early light of the morning, finding that Mary Magdalene had arrived. She had walked back to the tomb, still weeping. There was nothing we could say to comfort her. Mary would not leave, so we walked back to the upper room, not knowing what else to do. Later, Mary told us that in her confusion, she had forgotten to tell us to go to Galilee to meet Jesus.

She had stayed alone, remaining outside the sepulcher, still in tears. As she wept, she fell to her knees from exhaustion. She peered again into the sepulcher and saw that the angels had returned. One stood at the head and the other at the foot of where the body of Jesus had lain.

One of the angels said, "Woman, why do you weep?"

"Because they have taken away my Lord," she cried, "and I do not know where they have laid His body."

They offered no answer, so she stood and turned away to see a man standing behind her. It was Jesus, but she did not recognize Him at first because her eyes were blurred with tears. As she turned away from Him to leave the garden, Jesus said, "Woman, why do you weep? Whom do you seek?"

Mary, supposing Jesus to be the gardener, said, "Sir, if

you have borne Him away, tell me where you have laid Him, and I will take Him away."

Jesus comforted her, healing her heart with a single word, "Mary."

She immediately recognized His voice and spun around, exclaiming, "My Master!"

In her absolute joy, Mary rushed toward Jesus to embrace Him. He stopped her, saying, "Do not touch me because I have not yet ascended to my Father. Go to my brethren and tell them that I ascend unto my Father and your Father, and to my God and your God."

When Mary turned to leave, obeying His commandment, she saw her friends standing nearby, the other women who had witnessed her encounter with Jesus and saw her joyful smile. Jesus walked toward them and said, "Hail to all of you." They came and beheld him, falling at His feet to worship Him. Then Jesus said, "Do not be afraid. Go and tell my brethren to go into Galilee, and they shall see me there."

Mary obediently left and returned to us. When she told us that she had seen Jesus and that He was alive, once again we did not believe her. She told us to go to Galilee, and we would see Him! Frankly, what she said was difficult to believe.

THE CHIEF PRIESTS

When the chief priests heard what the Roman guards reported, they were not concerned that Jesus might be alive but that the people would believe He was alive. As Sadducees, the chief priests were bound by tradition to deny the possibility of resurrection, so despite hearing the report that an angel had rolled back the stone, they refused to believe.

They hurriedly called the elders into another council of conspiracy to determine their next move. They decided to bribe the soldiers, paying them a large sum of money to say that His disciples came in the night and stole Him away while they slept.

The Sadducees assured the soldiers that if Pilate heard the story, the Sadducees would go to him and say that the story was their invention. They promised to protect the soldiers from execution, which was the punishment for any caught sleeping on duty. The soldiers took the money and spread the story, which was widely believed and confirmed by the Jews.

While I knew that the Sadducees had successfully created a lie, they could not explain the other things that happened. When Jesus was resurrected, there were other graves opened too. Many of the saints who had died rose from their graves, going into Jerusalem and appearing to many people. Jesus was the first resurrection, but others were raised that day also. The Sadducees believed what they wanted to believe, and if it didn't fit the facts, they ignored the facts or distorted them to fit what they believed.

ON THE ROAD TO EMMAUS

Cleopas and another disciple shared an experience that happened later that day as they left Jerusalem to return to their home in Emmaus, a village located a bit more than seven miles northwest of Jerusalem. While traveling, they discussed all the things that had happened that day and what the events would mean to the disciples of Jesus. While they talked, another man joined them. They did not know it, but it was the resurrected Jesus, who appeared just as any man of flesh and bone. They did not recognize Him because their eyes were restrained from seeing who He was.

Jesus asked them, "What are you talking about that makes your conversation so sad?"

Cleopas answered Jesus, "Are you a stranger in Jerusalem? Do you not know what has happened there in these past days?"

"What things?" Jesus asked.

Cleopas answered, "Concerning Jesus of Nazareth, a prophet who was mighty in deed and word before God and before all the people. We trusted that He was the One that would redeem Israel, but the chief priests and our rulers delivered Him to be condemned to death, and they have crucified Him. Today is the third day since these things were done.

"Early this morning, some of the women of our company surprised us with the report that when they went to His sepulcher, His body was not there. They told us that they had seen a vision of angels who told them Jesus was alive. The women also claimed that they saw Jesus and that He was alive. Other men who were with us went to the sepulcher, and they found it empty, just as the women said, but they did not see Jesus."

Jesus asked them, "Oh, the unwise who are reluctant to believe all that the prophets have spoken! Should Christ have not suffered these things and not entered into His glory?"

Jesus then taught them, beginning with Moses and moving down through all of the prophets. He expounded to them from all the scriptures on the things concerning Himself. They were taught by the greatest Teacher in the history of the world.

As they drew near to Emmaus, He bid them farewell to continue His journey on to Galilee. They asked Him to stay the night with them. They said, "Abide with us because it is nearly evening, and the day is at an end."

Jesus went into their house as if to stay the night. As He sat to eat, He took bread, blessed it, broke it, then gave it to them. As He did, they finally recognized Him. And, in their words, "He vanished out of our sight."

When He was gone, they said, "Did not our hearts burn within us while He talked with us on our way here, and when He opened the scriptures to us?"

Cleopas and his fellow disciple had an experience that I was familiar with. Many times as I had listened to Jesus teach, my heart burned within me, but sometimes it was not until I reflected on what He said that I remembered that burning. I was so caught up in what He was teaching that I did not pay attention to how I felt. I knew that Jesus was the Christ because of the burning within when my spirit recognized the truth as He spoke. I knew things that I did not know I knew.

THE APOSTLES SEE JESUS

Although it was late in the day, Cleopas and the other disciple immediately rose from their meal and returned to Jerusalem to find me. I was in the upper room with the other Apostles, the same place we were when they left us. Thomas was the only Apostle not present. By the time the disciples arrived, it was night, and we were behind locked doors, doing our best to keep out of the sight of any Pharisees or Sadducees who might be looking for us. Cleopas told the story of how Jesus had taught them as they traveled to Emmaus and that they recognized Him only when He broke bread for them. In spite of his testimony, there were some in the room who did not accept what Cleopas or the other disciple said. I listened quietly and said nothing about believing or disbelieving their story.

In frustration, the friend of Cleopas observed that Mary Magdalene had also seen Jesus and so did the women who were with Mary at the tomb. Some of the Apostles were bothered that two disciples had seen Jesus, yet His Apostles had not. It did not make sense to them. "Were we not as important as them? Were we not His brethren, His Apostles?" they asked.

Cleopas was greatly disturbed at their reluctance to believe his testimony. Finally he testified of his own experience, insisting, "The Lord has risen indeed!" When no one accepted his witness, Cleopas gestured toward me and added, "Jesus has appeared to Simon."

My secret was out. Jesus truly had appeared to me, but He had commanded me to tell no one. Immediately, everyone wanted to know the truthfulness of Cleopas' statement. If he spoke the truth, why had I not told them? When I said, "I cannot speak of it," they became quite forceful in demanding that I explain. I could not and would not confirm that Jesus had indeed appeared to me, the senior Apostle.

The truth is that when Jesus appeared to me, He did so to comfort me and relieve me of the great anguish I was suffering for the three times I denied knowing Him. Yes, I knew that Jesus was alive. He showed me the wounds in His hands and feet and side. Yes, He was resurrected, but He commanded me not to tell anyone, saying that He would show Himself to the Apostles when the time was right. Obediently, I had kept quiet, waiting for Him but not knowing when He would come.

While I was thusly interrogated by my obviously irritated brethren, Jesus appeared in the room, standing in the middle of us. He said, "Peace be unto you." The rest of those around me looked at me with shock—fear, even—as if they had seen a spirit.

I was at total peace just to hear His familiar voice. His arrival conveniently saved me from the wrath of my fellow Apostles. I had waited for Jesus to speak and show His body to them, and He did as He promised.

"Why are you troubled?" He asked. "Why do you have doubts in your hearts?"

They remained silent and continued to stare at Him as if He was an apparition they should fear. We knew that evil spirits were easy to detect because they had no bodies of their own. That's why they often tried to inhabit other people. We had been taught that if we suspected someone was a spirit, we only needed to touch him, and we would immediately know if he was.

Jesus told them, "Look at my hands and my feet and see that it is me, because a spirit does not have flesh and bones, as you see I have." And then He put out His hands for all to see His wounds. They stared at His hands and touched them, and then His feet, and they looked at the wound in His side too. I joined the others, looking again and knowing for a certainty that He was resurrected. As He said, His was a tangible body of flesh and bones. I testify that He told the truth.

My fellow brethren were so overwhelmed with joy that they were incredulous. Tears flowed freely from their eyes, and smiles never left their faces. They wanted to believe what they were seeing, but they still wondered if this was an apparition, even after they had touched Jesus and knew better.

Jesus, knowing their thoughts, did not chastise them, but instead asked, "Do you have any meat here?"

I handed Him a piece of broiled fish and a piece of honeycomb. Jesus took it and ate it to demonstrate that He was neither an apparition nor a spirit. They watched silently, and expressions of peace and joy filled their faces. He was indeed alive with a body of flesh and bone.

I testify that His divine spirit was reunited with His resurrected body, and it was that living body of flesh and bone, not some unknown "substance," that we saw. That is what is meant when I testify that He has been resurrected.

Jesus spoke to the Apostles that evening, saying, "This is in fulfillment of the words I spoke to you while I was yet with you. All things that were written in the law of Moses and in the prophets and in the psalms concerning me must all be fulfilled."

Then Jesus taught us from the scriptures as He had taught Cleopas and his friend. Jesus opened the eyes of our spiritual comprehension that we might understand all of the scriptures that testified of Him. For the first time, we truly understood what the esurrection was about, why He had to die, and why

He was raised from the dead. We understood! Can I repeat that? We understood! Jesus said, "Thus it is written, and thus it was necessary for Christ to suffer and to rise from the dead on the third day. And, beginning at Jerusalem, repentance and remission of sins should be preached in His name, so go among all nations and bear witness of what you have seen, because you are witnesses of these things.

"Peace be unto you. As my Father has sent me, even so, I now send you."

Then Jesus breathed on each of us, one by one, and said to each of us, "Receive the Holy Ghost. Whosoever sins you remit, they are remitted unto them, and whosoever sins you retain, they are retained."

We had received the baptism that John the Baptist taught, the baptism of the Holy Ghost, but we had yet to be baptized with fire. We had also received a power that I did not comprehend, the power to remit or retain sins. In my mind, only God had the power to do that, but Jesus had just given us the same power.

Afterward, my fellow Apostles believed everything Cleopas had tried to tell them. I understood why Jesus commanded me to be silent about His visit with me. He wanted to visit them in person so that they would witness and believe that He was resurrected. After all He had taught us, after the many times He told us that He would be raised from the dead, we finally understood the need for His crucifixion and His Resurrection. Our eyes truly were opened.

We could then speak and testify as witnesses with greater credibility than teachers or believers.

I am Peter—disciple, Apostle, and witness of the Son of God.

DOUBTING THOMAS

Thomas was not present when Jesus came into our midst in the upper room. When Thomas did arrive, we all joyfully testified to him, saying, "We have seen the Lord!" But Thomas did not believe us, just as the other Apostles did not believe Cleopas, and just as I had not believed Mary.

Thomas said, "Except I see the prints of the nails in His hands, and except I put my finger into the print of the nails, and except I thrust my hand into His side, I will not believe."

Some would criticize Thomas for not believing, but there were nine other Apostles in that room that Sunday evening. They, along with a number of disciples, did not believe Cleopas until they had experienced exactly what Thomas said he needed. I would not be the first to criticize him as being the only one having little faith. He was one among many. It was again clear to me why Jesus had forbidden me to testify that I had seen Him.

Eight days later, we were again gathered in the upper room behind locked doors. This time, however, Thomas was with us when Jesus appeared, again saying, "Peace be unto you."

Jesus addressed Thomas, "Put your finger here and look at my hands; put your hand here and thrust it into my side. Be not faithless but believe."

In reverence and awe, tears flowed from Thomas's eyes as he replied, "My Lord and my God."

Jesus said, "Thomas, you believe because you have seen

me. Blessed are they that have not seen me and have believed."

At that time in the upper room, Jesus showed many other signs to His Apostles, none of which are written. The things that are written were kept so readers might believe that Jesus is the Christ, the Son of God and that by believing on His name, they might have eternal life. And that is why I testify of Him too.

At the Sea of Galilee

After Jesus appeared to us and showed Himself to Thomas, He left us alone in the locked upper room. He also commanded us to go to Galilee, where He would join us. We all lived in Galilee, so it was fitting that Jesus would meet us there.

We journeyed back to Galilee as quickly as possible and gathered at my home each day to wait for Jesus. We missed Him, and we spent many hours waiting for Him to arrive and instruct us before we did anything else. One afternoon, after sitting and talking most of the day with Thomas, Nathanael, James, John, and two other Apostles, I grew impatient. Finally, as the sun was about to go down, I said, "I'm going fishing."

They followed my lead and said, "We're going with you," so we all went down to the Sea of Galilee and boarded my ship. We fished the whole night and caught nothing.

In the morning, we returned to shore with empty nets and empty hearts. Without Jesus to lead us, we were like ships without rudders. We had no direction. We moved back toward shore, distressed at our failure. Less than a hundred yards out, a man shouted across the smooth water, saying, "Children, have you any meat?" He wanted to know if we had caught any fish. It was not uncommon for someone to call to us from the shore, hoping to buy the freshest catch.

"No!" someone called back.

"Cast the net on the right side of the ship and you shall find fish," the man told us.

We tried it, and, to our surprise, the net was so full we could not draw it into the ship. I was struggling with the net when my young friend John reminded me that Jesus had done this earlier. I looked at him with a knowing smile, and he confirmed what I was thinking, saying, "Peter, it is the Lord!"

I was naked from the waist up, as was the custom when we fished, so I quickly pulled on my fisherman's coat and jumped into the sea. I swam to the shore as fast as my arms and legs allowed. The tears that flowed freely from my eyes were hidden by the splashing from the sea. My heart raced, not from swimming hard, but from knowing that I was approaching Jesus, the resurrected Son of God.

Even now, I do not have the words that would truly express my love for Him and the joy I have felt from knowing Him. At that moment, after waiting for Him in Galilee, desiring so much to see Him, I wished to be at His side more than anything in the world. I could not even waste the time to row the boat ashore.

The other Apostles slowly followed in the boat, dragging the net filled with fish. By the time they got ashore, I had already climbed over the rocks and greeted Jesus. I still stood in awe of Him being alive—being resurrected. I could not remove the lump in my throat or the grin on my face. I blinked my eyes to clear the tears of joy, but they would not stop flowing.

When the other Apostles arrived, they saw a bed of hot coals, on top of which fresh fish and new bread were cooking.

Jesus reminded us of our catch, saying, "Bring the fish you caught."

We went to the boat and dragged the overloaded net to the shore. There were one hundred and fifty-three large fish, but the net was not broken. I inwardly noted that when I did as Jesus commanded, I prospered. I was pleased to do as He commanded.

Jesus told us, "Come, eat."

He carefully removed the hot bread and cooked fish from the coals and served them to us. After we finished eating, Jesus gestured toward the net full of fish and said, "Simon, son of Jonah, do you love me more than these fish?"

I noticed that He called me Simon, not Peter. I responded without hesitation but with a bit of guilt, "Yes, Lord. You know that I love you."

I was the senior Apostle, charged with being His witness. And what was I doing when He came to Galilee? I was fishing! Certainly I loved Him more than fishing, but He needed to remind me of my priorities.

Jesus accepted my answer and responded, "Feed my lambs," gesturing toward my fellow Apostles.

Without pausing, Jesus asked me the second time, "Simon, son of Jonah, do you love me?"

I answered immediately, thinking maybe He had not heard me the first time, repeating my prior answer, "Yes, Lord. You know that I love you."

Jesus said, "Feed my sheep," and He gestured to the area around us, the people of Galilee.

When He said that, I knew that He had heard me; after all, He gave a different answer.

Without pausing, Jesus asked me a third time, "Simon, son of Jonah, do you love me?"

I was hurt to think that He would need to ask me three times if I loved Him. I answered, "Lord, you know all things. You know that I love you."

"Feed my sheep," He said, gesturing toward the horizon, suggesting to me that we teach the rest of the world, including the Gentiles. I was not completely sure of His meaning, but I thought I understood.

There was silence among my fellow Apostles as they watched us talk. Then there was silence as we watched the fire burn out and the ashes turn gray long after the fish and bread were all gone.

As I sat there contemplating His words, I realized that He had just offered me the opportunity to redeem myself from denying him three times by professing my love three times. I looked at Jesus, and He looked back, as if peering directly into my heart. He smiled, and I knew that He knew my thoughts. He loved me, and I loved Him.

Jesus broke the silence, saying to me, "In truth, when you were young, you put on your girdle the way you wanted, wore your sword if you wished, and you walked wherever you wanted. When you are old, you shall stretch forth your hands, and they shall be bound. Your girdle will be chosen by another, and you will be taken where you would not go."

I understood His imagery, remembering that I had told him in the Garden of Gethsemane that I would go to prison and to death with Him. He had confirmed that I would be arrested and crucified, but not until I was old.

I had resolved long before that day that death would not cause me to waver in my commitment to testify of Him. If I were to be crucified, it would not be a test for me but another opportunity to testify of my belief in Jesus. I did not fear dying.

Jesus looked at me again, gestured, and said, "Follow me." I knew those words. They were the same words He used to call me from my ship to be His disciple. "Follow me" rang in my ears as a tender invitation not only to be His Apostle but also as a solemn challenge to follow Him in crucifixion. At that moment, however, He invited me to walk with Him along the edge of the rocky shore of the Sea of Galilee.

He taught me what it meant to feed His lambs, referring to my leadership responsibilities as the senior Apostle. I was to preside in His absence. When He told me to feed His sheep, He was referring to taking the gospel to the house of

Israel. When He repeated that I was to feed His sheep, He was referring to taking the gospel to the Gentiles. His answers were not repetitive, but instructional, and I understood and accepted them.

As we walked, I looked behind us and saw that John was following along at a respectful distance. John was the youngest of all of us, and Jesus treated him like His own little brother. We all seemed to do so, but Jesus protected him even when he was a little more outspoken than he should have been. In my concern for young John, I nodded over my shoulder toward him and asked, "Lord, what shall this man do?"

Jesus answered, "If I will that he remain until I return, what is it to you? You are to follow me."

I remembered that He had told us that some Apostles would not taste of death until they saw the Son of Man and His kingdom come with power. I learned then that John was to be one of them. I also learned that my future did not depend on what might happen to John or any of the other Apostles. Still, I asked because I was greatly concerned for my young friend. I hoped he would not suffer what I would.

My fellow Apostles talked among themselves that John the Apostle would not die; rather, he would stay until Jesus returned. We all testified of the truthfulness of those words.

John observed that if everything Jesus said and did were written, "the world could not contain the books that would be written," because He said and did many things.

HIS ASCENSION

After our time on the shore of the Sea of Galilee, Jesus stayed at my home for a few days. He called us together to give us hours of intense, private instruction. Multitudes gathered outside my home, but they were not allowed to enter. Our private time with Jesus was filled with instruction and preparation.

One morning, Jesus told us that it was time for Him to leave. I knew it was coming, but I was deeply disappointed. As He departed, Jesus told us that He would meet us at a particular place we knew on the Mount of Olives. He left Capernaum, but I did not know where He was going.

As we prepared to leave for Jerusalem, a few people gathered to follow along. The further we traveled, the greater their numbers grew. By the time we arrived at the place Jesus had appointed, we were followed by multitudes. Some were there to see or worship the resurrected Son of God, but an even greater number were doubters, curious to see if He had actually been resurrected.

We found Jesus where He said He would be. He called the Apostles to His side and spoke to us privately, saying, "All power has been given to me, both in heaven and on earth." That was when I understood why He had left us in Capernaum. He had been with His Father and had received all that His Father had promised Him, including the power of His Father. I understood only part of what that meant.

Not knowing what His brief comment implied, I asked

Jesus, "Will you now restore the kingdom of Israel?"

He answered, saying, "It is not for you to know the times or the seasons, which the Father has put in His power, but you shall receive certain power after the Holy Ghost has come upon you. You shall be witnesses of me, both in Jerusalem and in all Judea and in Samaria, and then to the uttermost parts of the earth."

Jesus thus commanded us to go out as missionaries and teach. He expanded our call, saying, "Go out and teach all nations. Preach the gospel to every creature and baptize them in the name of the Father, and of the Son, and of the Holy Ghost. Teach them to obey all of the things I have commanded you.

"He that believes and is baptized shall be saved, but he that does not believe shall be damned. These are the signs that shall follow them that believe. They shall cast out devils in my name; they shall speak in new tongues; they shall pick up serpents and not be harmed; if they drink any deadly thing, it shall not harm them; and they shall lay hands on the sick and they shall recover."

Then, finishing His charge to the Apostles, Jesus said, "I will send the power of my Father upon you, but stay in Jerusalem until you are endowed with that power from on High. John baptized with water, but you shall be baptized with the Holy Ghost not many days from now."

Jesus laid His hands on us and gave us each a blessing. After He finished His farewell instructions, He offered a final word of comfort, saying, "Know that I am with you always, even unto the end of the world. Amen."

After saying His farewells, He was taken from us and carried up into heaven, where we saw Him sit at the right hand of God! We saw Jesus with His Father. Many who were with us were astonished, and they knelt and worshipped God. Jesus had been with us for forty days following His resurrection, and now He had gone to His Father.

As He went up to heaven, we looked steadfastly toward Him until a cloud obscured them from our sight. While we were thus engaged, we did not notice that two men, clothed in bright white clothing, had joined us. They were angels.

The angels said, "Men of Galilee, why do you stand gazing into heaven? The same Jesus that is taken from you up into heaven shall return in the same manner you saw Him go into heaven."

They reminded us to go to Jerusalem and remain there, as Jesus had instructed us, and we joyfully obeyed. We went into Jerusalem and then to the temple, where we spoke openly of Jesus, continually praising and blessing God.

At night, we stayed in the same upper room in Jerusalem where we received what is now known as the Last Supper. Chosen by Jesus, we found it to be a good place to meet. I was there, along with James, John, Andrew, Philip, Thomas, Bartholomew, Matthew, James the son of Alphaeus, Simon Zelotes, and Judas the brother of James. We continued in prayer and supplication to God, asking Him to send the Holy Ghost He promised. We were joined by the women who had been there with Jesus at the crucifixion and at the tomb. We all prayed together. Mary, the beloved mother of Jesus, was there also, along with her sons, the brothers of Jesus. After several days of prayer, the day of the Feast of Pentecost arrived, and we remained together still.

The Feast of the Harvest was more commonly known as the Pentecost because it took place fifty days after the weekly Sabbath following the holy day of the Passover. God gave a commandment to Moses that this feast should be observed the day after seven Sabbaths, which would be on a Sunday.

We were sitting in the upper room when there came a great sound from heaven, as if it were a mighty rushing wind, filling the house with that wonderful sound. The presence of the Holy Spirit made the house and everything in it glow as if it were ablaze. We sat in awe of a feeling that we had never felt before, as if an unseen fire warmed us from within. My body tingled all over, and I felt an indescribable peace come over me, a feeling I could not compare to anything I had ever felt before.

The sound and the glowing of the building caused many curious people to come and enter. Within a short time, people overflowed the upper room and the adjoining rooms. They stood outside and crowded the doorways. As we were filled with the Holy Ghost, we spoke the words given us by the Spirit.

In the crowded room, there were people from every nation who were visiting Jerusalem for the Pentecost. As we spoke and testified of Christ, we spoke in our own tongue, but they each understood in their own tongue. It was said that we spoke with "cloven tongues," because we spoke in our language, but they understood our words in their own. It was as if we were speaking in multiple languages at the same time.

This "cloven tongue" event caused quite a stir, almost as much as the amber glow of the building and the noise that had attracted the attention of everyone in Jerusalem. Word of the variety of languages we had spoken spread quickly, and people marveled one to another. "Are not these men that are speaking all from Galilee?" they wondered. "How is it we hear them speak in the tongues where we were born?"

These visitors to Jerusalem were Parthians, Medes, and Elamites. There were also people from Mesopotamia, Judea, Cappadocia, Pontus, Asia, Phrygia, Pamphylia, Egypt, Kyrene, Rome, Crete, and Arabia, and all marveled. "We hear them speak the wonderful things of God in our own languages."

The experience amazed them, and then they expressed their doubt, saying, "What does this mean?"

Other Jews doubted the men from other lands and

mocked them, saying, "These men are full of new wine."

As the presiding Apostle, I stood to address them. I said, "Men of Judea and all that dwell in Jerusalem, know this and hearken to my words. These men are not drunk, as you suppose. It is but nine o'clock in the morning. What you see and hear was spoken of by the prophet Joel when he said, 'And it shall come to pass afterward, that I will pour out my Spirit upon all flesh; and your sons and your daughters shall prophesy, your old men shall dream dreams, your young men shall see visions. And also upon the servants and upon the handmaids in those days I will pour out my Spirit. And I will show wonders in the heavens and in the earth. There will be blood, and fire, and pillars of smoke. The sun shall be turned into darkness, and the moon shall be turned into blood before the great and the glorious day of the Lord's coming. And it shall come to pass that whosoever shall call on the name of the Lord shall be delivered in Mount Zion, and in Jerusalem there shall be deliverance, as the Lord has said.'"

I continued to teach and warn them, saying, "Men of Israel, hear these words. Jesus of Nazareth, a man approved by God, did miracles, wonders, and signs among you, as you well know. He is the same man who was delivered into your hands by the appointed counsel and foreknowledge of God, and you took Him, and by your wicked hands, you crucified and you killed Him. God loosed the bands of death and raised Him up because it was not possible that He could be held by death.

"David spoke concerning Him, saying, 'I have always set the Lord before me. Because He is at my right hand, I shall not be moved. Therefore, my heart is glad, and my glory rejoices, and my flesh shall rest in hope. For God will not leave my soul in hell. Neither will He suffer His Holy One to see corruption. He will show me the path of life. In His presence is found the fullness of joy, and at His right hand, pleasures forevermore.'

"Men and brethren, let me speak freely to you about the patriarch David. He is both dead and buried. His sepulcher is here today. David was a prophet, and he knew that God swore an oath to him, that from the fruit of David's loins, according to the flesh, the Messiah, the Christ, would be raised up to sit on His throne. David saw the resurrection of Christ before he prophesied of it. He saw that His soul would not be left in hell and that His flesh would not see corruption. He was not in the tomb the fourth day."

My fellow Apostles stood with me as I testified, "We are all witnesses that God raised Jesus from the dead," I proclaimed. "Jesus is now exalted because we saw Him on the right hand of God. Jesus promised us that the Holy Ghost would be shed upon us. That is what you have seen and heard this day."

I bore testimony that day that the prophecies of David were fulfilled in Jesus Christ. Then I added, "He is this same Jesus who you have crucified, the Son of God, the Messiah."

When they heard my testimony and saw my fellow Apostles stand as witnesses of my testimony, they were pricked in their hearts, and they said to us, "What shall we do?"

I spoke plainly, saying, "Repent and be baptized, every one of you, in the name of Jesus Christ for the remission of sins, that you also shall receive the gift of the Holy Ghost. This promise is offered to you, even to your children, and to everyone that is afar off, even as many as the Lord God shall call.

"Save yourselves from this wicked generation."

It was a day to remember. The power of the Holy Ghost took my words into their softened hearts. Those that received my words repented, and there were about three thousand souls baptized that day. They had been changed by the out-pouring of the Spirit. They continued steadfastly in obedience to what we taught them. They ate together, fasted together, and believed together. All that believed stayed together and shared everything in common. They sold their possessions and their goods and shared the proceeds with one another, each man according to his need. They prayed in the temple, and they ate their bread with gratitude to God and singleness of heart. And the Church of Jesus Christ grew daily.

We went forth and preached to all nations. The Spirit of the Lord worked within us, and the signs that followed us confirmed the word of God to those that heard us speak.

Epilogue

When I visit with friends, I am often asked to take a moment and summarize my experiences with Jesus Christ, the Son of God. I am a fisherman and the son of a fisherman, but I was there when Jesus chose the ones He wanted to follow Him. I saw many great and wonderful things.

Skeptics always ask if I actually saw Jesus perform the miracles reported in the written record or if I took someone else's word. The answer is that I saw Him perform many miracles, many times, in many places—many more miracles than were recorded. I know there are people who deny that He performed any miracles because they claim to know that what He did could not have taken place. I would caution them about being so arrogant. Can an ordinary person know everything that is or was or may be? I know that I cannot, but I am an ordinary man. Only someone that has supernatural powers or is omniscient can know what these skeptics claim to know. Do they think they are gods? As an ordinary man, I had no idea of the extent or the nature of the power of the priesthood of the Son of God. I did not know what He could do until I saw Him do it. In my time, I would have denied that radio, television, and cellular telephones were anything more than fantasy, but they are a commonplace reality in this modern age. I testify that Jesus performed many miracles. I saw them myself. I saw many things, and I continue to testify of them.

I was at the wedding in Cana, and I saw Jesus change

water into wine. I met His wonderful mother—several times. I saw Him clear the temple—twice, when no man dared stand to resist! I was with Him the night He boldly instructed Nicodemus the Pharisee. I testify that Jesus baptized me in Judea. I watched the crowds gather to hear Him so many times in Judea and Galilee that I cannot number them. I traveled with Him to Samaria, and I heard the tender words He spoke to the woman at the well. I saw the Roman nobleman plead with Jesus on behalf of his son, and I heard Jesus tell him to return to his home, that his son would live—and it happened just as He said.

I was not with Him, but Jesus told me of His disappointment when He returned to His hometown of Nazareth, where the citizens tried to kill Him. I was with Him later when He returned to Capernaum, my hometown, and was received with love. I saw Him cast out devils in our synagogue.

I tenderly remember when Jesus called us to be fishers of men. I faithfully followed Him throughout Galilee as He preached, healed, and cast out devils. I testify that after I had an unsuccessful night of fishing, He told us to let down our nets and draw them in one more time, and they were filled with fish. Later I saw Him cleanse a leper, the first of many.

I often saw Him kneel and pray to His Father in Heaven. When He called me to be an Apostle, I watched Him pray all night long before He laid His hands on my head and ordained me to be His first Apostle, the senior Apostle, along with the rest of the Twelve.

I was there on the mountainside when He healed everyone that was brought forward until none remained, and then He taught His Sermon on the Mount. I was there when He instructed us how to pray. I heard Him tell the centurion that his servant would be healed, and I saw Him raise the widow's son in Nain. I was with Him when He ate in the uppermost room in the house of Simon the Pharisee. I am pleased to testify that He stayed in my home in Capernaum, where He performed many miracles, cast out devils, and healed many people.

I was in the boat when He spoke and calmed the Sea of Galilee. I went with Him to the far side of the Sea of Galilee, where He cast the devils out of a man and into a herd of pigs.

I testify that it was in my home that four men let their paralyzed friend down through the roof and Jesus healed Him. I ate with Jesus in the house of the publican. I walked with Jesus when the woman touched His garment and was healed. I saw Jesus raise the daughter of Jairus from the dead by saying, "Maiden, arise." I watched Him heal two blind men in Galilee.

I was with Him at Jerusalem when I saw Him heal a man that had been unable to walk for thirty-eight years. I was there when that miracle led to His first confrontation with the Pharisees and the Sadducees, evil men that I came to despise.

I was with Him when He returned to Galilee and was met by a group of women that included Mary Magdalene. I knew her because Jesus had previously cast evil spirits out of her, leading her to become one of His most loyal followers. I was there when He went into the synagogue and healed a man with a crippled hand on the Sabbath, infuriating the Pharisees and scribes.

I was on the rocky shore of the Sea of Galilee when the crowds became so large and aggressive that Jesus went into my boat to assure everyone's safety and taught from there. I had the honor of hosting Jesus in my home whenever He came to Capernaum, and my home became a gathering place for believers, disbelievers, truth-seekers, skeptics, and spies. It was in my home where people possessed of unclean spirits came forward, and those spirits testified that Jesus was the Son of God. I saw Jesus silence the evil spirits and cast them out. Shortly thereafter, I saw Jesus cast the devil out of a man that was both blind and dumb and give him sight and speech only to hear the Pharisees accuse Jesus of being Beelzebub.

I got to visit with Mary, the mother of Jesus, and her other sons when they came to my home to see Jesus. I was there when Jesus again went into one of my boats to teach the people in Capernaum, this time using a series of parables.

I was there when Jesus returned to His hometown of Nazareth to teach and to heal those in the surrounding villages. I saw the great grief Jesus suffered when He heard that John the Baptist had been beheaded. I took Jesus in my boat along the coast of the Sea of Galilee to Bethsaida, and we landed at a desert place where He fed five thousand men and their families with five barley loaves and two small fish.

When Jesus stayed on that mountainside, I sailed with my fellow Apostles on the Sea of Galilee, where a violent storm tossed us back and forth all night long. I testify that Jesus approached us in the early morning hours, walking on the water. I admit that I asked Him to have me walk on the water too, but my faith wavered until He lifted me by the hand. Afterward, I watched as the people of Gennesaret touched His robe and were healed.

I was also there when He first announced that He would be betrayed by one of us. This is one moment I do not remember with fondness because I learned that one of the Twelve was a traitor.

I was there when Jesus sat down to supper without washing His hands, intentionally offending the scribes and Pharisees. I was with Him when He left Galilee to travel to the Mediterranean seacoast to find respite from the multitudes that followed Him and those that were seeking His life. I was there when He cast the devil out of the daughter of the faithful Canaanite woman. I traveled with Him to Decapolis, where Jesus healed every person that was brought to Him. That was where I saw Him heal a deaf man with a speech impediment by putting His fingers in the man's ears and touching the man's tongue. I was on that hillside with Jesus when He took seven loaves and a few small fish and fed four thousand men, along with their families.

I sailed with Jesus across the Sea of Galilee to Dalmanutha, where more Pharisees and Sadducees asked for a sign. I was in the boat with Him when we returned to Bethsaida and were met by a blind man. That time, Jesus healed by spitting on the man's eyes, then laying His hands on the man and giving him a blessing. In fact, He blessed him two times, until the man could see.

When Jesus asked me who I told people He was, I testified that He was the Son of God. That was when Jesus told me that I knew it by revelation from His Father and it was upon the rock of revelation that He would build His Church. Contrary to what people may say, His Church was not to be built on me! I was there when Jesus warned us not to testify of Him any longer, to protect us from those that would kill Him. I objected to His declaration that He would die, but that was before I understood the need for His crucifixion and Resurrection.

I was there on the mountain near Caesarea Philippi when He was transfigured and spoke with Moses and Elijah. I testify that I heard the voice of God bear witness that Jesus was His Son. I stayed that night on the mountain with the Son of God. I was there at the bottom of the mountain when Jesus cast the evil spirit out of a young man after the other Apostles were unable to do it.

I was with Jesus in Capernaum when He sent me to catch a fish, and the mouth of that fish held the coin needed to pay the temple tribute for Jesus and for me. I was there when Jesus taught me that if any of us desired to be the first, he should be the servant of all of us. I watched as He held my son and told us to become as a little child. I was there when He taught us to leave the ninety-nine and seek after the one that is lost. I heard Him tell of the prodigal son. I was the one He told to forgive people seventy times seven. He taught me, stirring up my guilt for my weaknesses, then comforted me as I strived to do His will.

It was in my home that Jesus laid His hands on my head and bestowed upon me the keys of heaven. I was one of those Jesus sent to Samaria, where we were not well received. I heard Him caution the sons of Zebedee not to call down fire on those that did not welcome His visit. I was there when He sent the Seventy to teach those who were seeking Him, and I heard Him instruct the Seventy to curse those that rejected Him. I was there when He cursed all of Galilee for its unbelief. I was there when the Seventy returned to testify of all the things they were able to do by the power of His name.

I was with Jesus when He traveled through Samaria, where He was met and loved by the people. I was with Him in Judea when the lawyer came to test Jesus, and Jesus taught him a great truth by telling the story of the good Samaritan.

I was with Jesus in Bethany when I met the sisters, Mary and Martha and their brother Lazarus, a family that loved Jesus. I watched Jesus when He stopped to pray before we entered a city in Judea, something He did regularly. It was there that He taught us how to pray.

I was with Jesus in Judea on the Sabbath when He healed a woman that had not been able to stand straight for eighteen years. I traveled with Him when Nicodemus the Pharisee came to warn Jesus that Herod wanted to kill Him. I went with Jesus to the house of a Pharisee to eat supper on the Sabbath. I watched as a lame man entered the room and Jesus healed him. I heard Jesus challenge the Pharisee.

I was there when Jesus used parables to teach the people of Judea, and I observed the Pharisees that continued to spy on Him. I heard Him tell them the parable of Lazarus and the rich man, the only parable in which He gave a character a name.

I was in Samaria with Jesus when ten lepers asked Him to heal them, which He did, but only one of them thanked Him. I was with Him as He traveled into Jerusalem and was again met by Pharisees. I heard Him teach them and everyone in parables.

I was with Jesus in Jerusalem for the Feast of Tabernacles when He confronted the Pharisees over their conspiracy to kill Him. I was there in the temple when the scribes and Pharisees brought a woman taken in the act of adultery, asking Jesus to pronounce a sentence on her, to trap Him in His words. I saw them skulk away after He outwitted them and challenged their own virtue. I testify that it was in the temple when Jesus said, "I am the Light of the World." I was with Him in the temple when He rebuked the Pharisees, and I heard Him boldly testify of His divinity, saying, "Before Abraham was, I Am."

I was with Jesus as we left the temple and He healed another blind man, again on the Sabbath. I heard Jesus testify to him. I was there.

I was there when the Son of God told all men to marry, excusing only eunuchs from that requirement.

I was there when a rich young man came running toward Jesus to ask what he should do to inherit eternal life. I watched him walk away slowly after Jesus told him to give all he had to the poor and follow Him. I was there when Jesus said, "With God, all things are possible."

I was there when Jesus told the twelve Apostles that we would be the judges of the tribes of Israel. And I was in wonder that I would or could ever judge anyone.

I was with Jesus in Jerusalem in the winter for the Feast of Dedication. I heard him testify to the Pharisees that He was the Messiah, but they refused to listen.

I was with Jesus in Perea when Mary and Martha sent word from Bethany that their brother, Lazarus, was very sick. I confess that I wondered why Jesus stayed two more days before beginning the journey to Bethany.

I was with Jesus as we approached Jericho and the blind man called out for Jesus to heal Him. I watched Jesus touch the man's eyes, and he was healed.

I was there in Jericho when Jesus called to a man named Zacchaeus that had climbed a tree to see Jesus, and we went to his house for supper. I heard Him teach in parables as we ate.

I was with Jesus when He arrived in Bethany, and Mary and Martha wept. I also saw Jesus weep at their grief. I testify that Jesus called Lazarus forth from his grave, still wrapped in burial clothing, four days after he died. I was in the home of Mary and Martha when Mary anointed the feet of Jesus as we ate.

I was there on the fifth day before Passover when Jesus approached Jerusalem on the back of a colt. I watched as He paused on the journey and lamented over Jerusalem before He entered the city. I was there when people joyfully spread their clothes and palm fronds along the way to welcome Him.

I was with Jesus in the temple when I again heard the voice of God testify of Jesus. I testify that I heard it. I also heard Jesus confront those who were conspiring to kill Him. I was there when He drove the money changers out of the temple for the second time.

I was there on the way into Jerusalem when Jesus cursed the fig tree because it was barren. I was there when the chief priests questioned the authority of Jesus and He confounded them. I heard Him teach them with beautiful parables that further condemn their wickedness. I heard Him say, "Render unto Caesar the things which are Caesar's and unto God the things that are God's."

I was with Jesus in the treasury of the temple when the widow threw her two mites into the horn. I heard Him teach in the temple. I was also with Him in the house of another Pharisee when He again chose to provoke them by not washing His hands. I heard Him unmask their wickedness.

I stood in awe as Jesus walked along the Temple Mount and prophesied that not one stone of the temple would be left on another. I was next to Him when He stopped on the Mount of Olives and again lamented over Jerusalem.

I was with Him when He prophesied the destruction of Jerusalem and gave us the signs to watch for. I stayed with Him on the side of the mountain, listening to Him all night long. I heard Him prophesy of the terrible things that were going to happen to Jerusalem. I also heard Him tell the parables of the fig tree, the ten virgins, the talents, the sheep and the goats, and others. I was there to hear Him.

I was there when Jesus announced that in two days He would be betrayed and crucified. I was there when He ate supper at the home of Simon the leper. I watched the woman anoint His head with costly spikenard. I stayed with Jesus while Judas the traitor went into the night to betray Jesus to the chief priests.

I was the one that went and found the upper room to hold the Passover meal. I was there when we all sat to eat the meal of unleavened bread on the first day of Passover.

I was there when Jesus washed the feet of the Apostles, and I objected to having Him wash my feet. I was there when Jesus repeated that it would be one of us that would betray Him. I was there when Judas went into the darkness to do his evil work. I watched Jesus break bread and bless it and take the wine and bless it, instituting the sacrament. I was there when He blessed us with peace, and I felt that peace. I was there to receive His last instructions and when He prayed for us before He was betrayed into the hands of the Jewish rulers.

I heard Jesus tell me that I would deny Him three times before the cock crowed twice. I walked alongside Him to Gethsemane, and He asked us to watch while He prayed. I could not stay awake, but I saw what happened there, including the angel that came and ministered to Him as He suffered for our sins. I saw blood drip from His body as if it were sweat. I was there when the mob came to arrest Him and He boldly identified Himself. I drew my sword to defend Him, but He stopped me.

I escaped into the darkness, and I watched as He was taken, bound, and led away to be tried in the palace of Caiaphas. I followed to watch the proceedings. I admit that I denied knowing Him three times, and I was ashamed of myself.

I watched the illegal trial. I was there when the Jews accused Him before Pilate, then Herod, and then Pilate again. I watched their treachery and did nothing, as He had commanded.

I saw Jesus when He came before Pilate again after being beaten nearly to death. I watched Pilate try to release Jesus, but the Jews would not have it. I was there when Simon carried His crossbar to the hill. I watched as they nailed Jesus to the cross. I watched until He gave up the ghost. I heard the thunder, I saw the darkness, and I felt the earth rumble from within. I felt the grief of the earth, and it was like my own.

I was there in the upper room when Mary Magdalene came to tell us that His tomb was empty. I ran to the tomb, but His body was not there. Jesus knew of my own emptiness, and He appeared to me before He appeared to Cleopas. I was there when He appeared to us in the upper room—both times. I was there when He opened my eyes to the scriptures so that I finally understood the reason for and the meaning of His crucifixion and His Resurrection. I came to understand, as I hope others will.

I waited for Him in Capernaum, as He commanded, but I grew weary of doing nothing and went fishing, only to have Jesus come to us at the sea. I swam to shore to be next to Him. I testify that Jesus asked me if I loved Him three times in a row. I heard Him say that I would be taken captive and crucified. I was to follow Him in death, as I had once testified I was willing to do.

I was there at the Mount of Olives when He announced that He had been to His Father and had received all that His Father had for Him. I testify that Jesus ascended into heaven, and He sat on the right hand of God. I testify that I saw them both, sitting next to each other, separate beings.

I was there at the Feast of the Pentecost, when the sound of a great rushing wind and the fire of the Spirit made it look like the building was afire. I felt the Spirit of the Holy Ghost change me. I bear my testimony of Jesus Christ. He is the Son of God. I was there to see all that happened.

In the words of my fellow Apostle Paul, as he wrote to the saints of Corinth, "The Jews require a sign, and the Greeks seek after wisdom. We preach that Christ was crucified, which is a stumbling block to the Jews and is foolishness to the Greeks. But to both Jews and Greeks, I testify that Christ has the power of God and the wisdom of God."

Before I finish, I wish to share one more story. One day, at about three o'clock in the afternoon, my young friend John and I entered the temple at the gate called Beautiful, located between the Court of the Gentiles and the Women's Court. There was a lame man lying there asking for alms. He stared at the ground, not looking anyone in the eye. I said, "Look at us." He looked up, expecting us to give him money. Instead, I told him the truth, saying, "I have neither silver nor gold, but such as I have I give to you." Then, following the example of my Master, I said, "In the name of Jesus Christ of Nazareth, rise up and walk!"

I reached down and took him by the right hand and lifted him up. As he moved to stand, the bones in his feet and ankles received strength, and he leapt up, stood, and walked. He followed us into the temple, walking, leaping, and praising God. Everyone knew this man as the lame man from the gate of the temple. A crowd gathered at Solomon's Porch to watch, with wonder and amazement in their faces. The lame man stopped his leaping only long enough to hug John and me. Once more, I testified that I had not done this of myself but by the power and holiness of Jesus Christ, the Son of God.

I was once a crude man, seeking the Messiah, but I came to be a witness for the Son of God. Those things that were carnal and worldly were removed one layer at a time, leaving a vulnerable, childlike soul. What was rough and crude was smoothed and finished by the Son of a carpenter. I became His Apostle, built by His hands. I take no credit for who I became or what I did. Every good thing about me was because of Jesus Christ. I testify of His influence in my life. Everything I know came from Him, and I want everyone to know what I know.

As I told the lame man at the gate of the temple, I share with you what I have: my testimony that Jesus is the Son of God—the Messiah—that He was born of Mary, was crucified, and rose on the third day. I have no greater gift to give.

After His Resurrection and Ascension, we continued to testify of Him and perform many works in His name. Those acts of the Apostles and our many letters are recorded for all to read. I shall not include anything more of them because my desire is to testify of Jesus, not to recount what Peter, a lowly fisherman, did in His name.

If a man with a belief in God endures grief and suffers wrongly because of that belief, God is pleased with him. What glory is there in patiently paying the consequences for the things you do wrong? But if you do good and suffer for it patiently, that is what is meaningful to God. After all, Christ suffered for us, leaving an example for us to follow. Jesus committed no sin. There was no deceit in what He said. When He was reviled, He did not revile back. When He suffered, He made no threats. Instead, He submitted Himself to His Father, who judges righteously. He took upon Himself our sins in the Garden of Gethsemane, and He paid for them on the cross so that instead of being left to die in our sins, we might live righteously. It is by His stripes that we are healed. We were as sheep, gone astray, but we are returned to the Good Shepherd, who is the Bishop of our souls.

I testify that Jesus lives. I saw Him on the right hand of God, resurrected to a body of flesh and bone. I testify of Him in His holy name, even the name of Jesus Christ, whose name I love, honor, and revere.

I am strong, but my strength is not found in my hands or my back but in my faith in Jesus Christ. I am Peter—disciple, Apostle, and witness of the Son of God. Even so, amen.

AUTHOR'S NOTES

T he Bible is probably the most studied and written about book in history. Indeed, many scholars have spent their lives doing so. While sifting through this immense body of information and opinion, the author encountered a number of little-known but interesting facts, a few of which are shared below.

THE CALENDAR

Our current calendar is not the same as the one used in the time of Christ. There have been several modifications. In 45 BC, the Julian calendar changed the first day of the year from March 1 to January 1. In 5 AD 25, the abbreviation for Anno Domini, Latin for the year of our Lord, was introduced, and the years were renumbered to start at the year Jesus was thought to have been born. That date was designated as AD 1. The Gregorian calendar, our current calendar, was adopted in Rome in AD 1582, and a ten-day adjustment moved the first day of spring to March 21.

BC, the abbreviation for Before Christ, was used to designate the years before the birth of Jesus, 1 BC being the year just prior to His birth. Numerically, the years jumped from 1 BC to 1 AD, so there was neither a 0 BC nor a 0 AD.

The politically correct usage of BCE, meaning Before the Common Era, and CE, meaning Common Era is dismissed as the foolishness of men bent on denying the significance or the reality of Jesus Christ. There is nothing common about the birth of the Son of God.

Exactly When Was Jesus Born?

The exact date of Jesus's birth remains uncertain, but specific historical facts may be combined to arrive at a close approximation.

The wise men visited Herod in Jerusalem, then went on to Bethlehem in search of the young child. The wise men did not know when Jesus had been born, but apparently they told Herod that the star they were following had appeared less than two years earlier. They followed the star to find baby Jesus, not in a manger, but in a house in Bethlehem. Being a responsible man, it is likely that Joseph planned to return to Nazareth as soon as Mary could travel, suggesting that the wise men visited Jesus when He was not more than a few weeks old.

After finding Jesus, the wise men returned to their country by another route, and Joseph fled into Egypt with his family. The fact that Bethlehem is only five miles south of Jerusalem means Herod did not have to wait very long to conclude that he had been "mocked" by the wise men. Herod probably acted quickly, ordering the murder of all children in Bethlehem aged two and under.

How much time then passed before Herod died is the unknown fact. What is known is that not long after Herod died, his sons journeyed to Rome to petition Emperor Augustus for approval to succeed their father. Emperor Augustus agreed to Herod's will, letting them succeed him in 4 BC. Jesus, therefore, was born before Herod died in 4 BC.

Josephus noted that Herod died in Jericho shortly after a lunar eclipse and just before Passover. Such an eclipse occurred on March 13, 4 BC. This date coincides with Herod's sons' journey to Rome to receive approval for succession in 4 BC.

The final fact is that Jesus was born in the lambing season, which typically runs from February to early April. (The lambing season is the only time shepherds stay in the fields at night, protecting newborn lambs from predators.) This fact allows for Jesus to be born in 4 BC, just prior to Herod's death, but it does not prove it happened then. If Herod died only a few days or weeks after Jesus was born, there may not have been a need for Joseph to flee into Egypt. This combination of facts suggests that Jesus could have been born in the lambing season of 4 BC, but it may have been the prior year or even earlier.

When Did Peter Meet Jesus?

Two facts combine to suggest that Peter first met Jesus in the early spring of 29. First, Emperor Tiberius assumed the throne on August 19, AD 14. The fifteenth year of his reign referenced by Luke was August AD 28 to August AD 29. Second, Passover was at hand, and Passover occurs on the day of the first full moon following the vernal equinox (the first day of spring). These two dates suggest that this was the early spring of AD 29.

A confirmation of this date was given when Jesus was told that the temple, which started construction in 18 BC, had been ongoing for 46 years. Add 18 BC to AD 29, then subtract 1, and the answer is 46 years. (The minus 1 is because there was no 0 BC or AD 0.) As with many details, the exact date is interesting speculation but is not important.

In AD 29, Jesus would have been no less than 32 years of age (4 BC + AD 29 − 1 = 32). That Jesus may have been 32 years of age is interesting but is also unimportant.

Leprosy

At least some of the incidence of leprosy in the Holy Bible may not have been the well-known leprosy known as Hansen's Disease. Naaman's leprosy was probably a lack of pigment in the skin called leucoderma or vitiligo. Other Biblical references to leprosy include unpigmented skin (skin that looked "as white as snow"), pustules or boils, and white hair and skin.

DAY OF THE CRUCIFIXION

Scholars agree that the Sabbath of the crucifixion was not the weekly "Saturday" Sabbath but the "Sabbath of the Passover," a holy day of its own, subject to the same laws of observance as the weekly Saturday Sabbath. Their argument concludes that the crucifixion did not happen on Friday but more likely on Thursday because the Lord Himself said He would be in the heart of the earth three days and three nights, the same as Jonah, which would be Thursday night, Friday night, and Saturday night. Some scholars insist that Jesus was not in the grave all of Saturday night, indicating that He was necessarily crucified on Wednesday. No scholar argues that being crucified on Friday allowed Jesus to be in the grave for three nights. As with differences of opinion over other events, they are interesting to ponder, but the exact day is of no consequence to the reality of the crucifixion and the Resurrection. Christians celebrate His Resurrection, not his crucifixion.

FULFILLMENT OF THE PROPHECIES OF JESUS

Jesus spoke of many things that would befall Jerusalem, and His prophecies were all fulfilled.

Josephus wrote that within only a few years, the blood of Jews covered the floors of the temple when a false prophet attempted to lead his followers into the secret chambers of the temple and nearly 6,000 of them were burned alive by the Romans. It was truly a horrific scene. Other false prophets led many desperate people into the desert. The Jews had rejected the Messiah, the Son of God, who would give them eternal life, but willingly followed one false prophet after another to their mortal destruction.

The prophesied abomination of desolation was brought to Jerusalem. In AD 40, the gilded statue of Emperor Caligula, the mentally deranged successor to Tiberius, was brought into the temple. Jews were expected to worship it.

In AD 41, the momentum of the war with Rome was headed toward the total annihilation of all Jews from upon the face of the earth. Those who heeded the warnings Jesus gave, left Jerusalem and fled, many to Pella in Greece. There came a time when it looked as if Caligula were going to succeed in exterminating Israel, but as Jesus prophesied, the days of the mad emperor were shortened. Caligula was assassinated, and were it not so, a total destruction would surely have fallen upon Israel. Caligula was following the plan of Jewish extermination envisioned by Sejanus, Consul to Tiberius, which plan was later taken up by Claudius and Nero, Caligula's successors. They were of a similar mind, but not as driven as Caligula in their thirst for Jewish blood.

Early in AD 70, Roman soldiers under General Titus, the son of Emperor Vespasian, set up their ensigns in the temple and offered sacrifices to them. Later, as the Jews gathered for Passover, the Roman army surrounded Jerusalem and cut off all food supplies, causing mass starvation. When the Roman soldiers overran Jerusalem, they found terrible atrocities, including fulfillment of the prophesy by Moses that parents would eat their own children. Josephus wrote that 97,000 Jews were taken captive and 1.1 million were slain.

In addition to the sacking of Jerusalem, Josephus wrote that the Greeks and Syrians attacked the Jews, killing 50,000 at Seleucia on the Tigris, 20,000 at Caesarea in AD 66, 13,000 at Scythopolis, and 10,000 at Ascalon.

ABOUT THE AUTHOR

Arnold S. Grundvig, Jr. is the president and CEO of a software company. He is the author and founder of the nationally acclaimed entrepreneurial seminar, The 90-Minute MBA®. He has presented that seminar coast to coast to thousands of managers and small-business owners.

Arnold has a bachelor's degree in psychology and a master's degree in business administration. He is the author of *The 90-Minute MBA* and other books and has written several magazine articles.

Arnold grew up in Moab, Utah, descended of Mormon pioneers. He and his wife, Barbara, have three children and five grandchildren.

0 26575 57915 4